THE TIMEKEEPERS

JENN BREGMAN

TRIBOROUGH PUBLISHING

Published by Triborough Publishing
TriboroughPublishing.com

Cover & Interior Book Design by Monkey C Media.
MonkeyCMedia.com

Printed in the United States of America

ISBN: 978-0-9981441-0-8

Publisher's Cataloging in Publication Data:

Names: Bregman, Jenn, author.

Title: The timekeepers / Jenn Bregman.

Description: Westlake Village, California : Triborough Publishing, [2017]

Identifiers: ISBN: 978-0-9981441-0-8 (paperback) | 978-0-9981441-1-5 (ebook) | 978-0-9981441-2-2 (ePub) | LCCN: 2017900345

Subjects: LCSH: Law--United States--Fiction. | Lawyers--United States--Fiction. | Traffic accidents--California--Fiction. | Liability for traffic accidents--California--Fiction. | Conspiracies--United States--Fiction. | Corruption--United States--Fiction. | LCGFT: Thrillers (Fiction) | Detective and mystery fiction. | Romance fiction. | BISAC: FICTION / Thrillers / Legal. | FICTION / Legal. | FICTION / Thrillers / Suspense.

Classification: LCC: PS3602.R4437 T56 2017 | DDC: 813/.6--dc23

For my husband Jerry, my Mom and Dad,
and my sisters Gwen and Kaarin,
with my deepest love and gratitude.

CHAPTER ONE

She was going to win. The momentum in the courtroom was shifting her way. She could see the judge leaning forward, the court clerk highlighting sections of her brief, opposing counsel scribbling furiously on his notepad. Her voice was getting stronger, her back straighter. She was doing great. She made another convincing argument and watched opposing counsel grimace as he began hunting furiously through the papers next to him. She thrust out her hands to make a point. First, the right; then, the left. And with that tiniest of miscalculations, the tip of her finger grazed the papers stacked on the lectern, sending them—along with her iPhone, pens and highlighters, and her last gulp of coffee—onto the floor, where they landed in an unceremonious heap next to the clerk's foot. A hush filled the courtroom as the other lawyers on the four o'clock calendar put down their reading in anticipation of the carnage ahead. She couldn't believe this was happening. She wanted to cry, but pinched her thigh under her suit until the pain put an end to any thought of tears. She looked at Judge Schneider scowling at her from the bench and glanced down at her disgraced brief.

It hadn't always been like this. There was a time in the not so distant past when she had enjoyed all the luxury—both money and help—that a big law firm could offer. She had graduated Order of the Coif from UCLA Law School and had accepted an offer to become a litigation associate at the biggest, most prestigious firm in town. Not bad for a girl from the south end of San Bernardino County. She grew into a good and conscientious lawyer at Tate & Brown LLP. But after two years of associate work and accompanying big paychecks, she became restless and dissatisfied. The fact was, she was a plaintiff's lawyer. Always had been, always would be. It was a bent left over from her childhood that she couldn't deny no matter how hard she tried. Doing defense work for big insurance corporations was slowly but surely sucking the life right out of her. Jesse called it her own personal David-Goliath complex. And Jesse didn't like that she had it. It kept their relationship in a state of on-again, off-again suspension that he was beginning to hate.

When it came down to it, though, it wasn't an agonizing decision. In fact, it wasn't a decision at all, but a revelation that appeared to her early one morning last January. She had a vision of herself slaving away her youth, locked away in the ivory chamber of prestige and wealth, moving money around. It was always about the money and moving the money. Sometimes your client got more, sometimes less, but to her it was never anything more. On that frosty morning, she realized that either she didn't want to spend her life moving money or, if she was going to move money, she wanted to move it into the hands of people who needed it. So she gave notice and set out to open her own law firm with an emphasis on plaintiff's personal injury.

To say that things hadn't gone according to plan was a kind understatement. And it was on mornings such as this that she wondered if she had made the right decision or whether the revelation she experienced was just a psychotic episode brought on by too much Diet Coke and too little sleep.

She forced these thoughts from her head and began speaking carefully, her brain churning one step ahead.

"No, your Honor. I wasn't aware *Miramar* had been overturned. But I cite *Miramar* solely for the general proposition that a family member can recover damages for emotional distress when that member witnesses the death of a loved one." She took a deep breath and plunged ahead. "The fact that *Miramar* was overturned on other grounds is simply irrelevant."

"Irrelevant is a word I would use carefully, Ms. Brockman. Although I agree that *Miramar* correctly states the black letter law on this point, I don't enjoy seeing overturned cases cited in briefs filed with this court and I sincerely hope I won't see it again."

"No, Your Honor. You won't. My apologies to the Court."

Schneider rocked forward in his chair and leered over the bench. "Regardless of your glaring error, Ms. Brockman, I find you have met your burden of proof and I'm granting your motion. Submit your order to the clerk by noon tomorrow."

"Thank you, Your Honor." Sarah hastily gathered her papers and bee-lined for the door, scurrying quickly into the corridor in case the famously mercurial judge changed his mind.

"Nice save in there, counselor." She turned to see one of her law school classmates rapidly approaching from the courtroom. Sam Morrow. Smart, but unpretentious. She was glad it was Sam and not some other less than gracious classmate.

"Hi, Sam," she called. "I wish that hadn't happened in front of Schneider. But at least he wasn't at his nastiest today."

"Yeah, I know what you mean. I try to say as little as I can, stand up straight, and hope it's over as soon as possible." He shot a hand through his still jet black hair and scratched the back of his neck—a mannerism she remembered well from law school. "I heard you went out on your own. How's it going?"

"Not too bad." She felt she could be a little more honest with him than with other colleagues she ran into, to whom she usually replied, "Great. Couldn't be better," when asked the same question. "It's been a bit rocky in terms of money and time. I wish I could get more help without having to pay any more money."

She could see him shift uncomfortably and look down at his beautifully polished Allen Edmunds shoes. She suspected he was still at Cabot, Strickland & Baines LLP and making obscene amounts of money. Cabot had risen to prominence about seven years ago based on a couple of colossal class action judgments against Conran and Mumford, two Fortune 100 asbestos manufacturing companies. Since then, they had branched out into corporate work and different kinds of personal injury cases including, surprisingly, auto accidents, but they seemed to attract the higher end, bigger damages car cases—not the minor fender benders she got stuck with. She guessed these cases were extremely lucrative for them even with the tightfisted insurance companies on the other side. Brain damage or lost limbs simply paid more than a strained neck. She knew she shouldn't, but couldn't resist confirming the obvious. "You still at Cabot?"

"Yeah," he said. "Lots of hours though." He inspected his shoes again with renewed interest, and then had an idea. "Hey, how about we go and grab a drink? I think you deserve one after that run-in with Schneider."

She hesitated. It would be nice to share war stories with another lawyer for a change. Not only was her professional life challenging and stressful, it was lonely too. No one to bounce theories off of. No one to celebrate the successes or commiserate with about the failures. But as much as she wanted to go, she knew she couldn't. She had a summary judgment motion waiting on her desk that was due tomorrow. Needless to say, she hadn't even started it and it was already five o'clock. Maybe another time.

She said goodbye and walked out into the blinding late summer sun. She didn't see the truck roar around the corner and careen through the crosswalk. She just heard a sickening screech of tires and two deadly thuds. One when the truck hit the man in the crosswalk, the second when he slid off the hood and onto the pavement. She stood frozen for a second, stunned by the horror. Then her body was on automatic, racing to the corner, every nerve on fire.

Blood seemed to stream from every pore on the man's body. His face was a mangled mass of blood and tissue, jaw contorted at an impossible angle. She couldn't determine his race, let alone his age or nationality. He stared straight ahead, his eyes unblinking, unnerving in their focus.

"Call 911!" she yelled to a woman standing by, her mouth agape. Sarah grabbed the man's neck and felt for a pulse. It was there, but faint and erratic. The woman still hadn't moved. She lunged at the woman and thrust her into motion. "Call 911—now! Move it!"

She turned back to the man just as a college age, pimply faced boy rounded the corner and let out a blood-curdling, inhuman scream of anguish. He raced to the man and fell down next to him, cradling the blood-soaked head in his lap. "Dad, it's me, Andy. I'm here. Don't worry, Dad. Everything's going to be OK. You're going to be fine." Sarah was struck by the almost instantaneous composure the boy was demonstrating, far beyond his years and experience. She touched his arm gently and sat quietly at his side.

The shriek of the fire engines seemed to jolt the now numerous bystanders into action. Hands were everywhere. Pillows appeared, water was produced. Then, in a heartbeat, it was over. The paramedics arrived and rushed in with a flurry of activity and authority that would have put the cavalry to shame.

Sarah moved out of the way, sat down on the curb on the far corner and began sobbing uncontrollably. The tension flowed out of her and seemed to saturate the street. She couldn't remember ever feeling more spent.

"Thanks for your help." She looked up to see Andy standing next to her. Blood covered his shirt and pants. "Did you see what happened? Did you see who did this?" His face was imploring, almost as if an answer would somehow turn back the clock and retrieve his life.

"I didn't see his face. I'm sorry. It happened so quick. All I could tell was that it was a big, white commercial truck with some writing mostly etched out on the side. It had something to do with 'meat.' Like 'it's meat time' or 'meat so fine.' Something like that. He didn't even stop. Just kept driving as if he had run over a pile of trash." She paused, looked up, and saw the damage her ill-considered words had done.

"Oh, I didn't mean to say that. I didn't mean your dad was trash or . . . or, anything."

The look of pure anguish on the boy's face made her wince in sympathy and she reached out instinctively to embrace him and pull him close. He crumpled to her side—a blond shock of hair falling over his tear-streaked face. She saw the little boy he must have been at ten. So very small. So unbearably scared.

"My dad is the finest man I have ever known." He began quietly, almost in a whisper. "He never has a harsh word for anyone. He works so hard. Every day he works hard to provide for us, to care for us. He has taught me things I could never have learned on my own. He deserves better than this."

She fought for the ideal words, racking her brain for the perfect message, but all she could come up with was, "Don't worry. He'll be fine. I promise, everything will be OK." And with that, the boy took a long, deep look at her, squeezed her hand and walked away. She wouldn't hear from him again for six months.

CHAPTER TWO

It was on one of those impossibly rainy days at the end of winter that Andy reappeared, this time in the Law Offices of Sarah Brockman, Esq. She had just finished proofing a discovery motion for filing when she saw a familiar shock of blond hair skimming by the top of the hall credenza.

"What are you doing here?" she exclaimed, recognizing him immediately.

"Well, I was in the neighborhood and thought I'd drop in on you."

"I don't believe that for one minute. You don't even know my name. Well, I guess you do now, but you didn't then. How did you find me? Better yet, why did you want to find me? Wait, let me back up. How's your dad?"

"He's going to be OK. Just like you said. That first night was the toughest. He almost didn't make it, but my mom and I kept talking to him and reminding him of all the good times. Reminding him of us. I knew he wouldn't give up if he could help it. After that first night, the rest was one painful surgery after another. It took everything he had, but he made it.

My dad's going to be OK and I came to thank you for it."

"You've got to be kidding. I didn't do anything. In fact, I've gone over and over the accident in my head a zillion times and all I can think about is all the things I could have done and didn't. I didn't do anything to save your father."

"Maybe not directly, but you did everything to save me. See, you *promised* me that everything was going to be OK and I believed you. I believed you because I had to. I couldn't accept anything else. But because I did, I made my dad believe you too. And that's why he made it. That's why he's still here.

"Well, that's really a very sweet and dear thing to say, but I don't think I . . . I mean, well I . . . thank you."

"You're welcome." He grinned at her from beneath that ever-present shock of hair and glanced shyly at the forgotten shaft of papers in her hand. "Oh, there's one other thing I wanted to ask you. Everybody tells us that we should sue. That this man should have to pay for what he did to my father."

Sarah smoothed her jacket and assumed her plaintiff's lawyer demeanor. "They're absolutely correct. What that man did to your father was a horrible, vicious act and leaving the scene like he did was cowardly as well. He deserves to be punished and your father deserves to receive monetary compensation for all the pain, anguish, and suffering he's been through. God knows, he can never be made truly whole again, like the accident never happened, but money will help. And, in my experience, sometimes it can help a lot. But you know, what this man did was a crime as well. What's going on with that? Isn't this guy in jail?"

"Yeah, he *was* in jail. For about a day, I think, until he made bail. And now he's out on probation. He was tried for reckless driving and leaving the scene of an accident, but only convicted for leaving the scene. We couldn't believe it. My mom almost fainted. I mean even I remember seeing the screech marks on the pavement from how fast he was going. But the prosecutor didn't say anything about it, and the guy said the sun was in his eyes and he couldn't see the crosswalk for a second or so when he turned the corner, and by then it was too late. 'Freak timing' he said. He also said he was a recent immigrant with a wife and two kids and living on minimum wage. He left the scene because he was scared of going to jail and never getting out. So the judge sentenced him to a $200 fine and no jail time. *In the interests of justice*, he said. How can that be *in the interests of justice?* What does that even mean? The judge also gave him credit for turning himself in to the prosecutor's office a few days after the accident. We still can't believe it, but apparently there's nothing we can do."

"I don't know much about criminal law, but that sounds absolutely outrageous. Which judge was it?"

"Judge Schneider."

Sarah could barely contain her irritation. "Well, that doesn't surprise me. That judge is known for being extremely unpredictable. I've had plenty of run-ins with him myself. He seems to make rulings based on which side of the bed he gets up on in the morning. Still, this seems really far afield even for Schneider."

"Yeah, I don't get it either, but like I said, there's nothing we can do. That's why we figured we could at least try and make him pay by making him pay. And any money would help. Our medical bills are through the roof and insurance is only going to cover some of it."

"I think you're right. A lawsuit is your best bet at this point although there might not be much of a deep pocket around unless the guy was working for a business—hopefully, with insurance—at the time of the accident. You need to find out if he was an employee at the time of the accident. Also, you really need to do a background check and find out what his assets are. It doesn't make sense to spend a lot of time and money pursuing a case if it's never going to pay in the end." She suddenly checked herself, as she saw Andy's eyes getting bigger and bigger, filling with hope and potential. Oh no, she had done it again. She had the habit of getting so wrapped up in the initial possibilities and theories of a case that her excitement carried her away and swept everyone along with her. She ended up auditioning for cases and causes she didn't even want. Particularly, somehow, the ones that didn't pay. And she always got the part. Jesse would love this one. David and Goliath, Part 220.

"Well," she continued hurriedly. "I don't know if you have a lawyer to represent you yet, but I can certainly give you a great referral to someone experienced in this kind of law."

"What about you?" Andy asked expectantly. "Your brochure says that you do 'plaintiff's personal injury.' Isn't that what this is? Personal injury?"

"Deep breaths, deep breaths," she said silently. She simply couldn't afford another one of these time-intensive, probably cash-poor cases, no matter how sympathetic he was. She had to come up with some excuse and quick. "Yes, you're right, I do practice a lot of plaintiff's personal injury, but in this case, I *witnessed* the accident. You'll need me to testify as to what I saw so I really can't be your lawyer too. There's a huge legal conflict of interest."

"Isn't there any way around that? I mean, my family feels like there's a specialness between us. We feel kind of like you're our guardian angel." And then he said that thing that had gotten her into trouble in each of the previous David and Goliath episodes. "We really need you."

Sarah felt her resolve evaporate as she saw the unguarded vulnerability in Andy's eyes. She knew they needed her and she knew how much she could help. Maybe she could bring some peace and justice to this family who deserved it so much. So she said, "Let me look into it. It may be that you can just sign a written waiver of the conflict of interest and it will be fine."

"Thank you so much," he virtually squeaked with excitement. "My dad will be so happy. He doesn't remember you, of course. But he remembers a sensation, a sensation of someone being there with him—a kind, gentle presence. That's why he's convinced you're his guardian angel."

"Well, I'm not sure there's any part of me that qualifies for 'angel,' but he is sure sweet to think so. I'll look into the conflict issues and give you a call. Please meet my assistant in the front and she'll take all your information." And as Andy grabbed her in a spontaneous hug, blushed, and scurried for the lobby, Sarah started constructing "the spin" on this one for Jesse.

CHAPTER THREE

Sarah awoke the next morning with a splitting headache and accompanying foul mood. The fight with Jesse the night before had been the worst ever. She didn't understand why he got so upset about the way she ran her business. After all, it was her business. Not his. In retrospect, she didn't know why she had even brought up Andy and his father. Maybe she did it just to stir up a fight. She knew how he'd react and he didn't disappoint. Maybe her subconscious was telling her that it was time to move on. She dragged herself out of bed and brewed an impossibly strong cup of coffee, grabbed some aspirin, and headed for the shower.

Just then the ring from the phone cut through the apartment and lodged in her pounding head. What asshole could be calling at seven o'clock in the morning on a Saturday, she thought irritably as she dived for the phone to make the head exploding noise stop.

"What do you want?" Sarah screeched into the phone.

"Oh, oh, I'm so sorry. I thought you'd be up. I remember that you were always a morning girl. I'll call back later," Sam said.

Sarah just about dropped the phone in surprise and embarrassment. It was Sam Morrow. It had been so nice running into him after the court appearance the day of the accident that she'd called him about a week after, but he hadn't returned her call. She'd figured he wasn't interested and let it go at that. To hear from him at this late date was quite a surprise albeit a welcome one.

"I'm so sorry. I just woke up with this headache and feel exceptionally beastly. But you remember correctly, I am a morning person. I usually don't yell at people until much later in the day."

"I really do apologize for calling so early, but I wanted to catch you before you went out. I have an extra ticket for the Stones concert tonight and I was wondering if you wanted to go."

Even more waves of surprise washed over her and she broke out in a cold sweat. "I would love to go," she said excitedly, but caught herself as she remembered her previous plans. "I really would love to go, but my parents are having their thirty-fifth wedding anniversary party tonight. I need to go to that."

"How fantastic. Congratulations all around. I knew it was a long shot anyway, but I thought I'd give it a go. Maybe we can get together sometime next week? I'll call you."

The "I'll call you" lingered in the air like an overstuffed mosquito and then kept surfacing periodically at the party and all day Sunday. Sarah had decided not to work on Sunday for the first time in a very long time, but instead of resting, her mind had been scattered all day, flitting from thought to thought, and somehow, always coming back to the phone call from Sam. She didn't know what it meant and, God knows, she had considered every possible angle—ad nauseam. So by Monday, she was delighted to start working on some of the preliminary issues in Andy's case and turn her mind to something more productive.

She began with an analysis of the conflict issue and decided she could get around it with a written waiver and someone to either second chair her or actually try the case if it went to trial. Chances are she would settle the case anyway so she wasn't particularly concerned. Next, she started a background search of the driver. Andy had dropped off all his court papers over the weekend so she started with them. The driver's name was Paul Rodriguez. He was thirty-six years old, married, with two small children, ages three and five. He had only been in Los Angeles for about a year. He had no history of criminal behavior and, instead, appeared for all purposes like a stand-up family man who bolted the scene of the accident out of ignorance and fear rather than any kind of malicious intent. All in all it was a pretty tidy package. Sarah scanned the papers for evidence of insurance and employment, but the documents were silent on both. The public defender's mark-up sheet was only partially completed, with many questions unanswered and many other questions completed only with illegible handwritten notations. Now that's a practice for you, Sarah thought. Next time I complain about mine, I'll think about what goes on in the PD's office. Sarah made a cursory plan of action on the case, drafted the retainer agreement, and called her friend and background check expert, Duane Marcez.

The rest of her day was spent on other routine matters and then in preparation for her meeting with Andy's father, Murray, at five o'clock. She braced herself for the shock of seeing someone who had been through so much physically and emotionally. No matter how much personal injury work she did, she never got used to seeing the results of car accidents, especially when car met pedestrian. It wasn't just the physical horror that assaulted her when she walked in, but the emotional pain as well. It reached across the room and smothered her the moment she stepped through the door. She hated it. But it was unavoidable.

Sarah drove her never-die Honda to the Matthews' house, situated in an unremarkable middleclass neighborhood in the Valley. She always went to her client's house to sign the retainer because it made everyone feel much more comfortable and showed her client that she cared enough about them to make the trek. She pulled up in front of one of the ubiquitous 1950s style California ranch homes that characterize the older parts of the Valley and noted the de rigueur white shutters and decorative low-slung fence. She had grown up in a house like this and the memory still made her feel a bit claustrophobic. She barely had a leg out of the car door when Andy bounded out to meet her. He was so genuinely thrilled to see her that she responded in kind.

"Thank you so much for coming out," Andy said. Dad has been looking forward to meeting you all day. Mom too."

"I've been looking forward to it myself. How's school going? I bet you're starting to make spring break plans. That sure sounds good about now!"

"Actually, I'm not doing anything. I'd rather stay home and be with my mom and dad. That seems more important to me right now." He smiled that sweet, shy smile that she was growing to love and led the way up the walkway and into the house.

Nothing could have prepared Sarah for what greeted her

when she walked through the door. Murray was seated at the window in a well-worn blue and green plaid La-Z-Boy. His feet were carefully placed in pillowed grooves on the footrest, his body wrapped in layers of sweatshirts, sweaters, shawls and wraps. It was as if he couldn't get enough heat into his body even though the temperature in the house was beyond stifling. But it was his face that made her let out an involuntary gasp. Six plastic surgeries later and it was still contorted, almost inhuman. In the partial shadows cast by the late afternoon sun streaming through the window, it took on an eerie resemblance to the phantom of the opera that was almost overwhelming—half human, half mask.

She fought to regain her composure. But Murray was apparently used to this response and spoke quickly. "I'm sorry to frighten you. I know I'm a bit difficult to look at right now, but the doctors have a lot of hope for me and think they can get me back to almost normal in no time. I told them normal isn't good enough, and have officially placed my order for a young Carey Grant mug." He said it with a wink and a smile and Sarah felt her discomfort evaporate in his charm.

"It's really wonderful to finally meet you Mr. Matthews. Your son is a very special young man and I can see the apple's pretty close to the tree."

"Actually, if I can be so bold to correct my own attorney, it's nice to meet you *again*. I want to thank you from the bottom of my heart for being there with me at an awful time. Being there when I really needed someone to be there. Thank you."

She murmured something unintelligible in response just as Andy's mother walked into the room and took a position next to Murray on the matching couch. She was a slight woman with a warm smile and Sarah thought they looked like the kind of parents she had hoped Andy had. Loving, caring, without pretext—a couple who had aged perfectly together.

"Thank you for coming, Ms. Brockman," Alice said. "Andy has told us so many wonderful things about you. I can see he was right."

"I'm sure Andy's a bit of an exaggerator, but I think the world of him and look forward to all of us working together on this case." With everyone's head nodding in agreement, Sarah settled into the remaining living room chair and spent the next two hours going through her personal injury intake questionnaire. As always, she was meticulous in eliciting every possible fact and recollection from the Matthews so that she knew everything they knew. She did this with every new case she took—sometimes overkill, but usually critical to avoid surprises during the case and, especially, at trial. She was in the car and back over the hill by eight o'clock, signed retainer in hand.

The case seemed relatively run of the mill except for a few things that kept nagging at her as she drove through the gate and parked underground in her apartment building. The first was why didn't the prosecutor introduce any evidence about the speed Paul Rodriguez was going when he hit Murray? The officer on the scene marked excessive speed as the basis for the reckless driving charge in his accident report, but Alice and Andy were emphatic that the prosecutor said nothing about speed at trial. She would double-check that when she received the trial transcript later in the week, but if that was true, of course there was no evidence to support the reckless driving charge and Judge Schneider was right in dismissing it. Sarah knew the prosecutor's office was overworked and underpaid, but this kind of mistake would constitute an extraordinarily shoddy job even for them. And why the veritable dirth of information at trial about either Rodriguez's income, or his employment and ownership of the truck? At the very least, Schneider was required to make an evidentiary inquiry into Rodriguez's finances to impose an appropriate fine, since Schneider had reduced the fine from the statutory minimum *in the interests of justice*. But Andy and Alice said there was no financial evidence other than Rodriguez's testimony that he made minimum wage. Also, why did Rodriguez turn himself into the prosecutor's office instead of the police station? For someone who claimed to be generally ignorant about the legal system in this country and afraid that he would be thrown in jail, how did Rodriguez even know what a prosecutor did, let alone find his way to the appropriate office. Definitely odd.

Sarah poked around in the fridge for anything even vaguely edible and ended up with the questionable remainder of a tortilla pie and dried up Spanish rice from her visit home last week. Two glasses of cabernet later, she dropped off into a fitful sleep, her brain spinning with too many questions to allow anything else. But as she tossed and turned, another man waited, wide awake, across town, his eyes trained intently on an underground parking garage gate. As he stared, the gate opened and a recent model E550 Mercedes came into view. Sleek and black, with shiny custom hubcaps, it swung into view and then into focus as Duane used his night vision goggles to peer inside the passenger compartment. And as he looked, he caught his breath. It was Paul Rodriguez.

CHAPTER FOUR

When Sarah arrived at the office the next morning, she found two packages waiting for her: one from Jesse with all the belongings she had ever left at his apartment (along with a little yellow Post-it that read "The End") and Duane Marcez. As shocked as she was by the contemptible way Jesse had ended their relationship, she was even more surprised to see Duane. Duane was not a morning person, so much so that he adamantly refused to even turn on his cell phone before noon. To see him in her office, dressed and coherent, before nine o'clock in the morning was a shock indeed.

"What are you doing here?" Sarah asked as she shook off her umbrella and stashed it next to the door. "Did I forget to pay my bill?"

"And good morning to you too, Sarah," Duane said without a hint of a smile. "We need to talk. Can we go into your office, please?"

As soon as they were seated with the door closed, Duane began. "I started work on Paul Rodriguez right after you called.

I found things right away that didn't add up. Lots of joint credit cards, frequent address changes, and what seemed to be multiple aliases. What bothered me the most, though, was what appeared to be a pattern of carrying high balances on credit cards and other loans and then suddenly paying them off in full all about the same time. I don't think you can scream "illegal" louder than that. Rodriguez has got to be into gambling, drugs, or some other "under the radar" activity that produces these kinds of big hits. A guy making minimum wage just doesn't have the opportunity. I got so fired up that I decided to go take a look at this Mr. Paul Rodriguez before I called you. After a few dead ends and false addresses, I found Mr. Rodriguez . . . driving a spanking new E550 Mercedes."

Sarah gasped and leaned back heavily in her chair. "You've got to be kidding. This is a very different Paul Rodriguez than was painted at trial. Are you sure this is the *right* Paul Rodriguez?"

"You know me, you know my work. It's the right guy."

Sarah sat quietly, letting the enormity of the disclosure sink in. Suddenly, a case that had seemed pretty run-of-the-mill had morphed into something very different indeed. She felt her stomach muscles tighten and her jaw set. "Well, we're going to have to drill deep on this one. Do a full investigation. If anything leads offshore, go after that too. What do you think about surveillance?"

"I think we can start with a twenty-four-hour tail and then move up to electronic in a few days if we think it's warranted. I have a new guy I use who is cheaper and very good. I'll set him up right away."

"OK, that sounds great. I still can't believe this. Duane, is there any way I can stretch your bills out a bit? As you probably figured, I'm on contingency on this one."

"Sure, no problem. I'll be in touch as soon as I get a work-up or if I find something else too juicy to keep to myself. Mr. Paul Rodriguez and I are about to become intimately acquainted."

And with that, Duane was up and out, and as Sarah gathered her notes for filing, she felt an unexpected surge of buoyancy and freedom. For once, she didn't have to justify herself to Jesse. And it felt good.

◆ ◆ ◆

What didn't feel good was the level of irritation Maurice was feeling and so early in the morning. He hated it when his egg soufflé was overcooked. It should be light and airy, a delicate, refined kind of victual that almost vanished on the tongue. This, by contrast, sat heavily in his mouth like a vulgar impostor, too crude to even eat. He pushed his plate away and called for his chef. Yet another one would have to go. He would have Merrick do it later. No need for any unpleasantness now.

"Bring me a bowl of fresh strawberries and two raisin scones. This soufflé is inedible."

The chef scurried back to the kitchen, knowing his days were numbered, just as the iPhone in his soon to be ex-employer's robe pocket rang with an incoming call. "Yes? When? Who did you say? Never heard of her. Well, do the usual. Use Simon. Call him right away and call me with an update this afternoon."

Maurice settled back in his chair and reached for his still steaming espresso, his irritation increasing by the second. He hated to be bothered by the small details of his practice. He was a big idea man, a man of stature and prestige. He shouldn't have to deal with such pedantic matters as staffing a crappy little wipe-up. He could feel his blood pressure rising. He was in need of a fix. He checked his calendar and saw that he had a Republican fundraising dinner at the Marimont scheduled for seven o'clock in the evening. Maybe he could get set up before, or maybe after. He was due. He didn't even care if his bitch of a wife knew. Ever since she found out about his last episode a month ago, she had been distant, frigid. She wouldn't even come down for breakfast. Not that he cared about that. What he did care about was that it was just one more annoying detail he would have to take care of now sooner than he had planned. But that was all it was—a small detail. Neither she nor her lawyer would ever find the money. It was too well hidden. He made a mental note to transfer last month's draw to his accounts at Obelisk Holdings. Some details he did care about.

CHAPTER FIVE

Less than two hours later, Simon was already hunched over his computer, his bony fingers flying over the keys in a way that showed they had traveled this path many times before. Rodriguez had not yet been served, but Simon knew a complaint would be coming his way in short order. This was Simon's favorite part of any case. He loved thinking about how opposing counsel would recoil at the mound of discovery they would receive from him along with his answer to the complaint. He smiled gleefully as he made his way through his various personal injury discovery forms, interrogatories, requests for admission, deposition notices—it really was too much fun. He hadn't heard of this lawyer before, though. Sarah Brockman. Probably some newbie fresh from the bar exam. Who else would take this case? The criminal adjudication couldn't be clearer. Leaving the scene of an accident. Ha! He almost laughed out loud. They didn't even get a reckless driving through. He'd have to look at the transcript and see how they did it. Made his job too easy. Plus, on paper, Rodriguez looks like a down and outer, almost indigent—definitely not a source for ready cash. Simon could hardly wait for the games to begin. He would keep pounding the fact that there was no insurance and no money to be had from Rodriguez and probably settle the case for about $2,000 nuisance value. And probably within a few weeks. Maurice would be pleased. The only thing that marred an otherwise divine professional moment, however, was that it was Paul Rodriguez again. Rodriguez was getting sloppy—and from what he'd heard, cocky too. Something had to be done about the situation. He made a mental note to bring it up in the next meeting.

He picked up the phone to leave a message for Sam only to find Sam at the other end of the line. "Hey. Hi, Sam. The phone didn't even ring. One of those weird déjà vu kind of things. How are you? I was calling to see if you wanted to have lunch today."

"That sounds great," Sam said. "I have a bit of a headache from that stupid mixer last night, but should be feeling fine by then. Madriano's at noon? We can beat the rush."

"Perfect."

Sam hung up the phone, reconsidered, and dialed another number. Sarah's assistant answered the phone.

"I'm sorry Mr. Morrow, Sarah has her 'do not disturb' on. She's got a filing deadline this afternoon and is unavailable till then."

"Will you tell her I called and that she can reach me on my cell phone later this afternoon and evening? Thanks so much." Sam was surprised to feel disappointed at not connecting with Sarah. He wasn't sure why he didn't return her call all those months ago, but suspected a large degree of cowardice. He had convinced himself to call her for the concert by telling himself that he was just renewing an old law school friendship. Now he was just a bit sideways. He wandered down the hall to get some fresh coffee so he could tackle the pile of documents gathering dust on his credenza. As he walked, he sang the little private song he was working on in his head that went to the tune of "To Every Season, Turn, Turn, Turn," only his lyrics were along the lines of "For Simply No Reason, Churn, Churn, Churn." He thought it was pretty funny and it was really progressing quite nicely. He absently thought about whether *The Rodent* might be interested in publishing the lyrics—anonymously, of course. He looked up just as Maurice Strickland passed him in the hall. Mr. Strickland always intimidated him and, he thought, with good reason. A named partner of the firm, Strickland was a hulking brute of a man. He had played defensive tackle at USC and even been drafted by the Raiders, but had declined a football career to go to law school. Even now, thirty years later, he was still a physically imposing presence. When coupled with his exquisite taste in clothes and formidable intelligence, he was a force that overwhelmed even his most accomplished adversaries.

"Good morning Mr. Morrow."

"Good morning, sir."

"I understand you've been doing an exceptional job on the Escon matter and your hours are some of the best in the firm. You're a role model for all your classmates. Keep up the good work."

"Thank you, sir. You are so kind."

Maurice nodded and continued down the hall while Sam harangued himself for his idiotic "you are so kind." What kind of a comment was that? It sounded more like a doddering old aunt than a hard-hitting senior associate on the fast track to partnership. It never failed to amaze him. He said something stupid every time he talked to Strickland.

But Maurice didn't think so. He considered what he knew about Morrow. Straight shooter. No wife or kids. No known drug or alcohol problems. But no known financial pressures either. Smart. Hardworking. Maybe he was getting tired of working in corporate litigation. Maybe it was time to move him over to the personal injury side. He might enjoy the change of pace. Plus, he could tell him that working in the biggest grossing practice group in the firm would help his partnership chances. The fact was that the personal injury group was working at full throttle and stretched almost beyond its capacity. And the "press of business" would only increase. He smiled as he thought of the press of business. What a quaint term to describe what he did. He instructed his secretary to set a meeting with Sam later in the morning and began his review of the day's action memos. Watson had settled for $3.5 million, defense verdict on Manley, and Perrata had just gone to pre-trial conference. He would bring in a couple more big injury cases by the end of the week. With the winter rains making the freeways hazardous, a few more major accidents would not be unexpected. He made some notes in his calendar and headed into the conference room for his first meetings of the day.

Meanwhile, Sam had just got a call from Maurice's secretary and was bracing himself for the meeting ahead. He continued to alternately plow through his stupor-inducing pile of documents and berate himself for his idiotic interaction with Strickland. By half past eleven, he had put himself in such a tortured state that when the phone rang, he grabbed it like it was the last remaining life preserver on the Titanic.

"Sam Morrow."

"Oh, my . . . you must be billing in one-sixteenth intervals now if you can't afford the luxury of a 'hello.'"

It was Sarah.

His involuntary gasp gave him away. "I, uh . . . Sarah. I thought you were immersed in some form of legal tender due later today."

"I was, but decided that all available brilliance had been imparted by me in that brief by eleven. Any more, as they say, would have been commentary."

"Fewer words. That's a novel concept for a lawyer. You must just play one on TV."

"I wish. I'd have a much better wardrobe."

Sam caught himself smiling at their easy banter. What an unexpected treat to brighten his otherwise painful morning. "So what's going on with you? How are you doing?"

"Pretty good. Crazy busy. I just got in a new case that could be my biggest car case so far. And the clients are the sweetest dears you could ever meet. The weird thing is, I just got it in. I mean, I've only had it a few days and it's already taken some strange turns. Lots of conflicting versions of reality. Not that I care. If I can just find some cash on the backside, I'll be a happy camper."

"Sounds a lot more interesting than what I've been doing. Documents, documents, and more documents. Maybe I should claim a paper cut injury, collect worker's comp, and ride the gravy train."

"Now *that's* a plan, but if it's worker's comp, you will most likely be riding the Purina dog chow gravy train."

"Ha, ha. You're missing your calling." He looked up just in time to see his desk clock hit 11:40 a.m. "Oh, my god, I've got to go. I've got a meeting with Strickland in five minutes. Dinner later?"

And as Sarah squeaked out a spontaneous "OK," Sam grabbed his suit coat, muttered a garbled "goodbye" and raced down the hall past the associate offices and into the exalted regions of the firm's partnership.

CHAPTER SIX

Sarah walked into the lobby at Cabot, Strickland & Baines at exactly seven o'clock in the evening and literally stopped and stared. It was the most exquisite lobby she had ever seen, every inch bespeaking wealth and power. She involuntarily covered her mouth as she gasped at the magnificence of it all. The reception desk was cherry wood inlaid with mahogany and what appeared to be veins of green tourmaline. Pearled marble covered the floor and the walls were sheathed in rich Belgium damask. A hand-blown Venetian chandelier forced the eye upward in an almost heavenly reverence. The lobby was, in fact, divine. Sarah walked to the set of companion couches at the far end of the room and sat down opposite a woman like none she had ever seen before. To say that she was stunning was to capture only the most mundane of her gifts. She exuded an aura that was at once disarmingly charming while somehow reserved—seemingly intelligent, yet patently superficial. And all this without saying a word. She lifted her eyes from what appeared to be a loosely bound transcript of some kind and looked at Sarah with deep blue shimmering eyes. Eyes that men wrote songs about and got lost in. Eyes that belonged to the chosen, the privileged, to the homecoming queens and the Miss Americas. The kind of eyes that had taunted Sarah all her life, as she was dark haired, dark-eyed, thin in a too-thin kind of way, cute enough sometimes in certain circles, but never when compared to *those* kinds of girls. Sarah felt all the old embarrassed feelings of worthlessness rush over her. She almost couldn't breathe from the weight of it. She pulled her jacket tightly about her in a diminutive, protective manner and glanced up to see the eyes still watching her. And then they were gone. A brief nod, a hint of perfume, and the woman was up, elegance in motion, long shapely legs stretching through the interior doors of Cabot, Strickland & Baines.

Sarah reached for her bag and started the hunt for her iPhone just as Sam swung through the opposing set of mahogany doors and walked to her side.

"What are you doing, getting ready to bawl me out for being a minute late?"

"No way," Sarah laughed, easily shaking off the negative feelings she had just been experiencing. "I just figured I'd catch up on some e-mails while I had a few minutes."

"That was your few minutes. Let's go have some fun. Unless, of course, you want to see the little hovel I call home?"

"Sure, I'd love to."

Sam waived his security card on the door panel and Sarah followed him into the hallowed halls of the firm. It was every bit as impressive inside as the lobby. Colorful Persian rugs accented thick Berber carpeting. Important paintings. Important sculpture. Clearly a place to do serious work. But, surprisingly, here and there, in little out of the way nooks, stood amusingly whimsical sculptures of favorite fairy tales and nursery rhymes—the Mad Hatter, the Ugly Duckling, the Princess and the Pea, all lovingly detailed with comic genius. Hans Christian Anderson seemed to be a favorite subject. They were small, partially hidden, and always unexpected; Sarah laughed every time she came upon one.

"I love these!" Sarah exclaimed. "Who made these and, no offense, but what are they doing in your firm?"

"Well, there's a long story and a short story. Which one do you want?

"Both."

"The short story is that they were made by one of the retired partners of our firm. The long story is that they were made by retired partner Alexander Cabot, esteemed founder of Cabot, Strickland & Baines, and they were made for a reason."

Sam looked at Sarah to see if she was really interested or just being polite. "Are you sure you want to hear the long version? It's a bit of a tale."

"Absolutely. Go for it."

"Well, Alexander began the firm in Oklahoma City at the end of the Great Depression in 1939 when he was just twenty-five years old. Apparently he had become obsessed with Steinbeck's novel about the dust bowls and the lives of the farmers in *The Grapes of Wrath*. He couldn't get the farmers out of his mind. The gaunt faces and despairing eyes of the financially and emotionally bankrupt haunted him. Now, mind you, he was Order of the Coif from Columbia with five big-moneyed Wall Street law firm offers outstanding. Plus, he was Catholic and a Brooklyn boy. He had never even been out of New York. He had to look on an atlas to see where Oklahoma was, but he had to go.

He moved to Oklahoma City and set up shop in the parlor of one of the city's many boarding houses and lived in one of the rooms upstairs. Such as it was. The firm lore from those days is that Alexander's living quarters consisted of a bed and a wash basin, for which he paid by helping with various chores around the boarding house. An endless stream of farmers and those in need came at all hours without appointments and mostly without money. They came before the morning chores and after the evening ones. Some of the city women came in the middle of the night, having snuck out of their homes while their husbands slept, to seek advice or just a willing ear. They came, they were helped, and they went. And with each client, Alexander felt the promise of America returning and he was exhilarated. Over time, he moved his practice to other hot spots of the country—the coal fields of Kentucky, the Garment District in New York, and, eventually, to the immigrant workers in Southern California, which is where he sprang to national prominence and where you probably first heard about him.

The strange thing about his career though, was that he made money doing public interest law, almost in spite of himself. Since his clients had no money, they frequently paid him in trade. Among the farmers, it was produce, chickens, pies made by the wives, occasional homespun clothes, and quilts. On other occasions, it was deeds to mines in Appalachia, tracts of land, foreclosed industrial buildings, and bankrupt businesses. These properties were all virtually worthless, but Alexander accepted them because that was all his clients had to offer and because it was important to them to pay whatever they could.

Over time, and in a surprising twist of providence, some

of these previously worthless offerings turned into valuable assets. Property values reversed and, on a few occasions, skyrocketed. A big coal company bought his mineral rights in the Appalachians. The mega-developer McCormick Housing bought land he owned for a housing project. His industrial space was transformed into mini-storage. It was as if the great hand of God himself reached down to reward a man who had given so much to so many.

Of course the effect of the money on Alexander was much different than it would have been on just about anybody else. It wasn't that Alexander didn't care about the money. He did. But he cared about it because it gave him the freedom to do even more and give even more. He started to expand his public interest empire. He started taking on corporate clients and individuals of means. He added partners. He leased attractive space. He appeared to be a regular law firm. But he wasn't. For every full-fee paying client, he added at least two pro bono matters. Plus, and here's the genius of his passion, he made his paying clients donate a surcharge of an additional ten percent of their legal bill to his non-profit foundation. He felt that the simple act of donation, whether coerced or not, created a habit, and that habit created an effect that could multiply all over the world. He was a crafty soul with a brilliant mind and a heart of gold who built a public interest empire. And through it all, he never lost his sense of humor or his humanity.

Which brings us to Alice in Wonderland. You see, when Alexander was a young lawyer first starting out in Kansas City, he met a little girl. Her name was Elisabeth and she was a beautiful little girl with wide blue eyes and golden pigtails. Her parents brought her with them when they came to see him late one night. They were in the midst of a foreclosure on their farm and had nowhere to go and no way to live. He did what he could for them, which he felt was not enough, but it meant the world to them. And when they were packed and on their way to California to start a new life, they dropped in to say goodbye. After hugs and well wishes, Elisabeth shyly approached and pressed a small, hard object into his hand. Wrapped in old newspaper with a well-worn piece of red string, it looked like a lumpy piece of clay. But when he opened it, he saw the most delightful rendition of Alice in Wonderland that he had ever seen. It was clear that Elisabeth had made it and that she had labored over every detail. But the thing that was most astounding about it was its sense of humor and hope. Here in the darkest time was a glimmer of the human spirit. To this day, he still loves that piece more than any other art he owns. It sits in a special place of honor in his home, protected as well as anything can be, and he makes these figures to honor Elisabeth and honor the best that life has to offer."

"What a fantastic story," Sarah exclaimed. "I've heard and read a lot about Alexander Cabot, but I thought it was just hype and big firm marketing. I didn't think those kinds of lawyers actually existed anymore."

"Well, probably not for long. At his eighty-ninth birthday party a few weeks ago, he looked noticeably frailer than he did when I saw him at Christmas. I think time is catching up even with him. He's been out of the management of the firm since his retirement five years ago, but recently, he's stopped coming to all but the most significant firm functions. It's a sad thing to watch." Sam paused and tilted his head in thought. "Actually, I misspoke. It's not sad at all. When you meet him and see that sparkle in his eye, you know that you are meeting someone who is truly alive. I doubt that spark will be extinguished even when his body is."

"You must really love this man," Sarah said softly.

"I guess I do," Sam whispered self-consciously. "He's the reason I came to the firm and one of the reasons I decided to become a lawyer in the first place."

Sarah moved closer and put her hand in his. She could feel the heat of his body and the stocky maleness of his fingers—thick where hers were slender, coarse where hers were gentle. Both hands doing the same work, performing the same tasks, but hers very different from his.

He looked down at their hands and slowly intertwined his fingers with hers, one finger on top of the next, weaving, braiding, each finger falling comfortably in place, each filling the space where the other left off. And then she could feel his eyes on her. She could feel his thoughts. And as she raised her eyes to meet his, there was no mistaking his intention. Her breath stuck in her throat and her heart felt like it was beating out of her chest. She fought for composure. She turned to fully face him and felt his arms slide up, encircling her waist in a strong, possessive way.

"Hello, Sam. I thought that was you."

Sarah spun around at the unexpected voice and came face to face with the woman from the lobby.

"I didn't recognize you without a computer strapped to your chest. I didn't know you knew how to do anything other than bill hours." She said with a wry, sardonic wit. "I'm glad to see someone is having a little fun around here and happier still to see it's you, Sam. Why don't you introduce me?" And with that, she turned her hypnotic eyes to Sarah.

"Sarah Brockman, Ariel Strickland," Sam murmured.

"Pleased to meet you," Sarah responded in her best meet-the-parents voice.

"The pleasure is mine," Ariel said. "Didn't I see you in the waiting room?"

"Yes, you did. I was waiting for Sam."

"Well, he's certainly worth waiting for," Ariel paused. "I didn't know he had a girlfriend." She said it with a slight rise at the end, hinting at the question rather than asking it. Sarah could see her watching Sam carefully for a reaction.

"Ah, uh, we're just dating. Oh, I don't mean *just* dating, I just mean we've just started dating. In fact, this is our first date." Ariel watched him twist and turn about in obvious enjoyment. Maybe she was one of those women, Sarah thought, the black widow women, who collect men, use them, and then discard them once their usefulness has run out. Or maybe it was something else. Maybe there was, or had been, something else between them.

"Enjoy yourselves," Ariel said abruptly as she turned on her heel and disappeared down the hall.

"Nice to meet you," Sarah called in reflexive politeness. "She sure is interesting, isn't she?"

"You could say that." And Sarah could see a faint blush creep up the back of Sam's neck. "She has an MBA in finance from Wharton and JD from USC, but spends her time sitting on charity committees and volunteering for the Junior League. I think it's a huge waste of talent, but she definitely helps Strickland pull the work in. And she plays her role with perfection. If she's going to be the bitch on the back, though, I hope she wears a helmet. Ariel is Strickland's third wife and it's been more than a few years since he married her. Hell, even I know Strickland well enough to know that she's vulnerable. He's a son of a bitch when it comes to a lot of things, one of which is women. I respect him as a lawyer, but not as a husband."

He finished and leaned back against the wall, his hand making a subconscious pull through his hair. He really is gorgeous, Sarah thought. Almost too gorgeous. She had to find out why he wasn't married.

"Well, let's go grab some dinner and then I have a special treat."

"Oh, I can't wait."

CHAPTER SEVEN

Sarah woke up the next morning the happiest she could remember feeling for a very long time. She stretched her legs out long, like a cat, and felt how good they felt—long, still trim even without exercise, and shapely. Her mom always told her she had pretty legs and Sarah took a moment to enjoy them and appreciate them as the gift that they were. She smiled as she thought about last night. They had gone to dinner at a fabulous hole-in-the-wall Brazilian place she was surprised Sam even knew about. She loved it. The food was delicious, and everyone was so warm and welcoming she felt like part of an extended Brazilian family almost from the moment she walked in.

The chef made them a special appetizer with plantains and black beans and then proceeded to bring out one dish after another, each one more delicious than the last. They never looked at a menu and, truthfully, she wasn't sure she knew what she was eating half the time, but it was all fantastic. Then came the treat. After the last dish was cleared, everyone pulled their chairs into a circle around a little boy, not more than ten, who began playing the most exquisite guitar she had ever heard. He played beautiful haunting ballads and fast, spicy Brazilian salsas and, after a while, everyone began to sing. Some sang the melody while others improvised their own unique harmonies that wound through the melody in a mesmerizing dance of sound. The result was breathtaking and Sarah felt a lump rise in her throat in response to the magnificence of it all. She had one of those rare, elusive moments when she felt pure joy and peace. And she had Sam to share it with and to thank for it. As she thought of him, she could still feel his gentle touch on her shoulders, her hands, and on her lips. She couldn't help but imagine more. Her lips curled up in a subconscious smile at the thought and the early morning sun tickled the wisps of hair that framed her face in such a way that made Hector swallow hard.

"I wouldn't mind having a little piece of that myself," he muttered as he adjusted the binoculars to get a clearer view. He felt his senses responding to the eroticism of the picture and felt the familiar itch returning. He was going to get lit. He couldn't wait. It had been so long, but it wasn't something you could predict or make happen. It either happened or it didn't and this one was going to do it for him. He watched her make coffee and eat a bagel. It looked like blueberry, he thought, or raisin. He could see her scan the headlines and absently toss the paper into the recycle bin. He noted the particulars of her morning in his BlackBerry for erudition later. Erudition. What a great fucking word. A word a day and pretty soon he'd have as good a vocabulary as the rest of them. Pretty fucking erudite he was. He pocketed his BlackBerry and watched her move to the closet to get dressed. Goddammit. That fucking tree was blocking his view. He adjusted his position as best he could, but there was only so much room and it wasn't enough. Well, he sure was going to remember to get a better angle tomorrow. Now he'd just have to settle for a little imagery of his own. He snapped a few pictures as she gathered her things and headed for the door. Maurice always liked pictures. Pictures and memos. He started his car and waited until Sarah's car swung out from the underground parking and headed north on Tamino where he joined it three cars back and tailed it to her office. By this time he could hardly drive. His body felt like it was being electrocuted. Every nerve seemed exposed, rubbed raw from waiting. He somehow managed to log Sarah's arrival time at her office and make it to his friend's house where he launched himself into one of the most spectacular highs of his life.

◆ ◆ ◆

Meanwhile, Sarah practically glided into the office, still awash in delicious thoughts about her evening with Sam. She even felt hungry again for the first time in months and cornered the last of the office donuts before settling in to begin her second review of the public defender's report. This time she did it carefully and took notes. She wasn't sure exactly what she was looking for, but there was something gnawing at her subconscious that had bothered her since her cursory review of the file the other day. And then she saw it. Rodriguez had been represented at trial by the Bicknel Law Firm, not the public defender's office at all. That's why the PD's notes were so sketchy. With his alleged financial situation, she could understand that Rodriguez could have hired some run-of-the-mill kind of criminal defense attorney to represent him, but Bicknel was another story. It wasn't that Bicknel wasn't a good law firm. It was *too* good a law firm—one of the top defense firms in the city. There was no way Rodriguez could have afforded this firm. Either they handled the case pro bono or the Mercedes-driving Rodriguez had paid the fare. The larger issue, though, was that Bicknel was a civil defense firm, not a criminal defense firm. They made their money representing the insurance companies that nickeled and dimed her to death. To her knowledge, they had no criminal defense attorneys in their midst and had never handled a criminal trial before. Although in this case, Schneider and the prosecutor basically made their defense for them. She did a quick general Internet search, reviewed Bicknel's website, and checked court cases online. No, she was right. Bicknel was not in the criminal defense business. And she had never heard of the lawyer who represented Rodriguez, another strange fact given the transparency of the defense bar. Her eyes scanned the remaining entries by the PD. Nothing about any employer. No insurance. Turned himself in to ADA Wilkins, who later tried the case. Interesting. Maybe she should have a little chat with Wilkins and clear some of this up. She reached for the phone just as Christine popped her head sheepishly around the door.

"Sorry to bother you when you've got your DND on, but I just pulled the messages from the machine and Duane called twice last night asking that you call him as soon as possible. He says he couldn't reach you by cell or home phone and wondered if they might both be broken," Christine said with a teasing smirk. "How was your date with Sam anyway? I noticed you couldn't wait to gobble a donut this morning."

"None of your business," Sarah said feigning irritation. "He's a nice guy. That's all. We had a good time."

"Yeah, I bet. I can tell by that youthful glow," Christine said, dashing for the door as Sarah hit it with the remnant of a decrepit granola bar. Sarah reached for the phone again, but this time to leave a message for Duane, the vampire, who would not yet be receiving.

"Hello," came a Duane-like voice over the phone.

"It can't be you," Sarah exclaimed, startled to get a live body, "unless you're on East Coast time. It's only ten."

"Tell me about it," Duane said flatly. "My whole lifestyle is getting disrupted. This case—I mean *your* case—has really got me wound up. It wakes me up and keeps me up. You can count on one hand how often *that* has happened."

"Oh my god, Duane. What is it? What's going on?"

"I haven't really figured it out yet. I'm not sure what's going on."

Sarah pressed herself back into her chair and made herself breathe before continuing. "OK, well tell me what you know. I'm listening."

"After our meeting, I decided to tail Rodriguez myself and not give it to Mark like I originally thought. It just seemed too out there to hand off to him. So the next day? No sign of Rodriguez. He doesn't leave his apartment complex. Neither did his car or his truck. But it's a work day, you know? I figure he should be working. And that means working using his truck. Anyway, I move in and get the truck and Mercedes license plate numbers. Then I bring the almighty powers of the California DMV to bear on the identification . . . which reminds me, there will be a $200 charge for Dodger tickets on your next bill, Sarah. And voila, the Mercedes is registered to a Marion Morales at 1250 Timberline Road, and the truck is registered to a Nevada LLC called K-2 Financial. Suspicious on all fronts. First stop. Who is Marion Morales? I pull Mark in as an extra set of hands and he does some bang up work in short order. Guess what he finds? Guess who Marion Morales is." Duane was actually starting to sound gleeful, clearly enjoying his moment in the sun, but Sarah was having none of it.

"I am not playing," Sarah said sternly. "This is serious. What did he find?"

"OK, OK. Sorry. Marion Morales is Paul Rodriguez's wife. But it's an alias. That's why it didn't come up in the credit report.

"Unfuckingbelievable. So the car really is his. What's he doing driving what's gotta be at least a $65,000 car? Is it a lease?"

"No. He, or I should say, *she* owns it, but not outright. And here's where it gets really interesting."

"Great. I'm holding my breath."

"Well, it turns out that the lien holder for the truck is a company called Obelisk Holdings, LLC."

Sarah made some kind of humpf sound and Duane continued.

"I decided to do some quick research on K-2 and Obelisk to see what they do and if there's any connection between them. It turns out neither corporation is affiliated with meat or meat delivery. In fact, they're affiliated with nothing. They seem to be shells set up by God knows who to do God knows what. Obelisk just does it in a more exotic location—that location being the beautiful and oh so distant Cook Islands. Now, we all know that the Cook Islands have become, in the last five years, what the Cayman Islands were in the 90s: a place for all those Bens, Alexanders, and Jeffersons to lay their pretty little heads without any pesky reporting requirements."

"Yes indeed. A haven for hiders of lost money."

"You got it. So I try my powers of persuasion and every connection I have, but can't find out anything more about Obelisk other than that it has one managing agent with the initials A.C. Apparently under Cook Island banking laws, you don't even have to publicly list the name of the managing agent. It's enough to declare that the LLC has one. Which brings us to the trust. Obelisk Holdings, LLC is actually a shell itself that owns an irrevocable trust named 'The Rabbit Hole Trust.' In effect, Obelisk, together with its trust, is one big goodie bag filled with an unknown and unknowable amount of assets. It could just be the trust or it could be billions in cash or bonds, stocks, real estate or the Holy Grail for that matter. Interestingly," and Duane paused for dramatic effect, "there is only one beneficiary of the trust. Only one person in this whole world gets whatever is in that trust."

Sarah sucked in her breath and squeezed the phone into a strangle hold. "One beneficiary." She let the words slowly penetrate her brain. "Who is it?"

"I don't know yet," Duane said wryly, "I had to get at least one hour of sleep last night."

"Oh, I'm so sorry," Sarah said. "You've done absolutely amazing work in an unbelievably short period of time. Thank you very much. I really appreciate it."

"You're welcome. I'll admit, I got a bit rabid about it. It's like a treasure hunt. Each clue draws you to the next. I can't wait to find the chest at the end."

"I understand. Where do you go from here?"

"I'm going to make a visit to 1250 Timberline Road and see what's at that address and if I can make any sense of that part of the equation. I'll also do a full background check on good old Marion and probably have Mark do a little surveillance, depending on what surfaces in the background check."

"Great. Let me see what I can do on my end regarding Obelisk and K-2. I know a few asset protection attorneys who specialize in Cook Island transactions. If nothing else, at least I can understand how the legal structures fit together."

"Sounds like a plan. Oh, and by the way, don't be thinking that you can start calling me before noon just because I answered the phone once. You only *thought* that was me. Please leave a message after the beep. Beeeeeeeep." And with that, Duane Marcez, clearly sleep-deprived vampire investigator, hung up.

CHAPTER EIGHT

At another law office on the other side of town, Sam was still enjoying his own memories of his evening with Sarah. He was surprised by how little he actually knew her even though they had been in the same study group in law school and had spent countless hours together slaving over torts and criminal law. It was as if he was meeting her for the first time—sweet and gentle, but with a flash of spice that could surface at any time and a quirky sense of humor that he just loved. He couldn't wait to see her again. He checked the time. Too early to call. He didn't want to look desperate. Anyway, he needed to finish reviewing the last of that annoying document pile so he could work with Simon in the afternoon. To his surprise, he found that he was actually looking forward to learning the personal injury trade now that he'd had time for Maurice's directive to sink in. He thought he might actually enjoy it. Maybe the disillusionment he'd been feeling with his career stemmed from simple boredom. He had been doing the same thing for a very long time. There was, after all, only so much you could do with a contract.

The documents took just a bit longer than three hours, so when he finished he was hungry and ready for lunch. Even so, he couldn't resist calling Sarah.

"This is your doctor, uh . . . Dr. Hurtzless, and I was just calling to see if you took your prescription for a nutritious, well-balanced, relaxing lunch with a soothing companion yet?"

Sarah could barely contain herself. She had thought about Sam all morning in spite of the troublesome information conveyed by Duane. It was as if her brain was on replay. Every time she tried to think about something else, it kept rerouting back to thoughts of their evening together. Have to finish the interrogatories for Simpson. Sam. Pay the rent and utilities. Sam. Even her grocery list included Sam. But when he hadn't called by noon, she thought maybe he didn't feel the same way. Now this call and invitation had her floating above the clouds again.

"Well, actually I haven't, doctor. You see, I was a little confused about the prescription. Can I substitute the generic for the 'soothing companion' or does it have to be the name brand?"

"Oh no, you certainly cannot substitute the generic. A generic soothing companion simply will not do. The name brand is required."

"I understand, doctor, but I can't quite make out the writing. Who exactly is the name brand?"

"Let me check my records. Ah, here it is. The name brand required is a certain Sam Morrow. Are you familiar with this brand and do you know where to fill your prescription?"

"I am somewhat familiar with the brand, but definitely not

with all the side effects," Sarah said, stifling giggles. "And I have no idea where to fill it."

"I can help you with that. You need to go to the Hong Kong Koi Gardens in Marina del Rey to fill it. The exact address is: 1411 Fiji Way. I know it's out of the way, but that's the only place that can fill your prescription."

Sarah just about hooted with delight. How fun was this? She loved Marina del Rey, but rarely allowed herself the luxury of the travel time to the water. She would just have to make time for it today.

"Alright, doctor. I will leave now and should be there in about thirty-five minutes."

"Perfect. I'm glad I called to check up on you. And remember, this prescription has unlimited refills."

Sarah grabbed her purse and headed for the door. "I'll be back in a couple hours," she called to Christine, hoping it would be more than a few. She swung her car onto Tujunga and then onto the 10 Freeway, not noticing the dark colored sedan that fell in line a few cars back. She arrived at the restaurant exactly thirty minutes later and parked almost at the door since the lunch rush was long over. In fact, there were just three other cars in the parking lot, one of which she recognized as Sam's.

The restaurant was nestled right on the water between the boat basin and Spinnaker Park and, even now, at the end of winter, the front garden was breathtaking. Sago palms, Calla lilies and birds-of-paradise dotted a green background of lush moss and ferns. Two miniature waterfalls made the interlocking koi ponds even more enchanting. Seeing the garden, Sarah remembered that she had been to this place many years before and thought what a waste it was that she hadn't been here since. Oh well. She was here now and she was going to enjoy every minute of it. She swung open one of the enormous teak doors and allowed her eyes to adjust to the dim interior. Tasteful and simple, just what the good doctor ordered. There was no host at the podium, so she moved toward the sound of muffled voices coming from the garden room. She could just make out Sam's voice and a vaguely familiar woman's voice.

"Really, Sam, I don't know what you mean. You can't possibly think I'm stalking you," the voice teased. "Seeing you twice in twenty-four hours is just extremely good fortune."

And then another teasing voice, this one an older man's. "Besides, Sam, it's clear Ariel didn't come to see you. I mean, I don't see you sitting here at the table."

Everyone laughed heartily while Sarah braced herself for yet another meeting with Ariel Strickland.

"Hi, everyone. Sam. Nice to see you again, Ariel," she said with a smile as she entered the patio room and made her way to their table. Sam kissed her gently on the cheek and then grabbed her hand and held it while he made the introductions.

"Sarah, I want you to meet Mr. Alexander Cabot, brilliant lawyer, esteemed founder, apparent man about town," he said with a wink to Ariel, "and the heart and soul of our firm. Alexander, this is Sarah Brockman, who is also a brilliant lawyer with her own firm, smart, funny, gorgeous and who, for some unfathomable reason, has graciously consented to date me."

"Very nice to meet you," Alexander said. "If you hadn't been so prompt, I'm sure Sam would have told me even more wonderful things about you than he just did."

Sarah blushed and added, "As he has about you."

"Oh, what a quaint little love fest," Ariel chimed in playfully. "Can I play too?"

"Of course you can, my dear," Alexander said. "You know you're one of my favorite objects of flattery."

Everyone laughed and Sam said, "You better watch out, Alexander, or I'm going to have to tell Mr. Strickland about this." He wasn't sure, but he thought he detected a slight, almost imperceptible pause and then, finally, the laugh he was expecting from Alexander and Ariel.

"Oh no," Alexander said just a click too strongly. "I think this will be our little secret."

"Whatever you say, sir. You're the boss. Well, we'll leave you in peace to enjoy the rest of your lunch. It was wonderful seeing you both." And Sarah and Sam walked hand in hand back to the entrance where the owner himself greeted them and led them to what was most certainly the best ocean view table in the house.

"Oh, this is so beautiful, Sam. Thank you for filling my prescription."

"Believe me, the pleasure is all mine. I'm sorry about the surprise meeting back there. I didn't expect to see anyone here at this hour, let alone those two. Especially together. I don't think I've ever seen them together, even with their spouses. And when I walked in, they had their heads really close. Seemed like they were working on something."

"I hardly know them and it seems strange to me too." Sarah agreed. "Here. Way off the beaten path. At this time. Maybe Ariel is planning a surprise party for her hubby."

"Could be, but like I said, Strickland is a real asshole when it comes to women, especially his wives. And from the general gossip I've heard around the firm, I don't think everything is particularly delightful in the Strickland household anyway."

"What do you mean?"

"Apparently Strickland has been stepping out on her. People were saying that and then my secretary saw him going up to the concierge floor of The Palms Hotel with a room key in his hand. She said there was someone in front of him, but she couldn't see who it was."

"That doesn't sound good. I guess you never know what goes on behind closed doors."

"No, you don't. But I know what's going on inside my stomach and it's a whole lot of growling. Let's order."

As Sam and Sarah enjoyed a delicious blackened cod with a spicy Thai sauce, Alexander and Ariel were finishing their coffee and sharing green tea ice cream and almond cookies.

"That was certainly unfortunate," Ariel said dryly. "We're always so careful. The one time we decide to enjoy a nice lunch together, look what happens. Do you think Sam *would* say anything? I mean I think he understood what you were saying, don't you?"

"Don't worry, Ariel. I think he got it. Plus, why would he want to say anything to anyone? What could that possibly get him? And that's apart from the fact that we're like father and son. I know how much he respects and, I think, actually loves me. And he may even have stronger feelings for you," Alexander said with a mischievous wink.

Ariel lightened up and laughed a little. "Oh, cut it out, Alexander. It was such a shock seeing him, that's all."

"Let's finish then and head out. Next time, I pick the restaurant."

Luckily, the man in the dark sedan parked at the curb took no notice of them. He was the second shift man, hired just two days ago. His job was to follow the other lady, take pictures, write down what she did and who she did it with, and write memos. Hector said the boss liked a lot of detail and a lot of pictures and he wanted a memo a day. Francisco hadn't met the boss and didn't expect to. Hector was boss enough for him. So he waited. An hour and a half he waited. Finally she came out with a guy he hadn't seen before. The guy must have been inside already, Francisco decided. He picked up his telephoto and took lots of pictures. Rapid fire. Click, click, click. He got the man's face good enough to identify later. They walked over to what must be his car; the man opened the passenger door for the lady to get in. Click, click, click. Got the license plate number. Good. Then the lady's cell phone rings; she gets out of the car. She acts jumpy. She doesn't seem to be able to hear very well. She hugs the guy and gets in her car and drives off. Francisco tossed the rest of his smoke in the street and waited a few more seconds before picking up the tail.

Sarah was a lot more than jumpy. All she'd been able to make out was that the call was from Christine, who was borderline hysterical. And this was a girl who didn't upset easily. If Christine was upset, it was worth being upset over. Sarah slammed her worthless piece of crap cell phone down on the seat next to her and concentrated on getting back downtown as quickly as possible. She raced into her office and was greeted by a still visibly blanched Christine.

"OK, calm down. Have some water. Tell me step by step exactly what happened," Sarah said in the most reassuring tone she could muster.

"Well, I sent Randy out to serve the Rodriguez complaint instead of Corkin & Matlin, because I couldn't wait a week for them to do it." Christine began, her eyes starting to tear.

"Yes, that's right," Sarah confirmed strongly. With that stupid med cap bill sitting on the governor's desk, we don't have a week to waste."

"I hated doing it since Randy has really turned into a full paralegal for us and I didn't want him to feel like he was even expected to be available for process serving anymore, but I just really needed it done and I explained it to him and asked him and he said it would be fine and not to worry." Christine continued at break neck speed, her words jumbling over each other in her effort to get the story out as quickly as possible. "So he went over to Rodriguez's apartment and Rodriguez opened the door and Randy gave him the complaint and Rodriguez wasn't happy, but everything seemed fine and Randy turned to go. But out of the corner of his eye, he saw something move and he glanced back and saw Rodriguez reaching for what looked like a bat—some kind of stick thing."

Sarah felt her stomach grow tight and her breath quicken. She dreaded what she knew was coming next.

"Randy took off at a dead heat. I'm sure he was running as fast as he's ever run, but Rodriguez was somehow quicker and caught him just before he could throw himself over the fence." Christine was starting to cry now. The tears pooling on the table below. "He beat him, Sarah. He beat him with his bat or whatever it was. He might have killed him, but some guy came by and pulled him off." Christine choked the words out, as though the thought itself had stuck in her throat. She took a deep breath and continued. "The guy took Randy to USC Medical Center and Randy called me from there. Randy claims he's not that bad off. He says just some bumps and bruises. 'Nothing too serious.' At least he could talk. That has to be a good sign. Don't you think?" Christine looked up imploringly.

Sarah rapidly bobbed her head in agreement hoping Christine didn't know that she couldn't say a word; her own throat was too constricted with tears. How could something like this happen, she thought. It was a routine service. There was no indication that Rodriguez was a nut or that the situation was in any way unsafe. For God's sake he was a thirty-six year old "family man." And sending Randy out was the right call. She would have made the same call herself if it had come up. Absolutely bizarre and incredibly upsetting. She felt sick in every which way, but she knew she had to step up and handle the situation. She had to be the boss.

"OK. So you called me as soon as Randy called, right?"

"Yes."

"And no one's called Randy's mother?"

"Right."

"Alright. First thing's first. Let me call Randy's mother since she lives in Glendale and it's going to take her a while to get here. And then let's go to the hospital. Bring the number with you and we'll call from the car."

Christine looked relieved and rushed into action. Sarah made the difficult call to Randy's mother, to Randy, and then one more call to the police on the way over to the hospital. When they got there though, the police had already come and gone. Apparently the hospital had called them when Randy was admitted as part of their public safety reporting requirements and they had interviewed Randy, a few other hospital personnel, and left.

"Howdy," Randy called as soon as Sarah and Christine rounded the corner. "Good way to get out of an afternoon of work, wouldn't you say?" Randy joked as they came closer. Surprisingly, Randy looked pretty much like he had said. He had a few bad gashes on his legs and one at his hairline. He had bumps here and there that were going to be doozies when they turned black and blue, but generally, he looked like someone who had been in a minor fender-bender, not like someone who had been attacked by a crazy person with a bat.

"Oh my God, Randy, I'm so sorry. I can't believe this happened. It's all my fault. I should never have sent you over there." Christine started to cry again and Sarah turned and gave her a giant bear hug while Randy reached up and stroked her hand.

"Geez, Randy. What the fuck are you doing?" Christine started to giggle through her tears. "You're supposed to be the injured one."

"Apparently not. But like I said, Sarah, I am taking the rest of the day off."

"Randy," Sarah said holding his hand and looking directly into his eyes. "I'm so glad you're going to be OK. I can't even say how sorry I am that this happened. Please let me know what I can do for you. Of course, don't worry about any of this," and Sarah waved her arm around the room. "Our insurance will take care of it. And you need to stay home as long as you possibly can, until you're fully recovered. Whatever you need, we'll be here for you."

Randy smiled gently and nodded, visibly moved by her warmth and concern.

"Now," Sarah said breaking the mood. "What did the police say? Are they going to pick this freak up?"

"I told them everything. Not much to tell really, Rodriguez just went bonkers. I did sign a complaint report. I think the charge was assault with a deadly weapon. I still don't get why he did it. He seemed fine when I gave him our complaint. Oh, that's the silver lining. He *did* get served. Maybe he was on drugs or something. That's the only way it makes sense to me."

"What about the guy who helped you? It sounds like he just showed up out of thin air. Did you get his name or address? Any way to contact him? We would sure like to send him a little something to thank him."

"No," Randy said. "Nothing. I already asked the nurses. He just took me into the emergency room and disappeared. Maybe he didn't want to get involved in the investigation part of it. In any event, I am very thankful to him."

"We are too," Sarah said and Christine nodded vigorously. "OK, I'm going to go back to the office and find out what the cops are doing. Christine, you stay here and keep our warrior company. I'll come back later to check on you."

"Great," Christine and Randy said almost in unison.

Sarah made her way back out to her car and felt anger starting to seep up into her consciousness. What an asshole Rodriguez is, she thought. What kind of a monster would do something like that? Not only was he going to pay for what he did to Murray, Andy, and Alice, he was going to pay for what he did to Randy. Rodriguez had picked the wrong fucking victims and she was going to make sure it cost him, big time.

◆ ◆ ◆

Meanwhile, Sam was worried that he hadn't heard anything from Sarah yet, but didn't want to call and be a bother. Besides, he couldn't escape from his training session with Simon long enough to even make the kind of call he wanted to make. He would just have to focus on what Simon was trying to teach him, get done, and then go over and see if he could help. He retrained his attention on what Simon was saying.

"I first want to welcome you as the latest addition to our incomparable personal injury team. 'Bout time Maurice tapped you. I know you're not completely thrilled about it, but it can be a lot of fun and it's definitely good for your career. The P.I. group brings in more than twenty-five percent of the revenue of the firm and if you remember your Golden Rule—he with the gold rules? Nothing to snub your nose at. Especially when you're up for partner. The main thing you need to know is that we have devised an unbelievably efficient, lucrative and, from your vantage point, sterile system for handling car cases. I know you've heard tales around the firm about the efficiency and profitability of this practice group, but you probably don't know that the lawyers handling the cases never have to get their hands dirty or offend their oh-so-delicate sensibilities. We have investigators and paralegals for that," Simon deadpanned. "What this means is that you never have to actually see the grossly injured people who are your clients. They remain virtually anonymous. Just names on your pleadings. You are responsible for the law and applying the law to the facts, but others are responsible for obtaining those facts."

Sam took in what Simon was saying, but found it somewhat odd. "How do you make sure the investigators touch all the bases and ask the right questions? And how do you really connect with your plaintiff and with the jury later on, if need be, if you don't know your client?"

"Good questions, Sam," Simon nodded approvingly. "I can see why Strickland wanted you on his team. The short answers are that, no offense, it would take you a dozen years to become as experienced and savvy as these investigators. This is all they do and they've been doing it for a very long time. Plus, they have checklists they use to make sure they hit every possible angle. As for trial simpatico, only one in twenty cases actually goes to trial. And if one of your cases should go, don't worry about it, because you won't be doing the trial anyway. Sorry, but trial experience doesn't come with this job. Either Strickland or I do all the trials."

"Oh. Thanks for telling me. I thought I was the Marines."

"Far from it, dear boy," Simon said with a perfectly pathetic British accent. "You are merely my plebe. You will learn. You will grow and, eventually, if you're really nice to me and pay me lots of money, I'll let you second chair."

"Great. I'm glad we cleared that up. So let me get this straight. I'm just the paper guy. I do all my work and prepare my cases based exclusively on what I get in reports from other people."

"Correct," Simon confirmed. "Moreover, you are not permitted to speak with or, in any other way, contact your clients, witnesses, police, doctors, or any other individuals involved in the case. I know this sounds strange to you, crusading avenger, but it's why the process is so good. Only one talking head and one line of communication. Nothing is lost in multiple communications. One person is responsible for the facts. One person is responsible for the law. And the paralegals are there to assist. Over the years, we have found that this works the best. It's all about the system. And the system works."

"OK, OK, Simon, you're scaring me," Sam laughed. "You sound like a cult member. The system. The system. It's all about the system. OK, I get it and I'll do it, but I'd rather be a Marine."

"Alright, I'm glad you got it," Simon said with a smile.

And Simon was quite pleased that it had all gone so nicely. If he could control Sam, he could control anyone.

"I'm going to give you one case to get started on," Simon continued as he reached into the file cabinet and pulled out a thin manila folder. It's a straightforward case involving a sedan, a rainy road, and some relatively minor soft tissue injuries. Definitely the easiest case we have right now. Status conference in a week. Good luck, and keep me in the loop."

"Thanks, Simon. I will," Sam said as he accepted the folder. "I appreciate your primer. I'll bug you when I have to." And with that he was out the door, moving quickly toward his office so he could call Sarah.

CHAPTER NINE

Paul Rodriguez was not having a good day. He was presently sitting in the LA County Jail, Crenshaw precinct holding cell, but that was the least of his problems. The bigger problem was that he was starting to come down off his meth high and for every step down, his anxiety level was rising three. Hector was going to fucking kill him. Really. Paul had never seen him so mad. He was bright red and his eyes bulged out in this really amazing way. At the time he thought it was fantastically incredible—almost a psychedelic rainbow light show. Now he thought it was probably just really scary. Anyway, all he could remember was that he was hitting this creep who came to serve him with papers. It seemed like a good idea at the time. It was also a lot of fun. And then Hector showed up. He just appeared like Spider Man out of the blue. Hector yanked him off the creep and yelled at him to get the hell away. He wasn't sure, but he thought Hector hit *him* with the bat too, for good measure. Shit. How fucked up was that? Anyway, Hector put the guy in his car and drove off. Paul didn't know what to do and he couldn't really think of anything, so he went back home. The cops must have come some time after that, because here he was, in jail, waiting for God knows what. Well, at least he was safe from Hector. Jail was probably the safest place for him to be. He thought about that for a while and enjoyed thinking about how funny that was. Jail, the safest place to be. Ha ha. But that was it for enjoyment. He knew hours were passing because his body and brain were hurting more and in more places. Plus, he had a regular parade of cellmates. Finally, some time late in the evening he was called by the guard and escorted to what he assumed would be his arraignment. It all seemed pretty straightforward. The parts that got through to his rather disarranged senses anyway. Some guy in a suit was there and was helping him out. He figured the guy must be his lawyer. The guy said some things to the judge and then sat down. The other guy in a suit said some other things and then the judge granted him bail. Bail? Did the judge say bail? And all of a sudden he was being hustled back down the same hall he had come from and the guard was handing him a plastic bag with his watch and other stuff in it, and he signed a form, and then he was out in the cool dark Los Angeles night.

"Well hello, Paul," came an all-too-familiar voice from the shadows. "I bet you're happy to be out of that particular establishment with all your parts intact, aren't you?" The voice continued in a smooth, slippery way. "They are intact aren't they, Paul? Or has someone been kind enough to start the work that we'll be doing?"

And with that, Paul felt his arms being grabbed and harshly pinned behind his back while someone started punching him in the stomach. He shrieked in pain and tried to double up to protect himself, but instead, his knees buckled and he hit the pavement hard with his full dead weight, his head crashing down with enough force to knock him momentarily unconscious. He came to as they started kicking him.

"OK, OK, that's enough. We don't want to kill the son of a bitch." And then, seeing that Rodriguez was conscious, Hector added, "yet."

Paul was in complete misery. The pain of his physical injuries was one thing. The fact that it was Hector and his goons was something altogether different. What an idiot he was. He didn't even stop to think who had paid his bail before skipping excitedly out the door. He could have refused to go, stayed put in jail where it was safe. Fucking drugs. They had clouded his brain. The drugs probably were going to kill him, just not in the way anyone could have imagined. He tried to focus on what was going on around him. There didn't seem to be any way to escape. There were at least four of them. Four of them. Shit. Cocksuckers. Anyway, it was too late. They grabbed him by the arms and dragged him over to a van parked at the curb and tossed him in the back. He couldn't see anything, but he could hear Hector talking on the phone to someone about him. He could hear just enough to know that he would be meeting that someone in twenty-five minutes.

◆ ◆ ◆

Maurice hung up the phone and thought he was literally going to explode with anger. That goddamn fucking asshole Rodriguez. He could screw up everything. Or at least cause a lot of problems. Maurice chastised himself for his weakness six months ago.

He should have dropped Rodriguez then when he first started getting reports about sloppy work. This was especially true since the sloppiness seemed to result from cockiness and arrogance—two traits that had absolutely no place in this business. There was even some speculation from Hector that Rodriguez was into drugs. As incredible as that had sounded to Maurice at the time, he had to admit that drugs would explain a lot of Rodriguez's recent behavior. Well, that was all in the past now. Rodriguez had certainly forced his hand and he intended to do whatever he needed to do to protect his business. He made a decision to be even more careful with his communications, even in his own office. And he'd have to tell everyone else to do the same. He suspected that a little added vigilance might serve them extremely well right now. He finished his notes for the next day, packed up his briefcase, and walked down the hall to the kitchen to pick up some coffee to go. He definitely needed a fresh jolt of caffeine for the night ahead. As he turned the corner into the kitchen, he heard sounds coming from the other end of the hall. Normally he wouldn't be concerned; in a law firm of this size and caliber, associates frequently worked late, sometimes all night, but the events of the day coupled with the fact that he hadn't seen anyone for hours made him instantly nervous. He followed the sounds carefully, being sure not to make any of his own. As he got closer, he could make out paper shuffling and computer keyboard noises, not the sort of sinister thing he had been imagining. He followed the sounds until he reached the last associate office at the end of the hall and could see that Sam Morrow's light was still on. The sounds were coming from there. Maurice almost sighed with relief. Get a grip, he told himself. He was apparently so stressed that he had become a fucking paranoid. He hated paranoids. They were weak and small—neither of which he would ever allow himself to be. He mentally recalibrated himself and then jostled his briefcase and overcoat as best he could to make noise as he approached Sam's office. No sense scaring that poor bastard too, Maurice thought. He could hear the computer keys stop clacking as if someone was listening and decided to call from the hallway even before making the turn into Sam's office.

"Sam, what are you doing working so late? I hope we're not keeping you so busy that you can't get your beauty sleep."

In spite of the advance notice, Sam was shocked to hear another voice so late at night in an office he thought had been empty for hours. He bolted to his feet and accidentally knocked the remains of his afternoon coffee all over the files on his desk and right onto his computer keyboard. "Ooooohhhhh shit," he yelled, diving for the cup. Maurice muttered a companion "oh, shit," from the doorway and dove in to help with salvage. They managed to preserve all the files without any trouble, but the keyboard was a goner.

"Sam, my apologies about this. I tried not to scare you, but I see I wasn't successful," Maurice began.

"Oh, it's OK," Sam said. "I guess I was just a little jumpy."

"Anyway," Maurice continued. "Make sure you let the IT people know that the keyboard was my fault and have them charge it to me. However, I think this is an omen for you to go home and get some sleep."

"I would," Sam replied. "But I was out for a few hours today and need to draft a motion for filing tomorrow."

"Well, you know I never tell associates how to manage their time," Maurice said with a half-smile. "I must tell you though, that I am truly delighted that you've developed into such a fine writer here at CS & B that your work doesn't require more than a first draft." And while Maurice walked off down the hall, out the door and into the cool LA night, Sam stood there dumbfounded, amazed at the idiocy that could apparently erupt from his mouth at any time and in any place where Strickland was concerned. Absolutely astounding.

CHAPTER TEN

Hector and his associates had already arrived at The Lucky Seven, Rodriguez in tow. Hector hadn't been at the Seven for about two months, but it seemed the only thing that had changed was that it looked even more seedy and dirty. He couldn't believe Maurice was using it for his extracurricular activities. Not someone like Maurice anyway. Hector settled in and grabbed himself a beer. He motioned for his guys to get beers too. After all, no one had to be sharp for this one; it was about as penny ante as it got. Rodriguez was already so scared, he was just about shitting himself. That asshole Rodriguez. He had really fucked it up and caused a lot of problems. He was glad Maurice was finally taking care of this. Hector thought Maurice should have handled this months ago, but he was glad he was handling it now. Hector decided to chill out, enjoy his beer, and watch Rodriguez thrash around in his handcuffs and blindfold, being mindful to give him an occasional kick in the ribs as needed.

Hector had just given Rodriguez such a kick when Maurice arrived a little after two o'clock in the morning.

"Very nicely done, Mr. Skolnick. I hope Mr. Rodriguez appreciates your inestimable skill. If he doesn't now, I'm sure he will come to appreciate it as the night wears on." Maurice spoke with a flat, chilling tone that it caused Hector to shudder involuntarily. This was a Maurice Hector had never met before. It was as if Maurice had moved beyond the initial explosive anger that Hector had heard on the phone into a detached, almost nonhuman zone.

"You don't know who I am," Maurice continued, speaking to Rodriguez. "And you never will. Suffice it to say that this is my operation you've fucked up and I'm not happy about it. In fact, one might say I'm very unhappy about it."

Rodriguez started making unintelligible, squeaky kinds of sounds underneath his duct tape and recommenced thrashing about on the floor, which inspired Hector to walk over and kick him vigorously in the side. The kick apparently hit a little close to his kidneys though, since Rodriguez let out a horrible howl and immediately stopped moving.

"Well done, Mr. Skolnick," Maurice said approvingly. "Now let's get down to business. Mr. Skolnick, would you kindly ask your associates to wait outside? I'm sure we'll be fine by ourselves."

After the men had filed out, Maurice continued. "As I was saying, Mr. Rodriguez, I am acutely disheartened by your actions. You have betrayed the trust I placed in you and treated me with disrespect. I have never tolerated this from anyone and I am not about to start with you. I have come here tonight to exact my redress."

Shit. *Pulp Fiction* had nothing on this guy, Hector thought.

Maybe Maurice was enjoying being a bit over the top to freak Rodriguez out even more. But a quick sideways glance at Maurice confirmed that Maurice wasn't playing. He meant every word he said. Apparently the lump formerly known as Rodriguez knew it too, because he hadn't moved an inch since Hector's last well-placed kick. Hector wasn't even sure he was breathing, but then he saw Rodriguez sneak a small, shallow breath as if he was afraid his own breathing might piss off Maurice even more. If Maurice's goal was to scare the shit out of Rodriguez, he had accomplished it and more.

"I was deciding what to do with you on my way over," Maurice continued. "And I have determined that I'm not yet at the point of killing you." At that, the lump took a huge, shuddering breath and started twitching all over apparently in uncontrollable relief. Fuck. That Maurice was good, Hector thought. Rodriguez really thought Maurice might kill him.

"What I am going to do is this: you will be subjected to additional pain this evening involving various body parts as punishment and as a permanent reminder of your incredibly irresponsible and asinine act. You will be returned to your crappy apartment for a few hours while we wait for the night judge, a special friend of mine, to come on and then you will be returned to court and your bail will be revoked. You will accept the services of the lawyers at the Bicknel Law Firm. They will tell the court and prosecutor that you were on drugs, that you don't know why you attacked that man, and that you have no defense. You will plead guilty and accept whatever punishment is meted out upon you by the court. You will serve your time. Eventually, you will be released and you will return to what's left of your prior life.

Consider yourself persona non gratis from this moment on. If you ever say anything to anyone about this little business that you used to be a part of, we will hunt you down and kill you in a most painful way. Clear?"

Rodriguez bobbed his head violently up and down and winced as the abrasions on his face came in contact with his hot, salty tears of relief. Unfortunately for Rodriguez, his tears were premature. He should have saved some for what awaited him later in the night.

◆ ◆ ◆

Half past three in the morning and Maurice still wasn't home. What a bastard. It wasn't that Ariel cared that he wasn't home with her—far from it. Rather, she couldn't believe that he was at it again so soon after what had happened last time. Just another reason she was going to enjoy this divorce so much. She walked into her dressing room and turned on her full spectrum vanity mirror lights. She hated that she did this. She hated that she felt a need to do this, but the truth was that her self-esteem had been taking a beating ever since she found out that her own husband was fucking around. Every time he fucked someone else, he fucked her too. She carefully scrutinized every inch of her face, searching for any sign of new wrinkles or imperfections. Seeing none, she shook off her nightie and performed the same inspection on her naked body. She felt a momentary sense of relief upon declaring herself acceptable, but she couldn't smother the sadness that welled up from somewhere deep inside that mutely questioned how an accomplished woman like herself could still tie her self-worth to how she looked. She replaced her nightgown, turned off the lights, and returned to bed only to hear the garage door open. She was somewhat interested to see which bed he would choose. She had made some strategic mistakes early on when the marriage first started to sour, because she had thought there was a chance to save it. She was afraid those mistakes might have propelled the divorce forward and now might cause him to file before she was ready. In retrospect, she should have just smiled and nodded, been pleasant at the table and gracious in bed to buy time, since it was clear that he had intended to divorce her all along. Instead, she had acted like a hellion—starting fights, storming out of rooms, refusing to share her bed or even the table with him—making him want to get rid of her sooner. She had relapsed a bit since his last outing and had refused to come down to breakfast for a while, but she had eventually taken herself in hand and regained her mask of sainthood. No matter. It wasn't that much longer. She just needed a little more information and she would be set.

She was still grateful for the twist of fate that had exposed his true intentions six months ago. It was the annual partners' wives charity fashion show and auction. She smiled wryly as she thought how it was still—unfortunately—accurate to say partners' "wives." The party committee had selected the particularly beautiful bungalow gardens of the Beverly Hills Panorama Hotel for the event, and the gardens were magnificent with an especially lush end of summer bounty. The hotel's outdoor theme that summer was a version of "Escape to the Tropics," and the gardens were filled with orchids, dripping wisteria, and scents of hibiscus. All of the women were quite taken with the lavish display of Hawaiian proteas, which numbered in the hundreds.

Ariel had felt particularly happy and comfortable—even more so since she had splurged and bought a new Chanel suit just for the occasion. She was a little late, having stopped to pick up a few additional goodie bags as a favor to the committee, and the other women had clearly enjoyed at least a few glasses by the time she got there. As she was greeting her table, Katherine Baines complimented her beautiful suit. She could still hear the exchange as if it were yesterday.

"Oh, Ariel, you look absolutely gorgeous," Katherine had exclaimed, pulling Ariel to the side and smothering her with a generous, slightly inebriated hug. "Of course you should have the latest Chanel what with your husband doing so well at the firm. I don't want to talk out of school, but Jon told me he's almost up to a quarter of the firm's revenues now after a big six months. What *are* you doing with all that extra money?"

Ariel was stunned. She remembered groping for her chair and somehow dropping into it before her legs gave way beneath her. This was the first time she had heard anything about this. Her husband? Doing well? Money? He had always done well, maybe a million or so a year, but a quarter of the firm's revenues would put him somewhere in the five million dollar range. Definitely worth mentioning. Ariel looked up to see Katherine apparently still waiting for an answer, but then someone called to her from the auction podium and she was off, glass in hand, to handle the latest crisis. Luckily, the other women at her table had moved over to admire the ice sculpture the chef had unveiled and Ariel took the opportunity to catch her breath and calm her shaking hands. How long had this been going on? A long time, she guessed. You simply don't hit those kinds of numbers overnight unless you win a big jury verdict or settle something on contingency, neither of which was true. She had been so busy with her charity functions and social calendar that she hadn't kept up with her usual circle of partners' wives or she might have found out sooner. Interestingly, Maurice had been out of town that week, purportedly on business, and didn't know she was attending this function. If he had, he probably would have come up with some reason why she couldn't go.

Of course, the thing that hurt most was that she had thought they were happy. Six months ago he hadn't been sleeping with anyone else, that she knew of. Six months ago they went out on dates together every Friday, just the two of them. Six months ago they had passionate, impromptu sex, and fun, experimental sex, and just lots of sex. They laughed together and made plans together. They ate Jamoca Almond Fudge and read *The Times* together. She thought they told each other everything.

She'd sat for another minute, but as the women began drifting back to the table, she excused herself and went to the ladies' room at the farthest reaches of the hotel, where she made a hurried call of apology to Katherine for having to leave due to a family emergency. She was thankful that she hadn't been drinking and could drive, because the thing she needed most in the whole world was to run away as fast and as far from the hotel as she possibly could.

Hours later, she found herself at the top of Mulholland Drive. Her beautiful Chanel suit was ruined, tear soaked, with veins of black mascara running like hash marks across her destroyed life. She had never been dumb and only occasionally naïve, so she knew that there was only one explanation for what he was doing.

He was hiding money from her. Furthermore, there could be only one reason why he was hiding money; he was planning to divorce her and leave her with nothing. Ariel allowed the truth sink in. It was one thing to divorce someone. It happened all the time. It was sad. It was often tragic or pathetic, but it was the way to end a marriage. Each party got half of the assets and went their separate ways. What her own husband was trying to do, by contrast, was cruel and unjust. He was trying to screw her in the very worst way. As Ariel thought about it, her shock and sadness started to give way to anger. There was still time, she thought. She wasn't beat yet. And the more she thought, the angrier she became. She dabbed her face and smoothed her jacket. By the time she started her car to drive home, she had vowed to beat him at his own game.

CHAPTER ELEVEN

Sarah was still awake, her bed a smorgasbord of sheets, pillows, magazines, TV clickers, and animal cookie crumbs. None of her usual sleep helpers had worked and it was almost half past four in the morning. She decided to give up trying and face the fact that No-Doz would be her companion for the day. Almost on cue, her brain started reviewing again the shocking events of the previous twelve hours. After she had left Randy and Christine at the hospital, she called the precinct and eventually got through to the detective handling the case. He said they had already picked up Rodriguez and that he was due to arrive at the station house within minutes. That had made Sarah feel a little better. The detective went on to say that the arraignment would be later in the evening and that the judge would probably grant bail. Sarah's mental autopilot review stopped momentarily to allow a new and intensely upsetting thought. If Rodriguez had been able to make his bail, he was probably back on the streets right now. The thought forced Sarah out of bed and into the kitchen, where she paced back and forth for a while and eventually made a cup of tea that sat, forgotten, in the microwave. By then though, she had decided that Randy was probably safe from Rodriguez even though he was most likely out on bail, because there was no reason for Rodriguez to go after Randy again. Randy had already served him and been beaten for it. There was no continuing battle. If Rodriguez was going to be crazy over anyone, it would be her.

Sarah glanced out the window as she was digesting that thought and saw a light flash from the driver's side of a car parked across the street. With the little light out on the street, Sarah could just make out some kind of nondescript dark sedan with one occupant. The flash must have come from a cigarette lighter, Sarah thought. Probably a car service waiting to take some poor soul to the airport. She closed the drapes the rest of the way as she realized the driver had a well-illuminated view of her in her little-bit-too-revealing Dodgers t-shirt. A cigarette should be enough for him, she thought. He doesn't need a free peep show too.

She decided she might as well go into the office and make herself productive. At six o'clock in the morning, it was suddenly no longer too early to start the day. She could also leave a message for Sam that he would get as soon as he arrived, since she had forgotten to call him like she promised. She hoped he wasn't mad or worried, but the truth was she had been consumed by other things and had simply forgotten. She swung into high gear, but as she left her apartment at quarter to seven, her mind already on the day ahead, she failed to notice the dark blue sedan trailing a few cars behind her. This was a great idea, Sarah thought as she pulled into her parking spot fifteen minutes later—a clear record. A little counter-cyclical traffic shift every now and then could be a great way to free up more time, she decided.

But her office was another story. She had never been in this early and as she opened the outer door, she felt an eerie, creepy feeling coming over her. It felt like someone was there, watching her. She knew it was irrational and just plain stupid, but she couldn't seem to dispel it even after she turned on all the lights and opened the blinds. She scanned the credenzas and bookshelves. Everything was in its place, just as she had left it last night, and everything that had been left out of place was still out of place. Clearly, no overzealous elf had spent any time here. She moved to the kitchen and turned on the coffee pot to complete the business-as-usual office picture in her own psyche and retreated to her office. She decided that the best antidote for this kind of irrational creepdom was to get to work. She had a deposition later in the day on a slip and fall case and really wanted to make some headway on this Obelisk/K-2/Cook Island can of worms before then. Sarah noticed that the creepy feeling was finally starting to dissipate as she walked down the hall to the file cabinet to get the part of the Matthews' file she had put away yesterday. The only problem was the file wasn't where she had left it. She checked the drawer again and this time found her "Obelisk Research" file behind the "Damages" folder in the middle of the drawer. She felt the creepy feeling returning in droves. It was possible that someone else had used the file, but highly unlikely. She was the last person who'd left last night. It was possible that someone came back to do some catch-up work, but not on this case, and certainly not on this file. Plus, everyone in her office knew the particular way she liked her litigation files organized. It was different from the norm, but it was the way she liked it and everyone did it for her that way. Her brain told her the only suitable explanation was that she had simply misfiled it herself. Quite likely, actually, given the emotional rollercoaster of the day before, but not an explanation her creep-o-meter would accept. She took the file back to her office and scanned the contents. Everything in the file was just as she had left it, making it even more likely that she had just misfiled it herself. She decided to call Sam and leave her apology message as much to distract herself as to reach out to him. Given her state, she almost jumped out of her skin when he answered the phone.

"Sam . . . I, uh . . . I mean, uh . . . is your phone forwarded to your iPhone? I mean, did I wake you up? I'm so sorry to be calling so early."

"It's OK, Sarah. Are you OK? You don't sound so good."

"I'm fine. Where are you? Did I wake you up?"

"No way. I'm actually just finishing a motion from hell that's due today. I've been here all night. I'll be done in the next hour or so and will go home and crash for a few. What happened with Randy? I was worried when I didn't hear from you last night, but I figured you must be submerged in the situation and would call me when you could."

Sarah felt her eyes well up in response to his kindness. Most of the men she knew would either have yelled at her for not calling them or at least criticized her. Sam, on the other hand, was nothing but caring. She really did have to find out why he wasn't married yet.

"Oh, Sam, thank you for being so sweet. It was crazy and then I just got so upset and preoccupied. Anyway, Randy is going to be fine. He really only has bumps and bruises, which is amazing to me after being attacked by someone with a bat. Christine stayed with him for a while at the hospital and then his mom came, and by then he was about ready to be discharged. They arrested Rodriguez, but I expect he's probably out on bail by now. All in all, a much better ending than I first thought when I took the call. I'm sorry I got so freaked out and left our wonderful lunch so abruptly. Thank you again so much for such a fabulous time."

"You're welcome. I'm glad everything is working out. The whole thing still seems so bizarre. What would cause someone to just go insane like that? I guess I lead a rather sheltered life."

"Me too. It is bizarre." Sarah thought about mentioning the misplaced file to Sam, but decided it would just sound too paranoid and weird. "So why did you have to be there all night? Was it a last minute rush or a partner emergency?"

"I wish. It's called bad planning and, apparently, is a reflection of the fact that I don't know how to manage my time. I got busted by Maurice at around one in the morning for that. Of course, I'm the one who blurted out what I was doing in yet another example of Sam-idiocy with this guy. I even managed to spill my coffee and wipe out a keyboard."

Sarah started laughing in spite of herself. She thought she was the only one afflicted with almost predictable stupidity around certain people, Judge Schneider for one. "Well, I better let you get back to all that fun you're having. One quick legal question, though, if I might?"

"Sure. Pleased to be of even the slimmest value. What is it?"

"Do you know anything about asset protection in the Cook

Islands? Like, how are the regs different from the Caymans? And which banks are doing it?"

"Whoa, Nelly. I thought you said you were just making ends meet," Sam said jokingly.

"Yeah right. Sometimes those ends aren't even meeting. No, one of my cases has a Cook Islands LLC and trust."

"Interesting," Sam said seriously. "I, of course, won't ask you which case it is, but it must be a big one, because the Cook Islands are big business. All our high-net-worth clients use the Cooks and, a few years ago, most of the partners set up LLCs and God knows what else there, too. None of the associates were supposed to know about it since it just appears a bit improper, even though it's perfectly legal, but I found out about it through my friendship with Alexander Cabot. I don't know why he wanted me to know that partners were doing it, but he did and he told me."

"That's odd, but it must be nice to have the biggest cheese in the firm watching out for you."

"Big time. Anyway, the reasons everyone likes the Cooks now as opposed to the Caymans are that the banks actively demonstrate an extreme distaste for creditors and their requests, and the reporting requirements are virtually nonexistent in the Cooks. The government doesn't want to be anybody's 'nanny,' as one official is famous for saying. All you do is set up the basic legal structures, LLCs, revocable or irrevocable trusts, whatever, and attach some bank accounts and safe deposit boxes to them, and you're set. Of course, like any *legal* asset protection scheme, eventually creditors can get the goodies, but with the layering in the Cooks, it takes a very, very long time and can be very, very expensive. Most creditors just give up. And therein lies the real benefit of the Cooks. The banks there have incredibly strong stomachs for conflict and the police always seem to be too busy to enforce any out-of-jurisdiction judgments. No one is fazed by lawsuits or court orders or even the personal appearance of sometimes livid creditors. They just placidly ignore the creditors and, eventually, the creditors go away. Pretty nifty system. Takes the meaning of stonewall to a whole other level."

"Interesting. I had heard rumblings about the Cooks, but I thought they had to be exaggerations. It's a bit disheartening to hear that it's all true. Why do you know so much about all this? Do you have crown jewels hidden away?"

"I wish. No, I actually had a client that was pursuing some assets in the Cooks. I hate to admit it, but we ended up being one of those creditors who had to give up and go away. It just got too expensive, considering the amount of the judgment and the obstacles the islanders were throwing up. All in all it was a crappy experience."

"It still sounds a bit raw. Sorry for bringing it up," Sarah said apologetically.

"Oh, it's OK. God knows I've had worse experiences in the law."

"Me too."

"Well, I better get back to the beast. Dinner later? Maybe I'll cook."

"Maybe you won't. My treat. We'll go someplace cheap."

"Deal. I'll pick you up at seven?"

"OK, but I'm going to be ashamed of my offices, especially after I've seen yours."

"Better now, while we're in our honeymoon phase. I won't tell you what I really think."

"Thanks a lot. See you later. And Sam . . .?"

Sarah said 'Sam' with a slight feminine lilt that caused Sam to swallow hard and garble out some kind of a "yes?"

"Maybe I'll even let you see my apartment."

Sarah hung up the phone feeling a wonderful sense of mischief and fun. It was so nice being with him. So very nice.

"By the looks of that grin, I bet you'll be eatin' the donuts again this morning."

Sarah started and looked up to see a rather smug Christine in the doorway, coffee in hand, obviously enjoying catching Sarah in an unguarded moment.

Sarah feigned consternation and said, "My dear, you do recall that I am your boss, don't you? And that I sign your paychecks? I believe a little respect and deference are in order."

"Most assuredly, Ms. Brockman," Christine responded, pretending to cower against the door. "I promise you, it won't happen again."

"See that it doesn't," Sarah replied and they both laughed good, real laughs and each thought how much they enjoyed working together.

Christine moved into the office and sat down across from Sarah. "What are you doing here so early? Not to be rude, but you're *never* here early."

"You know, I honestly couldn't sleep. This whole thing with Randy yesterday was so upsetting. I can't believe he's in such good shape. It's amazing he didn't get seriously injured."

"I know. I think God stepped in and helped. His mom thinks

so too. Anyway, I want us to cream this guy. Whatever it takes. I'm here."

"I'm with you. Maybe you can take a few minutes and do some research on that Nevada LLC, K-2 Financial. See what you can dig up. Duane's going to be in around ten to give me an update on Marion Morales and Timberline Road. I can't wait to hear what he's dug up."

"Me either."

"By the way, did you come back to the office after I dropped you off last night from the hospital?"

"No, are you kidding? I was exhausted. Why?"

"Nothing really. Just one of my files was misplaced and you know how nuts I am about proper filing. I was just trying to find out who to yell at. I guess I get to yell at me." But even as she said it, Sarah still didn't think she was the one who had misfiled the folder, even though there was no other rational explanation. She felt the creep-o-meter start running again.

Christine headed out to start her research and Sarah willfully turned her attention to her slip and fall deposition preparation. By ten, she was ready for Duane. A few minutes later, both Duane and Christine popped their heads around her door and came in.

"Sorry to barge in," Christine said, "but a messenger just dropped this off and I figured you'd want to see what it is right away."

"You got that right. Now let's see what good tidings this five pounder holds," Sarah said wryly as she noted the Bicknel Law Firm, LLC return address. "I hope it's the last of their Christmas fruitcake."

She ripped open the package to reveal reams of interrogatories, deposition notices, requests for admission and, finally, Rodriquez's answer to the complaint. At least there was no mistaking it. Bicknel meant war.

"Christine, take these poor dead trees and calendar the response dates, make copies for the Matthews, and a working copy for me, and then file the whole mess in the monstrous file cabinet at the end of the hall. That should hold it for awhile."

"Will do. Let me know when I can help."

"Thank you. I really appreciate it." And Sarah thought again about how lucky she was to have found Christine, assistant extraordinaire, who was never afraid to dive into any project no matter how overwhelming or scary. She's a great role model for me, Sarah thought. And she felt her determination growing as she decided that she would no longer be afraid of "the big boys." She was going to take on Bicknel and she was going to win.

"Damn, you look like you're either going to eat a Brontosaurus or slay one," Duane said as he slid into the chair across from hers.

"You got that right. And it's only 10:00 a.m. Wait till you see what I'm going to do by noon," Sarah said with obvious gusto as she spun around and whipped open her laptop. "I know what you mean about this case; it's worse than quicksand. Quicksand is at least a slow, piece-by-piece submersion. This just swallows you whole. Did you hear what happened to Randy?"

"Yeah," Duane said. "Christine told me."

"Be careful with this guy. He's a scary customer and we now know, violent and unpredictable. I don't want you to get hurt too," Sarah said forcefully, looking Duane directly in the eyes. "So take it easy."

"I will," Duane promised. "The more I learn, the more careful I am, which brings me to Marion Morales and 1250 Timberline Road."

"I'm all ears."

"Well, I started by doing some more research on Miss Marion and the lovely Timberline Road property and quickly found out that 1250 Timberline Road is owned by, you guessed it, Miss Marion Morales."

"She certainly is doing well for herself, isn't she?" Sarah asked sardonically. "A spanking new Mercedes and a house too? Tell me about the house. Probably not a wreck, I bet."

"Far from it. It's a new—looks like spec—McMansion with all the trimmings. Four bedrooms, three full baths, pool and jacuzzi, landscaped grounds and, as best as I could tell, chef's kitchen with a Viking stove, Sub-zero, and God knows what other high-end stuff in there. The tax rolls have it at $1,100,000 a year ago. Nice suburban neighborhood. Wouldn't mind owning that myself."

"Me either, although I'm sure we'd sorely miss the apartment lifestyle."

"Right. Anyway, between Mark and me, we staked the place out for twenty-four hours and engaged in a little noninvasive reconnaissance of the house and grounds. I see that look, Sarah. I said *noninvasive.* We didn't treat ourselves to a house tour, just scoped the outside, for now," Duane said with a mischievous wink. "Here's what we learned. First, just Marion and a man live there. We did our usual sign for delivery scam, so we know the woman was Marion. We didn't ever see a man, but there was a full walk-in closet with men's clothes and there are pictures of

Rodriguez and Marion all over the house. I think we can be pretty confident that Rodriguez and Marion live there together. But why does Rodriguez also have that crappy apartment? I don't think it's a little love nest that Rodriguez keeps for the lady folk—it's just too skuzzy and too uninhabited. I know. I checked. It's basically just a bed, a TV, and some dishes, nothing that would inspire any romantic flights of fancy in my book. It's like a set in a movie, more for show than for living. I think he's trying to pull off some really lame asset protection by putting the assets in his wife's name and by running two separate lives. Probably got the idea from TV. In one life, he's the poor immigrant family man and in the other, he gets to be part of a well-off suburbanite yuppie couple. No sign of kids, though. I guess he couldn't hire any."

"Interesting. I'm sure he amazes himself with his cleverness. Question is, who is he hiding assets from? And, second, how did he even get the assets?"

"Those are the biggies. Of course, we'd also like to know who he works for and what's the story with the truck and that Nevada LLC."

"Right," Sarah paused. "K-2 Financial. Lien held by Obelisk Holdings, part of the black hole of Cook Islands banking.

"That bad, huh? I guess your research on the Cooks didn't go the way you hoped."

"That's putting it mildly." Sarah shrugged. "Anyway, let's keep doing what we're doing only deeper. I'm not sure how this is going to pan out, or even how any of it might be relevant to our case, but I just have a gut feeling that it is and that we have to follow it through."

"I agree. We'll keep peeling the onion," Duane said as he stood up to leave.

"Thank you again so much for everything you're doing," Sarah said sincerely. "You're just the best."

"You're pretty impressive yourself, ma'am," Duane said as he doffed an imaginary hat and backed himself out of the door.

He was definitely getting more quirky all the time, Sarah thought as she smiled to herself and picked up the phone to call the Matthews. It had been a few days since she had checked in with them and she was sure they were anxious to receive an update.

"Hi, Alice. This is Sarah. How are you?"

"Just fine, Sarah. Nice of you to call. How have you been holding up? We spoke to Christine briefly this morning and she said there's been a lot of activity on the case."

"That's an understatement. We served Rodriguez yesterday and already received discovery and his response to our complaint today—about half of a tree of discovery. I'll send copies of it over so you and Murray can start looking at it and formulating some answers. Just do what you can. We'll fill in the rest. We've got the Bicknel Law Firm on the other side and they're apparently going to start by papering us to death. Also . . ." Sarah had been about to tell Alice about Randy's beating, but then reconsidered it, since all it would do was upset Alice unnecessarily. "Also, be sure to send over Murray's most recent medical expenses so we can make sure we're keeping track of all of the damages."

"No problem. Andy makes copies of them when they come in so we always have an extra set ready for you. You know, I think Murray is doing even better now that you're on board. He trusts you implicitly, as we all do, and I think it makes him feel good to do something instead of just sitting around. He's getting even more lively every day."

"Whoa, that's scary. He was pretty incredible when I saw him last week. Was it only last week? It seems a heck of a lot longer than that."

"I know," Alice agreed. It seems like this case is going faster than the POS was going when he hit my Murray." Alice had taken to calling Rodriguez "the POS" a few days after they met. Sarah didn't know what it meant and didn't want to ask, but could tell that it gave Alice an inordinate amount of pleasure. Sarah suspected it contained words not normally found in Alice's lexicon.

"Oh, I'm glad you brought that up. I've been meaning to ask you what else you remember about the prosecutor's failure to raise excessive speed as an issue at trial. I've read the trial transcript thoroughly and it still doesn't make any sense to me. How could any prosecutor, let alone an experienced prosecutor like Wilkins, make a blunder like that? He should be fired or at least moved down to juvie for a while. My contact in the department says he seems to be trying the same cases and doing the same work. Absolutely unbelievable."

"I know. That's what we thought. But there was nothing we could do. Wilkins was talking, putting on some kind of a case and then all of a sudden apparently decided he was done and rested his case. The defense lawyer put the POS on the stand to talk about why he left the scene and then moved for dismissal on the reckless driving charge, which the judge granted. Oh wait, one thing. Wilkins did look a little flustered when this guy walked into the courtroom about midway through his presentation. It looked like he got nervous, but just a little. He started sweating and drank some water, but his voice remained strong." Alice paused a moment and thought deeply, pulled back in time to that miserable scene so many months ago. "Wilkins also looked at the judge."

"Why do you say that?" Sarah asked clearly confused. "What do you mean, he looked at the judge?"

"Well, I remember him looking at the judge because it was an odd look. It was kind of a communicative look, like they were saying something without words. Even Andy picked up on it and asked me if I'd noticed it. It was certainly unusual."

"Do you think the jury saw it?"

"There wasn't any jury. It was just the judge and the lawyers."

Sarah felt stupid. She had read the transcript carefully, but had apparently skimmed through those rote parts she assumed she knew, like appearances of counsel, charges, and the like. Obviously she had missed the statement about it being a judge trial, but probably because she wasn't looking for it. Criminal defendants almost always thought they had a better chance with a jury, especially the guilty ones. It didn't make sense that Rodriguez would want to be tried by a judge.

"It just makes the exchange between Wilkins and Schneider that much worse," Sarah said definitively.

"I know it. Plus, Andy saw it too, so I wasn't imagining things."

"Yeah, I'll want to talk to Andy about this when he has a minute. Now tell me about the man that walked into the courtroom who shook up Wilkins a bit."

"That's right. It was just a bit. Wilkins didn't get panicked or anything like that. He just became more focused and maybe ramped himself up a notch."

"What did the man look like and what did he do?" Sarah asked.

"You can probably get a better description from Andy, but I remember that he was about six feet tall with black hair that had some streaks of gray in it, especially around his forehead. Based on his hair, he was probably in his fifties, but he seemed really athletic and fit. I really don't know how old he was. Oh, he had jeans on, but I don't remember what kind of shirt he had."

"That's a pretty darn good description, Alice. You're better than you think. What did he do after he stepped into the courtroom?"

"At first, he just stood in the back. The reason I noticed him at all was that I happened to be looking at Wilkins when the man arrived, so I saw Wilkins notice the man. Then he took a seat in the last row, dead center. Wilkins couldn't help but look at him while he was presenting his case. In fact, the man seemed to draw Wilkins' attention to him like a magnet. After the trial was over, the man got up and walked out without speaking to anyone. You could see Wilkins visibly deflate after the man left. It was as if he had been holding his breath the whole time. But all the man did was come in, sit down, watch the trial, and leave."

"I sure would love to know who that was and the nature of his relationship with Wilkins. What about Rodriguez? Any response from Rodriguez to the man?"

"Don't really know. POS had already testified when the man came in and had his back to the door the whole rest of the trial so he couldn't see the man."

"Interesting. What about Judge Schneider? Any interplay with the man?"

"No. I don't think so, but you should ask Andy, too. I was mostly watching Wilkins."

"Hopefully I'll talk to Wilkins in the next few days and see if I can gather any new information. I've already left four messages for him that he hasn't returned, but for the present, I'm just going to assume he is extraordinarily busy. If I don't speak with him soon though, I'll resort to my tried and true telephone guerilla tactics. That will probably shake him loose."

"Sounds unpleasant," Alice said sympathetically. "It would be hard for me to do anything so confrontational. We really appreciate all the hard work you're doing for us."

"My pleasure. I'll talk to you soon." And as she hung up the phone, Sarah allowed herself to feel just a bit proud that she was able to make the tough calls and do what was needed to zealously represent her clients. She hadn't always been so thick-skinned and courageous. Fact was, it took a lot to scare Sarah Brockman now. And with this case, that was a very good thing.

CHAPTER TWELVE

Simon paced back and forth in his tiny associate office, intently willing his Morengo desk clock to turn to quarter to ten. He tried to remember when their last meeting was and thought it might have been as long as a month ago. Absolute bullshit. It was as if Maurice had forgotten that there were members of "the team" other than himself. All Simon had received from Maurice lately were orders. No status updates. No financials. No nothing. Simon had had to demand this meeting himself or it wouldn't be taking place even today. Maurice was just getting too big for his britches, Simon thought. Being a partner in the firm didn't make Maurice ruler of the world in their private little club, and it seemed Maurice needed to be reminded of that. Luckily, Simon was just the one to do it. The more Simon thought about the state of affairs, the angrier he became. When the clock finally registered the appointed time, Simon was out the door like a Fury, almost running for his car.

Had he known what he had left out on his desk, he certainly would have taken the time to calm down and go through his usual office exit checklist.

As it was, Sam had just finished his motion from hell and was on his way out to grab a few hours of sleep when he decided to drop by Simon's office and ask him if he wanted to double with him and Sarah later in the week.

"He's not there," Simon's secretary called from her cubicle. "He went out to a meeting and will be back in a few hours."

"Thanks so much, Lorraine. I'll just leave him a note." Sam walked into Simon's office and easily found a pen and yellow sticky note on Simon's overflowing desk. Finding a place to leave the note where Simon would find it was another story. He eventually decided on the bottom corner of the computer monitor, but as he reached over the piles, a letter on Bicknel Law Firm letterhead caught his eye. He had heard of Bicknel. They were a prominent insurance defense firm in town that had actually beaten CS & B at trial on more than one occasion. So Simon had a case against them now, he thought. Tough luck. His eye drifted absently down the letter as he stuck the note on the computer. A settlement letter for $2,000 nuisance value. Must be a real minor car accident, he thought. That amount wouldn't even pay . . . the thought froze in Sam's mind as he saw the name at the bottom. It was Simon's. Simon's name and signature. His Simon.

Sam stood there, dumbfounded, as the questions started racing through his head. What the hell was Simon doing signing a Bicknel letter? Was he trying to help a friend out at that firm? Was Simon somehow moonlighting at the Bicknel Law Firm? Was he working for two firms at once? What the hell was going on here? Sam couldn't understand anything about the letter, but instinctively knew he wasn't intended to see it. After throwing a backward glance to the cubicles and seeing Lorraine hard at work on a document revision, he scanned the letter for any more information. It was just what he thought: a $2,000 settlement on what had to be a minor car accident case. It looked like Simon was representing a defendant through the Bicknel Law Firm. But how was this possible? More importantly, how could Simon do something like that, ethically and logistically? It just didn't make any sense. Sam put the letter down where he had found it and, again taking a furtive backward glance at Lorraine, picked up the case file lying next to it. It consisted of some handwritten notes he couldn't make out and an almost illegible messenger receipt. No help at all, Sam thought as he closed the file and replaced it on the desk.

By this time, he had broken out in a cold sweat, his palms almost too clammy to touch any papers without leaving a mark. I better get out of here, Sam thought, before I smear something. He turned for the door just as Lorraine called out: "Were you able to find some stickies, Sam?"

He just about jumped out of his skin as waves of panic started racing over his whole body.

"Whaaaat?" He sputtered.

"I said: Did you find some stickies?" Lorraine playfully over enunciated each word to tease one of her favorite associates. "It's not rocket science, Sam, just stickies."

"I, ugh . . . no . . . I . . . decided to talk to him myself," Sam finally stammered. "Thanks for your help, though." And Sam fervently meant it as he dived back to Simon's desk and collected the telltale stickie from the computer. He stuffed it deep into his pocket as he strode, in as purposefully a way as he could muster, down the hall, past the kitchen, and collapsed into the private sanctum of his own office.

◆ ◆ ◆

Meanwhile, Simon had just arrived at The Lucky Seven. Of course I'm the first one here, Simon thought disgustedly. And why we have to meet at this hellhole, I'll never know. He had hated The Lucky Seven from the first moment he saw it and his loathing just increased with every visit. Always seedy, dirty, and sometimes even smelly, depending on the number of festering take-out bags strewn about, Simon hated every moment. But Simon had nothing to say about where this meeting was taking place, just as he knew he had little to say about much else.

Simon shook his head in obvious revulsion and made his way inside, past the bar area, to what had been the main dining room. He had no idea where the light switch was, and didn't know if the power was on anyway, so he paused at the door to give his eyes a chance to adjust to the dim light before going inside. As he did, he noticed a strange smell he didn't recognize. It was sweet, but not food sweet. It seemed sweet and thick at the same time. And then his eyes focused enough to see what was making that smell. It was blood. Fresh, sticky blood splattered along the baseboards and on the lower portions of the walls.

He lurched into the wall next to the doorway and crumpled to the floor in a kind of distorted fetal position, his breath ragged with horror and disbelief. He had never seen anything like this before and the shock of it left him momentarily stunned and, in large part, physically paralyzed. After what seemed like an eternity, Simon was able to move himself out of his embryonic position and stand up. The room looked like a scene out of some terrorist videotape. There were beer bottles strewn over the floor, along with empty bags of chips and cigarette butts. The only piece of furniture remaining was a hard wooden chair that had been fixed in the middle of the room. It was clear that something sinister and macabre had taken place a very short time ago. His first impulse was to run away as fast and as far as he possibly could, not only out of revulsion, but out of fear for his own safety. Just because they weren't here now didn't mean they weren't coming back, Simon thought as a grimace passed over his face. He started for the door, but by this time, his eyes had become accustomed to the weak light in the room and his peripheral vision caught something that registered deep within his limbic cortex. Despite his better judgment, he was drawn to it like a moth to a flame and when he stooped down and looked at it, his whole body convulsed and shuddered as he vomited all over the severed human finger at his feet.

"Oh my God! Oh my God" he shrieked as he fell backwards and cracked his head on the hard wooden floor. The pain rocketed through his brain and stunned him into submission. Searing red flames pierced his vision. And then he was grunting and crying. He couldn't breathe. He was hyperventilating. He rolled over onto all fours and started gagging, spewing vomit spittle and blood in a putrid addition to the thoroughly gruesome mess already there. And then, almost at a primordial level, he noticed that someone was there.

"You wanted the meeting," Maurice said in an icy cold tone. "You thought I was keeping things from you. You said you wanted to know everything about the business. Well, you were right. I was keeping certain things from you. Tell me, Simon. Are you happier now that you know?" Maurice asked with a patronizing smirk.

By this time, Simon had managed to right himself into a sitting position and was trying to comprehend who was standing in front of him and what in the hell he was saying. He looked up sideways through the haze of shooting pain and managed some kind of incoherent response.

"My, my," Maurice said mockingly, in a cruelly sadistic way. "It looks like you've had a rather unpleasant time of it here at the old Lucky Seven. Still, it's nothing compared to what someone else went through right before you got here." Maurice moved to the pool of vomit and kicked absent-mindedly at the severed appendage. "I guess I should have invited you last night. Although, by the looks of things, you might not have had the best time. The rest of us did."

"You're fuckin' insane!" Simon shrieked out through the pain and mind-numbing red torpedoes that kept shooting across his vision. "You're insane! You fuckin' monster! What happened to the guy? Did you fuckin' kill him?"

"Don't be so silly, Simon." Maurice said in what seemed to be his favorite patronizing tone of the day. "*Killing* him wouldn't have achieved our goals. *Maiming* him did."

"What the fuck, Maurice? What you did, you did on your own. I didn't sign up for this kind of shit. That was what was so ingenious about the whole plan. No one could ever get hurt. But you went ahead and turned that into total and complete bullshit." By now the excruciating pain had receded and Simon was left with a horrendous headache and dull generalized throbbing, but at least he was able to formulate sentences.

"Oh, my dear Simon," Maurice replied in that same supercilious tone. "Have you already forgotten your criminal law class? When you, as you say, 'signed up' with me, you signed up for everything I chose to do as a part of our little business enterprise. That's right, Simon. Can you say 'co-conspirator'? Because that's what you are, and you're as much on the hook for this as I am." Maurice took a step back as if wanting to take in fully and enjoy the spectacle he knew would follow. Simon didn't disappoint. By this time he had risen to his feet in spite of the pain and was listening intently to Maurice, eyes glued to his face. Then, in a surprisingly quick move, Simon lunged at Maurice with all his weight and tackled him to the floor. Maurice felt the air suck out of his lungs from the force of the blow, but the countless hours he had spent on the playing field made his response almost instinctive. He easily found his tackle hold and flipped Simon flat on his back in a remarkable display of brawn and muscle memory.

"You little cocksucker," Maurice spit out the words like they were daggers. "Who do you think you are, you fuckin' piece of shit?" Maurice stood up and stood menacingly over Simon, his fists clenching and unclenching in a seething rage.

Simon instantly realized what he had done and started backing up on the floor, scooting along like an inverted crab, trying to get beyond Maurice's reach. But it was too late. Maurice swung with all the force of his impressive physicality and his anger, landing a perfect four-point punch on Simon's jaw. Simon was out cold. Maurice looked long and hard at Simon sprawled out on the floor and felt a deep sense of satisfaction and actual pleasure. It had been a long time since he had decked anyone that hard and it felt better than he remembered. He allowed himself to revisit the last time he had cleaned someone's clock. It was against Notre Dame, more than thirty years ago. He had pursued that little pipsqueak of a quarterback from the kick-off, but he couldn't sack him. He was even quicker than Maurice. But as fast as Maurice was, he had another ability that wasn't always so apparent, though it was equally important: he could read the offense. He knew where they were going almost as soon as they did. But for some reason, his skill wasn't working against this team. Every time he zigged, they had zagged. Cat and mouse, with the cat getting hungrier by the minute. Finally, by the fourth quarter, his frustration had reached a boiling point. He prided himself on his ability. His team depended on it and he hadn't been able to come up with one sack. It didn't matter to him that no one else had been able to come up with one either. It was then, at that almost overwhelming moment of frustration that he learned the skill that would serve him so well in years to come and figure prominently in his later success as a trial lawyer. He learned how to read the tells. That's probably what he had been doing on a subconscious level all along. In a flash, his brain made the connection that every time the quarterback went right, his foot moved, almost imperceptibly, to the right. Once he saw that, the rest of the quarterback's tells were glaringly obvious to him and Maurice was unstoppable. He sacked that little turd of a quarterback three times and was named most valuable player. In fact, that trophy was still, to this day, the most valuable trophy in his entire case. He used a specially designed spotlight on it so it was always the first thing anyone saw when they walked into his study, "Maurice Strickland, MVP – USC v. Notre Dame."

He wasn't sure anything could ever top that. But his later financial success and the prestige of being a named partner of a highly regarded firm came close. The problem was, though, that it wasn't enough. It was never enough. He was always hungry for more. Every time he achieved one goal, he was already sprinting for the next. It was to the point that he hardly even paused when he reached an important goal, let alone felt any sense of accomplishment or satisfaction. He seemed to have a voracious appetite for more, more, more. And the more he got or accomplished, the more he wanted. He was never full. Well, actually that wasn't true. He was only satisfied when he got his fix and then only for days afterward, not weeks like it used to be. He had to tell Hector to set something up for him now—tonight, if possible. He was so long overdue that he felt unbalanced and fragmented. Simon could be right, he admitted quietly to himself. His judgment might be impaired.

Maurice made a perfunctory check on Simon to make sure he was still breathing and then lit a cigar and took a seat on the wooden chair as he waited for Simon to regain consciousness. He was about half of the way finished when Hector walked in.

"Jesus Christ, Maurice! What the fuck happened here?" Hector seemed sincerely shocked and upset, moving quickly to where Simon lay still unconscious, flat on his back in a pool of vomit and blood.

"Thank God he's alive," Hector exclaimed after a cursory check of his breathing and pulse. "What the fuck happened?

Hector turned to Maurice with a hostile, accusatory look on his face. "Did you do this?"

Maurice took a last draw on his cigar and then slowly and deliberately snubbed out the remainder on the floor by his foot.

"Excuse me, Mr. Skolnick, but that's really none of your business, is it?" Maurice asked as he stood up and moved toward Hector in a rapid advance that left him two feet from Hector's face. "No, that's right, Mr. Skolnick. It's *my* business and how I run *my* business is completely up to me."

Hector didn't need to be told twice. "Of course, Mr. Strickland. I guess I overreacted. It won't happen again." It was still hard for Hector to believe that those kinds of words could come out of his mouth. What a sniveling putz. He felt like some scrawny kitchen boy from *Gone with the Wind*. Yes'm, Massa. No, Massa. Can I help you wipe yo' ass, Massa? No matter. It would all be over soon enough. He needed to suck it up, stay the course, and keep his eye on the long ball. He had no doubt that it would be worth it.

"How long has he been out?" Hector asked in a conciliatory tone, moving cautiously out of Maurice's range.

"Not long. Time to wake him up though. See if some water will do the trick."

Hector moved off to the bar area as Maurice nudged Simon with his shoe. The touch was enough to trigger Simon's consciousness and Simon started rolling his head and making soft, whimpering noises. What a pussy, Maurice thought. What a fucking little baby. This is probably the closest he's ever come to a fight in his life. Fucking pathetic. That's the problem with American society today, Maurice thought contemptuously. No real men left. Just girlie-men and fags. Maurice moved around to Simon's other side and gave him another prod—quite a bit harder—in the ribs.

This time Simon's eyes flew open in surprise. Maurice could see Simon take a moment to try and figure out where he was, who Maurice was, and what the hell had happened to him. Maurice knew Simon remembered when he saw Simon's eyes fill with fear and begin batting around looking for an escape route. But as much as Maurice would have liked to punish Simon some more for his egregious behavior, he decided, as he most often did, to put business first.

"Simon," Maurice began in his most congenial way as he stooped down and positioned himself close to Simon's face. "I am so sorry this happened and I want to apologize to you. I'm afraid my reflexes just went off and I was on autopilot, responding to a perceived attack. I am deeply sorry for the pain I caused you and I hope you will forgive me." And although Maurice said it with as much sincerity as a reverend on Easter Sunday, both of them knew he didn't mean a word of it, that their relationship was changed forever.

"Oh . . . uh . . . thanks for saying that, Maurice. I understand how that could happen. I'm sorry I dived at you."

By this time, Simon had taken an internal inventory of his injuries and decided there was nothing serious. No broken bones or teeth, or sharp pains. Just a grade A headache and lots of extremely tender areas, which he was sure would be noteworthy bruises by tomorrow.

"How are you feeling?" Maurice asked. "Do you need to go to the hospital or to a doctor?"

"No, no. I'll be fine. Just a little worse for wear," Simon said as he gingerly stood up.

"Glad to see you up," Hector said as he came into the room with a chipped margarita glass filled with water. "I'm sorry it took me so long," he said to Maurice, "but there aren't a lot of glasses left in this place." He handed the water to Simon, who drank it greedily.

"I'm going to get more water and clean up," Simon announced. "I'll be back in a few minutes and then we can have our meeting."

"OK," Maurice agreed. "If you think you're up to it."

"Definitely," Simon said as he moved slowly toward the restrooms.

When Simon returned five minutes later, Hector and Maurice had settled into the lounge chairs in the bar area and appeared to be ready to meet. Simon was ready to meet too, but he wasn't the same Simon who had authoritatively demanded the meeting from Maurice a few days ago and he wasn't the same Simon who had come to the meeting less than an hour ago. The fact was he was scared of Maurice now and, by extension, Hector as well. Simon sat down in the last available lounge chair and gingerly held a cold wet glob of toilet paper to his rapidly swelling face.

"Well, let me begin by extending my—and I'm sure Hector's—sincerest sympathies to you." Maurice said with a nod in Simon's direction and then turned to face Simon directly as he continued. "I'm sure the firm will understand if you need to take a few days off to recuperate after such an unfortunate car accident." And there it was. Not so much in his words as in his tone and bearing. In the blink of an eye, Maurice, the chameleon, had transformed himself from vicious thug to supreme commander of their shared universe, and Simon couldn't even muster the energy to be indignant or surprised. All he could feel was a strong sense of irony that Maurice wanted him to feign being a car accident victim.

"Yes, I'm sure that's the best explanation," Simon said. "My secretary knew I went out of the office for a meeting, so a car accident on the way back would be completely plausible."

"Good. Now on to other matters. First, status of pending matters and recently resolved matters. *Watson* settled for $550,000; defense verdict on *Manley*; and *Perrata* has just gone to pre-trial conference. I think I'm going to tell the boys to settle *Perrata* since we just had a trial for that insurance company three months ago that they won. We'll have them pay a little on this one to keep them realistic. After all, we don't want them to think we're *too* good," Maurice chuckled happily. "And now for the big news: *Samuelson* just settled last night for $2.5 million." Maurice paused a moment to let that sink in. "*Manner*, *Idelson,* and *Sanchez* have settlement conferences this week. *Turjilo* and *Vargas* are still in discovery. Those are the biggies. And here's a quick overview of the thirty-eight other pending matters," Maurice said as he stood up and handed Simon and Hector a one-page document. "I think I'll bring in two or three more cases in the next few days based on the weather report for continuing rain, so we should be nice and busy for awhile. Plus we have Sam Morrow starting up in the group to help. How's he doing anyway, Simon?"

"Just fine. He initially had some issues with the division of labor concept and wanted to do his own fact discovery and interact with the clients, but he accepted it after I explained the efficiencies and even seemed to like the structure by the end of our meeting. I gave him that tiny *Rivas* case to get started and told him to check in with me regularly. I think he's going to make a stellar addition."

"Glad to hear it. What about *Matthews v. Rodriguez*? How far are you on that?"

"Just answered the complaint and sent along my usual packet of discovery. I'll give them a few days and send over a $2,000 settlement offer. That should take care of it, since the Matthews are represented by some newbie P.I. lawyer that I've never heard of. Sarah Brockman. I looked her up on Martindale Hubbell and, although she went to a good school and has big firm experience, she's only been out of school a few years. I can't imagine she's any threat."

"That sounds right. Wrap it up as soon as you can," Maurice said. "Also, you should know that Rodriguez won't be working with us any more. Hector can fill you in with all the details later if you wish, but suffice it to say that Rodriguez assaulted Sarah Brockman's process server. Rodriguez was clearly on some kind of drugs. If Hector hadn't shown up when he did, who knows what would have happened."

Simon leaned back in his chair and let a wave of irritation pass over him before speaking. "I'm glad to hear that. He was stepping out of line and getting sloppy. I'm sure he didn't take it very well."

"That, dear Simon, is a gross understatement." And in that instant Simon knew who had been the hapless guest at The Lucky Seven last night. He felt a chill rush over his body, followed by a smothering fear that closed in on him like a fog.

If Maurice could do this hideous thing to Rodriguez, he was capable of doing anything to anybody. And that included him. In a flash, he knew he had to get out. Get out of the business. Get out of the firm. Get out of everything. Now. Quick. As soon as possible. It had all gone too far, and Maurice was unstable if not actually insane. He forced himself to stay in his chair and look normal even though every particle of his being was screaming for him to run. His forehead beaded with sweat and he hastily dabbed at it with his wad of toilet paper, clasping his hands in his lap to mask any telltale trembling. He fought desperately for composure, calling upon his experience gained through years of trial work. And then the miracle happened. Just when Simon thought he could no longer contain himself, Maurice said, "OK, well that about wraps it up. Hector could you stay a minute to finish up some other loose ends? Simon, you're fine to go, but don't forget to check in with the firm about your accident."

Simon was giddy with relief. Apparently, he had fooled Maurice and successfully hid what was going on inside him. He was going to be safe. Simon nodded, mumbled some kind of appreciation for the meeting and shuffled out the door, where he leaned against the door post and took the deepest breath of his life.

Maurice, in contrast, made a mental note to watch Simon. Of course, he had intentionally let Simon know that Rodriguez had been the casualty last night. He had done it specifically to watch Simon and see how he would react. Unfortunately, Simon had reacted just the way Maurice had hoped he wouldn't. If it all wasn't so serious, Maurice would have enjoyed watching Simon even more. He reminded him of a parfait. Simon, starting out bright red like the Jell-O layer at the bottom as he figured out Rodriguez was the unwilling guest, through a kind of roiling whipped cream and Jell-O layer as the significance of what had happened to Rodriguez sunk in, then moving to a thoroughly fear-blanched, white whipped cream top. Fascinating really. In any event, Maurice had learned just about everything he needed to know about Simon's commitment to their business and his capacity to do whatever it took to protect it. Low on both fronts. Plus, Simon had shown himself to be a lily-livered pussy, the kind Maurice abhorred. The fact that Simon had dive-bombed Maurice was just a reflexive aberration. Maurice had seen the enormous fear in his eyes, seen him try to scamper away like some kind of cockroach when confronted with a fight and, worse yet, seen him collapse so easily in defeat at the end. Maurice had let him leave now because he hadn't decided what course was best for him and the business. If Simon thought he had Maurice duped, all the better.

Maurice turned to Hector as soon as Simon had left. "Sorry about all this mess with Simon, Hector. I didn't want him to get hurt, just shocked."

"No problem at all, Mr. Strickland. I was out of line. When I first walked in, I thought Simon was dead. That's why I came at you so hard. I'm sorry I overreacted."

"No harm. He did look a bit defunct, didn't he?" And Maurice nudged Hector and laughed conspiratorially. "We sure know who the real men are around here, don't we?"

"You got that right, Mr. Strickland." And Hector shared the laugh and the wink from Maurice that followed, because he knew Simon was on his way out and he wanted to be sure that he wasn't joining him.

"So, Hector, what's the real story with Miss Sarah Brockman? Learn anything interesting?"

"We've only been on her a few days and she seems pretty run-of-the-mill. Lives alone in a small apartment. Works a lot. No pets. Kills her plants. No sleep-in boyfriend. Doesn't eat real well, and seems to have the normal assortment of friends and acquaintances, a few of which we still need to run down. I had my new hire, Francisco, tail her yesterday so I could check in on Rodriguez and see if he was getting high like you thought. Turned out to be a fuckin' miracle. Who knows where that poor shithead process server would be right now if I hadn't caught Rodriguez when I did. Probably in the morgue. Rodriguez was a fuckin' maniac. I even had trouble pulling him off, because he was this super-high-superman kind of guy. What a fuckin' bitch. Anyway, it all worked out OK."

"It sure did. Good riddance to that asshole," Maurice concurred. What about the important stuff? What's the status on Obelisk?"

"Sorry, I should have gotten to that first. I just wanted you to know that we're being really thorough with this one—doing a full tail and all. It just made sense since the truck was involved."

"No, you're absolutely right. Of course, I want a full tail, and probably a wiretap on Brockman as well, since that moron Rodriguez was driving the truck. It's my own damn fault for not taking care of that truck soon enough and being such a cheap bastard that I didn't just junk it. Once we moved all to paper, it was an idiot move to keep that thing around with the Obelisk lien on it. Fact is, I thought telling Rodriguez not to drive it would be sufficient. Shit."

Hector was watching Maurice out of the corner of his eye with fixed interest. He knew it was all bullshit. Maurice admitting a mistake? Saying he did something idiotic? Yeah, right. In another lifetime, maybe, but definitely not this one. Hector figured Maurice was just being chummy to make sure he was still part of the team.

"Anyway," Maurice was continuing. "Talk to me about Obelisk."

"Well, I got in there last night before I hooked up with Rodriguez and found a research file on Obelisk. I was surprised that Brockman had already found Obelisk and even more surprised to see that she had already started research on it based on what we know about her and her crappy little P.I. practice. But she had. The file was just her notes and was all very sketchy, but it looks like she knows about the Rabbit Hole Trust and K-2 Financial. At least that they exist, anyway. It also looks like she's got a private investigator working for her, but I couldn't find his name in the file. It will take more digging than I had time for then."

"Not great news," Maurice said stiffly. "This is why I sent you out on her right away. It's always the young, hungry lawyers who cause the problems, because they think they have so much to prove. If a bigger firm had this case, they'd still have their thumbs up their asses and not even look at the damn case until the night before the first status conference." Maurice was irritated now by the sheer thought of young, zealous lawyers making his life difficult. "Well, that fuckin' Simon's going to have more on his plate than he imagined. I'll make sure he has a fuller understanding of who he's dealing with in little Miss Sarah Brockman."

Hector nodded his head in agreement and thanked his lucky stars that he had gotten into Brockman's office last night instead of doing it tonight as he had originally planned. You can never be too responsive to a crazy person, Hector thought.

"Well, that's it," Maurice said as he closed his file and started packing up his briefcase. "Oh, one other thing," Maurice said with a certain studied nonchalance that was uncomfortably familiar to Hector. "I need services tonight after my Leaders of Tomorrow dinner. Can something be arranged?" Maurice said it politely, almost sweetly, which made the request even more grotesque.

Hector swallowed hard and gritted his teeth. "Of course, Mr. Strickland. No problem. Just tell me when and where."

"It will be an early dinner, so I think nine should be fine. The Beverly Hills Panorama Hotel. Bungalow no. 8. And make sure, what's his name? Francisco? Cleans up this mess. I want it spotless by the end of the day today, got it?"

"Absolutely, Mr. Strickland. Will do."

CHAPTER THIRTEEN

It was nice every now and then to reminisce, to remember the people he had known and those he had loved, to visit once again cherished times and treasured places and relive a life he had made rich with use. Alexander found himself searching back more and more these last few months. Maybe it was the stillness of his advancing years that made the contests of youth seem so much more alive than those events that happened yesterday. Maybe the contests of youth were really that affecting. In any event, he found a certain comfort and deep sense of satisfaction in replaying tapes in his mind, most now decades old, that captured the vitality of his life and, he felt, its essence. Many of these tapes recalled the great history of his firm. He loved remembering the difficult beginning and the equally challenging transition to becoming a corporate firm with a pro bono core. He was pleased and proud of what his life had been about and he felt that it had been well spent. So it was with great sadness and a profound sense of loss that he had watched his legacy falter over these past few years. He was deeply pained by the changes that were taking place in his firm. It wasn't that he objected to the increasingly predominant personal injury bent of CS & B. Indeed, helping those mostly poor, injured victims obtain justice against often arrogant, bullying insurance companies was right in line with his philosophy. Rather, he objected to the increasing emphasis by the majority of the partnership on lining their own pockets instead of caring most about their clients. The firm's philosophy was changing from service to greed, and the biggest offender was Maurice Strickland.

Maurice had burst into Alexander's world about ten years ago like a comet streaking across the night sky. They first met at a fundraiser for UCLA's pro bono program when they happened to be seated next to each other at dinner. Of course they knew each other by reputation, since Maurice had been a partner at a prestigious Century City boutique for many years, but this was the first time their paths had actually crossed. Alexander was completely taken with Maurice—so charming and smart, so focused and insightful. When Maurice told Alexander that he had begun a personal crusade to add more meaning to his life through charity and service, Alexander thought he'd found a long-lost brother. At that time, and for many years after, Alexander had viewed this chance meeting as divine providence. The shock of finding out two years ago that Maurice had orchestrated this purported coincidence with a special contribution to the pro bono fund still made him wince with pain and embarrassment. What a sucker he was, and at such an advanced age. He still couldn't believe he'd been so badly deceived by a man who was either a conman or an extremely shrewd businessman. It really didn't matter; the effect was the same. Over that dinner and many meetings that followed, Strickland explained that he felt that his personal and professional growth were being stymied by what he described as a controlling and narrow-minded managing committee at his firm that was only motivated by making money. He explained that he wanted to be part of something bigger, something like Cabot & Swain. During the three months that followed, Maurice impressed, ingratiated, charmed, cajoled, and eventually won a place in Alexander's heart and in Cabot & Swain as a partner. And no one was happier than Alexander. Maurice and Alexander were, in fact, a perfect fit. They seemed to agree on just about everything that mattered and their working styles meshed seamlessly, enabling them to accomplish tremendous things in record time. And Maurice was a dreamer. He was able to embrace visions Alexander had for the firm that even Richard Swain found too daunting.

But then it all started to change. It began so slowly and so inconspicuously that Alexander still couldn't identify exactly when it began, but it was probably in their third year of partnership, soon after Maurice was added to the letterhead. Maurice started bringing in car accident cases. The first few were friends of the family or friends of friends who'd had some tough luck and just needed a little help from a competent attorney. Alexander thought nothing of it. Little by little, however, Alexander started noticing more and more accident cases making their way through his firm's doors. He didn't know what to think. It was a different paradigm, but none of the other partners seemed to care. They had always gone to bat for the little guy, even before the big asbestos cases years ago that had put them on the map. They saw nothing different between car accident cases and other personal injury matters, but Alexander did and he didn't know why. Maybe he was getting snobbish in his old age and thought his firm was above handling run of the mill car accidents, but he didn't think so. No, something else was bothering him, and when Ariel Strickland came to see him, the bother just got worse.

She had shown up at his door unannounced sometime in late August of last year. Alexander and Ariel knew each other casually through firm-related contact, but were acquaintances at best, so it was quite a surprise when Alexander's wife showed her in.

"Good afternoon, Millie, Alexander," Ariel said nodding in acknowledgement. "I am so sorry to barge in on you this way. I hope you don't mind. I just thought if I didn't come right now, I never would."

"Oh it's wonderful to see you, Ariel," Millie said, giving her a hug. "We're delighted you came by."

"I'll second that," Alexander said with a hug of his own.

"Thank you very much for saying that. I do apologize for the inconvenience." By this time Ariel was seated on the Queen Anne tufted sofa across from the Cabots, nervously twisting the leather straps on her Gucci bag. She shifted agitatedly in her seat as if trying to find some elusive level of comfort and busily smoothed invisible wrinkles from her slacks. Alexander and Millie exchanged quizzical glances. They had never seen Ariel Strickland dispossessed of her trademark charm and decorum, let alone exhibiting obvious nervousness. Finally, Ariel leaned forward and was able to speak.

"I need your help," she said. "I'm sorry I have to ask for it and I'm sorry I have to tell you what I have to tell you, but I think you're the only people who can help me, if you're willing to." Ariel looked so small and sad sitting on such an imposing couch that Millie moved next to her and squeezed her hand. "Maurice is planning to divorce me and leave me with nothing." An involuntary gasp escaped from Alexander and Millie almost simultaneously.

"Oh my god, Ariel. How do you know? I mean, are you sure?" Millie asked incredulously. "He loves you. He worships you. He always tells Alexander you're the best thing that ever happened to him."

"It's true, Ariel," Alexander said. "He talks about you all the time. And not just to me, to everybody. Are you really sure this is true?"

Ariel looked up with the saddest eyes Alexander had ever seen. And in an instant he was back in the dust bowls of Oklahoma, in the coal mines and the textile mills, looking into the eyes that had haunted him all his life—eyes that had driven him, either through guilt or goodness, to do better and be better—these same eyes of inscrutable sorrow. He straightened in his chair and took a deep breath.

"Ariel, tell us what happened," Alexander said paternally. Millie nodded her assent and moved closer to Ariel on the couch.

"The first time I knew anything was wrong was at the partners' wives benefit luncheon a week ago."

"I saw you there before lunch," Millie interjected, "but couldn't find you later."

"That's because I left right after I found out that my husband had been making many more millions of dollars than he had told me about. Katherine was just being sweet and congratulating me on my newfound wealth. That was the first time I had heard or seen anything about more money. *And* the first time I knew there was anything wrong with our marriage, I might add," Ariel said sardonically. "Hidden money only means one thing. The fact that I caught him virtually flagrante delicto two days later was just a rude confirmation."

"This is truly awful, Ariel," Millie said. We're so sorry this is happening to you. What can we do to help?"

Ariel took a deep breath and turned to face Alexander. "I've decided to fight. I've decided to fight Maurice with every inch and fiber of my being. If I don't win, at least I'll know I gave it everything I had. But if I *do* win, I'll have taken from Maurice the only things that ever mattered to him—money and power." She said those words wistfully, cradling them in sadness and regret and showing Alexander, at least in part, the pain that realization had cost her. And then in an instant, that part of Ariel was gone, replaced by a hard steeliness that made Alexander recoil as she said, "Most importantly, he'll know I was the one who did it."

Her words lay heavy in the room. And after a moment of silence, it was Millie who spoke first. "We'll do anything we can to help you, Ariel. Just tell us what you need."

"Thank you so much. Thank you from the bottom of my heart," Ariel began. "This means everything to me. What I really need is information, financial information about the firm. I'm not sure how much you can tell me about the firm's financial structure, especially its compensation formulas, but I need to know anything you're willing to tell me. The only way I can even begin to take on Maurice is to know how he gets paid, to understand how the compensation structure works. After I know that, then I have a much better chance at finding where he's stashed all our money."

"I agree," Alexander said. "At the very least, you would know when draw and bonus payments are made and can look for assets based on that timing. Plus, it will give you broader information that might tie in to other information and help in ways we can't foresee now."

"Exactly," Ariel agreed. "I'm never going to get close to equal footing, but this kind of confidential information is the only way I'm going to have a chance at Maurice at all."

"It's really a pretty basic compensation structure," Alexander began. I set it up when I went corporate with my firm twenty years ago and it has suffered only minor alterations since then. My goal was to maintain a collegial partnership environment while still rewarding those who brought in the work. Even though I didn't particularly care for this kind of 'eat what you kill' component, I knew I needed specific financial incentives if I wanted my firm to continue to grow and flourish. I do have a basic understanding of human behavior after all," Alexander said with a wink to Millie, clearly a private joke. "Here's the way it works: every partner gets the same predetermined draw each month, which gets set at the start of each fiscal year based on projected income. A year-end accounting justifies the real numbers with the projected numbers and a bonus draw is paid. Of course, if there was a shortfall between the real numbers and the draw that had been paid, the partners would have to refund that money, but that has never happened, since the projected income is always calculated conservatively. This year the draw is $60,000 per month. In addition, the 'eat what you kill' component gives the partner who brings in the work 20 percent of all the fees billed on that matter. Obviously, this is where the real money is. Those fees are paid out quarterly."

"Sounds like a fair system to me," Ariel commented. And it's clearly working. When does your fiscal year start?"

"Actually, we just made it the same as the calendar year. Seemed much easier."

"Well, I knew about the monthly draw, but that's all," Ariel continued. "I asked Maurice once, a while ago, about whether CS & B was going to consider paying bonuses based on work brought in, since all the other firms were doing it. He said that was highly unlikely based on your particular ideological bent."

"Interesting characterization," Alexander said. "What else?"

"He also told me that the monthly draw had been frozen at $50,000 for the last two years to save up for necessary capital improvements in the building's heating and cooling systems."

"Another interesting but completely false statement."

"Plus, last year he said that there had been a shortfall in the annual realized income and that each partner had to refund $75,000 to the partnership."

"Astounding."

"I know." Ariel nodded her head somberly. "So let me get this straight. He's been hiding his 'eat what you kill' bonus since we've been married and he's just stolen another $315,000 in the last two years." She shook her head in disgust. "I'm almost immune to the fact that our marriage was built on deceit, but why this escalation now?" It was meant rhetorically, but an answer suddenly popped into her brain with startling clarity. Their ten-year wedding anniversary was this June. That would make their marriage a "long-term marriage" for purposes of asset distribution should they ever divorce. If they divorced after June, she would get more money. If they divorced before, she would get much less. Not only was Maurice planning to divorce her, he was planning to divorce her before June and leave her with an even smaller pittance than she had ever imagined. Her mind struggled to comprehend this new piece of information. It was as if she didn't know Maurice Strickland at all.

"Are you alright?" Millie asked, noticing the blanched look on Ariel's face.

"Yes, I'm fine," Ariel said hollowly. "I just realized why Maurice has been in such a hurry up offense. Our ten-year wedding anniversary is this June." She turned to face Millie and Alexander. "I think we all know what that means. So I'm going to have to execute the finest two-minute drill that's ever been seen. And," she said fixedly, "I can do it."

"We know you can, Ariel," Alexander said. But what exactly do you have in mind? I mean, are you just seeking your half of the community assets or are you wanting more?"

"No, Alexander. I just want what is fair. What the law entitles me to. I wouldn't steal from him the way he has stolen from me. But I want my half of the *hidden* assets too."

"I understand. I hope that what I've told you about the financial structuring of the firm has helped. Unfortunately, Millie and I have an engagement at the club that we have to get ready for, so we're going to have to say goodbye at this point."

"Oh, I'm so sorry," Ariel exclaimed as she stood up to go. I knew I was barging in. Thank you so much for seeing me and telling me what you did. It helps enormously."

"You're quite welcome," Alexander said as Millie showed Ariel to the door and closed it firmly behind her.

"What engagement at the club, Alexander?" Millie asked, perplexed. "I don't have anything on the calendar."

"I'm sorry, honey. I had to lie. I'm just not sure how far I'm willing to go with Ariel on this, and I needed some time to sort it out. I mean, I was happy to give her that general CS & B financial information because, frankly, it's just not that confidential. She could get that from any number of sources. But I'm not sure how I feel about giving her more information or offering to help her against Maurice. I mean, he is my partner. I've worked with him for over ten years, many of those years very closely. We've been through a lot together. And though I'm seriously concerned about the direction of the firm and feel that Maurice is primarily to blame, I can't just wipe out all those years of partnership. You know I don't like what he's doing to Ariel, but I just have to figure out where I fit into it all."

"Well, I'm glad I didn't offer up any more of you," Millie said apologetically. "I didn't stop to think that you might have any reservations about helping Ariel when I offered. It was a bit of a spontaneous outpouring, I'm afraid."

"I know, you sweet dear," as he kissed her and gave her one of his famous bear hugs. "And that's just one of the reasons I love you so very much."

CHAPTER FOURTEEN

Sam was still twitching. It had been over an hour since he'd escaped to his office, but he was still in a very bad way. He didn't understand why he was so freaked out. It was just a settlement offer on Bicknel stationary signed by Simon. Of course there was some reasonable explanation. He wished he had taken the time to read the letter more carefully and see which firm was representing the plaintiff. That might have given him more information as to what the hell was going on. He needed to get himself together so he could go home, get some sleep, and approach this thing again when he was more sane, but he couldn't leave his office until he was in a better state. Anyone who saw him now would think something was wrong with him. And they'd be right. In any event, he needed to get out before Simon got back. He couldn't risk seeing Simon before he'd figured out how he was going to handle the whole situation. He thought about calling Sarah to get her take on things, but decided against it. After all she'd been through in the last forty-eight hours, she didn't need to be involved in his little drama as well. He forced himself into his cushy client chair and took a number of deep breaths, trying out the little meditation tips he'd learned in a firm stress class years ago. Surprisingly, he felt a lot better quicker than he thought possible. He grabbed his coat and moved for the door, only to have his phone ring right as he got to the hallway. It was Lorraine. He could just make out the phone display from where he stood. He lunged for the phone only to catch himself and pull back at the last second. He didn't know what to do. Lorraine rarely called, even to set up appointments for Simon, so it was unlikely she was calling on Simon's behalf. That could only mean one thing. It had something to do with his visit to Simon's office this morning. He decided to take the call.

"Hi Lorraine," he said in the most casual voice he could muster. "I was just on my way out, but saw it was you. What's up?"

Instead of the chirpiness he was expecting, there was nothing, just dead silence on the other end of the line.

"Lorraine?"

"Oh, Sam," came a wail from the other end of the line. "Simon's been in a car accident."

"Oh my God, Lorraine. Is he OK?"

"Yes," she sniffed. "He said it's just minor cuts and bruises. He said he's going to be fine. He just needs to take a few days off work. I'm sorry to be so emotional. It was just kind of a surprise, you know?"

"I understand completely. It's really upsetting. How many days do you think he'll be out?"

"Just a few, I hope. He said the main reason he's going to stay home, apart from the aches and pains, is the Frankenstein effect—that he would scare small children."

"Well, if he can still make jokes, I'm sure he's going to be OK. Now you take care of yourself. Get yourself a nice cup of coffee and relax. It's going to be just fine."

"Thank you, Sam, for being so sweet. Simon wanted me to call Mr. Strickland first, but I'm so glad I called you. You made me feel so much better."

Sam replaced the receiver and thought about the call. Whatever distressed, confused thoughts Sam had about Simon and the Bicknel letter evaporated in his immediate concern for the welfare of his friend. He was sure there was some wholly appropriate explanation for the letter. He would just have to ask Simon when Simon was feeling better. He moved toward the hall again, this time e-mailing Simon get well wishes on his iPhone as he walked.

"You better watch where you're going," came a stern voice from his side. "You just about ran me over, Sam."

Sam looked up to see Mr. Strickland glowering down at him from his exalted 6'2" height, briefcase in one hand, coat in the other, thoroughly unamused at having to defend himself in the hall of his own firm.

"I . . . I'm sorry, Mr. Strickland. I wasn't watching where I was going."

"Clearly. I trust you got the motion done after all."

"Yes, sir. No problem. Went out the door this morning."

"Good. Oh, I wanted to mention to you that Simon will be out for a few days due to a minor fender bender he had this morning. I know you'll be available to step in should we need you, and I assume Simon will be working from home, so it shouldn't be much of an issue."

"No problem, sir. Let me know if I can help in any way."

"Fine, now you'll excuse me if I continue on to my office to start my day."

Sam stepped aside to allow Maurice to pass, pocketed his iPhone, and made a straight shot for the elevator. Frankly, he had had enough of all of it and desperately needed some air and a little sun if he could get it. As he exited the building, the ubiquitous Los Angeles sun hit him full in the face and, for once, he didn't mind the smog that went with it. It just felt good to be out. It seemed strange though that Maurice already knew about Simon's accident. Sam thought Lorraine had said she'd told him first and Maurice had evidently just arrived at the firm when they met up so he hadn't even made it to his office. No matter. That was the kind of information network you needed if you were a named partner at CS & B, Sam decided.

Meanwhile, Strickland had spent the last five minutes berating himself for his own inexcusable sloppiness. How could he mention Simon's accident to Sam? He wasn't even supposed to know about it yet. What a fuckin' idiot. He definitely was getting more and more unbalanced. And that translated into poor judgment. Thank god Hector would fix him up tonight. He heaved open his briefcase and began flinging files and papers all over his desk and credenza creating a virtual beehive of activity. It was his best effort at absolution.

"Hello, Marjorie. I'm in. Please bring my schedule and today's phone messages."

"Yes, sir. Right away," Marjorie responded briskly over the speaker phone, Maurice's schedule already in hand. She readjusted her jacket, grabbed the phone messages and strode toward his office, fixing a cup of coffee for him on her way. She didn't mind Maurice the way everyone else did and didn't mind showing him a little extra courtesy. The fact was she liked his brusqueness and efficiency and liked succeeding where so many others had failed.

"Good morning," she said as she entered his office. "Looks like you're already humming."

"Yes, Marjorie. That meeting this morning put me behind. I have a lot on my plate today and want to make sure I finish with enough time to go to that Leaders of Tomorrow dinner."

"Right. OK. Where do we start?"

"Schedule. Let's hear it."

"You have a conference call on Sweet Farm Distributors in ten minutes, lunch with Jeb Miller at Sabucco at one, the preliminary injunction hearing on Roper Technologies at two thirty, LASC dept. 10, and then meetings with Manuel and Jose Vargas out of the office at five. If the prelim hearing doesn't go long, you should be fine time-wise."

"Good. Phone messages?"

Michael Bodin, Stuart Teichmann, Emily Prager. And John Wilkins keeps calling from the prosecutor's office. He's already called three times today and sounds kind of stressed."

"OK. I'll call him. Anything else?"

"No, that's it for now."

"Alright. Thanks. Finish that tape I left you last night and then turn to the filing in *Figueroa*. Make sure to send a courtesy copy to the judge that gets to his chambers before three. After that, you can work with the paralegals to start organizing my Merrick trial exhibits."

"Great."

"Oh, and confirm my Bungalow no. 8 reservation at the Beverly Hills Panorama Hotel tonight. The dinner is going to go long and I know I'm not going to feel like driving all the way home after that."

Marjorie nodded as she backed out the door and adjourned to her desk to start working. Maurice sat back in his chair, immediately enraged. What the fuck was wrong with that moron Wilkins? Stupid cocksucker knows he is never to call me at the firm. Never. For any reason, ever. Goddammit. What does that idiot think this fuckin' iPhone is for? Maurice picked up his phone for emphasis and instantly saw that something was wrong. No lights were flashing and the screen was dark. Fuck. When did this thing die, Maurice thought in total frustration. Probably during the little get together with Simon this morning. Fuck. That's why Wilkins is calling here. And it must be important. Fuck.

Maurice looked at the clock and saw that he only had two minutes before his conference call. He couldn't reschedule—twelve lawyers and a judge were going to be on the line and he was the one who had called for the conference in the first place. There was no time. He couldn't get to another phone out of the office. He had to call now.

"Wilkins? What the fuck? Why are you calling me at my firm? I'm going to have your ass. You know there is absolutely no possible scenario that would authorize a call to my firm."

By this time, Wilkins had wound himself up into a state of near-hysteria, having waited by the phone for the past two hours. He was a meek, docile man who had found himself, first, in law school, and later, in the prosecutor's office by sheer paternal fiat. And it was this same wimpy nature that had led him into the kind of trouble he was in now.

"Oh, God . . . thank God it's you," Wilkins cried into the phone. I've been waiting for two hours to talk to you. Your cell phone isn't working and I didn't know what else to do." His voice sounded high and tight and whiny. Almost like my first wife, Maurice thought as he tried to push that visual out of his brain.

"Well, I came in early this morning like always and there was this man sitting in the lobby waiting. So I asked him how he got in, because you need a key and a card to get in before nine, you know? And what he wanted." Wilkins paused and took a few deep breaths to try and keep himself from hyperventilating. "He said he wanted to see me. I didn't know what else to do because he was so big and it was just me and him in the whole office, so I said sure. He said he wanted private and by this time I was so freaked out I just said OK and I took him into my office and we sat down. He said he was investigating the *Rodriguez* case that I had tried a few months ago. Well, I got all clammy, but I think I did pretty good under the circumstances. I said, 'well what about it?' And he said, 'well there's something fishy about it and I think you and the judge are in cahoots on it.' He just tossed it out there like that. My stomach was doing flip-flops, but I just looked at him hard and said no, that he was crazy and where could he ever possibly come up with such an insane thought. And he said he thought it was kind of strange that Rodriguez didn't even get reckless driving and there was no testimony about excess speed. And here's where I did good. I said, 'you know, you're right. I screwed up. I should have put in the evidence, but I just lost track during the trial and forgot to get it in.'"

"You fuckin' moron!" Maurice screamed into the phone. "What are you trying to do to me, you stupid son of a bitch?" He smashed his fist down on the desk with such force that his laptop lurched dangerously toward the edge, but the impact instantly brought him back to current reality. He lowered his voice and continued. "You just gave him our heads on a silver platter. You pointed him exactly where he needs to look, to the one big fat weakness in the whole thing if he's smart enough to catch it. The estimated speed and 'excessive speed' were noted by the cop at the scene who took, filed, and signed the police report. You admitted the police report as an exhibit, therefore you admitted those notations as well, you dumb fuck, even though you didn't admit any of it specifically as any competent prosecutor would have done. Any judge worth his salt would have caught the information in the police report and convicted that asshole Rodriguez on reckless driving, too. Gross incompetence just doesn't fly for both you *and* Schneider, so the only explanation is some kind of conspiracy between you two—a prosecutor and a judge. Brilliant job, asshole. You may as well have told the investigator that I was the one behind all of it. It's a small step from you two to me. I told you *never* to answer any inquiries. The fact that I decided to take out the reckless driving charge is laughable now thanks to you, you stupid fuck. I am so pissed right now I could come over and strangle your little scrawny neck myself. Whatever you do, don't say anything more to anyone about this case. And I mean not one thing. You are an officer of the court and you simply can't comment. Got it? I'll figure out where to go from here, but in the meantime, you should be very concerned about the trouble you have caused."

Maurice slammed down the receiver and sat for a moment, his chest heaving up and down with exertion. He couldn't believe how fucked up everything had gotten in such a short period of time. He had to figure out how to fix this mess too, but first he had to figure out who this investigator was and who he was working for.

Meanwhile, at the other end of the line, poor John Wilkins hung up the receiver, put his head in his hands, and cried.

◆ ◆ ◆

But crying wasn't a luxury Simon could afford. He had somehow managed to drive himself home from The Lucky Seven and was lying prone on the couch, his vision a psychedelic palette of reds, blues, and purples with an occasional orange thrown in for effect. His body didn't just ache; it throbbed, and then convulsed in the weirdest places. And he knew it would only get worse. He tried to make some sense of what had just happened, but he was still too crazed with what had gone on. He was only clear about one thing. He had to get out now. Right now. He had seen, for the first time, who Maurice really was and he was more scared than he had ever been in his life. Plus, the nagging question about Michael Byrne kept resurfacing in his mind. Michael had also been a senior litigator primarily working in Maurice's personal injury group when he disappeared. They had found his sailboat right off the Marina del Rey coast, but no one could say for sure that he had been on it and there were no signs of any struggle. The best the police could come up with was that Michael had gone out for a sunset sail, had some kind of medical emergency, and fallen overboard and drowned. The fact that no body was ever found was only slightly irritating to the cops and didn't prevent them from closing the file. The firm had mourned the loss and offered grievance counseling but, in time, everyone had pretty well forgotten Michael and moved on. Everyone except Simon.

Simon gingerly moved himself to the bathroom, where he did what he could for his face and tossed down three aspirin. What were his options? One, he could go to the police and tell them everything. Sure, his life and career would be over, but at least he would be alive. Or would he? Having seen what Maurice did to Rodriguez and what Simon suspected he did to Michael Byrne, there was no telling what Maurice would do to him. Two, he could tell Maurice that he wanted out. That he was done with the whole thing and wanted to just go back to being a regular associate in the firm. But even as he thought it, he knew it wasn't possible. He knew too much, he was too involved. Maurice wouldn't stand for a liability like him walking around free to shoot his mouth off at will. No, his only hope was to run—to take with him as much cash as he could and leave the country. But what did that even mean, leave the country? Where would he go? What would he do? Could he ever come back? Wasn't he just being totally paranoid? Maurice hurt Rodriguez; he didn't kill him. Simon sat down heavily at the kitchen table and let a wave of pain pass over him. His head hurt so much that he could barely keep it up. He knew he was in no condition to evaluate what was going on, let alone make a decision, but he felt like he didn't have the luxury of waiting until he felt better. He could almost hear all of the clocks in his house marking off the few minutes he had left. Tick-tock, tick-tock. What are you going to do, Simon? Tick-tock, tick-tock. You better do something fast, Simon. Tick-tock, tick-tock. Or you might end up dead. Tick-tock, tick-tock.

CHAPTER FIFTEEN

It was all Sam could do to throw himself in his car and get home after the exhaustion from his all-nighter kicked in. He was usually so good with all-nighters, having acquired a handy tolerance during law school and in his early years at the firm, but today was something different. He was absolutely beat. He cranked the sunroof and the radio, and made the normally thirty-minute drive home in twenty-five minutes, then he crashed on the bed and slept.

Luckily, the mailman woke him at four in the afternoon, or he might have slept right through the rest of the workday and his dinner with Sarah later. He hurriedly jumped into the shower, put on a fresh suit and tie, and headed for the door, grabbing a power bar on his way. He had just reached the car when his iPhone started ringing.

"Hello? What an unexpected treat," Sam said. "I was just thinking of you and wondering where we should go for dinner."

"Well, if I'm not cooking, at least I'm buying, so it better be someplace cheap." Sarah started laughing. "How crass. I mean someplace that offers exceptional value."

"Right."

"I'm glad I caught you. I knew you were snoozing, so I didn't want to call earlier, but I wanted to pick your brain about a prosecutor named John Wilkins."

"I wish you could, but I've never heard of him. What's up?"

"My investigator just had a rather strange interaction with him and I wanted to see if I could get more intelligence on the guy. Plus, there's some kind of connection between him and Schneider that may not be totally above board."

"Whoa, that sounds a bit creepy. Why do you think that? I mean, we both know Schneider's an asshole, but I can't see him being involved in anything that's not right ethically. If anything, he seems to me to be a fire and brimstone kind of guy. For him it's either right or it's wrong, and if it's wrong, that makes you wrong and you should be punished."

"I know. That's how I've always thought of Schneider, too. God knows I've been on the fire and brimstone end of it enough times."

"So what's the story?"

"Well, I'll just tell you what I can without naming any client names, but basically, Schneider dismissed a reckless driving charge on a guy for lack of evidence even though the evidence had been admitted in the police report. So it could just be Schneider having a bad day, except for this weird communication that transpired between Wilkins and Schneider at trial."

"What the hell does that mean?"

Both of my clients independently saw Wilkins and Schneider exchange some kind of communicative look at trial. I know how that sounds—what's a look?—but my clients saw some kind of communication between them during the trial when this guy walked into the courtroom."

"Weird. That does sound strange. What guy?"

"I don't know and they don't know either. And he didn't do anything either. Just sat at the back of the courtroom and watched. Anyway, I kept wondering how the reckless driving charge got dismissed and I kept calling Wilkins, but he wouldn't call me back. So I sent my investigator over to talk to him this morning."

"Good use. I'm sure that's exactly how Wilkins wanted his day to start off." Sam laughed.

"I know. It was a little mercenary, but I had called the guy six times with no response. What was I going to do, send a letter?"

"So what did Wilkins say?"

"Only that he made a mistake. He claims that he just screwed up, which I find a little hard to believe."

"No kiddin'. Anything else about this guy and this look?"

"No, just what I told you. My clients said that this guy walked in and Wilkins got nervous and seemed to try and communicate something with the judge."

"Hmm," Sam mused. "Who knows? There could be something to it. I wish I knew something that could help you. I feel like a dolt not being able to offer anything. But at least I can ask around the firm and see if anyone has any intelligence on Wilkins or Schneider."

"I would really appreciate that," Sarah said sincerely. "Now I definitely owe you dinner."

"Why yes you do. Big slabs of steak and martinis, but I'm buying. You can buy tomorrow." Good one, Sam thought. Good and sneaky. He waited to see if she would bite.

"We'll just have to see about that, Mr. Morrow," Sarah said playfully. "You can't expect to hog my whole dance card, can you?"

"Well, yes m'am, I can," Sam teased back. "But in the meantime, see you at Brevard's at seven? I'm sorry I can't pick you up, but the way things are going, I know I'll otherwise be unacceptably late."

"Oh, you mean there's a late that's acceptable?"

"Ugh," Sam groaned. "I'll see you at seven."

They both hung up their phones and smiled. Neither could wait to see each other later. Sarah was still smiling when Christine walked in.

"Girlfriend, I'm gonna plant a giant wet one on Sam when I see him," Christine said in passable street jive. "He's turning you into a real bona fide human being."

"You must be standing out there with a glass pressed to my door," Sarah said laughing. "Have you just come in to harass me, or do you have proper business with my Royal Highness?"

"I actually do. I wanted to give you an update on the research I started on that Nevada corp."

"Great. That was really quick. What did you find out?"

"Well, it was set up five years ago. It's current on all its fees and taxes, and its registered agent is one of those Nevada corporate 'service of process' companies. There doesn't seem to be any operating business tied to the LLC, even though the truck had some kind of logo on it.

"The writing was 'Best Meats Food Co.'," Sarah interjected. "It came up at trial. I've done a search for Best Meats and had Duane look into it too from his end, and neither of us has found any business attached to that name."

"OK. So it's a company truck with no company, that's driven by Rodriguez and owned by Obelisk Holdings. But who owns Obelisk? Do you think this was all set up by Rodriguez? I mean, in spite of his other lame attempts at asset protection, do you think Rodriguez did this?"

"I would find that extremely hard to believe," Sarah said. We're obviously clueless about who the real Paul Rodriguez is, but I just don't think he has the wherewithal to set up something this advanced. It's not only the Nevada LLC, but Obelisk and the Rabbit Hole Trust. Pretty complicated stuff."

"I know. Plus, what's the deal with the truck anyway? Does Rodriguez use it for work or does it just sit there?"

I'm having Duane watch Rodriguez's apartment and house as best as he can, but he's got other cases he's working on. Cases that are presently paying his rent, so it's not going to be 100 percent. We just have to do our best to get more information about Rodriguez now, since you know we'll never get anything out of him in a deposition anyway."

"Right. I know Duane has a new assistant, so maybe he can help too. Oh, and I also took a quick peak at Obelisk—mainly because I couldn't resist it."

"I know how that is," Sarah nodded.

"I was actually able to look at a lot of the Obelisk documents online and there's still no answer as to who 'A.C.' is. The initials are all over the place, but A.C. isn't spelled out anywhere."

"Great," Sarah said sarcastically. "No surprise there. Not that I think finding out who 'A.C.' is would give us the mother lode, but I think it could lead to more information. It looks like K-2 Financial is a shell, and Obelisk Holdings is a shell, and everything is really owned by the beneficiary of the Rabbit Hole Trust. So as it stands right now, all we have is Rodriguez's Timberline house and the Mercedes, both of which we could attach after we win our judgment except for one problem. They're both encumbered to their respective roofs. There's no equity left for us to attach and Duane hasn't been able to find any more assets in either Rodriguez or his wife's name. This is why we're working so hard to pierce this corporate shell game. Any bread crumb could lead to something bigger."

"Gotcha. If we can't get through the corporate entities and can't find any more assets, are we going to have to drop the case? I mean, there would be nothing to get even if we did win."

Sarah paused for a moment, letting the enormity of the question sink in. "I just can't go there yet. We'll see what shakes out. I can't stand the thought of Murray, Alice, and Andy getting nothing for all this. It would break my heart. We just have to look harder and try harder. I know we can do it."

"I know we can too," Christine said defiantly as she turned toward the door. "They've got nothing on us."

But Sarah wasn't so sure. She had been worrying about the financial issues with the case for days now, actually since day one, and she was getting more and more concerned. The costs were mounting. Dun & Bradstreet searches, LexisNexis research, and the cost of Duane, Christine, and her time were all making a heavy dent in her operating expenses. She was already out thousands of dollars. Thousands of dollars she didn't have, with no end in sight. She took a deep breath and told herself it was going to be OK. It had to be OK. After all, they were the good guys.

CHAPTER SIXTEEN

Hector was trying to psych himself up to do what he had to do for Maurice. The couple of shots he'd had an hour ago hadn't helped at all, and he didn't feel that he could have any more and still be able to drive over to Rodriguez's later. He needed to pull himself together, stop thinking about it and just do it. He'd been assured that this was absolutely the last time and he believed it. That should be enough, for God's sake. He turned to the job at hand. He picked up his cell phone, punched in a number and waited.

"Hi, Mikey? Yeah, I need a lamb tonight. No, same guy. But he doesn't want anything he's seen before. Wants fresh blood, so to speak. Right. And he wants something, as he says, 'sweet,' 'fresh' and, of course, young. The last one was apparently too old. For once though he doesn't care about color, so that should make it a little easier." He listened for a moment and said, "eight thirty pick-up? I'll meet you at the fountain. Thanks a lot."

Hector flipped his phone closed and couldn't contain an involuntary shudder. This whole business made him physically sick. If, for whatever reason, this was not the last time, it was his last time. He simply would not do this again. Not ever. Maurice would have to go fuck himself. He got up, walked to the kitchen, and slammed down another tequila shot despite what he'd told himself earlier. He would just have to go over to Rodriguez's a little later. He thought back to when this whole repulsive business began.

It had started out as a beautiful night. It was his twentieth anniversary at the firm and he was being treated to a fantastic party at the Baja Cabana. Everything was perfect, just like he liked it—lots of friends, Mexican food, and margaritas. And no one was shy about ordering extra tequila shots to supplement the already super juiced Cadillac Margaritas. He remembered looking over at Alexander and thinking how much he liked working for him and how sad he was going to be when the old patriarch retired. It wasn't that he didn't enjoy working for the new guy, Maurice. It was just that he really liked and respected Alexander and would miss having Alexander in his daily life. Plus, he owed Alexander a lot. Alexander had given him a steady job when he really needed it and a job that he was proud of. Twenty years ago, Hector was a struggling penny ante private investigator trying to get by. He'd been released from Cold Springs Penitentiary six months before, and he was really working to stay legit, but it wasn't going well. He had thought private investigation was a perfect fit for him, but he was having trouble not only getting work, but getting paid. He was on the verge of calling his old pals and putting together another car heist when he met Alexander.

Everyone had a story about meeting Alexander. It was rare that anyone ever met him in line at the checkout or at some common cocktail party. No, people always seemed to meet him in unusual situations, when they needed him most. Alexander would somehow appear and rescue them. Like a shining knight rescuing the Sleeping Beauties of the world. But it wasn't that they were such outstanding Sleeping Beauties that they commanded rescue. Rather, it was that Alexander was just so much the shining knight.

Hector had been working on a crappy little divorce case, trying to get some dirt on the wife to embarrass her into giving up more in the split. It was shameful work for Hector, since he found that he really liked the wife and thought his own client was a jerk. His surveillance had revealed that the wife, Emily, was seeing someone, but it was platonic. They met for drinks and dinner and occasional tennis, but never for a romp in the hay. Meanwhile, his client, Michael, bragged about conquests with different women in every phone call. Michael then told Hector to try and catch certain photos that made it look like there was something going on between Emily and her friend even though there wasn't. Seedy and disgusting, he thought, but he was doing it because he desperately needed the money.

After about two weeks of surveillance, Michael was just about ready to pack it in and go with the less than perfect evidence he had when it happened. Hector was watching the end of a tennis match between Emily and her friend when a tennis ball from another court bounced in and hit Emily smack on the forehead. She went down hard, out cold on the court. Her friend rushed to her side, brought her to, and carried her to the benches where he put a cold compress on her forehead and supported her in his arms. Hector couldn't help but notice the gentle way he cared for her. His touch, his extreme concern, all pointed to more than just friends. And later, when they moved from the benches to their cars, she leaned on him in a way that told Hector the feelings were mutual. They ended up at Steps at the Beach, a hotel known for its discretion, where they got a room with a balcony and a view of the ocean. Hector took all the pictures he could, but when it came time to give that week's photos to Michael, those pictures weren't part of the packet. He's still not sure why he did it. Maybe it was because he liked Emily that much, or maybe because he was tired of being bitchslapped by his client. In any event, he kept the photos and burned them that Sunday at a bonfire on the beach. Fitting, he thought. He had already closed the file and was urgently hunting for his next job when he got a call from a Mr. Cabot at the law firm of Cabot & Swain.

"Mr. Skolnick? Yes, this is Alexander Cabot. I'm a lawyer. I'd like to talk to you for a few moments if you have time."

"Sure, no problem," Hector had said. He couldn't remember any lawyer ever asking him if he had time to talk, let alone seeming so nice about it. "Go ahead. Shoot."

"I represent Mrs. Emily Westerly in her divorce case. You know her as Michael Westerly's wife."

"Oh." Hector braced himself for the worst. There was never anything good about lawyers and if Cabot represented Emily, it wasn't going to be good for him.

"I want to ask you a question. I'd love it if you could give me an honest answer, but I understand if you can't."

"Shoot."

"I met with Michael Westerly's lawyer the other day. He was

delighted to show me a packet of pictures of Emily and her friend 'at play' as he said. He was trying to tell me that they were having an affair, but despite some disingenuous attempts to embellish the pictures, I could tell that they weren't. I took them to my client to get her take on them and she said the tennis pictures of the day she got hit by the ball seemed incomplete. She wondered if there might be others. So my question to you is, are there other pictures that you're holding back or is that it?"

Hector smiled. So that's all it was. "You know I can't answer your questions," Hector began. "You know more than me about that attorney privacy thing, but even I know I can't say anything. Plus, how'd you get my name anyway?"

"I got your name from a photo stub that was inadvertently given to me in the packet of pictures I got from Michael Westerly's lawyer. His paralegal obviously made a mistake. The reason I decided to call you, though, is because I have an idea about you that I don't think is wrong." Alexander paused long enough to let those words sink in. "I think you took some pictures that you didn't like taking and you either kept them or destroyed them. In any event, I think you know more than your pictures reflect."

Hector sat down and took a sip of his now cold coffee. "Why would you think that?"

"Well, Emily and I are not only attorney and client, but we've been friends for fifteen years, so she tells me just about everything. She said she'd noticed a paneled pick-up truck that seemed to be in a lot of the same places she'd been over the last few weeks. She only noticed it because her dad had one just like it when she was growing up and she admired how well maintained it was. She said she saw it last week at the tennis courts and then later at Steps. I checked. You are the registered owner of a paneled pick-up truck and I think you used this truck to take your pictures. If this is the case, you took those tennis court pictures and you took pictures at Steps as well. Am I right? Did you take pictures at Steps? If so, where are those pictures?"

"I don't know what you're talking about. I admit I was hired by Michael Westerly to take pictures, but I won't say anything more than that."

"I understand and I respect your position. I knew it was a long shot. I guess I really called you more as Emily's friend than her lawyer. She's such a sweet, gentle person. I'm sure you see that too. If there are pictures out there that might show up later, especially at the divorce trial, I want to be able to prepare for them. I just want to know what to expect—if there are any more pictures coming."

"Like I said, I'm not saying anything more than I already said. I took pictures of her. You have the pictures. There aren't any more."

"Thank you Mr. Skolnick. That's the most I could ask for. You know, she really is a special person. She's a good and kind person."

"I like that her name is Emily. It should be Emily. You know the Moody Blues wrote a song about Emily. A real pretty song."

"Yes, I know."

"I hope she knows too."

Alexander hung up his phone and knew he'd been right. Emily had told him about the liaison at Steps and the pick-up truck. Hector must have taken pictures, yet none of them were in the packet. It had to be one of two things: either Michael's attorney was holding them back and waiting to spring them on him at a more critical juncture in the proceedings or Hector had not given up the pictures. Alexander had to find out, if he could, whether those pictures were ever going to surface. He was now pretty sure they wouldn't. The more interesting question was, "Why not?" And it seemed the answer was that Hector liked Emily. What a surprise, Alexander thought. Alexander had always liked a man who thought with his heart, even in the business world. He didn't think passion should be reserved for the bedroom. It was what made the world tick. But in the seedy world of private investigation, it was even more unexpected. He decided he liked Hector Skolnick and, since he was looking for a private investigator for his firm, he decided to hire him.

Alexander and Hector had laughed about "Hector the Romantic" over the years and many, many other things. Alexander had become one of Hector's most cherished friends and Alexander cared about him like a brother. This whole twentieth anniversary party had been Alexander's idea and Alexander had given the toast and coordinated the gift—a two week vacation to Belize. For a diving fanatic like Hector, it was going to be paradise. Later in the evening, after other people had made generous, heartfelt toasts, Hector felt that the warmth of this night would stay with him forever. But that was before Maurice cornered him in the hallway.

"Congratulations, Hector. Some party. You must mean a lot to the old man." Maurice liked to call Alexander "the old man" after a few martinis. After a few more, Alexander became "the old coot" and after even more, he was "His Royal Fucking

Highness." Hector had never seen what came after that and he didn't want to. He generally tried to close Maurice down when he got to "the old man." This night was going to be no exception.

"Hi, Mr. Strickland. What a great party. I'm glad I saw you. I wanted to thank you and all the other partners for hosting. You really outdid yourselves."

"Oh, this is nothing. Just a little thanks for our number one private investigator." Maurice was slurring his words now and Hector figured that he had probably moved on to "the old coot" stage of drunkenness.

"Well, I sure appreciate it. Thanks again. I better get back to the party," Hector said as he turned to go.

"No rush, Hector," Maurice said as he grabbed his arm to detain him. "I want to talk to you for a few minutes about some things."

"Sure, Mr. Strickland. Whatever you say." The words didn't sound terrible coming out of his mouth, it was just how they made him feel after he said them—worse than a subordinate, almost like a servant. But that was the kind of subservience Maurice required and that was another thing Hector loved so much about Alexander. Alexander made you feel like an equal. He made everyone feel like an equal—no matter what class of people or what circumstances. Maurice, by contrast, made everyone feel crappy. Apparently, he liked the power and the ego rush of being king. Hector thought that if Alexander retired and he had to work full time for Maurice, he would probably retire too or go back to running a solo shop. He simply couldn't stomach the demeaning treatment. And after twenty years on a nice salary, he wouldn't have to.

By this time Maurice was draped over him in a familiar way. One arm was looped over his neck and the other was still clutching his most recent martini. Maurice pulled Hector's head close to him and whispered conspiratorially in his ear.

"I know things about you, Hector," Maurice said in his drunken whisper. "I know that you like to smoke crack, Hector." He paused and smiled a particularly malevolent smile. "I know that you're a felon, Hector." His grip tightened and he pulled Hector even closer. "And I know that Alexander doesn't know either of these things."

Hector was stunned. Maurice released his grip and Hector fell back against the wall, chest heaving, trying to catch even the smallest breath. Questions were racing through his head. How could Maurice have found out? When did he find out? What exactly did he know? Why hadn't he told Alexander? Finally, after his brain cleared enough to make a more coherent association, what did Maurice want?

"I don't know what you're talking about Maurice and I don't know why you're telling me these things. Maybe you should go home and sleep off a few of those martinis. Let me get you a taxi."

"I don't need a taxi," Maurice hissed as he grabbed Hector's arm and spun him around. "What I need is a real conversation with you."

Hector was sober enough to know that Maurice meant business and wouldn't be deterred. Thinking quickly, he told Maurice to follow him outside where it was quieter. Hector was really thinking more private. As far as he knew, Maurice was the only one who knew these things. He sure as hell didn't need anyone else overhearing their conversation.

Once outside, Hector figured he would try one last stab at denial. "Not to be disrespectful, Maurice, but where in the world did you get this crazy information?"

"Shit, Hector. I'm surprised that you would even try and deny it. You know I'm not a careless man. My information is good." He had stopped slurring his words and appeared to be completely sober. Apparently the cool ocean air had snapped the drunk right out of him.

Hector knew he was screwed. "What do you want, Maurice?" He said it so quietly that Maurice had to lean in to hear him.

It was Maurice's turn to play dumb. "I don't know what you mean, Hector. Why do you think I, as you say, want something?"

"Well, I don't think anyone shares that kind of information just for fun. I think you have a reason. So I ask again. What do you want, Maurice?" This time there was a band of steel under the question. Hector wanted a no bullshit answer and he wanted it quick.

Maurice didn't care. He was having too much fun at one of his favorite games, cat and mouse. "You know, if Alexander found out about either of these, shall we say, indiscretions, you'd be out of the firm so fast your head would spin. The firm that you love. The firm that loves you so much they gave you this spectacular party." Maurice gestured toward the restaurant. "Think of the humiliation you would feel. Think of the look on the old coot's face. Think about not having this job. Think about being a bum again." It was clear Maurice really enjoyed that last line. Especially when he saw the response it elicited from Hector. "You would lose just about everything that's important to you in your life. What a shame. But the way I see it, you can help me and I will help you by not disclosing what I know. It'll be a win-win." Maurice was warming up to his win-win characterization, even though nothing could be farther from the truth. "You just need to do a little something for me."

He paused and looked over Hector's head at a point somewhere off in the distance and continued. "When I was growing up I knew I was different from all the other kids. I knew I was special. Even though I did all the things that everyone else did, I always did them a little better. It was never enough for me to be a participant. I had to be athlete of the year, student body president, debate champion. And I did it all with ease. I knew then that I had a date with destiny and so it is coming to pass. Who knows what the next years will bring. Congressman? Senator? The sky's the limit for me. But, as you may or may not know, all great men have weaknesses. Many would say that the weakness is, in part, responsible for their greatness. If they're smart, they keep their weakness controlled. If they're not, the weakness becomes the fatal flaw that results in their downfall. I happen to be one of the smart ones."

He trained his gaze back on Hector and continued. "The problem I have is that I am presently without a supplier for the need that I have. I suspect that you, with your underworld connections, can help."

"That was a long time ago," Hector interjected. "Twenty years ago."

"Yes, but even if you haven't kept up other relationships, I don't believe your present crackhead friends are completely without connections. Frankly, I don't care how you get it done, just that you get it done. If you don't get it done, I'll have you tossed out of Cabot, Strickland & Baines so fast you won't even be able to tell your beloved Alexander goodbye."

Hector was still in shock about what was happening. Twenty years at the firm, a beautiful party, and now this. It was some kind of macabre joke. But he knew he had to do it, whatever it was. He just couldn't give up everything. He had worked too hard to create a life that he loved so much. He was willing to do anything to keep it.

So that's how it had started all those years ago, Hector thought. God, how he hated what he had done. He didn't know if there was a hell, but he sure belonged in it. But he had to be honest with himself. If he had it to do over again, he would do the same thing. I guess I'm just a selfish bastard, Hector thought as the last tequila shot finally started to take hold. Selfish, greedy bastard. Selfish, greedy, fucked up bastard. And he was out like a light, still sitting at the kitchen table, head cradled in his hands.

CHAPTER SEVENTEEN

Marion Rodriguez was about as far away from drunk as you could get. She had rocketed past angry and was hip deep in payback. Those men would pay for what they did to her Paulie. They would pay more than they could ever imagine. She would see that they did.

Paul had called her from the apartment at half past five in the morning, his voice so faint she could hardly hear it. All she could make out was, "come" and "help." She didn't need to be told twice. She threw on some sweats and a coat, jumped into the Mercedes, and raced to the apartment. By the time she got there, the sky was beginning to turn light and she could just make out a huddled body on the couch. Paul was crying softly, shivering and crying. He had been trying to cover himself with some neglected t-shirts that had been strewn around the apartment. He looked horrible.

She gently approached, whispering his name as she walked. He was able to raise his head ever so slightly and see that it was her.

"*Gracias Dios, gracias, gracias. Mari, mia angel.* Thank God you are here." He was sobbing now, his shoulders heaving with the effort. Marion rushed to his side and held him in her arms. She blanketed him with her body in an instinctive attempt to warm and comfort him and he grabbed for her desperately like a swimmer drowning at sea. She was crying now too and they held each other for a long time and didn't say a word.

As dawn filtered through the windows of the apartment, Marion could see the extent of Paul's injuries. His body was a grim testament to the damage man did to man. He was bruised and battered seemingly from head to toe. There was blood still oozing from gashes on his face and his left hand was wrapped in a giant blood soaked swath of gauze. He had a huge egg-shaped welt under his right eye and his face was so grotesquely swollen that he could barely see through either eye. He looked perfectly ghastly, but Marion had grown up in a family of four brothers, so there was little that could unnerve her. She knew how to be strong and she knew Paulie would talk when he was ready.

She went to the kitchen for a bowl of warm water and a washcloth, and to take a moment to collect herself. She had been through a whirlwind with Paul Rodriguez. When she first met him he was the classic stereotype of the immigrant Mexican in Southern California. He was a picker and he worked the fields thirteen hours a day, six days a week. She was a maid at the Santa Barbara Surf Hotel. He was so happy and funny and optimistic about his future and everything American. And although she fell for him hard and married him five months later, Marion knew who she had married. She knew Paul was a simple, sweet man who sometimes drank too much and bet too much on the dogs. And she knew that he was loyal and true, and that he would never hurt or leave her. That was good enough for Marion. So when Paul got hooked up in this car thing with Hector and this big fancy law firm, she didn't know what to think. She did what she thought any good wife would do—she kept her mouth shut and supported her husband. It had been good. She loved her new fabulous house and car, clothes, trips, and eating out. She loved showing off to her friends and being able to send money home. She felt important and happy. She didn't understand where the money was coming from, but she was determined not to pry. She knew Paul wouldn't be involved in anything shady. She knew him too well. Now she felt like a fool.

She grabbed the edges of the sink to brace herself and tried to calm down as best she could. This was one of those critical times; she needed to step up. She would get to the bottom of it all soon enough, but what she needed to do right now was be there for her husband. Help him, support him, and not judge him. She smoothed her hair, warmed the water and went back to the living room. By this time, Paul had moved himself into an upright position on the couch and was fumbling with the bandage on his hand. He couldn't get it off immediately and he started pawing at it like an animal. He was getting more and more agitated as he pawed. Finally, he got it off and sat, stunned, looking at his hand as if he'd never seen it before. Swaths of dried blood covered his fingers and the top of his hand, but otherwise no bruises or cuts. Paul moved each finger slowly, independently of each other, watching with fascination as he moved each one. He turned his hand over and over, watching each turn, marveling at his ability to turn his hand. And then he started laughing. He laughed big, weird laughs that made Marion wonder if he was delirious. But his forehead was still cool to the touch, so she just let it run its course. Finally, he had exhausted himself enough that his laughs turned to ragged giggles.

"What it is, Paulie?" Marion asked anxiously. "How can you possibly laugh at a time like this?"

Paul looked into the sweet loving face that was overflowing with worry.

"Oh, I'm so sorry, Mari. I'm such an ass. I was just so relieved, I couldn't control myself."

"What do you mean, relieved?" Marion asked as she stroked his hair.

"Well, Hector told me that he cut off my finger. But he didn't because I have all ten. See?" Paul proudly wiggled his fingers in front of him like a little kid as he spoke, but dropped them the moment he saw Marion's ashen face.

"Oh, my God, Paulie," Marion screamed, crazy with shock and fear. "What have you gotten yourself into? Was it Hector who beat you up? Who was with him? How many were there? Were you doing drugs again?"

"Calm down. Calm down." Paul was now the soothing voice, the voice of lucidity and sanity. "Whatever happened, it's OK now. See? I'm going to be fine. I'll just have some aches and pains to get over, but nothing that a little rest and some of your sweet kindness won't cure."

"I don't think so, Paulie," Marion said frostily. "Not until you tell me what's going on here. And I mean from the beginning." She had had enough. She'd been the good wife and, true, she'd enjoyed the benefits, but this was the end of the line. She loved Paulie more than anything in the world and she was not going to stand by and let him get hurt or even killed. She knew how to fight and if she needed to fight to protect her Paulie, she would do it in a heartbeat.

"I don't think that's a good idea, Mari," Paul said quietly. "You don't know who these people are and what they can do, and that's the way I want it. I'm only beginning to understand who they are myself," Paul touched his face gingerly. "This is serious stuff. I think maybe deadly stuff, and I don't want you involved."

"That's not fair, Paulie," Marion said earnestly. "I'm your wife. I'm your best friend. I care for you more than anyone in this world cares for you. You can't keep this from me anymore. It has gone on too long and it's gotten too big. You need me. You need my help. And I need to give you my help." She was hugging him and holding his hands and kissing them, her tears stinging his wounds where they fell.

"No, Mari, no. I can't do it. I won't do it. If they thought you knew something, they might do something to you too. And I couldn't bear that." Paul was adamant. Marion knew there was no chance of getting anything out of him then, so she decided to back off and come back at it later.

"I understand, Paulie. You know how much I love you. I just want to help. It makes me crazy to see you hurting, but I'll do whatever you want. Just tell me one thing: What were you talking about with your finger?"

"Thanks for understanding, Mari. I love you so much. You're the world to me. The finger seems kind of like a crazy thing now. I'll just tell you what I remember and you can see if it makes any sense. First off, I didn't play poker last night like I planned. I got into a little mess with this guy and ended up getting in worse trouble with Hector, so that took me out of the game."

"And you didn't call me because?"

"You knew I'd be gone all night anyway, so I didn't see any reason to wake you up in the middle of the night just to tell you I wouldn't be home when you already knew it."

"OK, OK. What next?"

"Well, there were these guys and Hector was one of them and he was mad 'cause of something I did. So they beat me up and then when I hurt so bad I couldn't see straight, Hector told me he was going to cut off one of my fingers to teach me a lesson."

"Oh my God, I can't stand even hearing about it."

"I know, I know, but it didn't happen. I think what really happened was that I was so freaked out by what was going on and in pain and maybe just a little high that I couldn't connect the dots on my body parts. I mean, I really thought he did it. Plus, he's such an asshole. He bandaged my hand so I would still think I didn't have a finger until I got the bandage off. What a fucking asshole. Hector and his pals must have really laughed at that one. They must have thought that was the most goddamm funniest thing they'd ever seen. And I know who thought it up—that fucker Hector, of course. None of the other four guys would take a leak without Hector tellin' 'em it was OK. Fuckin' cocksucker." Paul was getting mad now, thinking about all the abuse he'd suffered, and the humiliation. "I'm going to get that fuckin' cocksucker."

"It's alright, honey," Marion said as she gently cradled his head on her breast. "Try not to get too worked up. You need to rest and get better now. There will be time to figure this all out later." Marion meant what she said, plus she had already learned more than she thought she would about what happened last night. Hector and four guys; Hector was the ringleader. If she could find Hector, she would get the rest.

"I'll calm down, Mari, just as soon as I kick the shit out of all of them."

"I know you will. In the meantime, how about a little clean-up, some Bactine, and a few aspirin? A little nap wouldn't hurt you either."

"Yeah, I suppose there's nothing I can do right this minute."

"No, not this minute," Marion said as she got up to get the supplies. When she got back, he was already asleep.

She stayed with him all day, watching him sleep until he finally started to stir at about six. She had moved through a parade of emotions and was now calm and contained, knowing that what she needed to do, she would be able to do in due course. Hector and his gang wouldn't get away with this. She would protect her Paulie.

"How long did I sleep," Paulie asked, wiping his eyes.

"All day. It's the best thing you could have done. How do you feel?"

"Like shit. I have a raging headache and my stomach is kind of pukey."

"You probably need some food. Let me get you cleaned up and then I'll get some soup or something. Sound good?"

"Amazing. I'm actually starving. I'm not sure when I ate last. How about some chicken soup and bread?"

"You got it," Marion said as she cleaned and dressed his

wounds and gave him some aspirin. I'll go to the deli. I'll be back in a few minutes."

"Thank you, Mari, I'm so lucky to have you."

Paul settled into the couch, starting to feel better than he had felt for many hours. He heard the door open and close, and the rustling of a coat.

"Thank you, Mari. Soup will really hit the spot." Paul called out, his stomach making loud growling sounds in anticipation.

"Which spot, Paul? I thought I hit them all last night?" Hector said as he stepped through the doorway and stood, outlined in the setting rays like an ersatz John Wayne.

Paul reflexively recoiled on the couch shoving his hands up to protect his face.

"The door was open. I didn't think you'd mind if I just came in," Hector continued as he moved into the apartment and stood next to the couch.

Paul's anger and boasted threats of retribution evaporated when confronted with the immediate flesh and blood person of Hector Skolnick. It wasn't that Hector was a particularly large man or well-built. True, he was fit and looked strong, but he wasn't imposing in a physical sense. Rather, he was imposing in a true personal sense. His presence simply overwhelmed those less endowed who crossed his path, especially those who crossed him first. Paul Rodriguez was one of those.

"You don't look like you're doing too badly, Paul. Nice that you've got the little missus fetching your soup. She must really give a shit about you. What's her name again, Paul? Is it Mary? Maryanne?"

Paul didn't say a word. He had reverted to the same mute

creature he had been last night, trying not to offend, just trying to survive.

But Hector was having none of it. "I asked you a question, Paul. I said, what's your wife's name?"

"I, . . . ugh, ah, . . . it's Marion," Paul managed to spit out. "Marion Rodriguez."

"I could figure that last part out myself, you moron." Hector turned to the kitchen. "You got any beer, Paul? Any beverage for your guest. I'm feeling a bit thirsty."

"Ah, . . . yeah . . . I mean, yes, there's some beer in the fridge."

"Why thank you. No, no, don't get up. You seem a little under the weather. I'll get it myself." Hector turned and started to walk into the kitchen just as Marion passed by the large front picture window on her way to the door. Glancing inside to see if Paul was sleeping, she saw a man moving into the kitchen. Instinctively, she knew it was Hector. She clutched her grocery bag and purse tight against her chest and quietly stepped to the side of the window. She needed to hide, Marion thought. If Hector meant trouble, she would at least be able to get away and call the police. But she also needed to find out what was going on in there. She carefully made her way past the door and down the walk past the other two apartments. As soon as she was at the end, she ran down the stairs and around to the back of the apartment complex. If she could just get on top of the building's storage sheds that were under their kitchen window, she could probably hear what was going on in the apartment. She hoisted herself up onto the first storage shed and eyeballed the second. It was much older than the first and rusted through in places on some of the seams. She desperately hoped that it would hold her weight. She could hear the aluminum creaking and scraping together as she swung herself up onto the roof, but it held. She breathed a sigh of relief and gingerly crawled to the far side of the roof where she pressed herself up to the window and waited. She didn't have to wait long.

"You're fuckin' lucky I didn't kill you last night," came Hector's voice through the mostly open window. "I think my boss would've been happy if I had."

Marion could hear Paul mumble something in response, but she couldn't make it out.

"I'm here to enforce what my boss ordered last night. You fucked up, Rodriguez. You fucked up big time and now you have to bear the cost. There's nothing you can say or do. The decision has already been made. Now listen up and get it. You have exactly five hours to clean yourself up, pack up what little crappy shit you and Marion have and go back to Mexico. I will dispose of your car and your house. Surprised I know about those? Well, you dumb fuck. Everybody knows about those. That's another reason you're gone. You're a stupid fuck and you got sloppy. You must have decided that the rules of the business somehow didn't apply to you. But guess what, super genius, they did. And the fact that you put your stuff in your wife's name just makes you more pathetic and stupid. Anyway, that's all over now. Just like you're all over now. You ungrateful son of a bitch. At midnight I'm going to meet you and Marion at the bus station. I'm going to give you two tickets to Tijuana and you're going to give me your passports. God knows the Mexican government doesn't give a shit about who tries to get into their country, just who tries to get out. That'll insure that you don't try and sneak your nasty selves back into this country. You'll be a fugitive. You'll have jumped bail so there's no chance that the government of these fine United States is going to let you back in. No. Just remember what a lovely time you had here and how you fucked it up. I'll see you at midnight. Downtown bus station. Adios."

Marion could hear the door close behind Hector as he left. She scooted down from the roofs of the sheds and ran back to the apartment. Paul seemed to be in shock. He was just sitting motionless on the couch with a far off gaze in his eyes.

"Paulie, Paulie, are you OK?" Marion asked as she sat down next to him and took his hand.

He looked at her with a blank stare. "What?"

"I said, are you alright? I saw a man was here. It was Hector, wasn't it? What did he want?"

"Ah, . . . ah, nothing. He just wanted to see how I was doing."

"Bullshit, Paulie," Marion said angrily. "I was here. I heard everything. I just gave you a chance to tell the truth and be honest with me and you blew it. Fact is, we're history. He wants us back in Mexico with all our stuff gone. Bullshit. Who is he to tell us to do anything?" Marion was infuriated and frustrated. The thought of going back to Mexico was enough to send her over the edge, but coupled with losing her beautiful home and car, all in the blink of an eye, was just too much to even contemplate. "What're we going to do?"

Paul was still trying to digest this change in plans and force his brain to remember exactly what had happened last night. He thought he was supposed to plead guilty and go to jail, but now somehow it was all about Mexico. But it didn't matter. They still had no choice. "We're going to do exactly what Hector says.

We're going to go home, collect our things, and meet him at the bus station at midnight. We're going to return to Mexico and we're going to live there the rest of our lives," Paul Rodriguez said woodenly. "It's either that or get hurt bad or killed."

Marion had never seen her husband defeated before and it pained her to see it now. He had given up; he was done. But she was not. She was a fighter and a survivor and she couldn't stand the thought of going back to a country that held no future for either of them.

"No, Paulie. No. We can't go back. I don't care so much about the house and car, but I can't go back to Mexico. I can't. We've got to do something. We've got to fight this."

"I don't see how, Mari," Paul said still blankly staring at the wall. "You don't know these men. They almost killed me last night. Why wouldn't they just kill us and dump our bodies in the ocean? We don't know that many people here and most of our friends move around all the time. No one would miss us for a long time and by then it would be too late. No, it's better to be alive in Mexico than dead here."

"You must have something to use against them, Paulie. You must know things they don't want you telling."

"Actually telling and showing, but that's just another reason to kill us. Letting us go to Mexico is actually a gift."

"Some gift," Marion said spitefully. "I can't believe you got us into this mess. I trusted you and you screwed it up. Now my baby . . ." Marion gasped. She couldn't believe that it had just come out of her mouth.

"What did you say?" Paul said suddenly coming alive. "What did you say?"

"I said 'baby,' Paulie. I said 'baby.' We're going to have a baby and now it's going to be born in Mexico."

"Holy shit! Gracias Dio!" Paulie exclaimed jumping up from the couch. "Baby? My baby? We're having a baby! When did you find out? I mean, why didn't you tell me? We're having a baby!"

Paulie was so excited he was flying around the room, bruises and all. Marion had never seen him so happy. She felt a little guilty for lying about the baby, but it was the only thing she could come up with right on the spot to bring out the fighter in him. And she needed that fighter now. There was no way she was going back to Mexico.

"I just found out yesterday," Mari said smiling as broadly as she could. "I was waiting for the perfect time to tell you, but then it just slipped out when I got upset."

"Any time is perfect when we're having a baby!" Paul exclaimed grabbing Mari and dancing her around. "We've got so many plans to make, so much to do." He stopped dead in the center of the living room and dropped his arms heavily to his sides. "Oh, shit, Mari. Hector. What am I going to do about Hector?"

Marion knew she had to be very careful. Everything rested on how she handled the next few minutes. She gently led Paul back to the couch and sat down next to him, holding his hand and stroking his hair in her most loving way.

"Paulie," she began looking into his eyes. "You know I would rather stay in America and I know you would too, but none of that matters now. What really matters is what's best for our baby. Where should we raise our baby? Where is our baby going to get the best future? Where is our baby going to be the happiest and have the best life?" She gazed even deeper into his eyes. "We have a responsibility now, not just to ourselves, but to a whole other human being we're bringing into this world. We have to think about that, and that alone." There, she had done it. The best she could do. She sat quietly and waited.

"Mari," Paul said after a few moments of silence. "God has given us this enormous blessing of a baby. There is nothing greater. We must protect our baby and give our baby the best life that we can. It is clear to me that life must be here, in America."

Marion felt as though her own life had been given back to her. Tears filled her eyes and spilled down in cascades of joy that ran down her face and mingled with Paul's own. They held each other and cried, she for herself and he for them.

"OK, OK," Mari interrupted after just a few minutes. "We've got to get going. We don't have much time. What are we going to do?"

"Well, the hard truth is that we're going to lose our house and car. Plain and simple. We should just try and figure out a way to stay in this country and not have to be looking over our shoulders every day. If we have to do that, it wouldn't be any better than Mexico."

"I agree," Marion said, and actually she did too. She didn't want to be scared the rest of her life. No, it was either stay in America undetected or go to Mexico forever. "We can either get on the bus or not get on the bus. If we don't get on the bus, we don't have much lead time—a couple hours at best. If we do get on the bus, but then get off the bus before it gets to Tijuana, we have a better chance. It would take Hector at least some time to find out we didn't go all the way to Mexico."

"Right. That's what we need to do. We'll act like we're fine with the whole thing and then just get off early – probably San Clemente. The bus stop is right across from the train station so it would be easy for us to get back up to LA. We do want to go back to LA, don't we?"

"I do, but I think it might be too dangerous. Even if we move to the Valley, there's a chance we might get spotted and caught."

"That's true. We need to figure something out. But, you know, even if we went to another city, hell, even if we went out of state, Hector would be looking for us. Once he finds out we didn't arrive in Tijuana, he'll go nuts trying to find us. He's like a bulldog. Once he latches on, he doesn't let up. Plus the big boss would be so pissed, he'd make doubly sure Hector turned over every rock looking for us."

Marion knew Paul was right. How could they stay in America and be free of Hector, too? "Jeez, Paulie, there has to be some way to do this. There has to be. God wouldn't have given us such a gift without giving us the way to care for our gift. He just wouldn't." She wondered if she was going to hell for blaspheming God this way. Probably. But at least she'd be in America until then.

"We'll just have to make it up as we go. Let's go get our stuff and get me fixed up as much as possible. That fucker Hector really jammed me up good."

"He'll pay for what he did to you, Paulie, I swear he will." Marion said under her breath.

Had they known that Hector was the reason Paul still had all his fingers and probably his life, they undoubtedly would have been a bit more gracious. As it was, they fiercely blamed Hector for everything that had happened to Paul and, consequently, remained altogether ignorant of the true culprit, Maurice.

Maurice had taken Hector aside during the incident last night and told him that what Paul had done was very serious and that Paul had to be taught a lasting and meaningful lesson.

"What exactly does that mean?" Hector had asked.

Maurice was instantly irritated. "What do you think it means, you idiot. Do I have to spell everything out for you? I want something permanent. I want Rodriguez to think of me and what he did to me every day. I want him to remember me as long as he lives."

Hector continued to look at him blankly.

"I want a body part, you dumb fuck. No . . . wait . . . better still, I want a finger. A toe is too easy. I want you to separate Rodriguez from one of his fingers. The method is up to you."

Hector didn't say a word. It was clear Maurice was serious and it was clear Maurice was out of his mind, consumed by some kind of blood lust that was turning him into an animal. He hastily weighed his options. If he said no, Maurice would turn on him. There was no question about it in his present state. He could try and talk him out of it, but a glance at Maurice showed him that Maurice was too far gone. Maurice was smiling at the thought of the mutilation, almost panting with excitement. No, he had to go with it. He still had that old girlfriend in receiving over at the medical school. Maybe she could help out.

"Sure, Maurice, whatever you say. You better hightail it out of here though. You can't risk getting connected with all this."

"I suppose you're right," Maurice said as his face slumped with disappointment. "It's too risky for me. I want to see it though, got it? Leave it here. I'll see it at the meeting in the morning. And don't clean up, I want our little pussy Simon to get a taste of the real world." Maurice started to put on his coat and collect his briefcase. "When you're done with Rodriguez, patch him up as best you can, but if it looks too bad, take him over to that crappy little clinic on Crenshaw. If you have cash in your pocket, they won't ask any questions. I don't want that fucker dying on me until I'm ready. Dump him off at his apartment and put a tail on him for the day. By then I should have his bail revoked. Go over later and haul his ass back to jail. I'll have a specially selected jail cell waiting for him complete with very special friends. Clear?"

"Clear." Hector didn't like the sound of the "specially selected jail cell and special friends." Who knew what was in that twisted fucked up mind of his. At least he got rid of Maurice with that bullshit about getting caught. He knew he would always win playing the card of Maurice's self-interest. Now all he had to do was keep his guys in the other room, do some bandage work, and call on his old girlfriend. He could do it. He could survive.

His fraudulent finger had passed the test at the morning meeting. It went better than he could have hoped. Too bad he wasn't there when Simon found the finger. That must have been hysterical. And Simon getting hammered by Maurice was unfortunate, but he couldn't control everything in this little psychodrama. Hector would have had an OK day except for having to deal with Maurice's fucked up request and this unsettled feeling that kept gnawing at his subconscious. Something wasn't right; he felt it. And if his twenty-plus years in surveillance and investigation had taught him anything, they had taught him to pay attention to his intuition. He didn't like that Maurice was causing Rodriguez's bail to be revoked. He didn't like the specially selected jail cell. It all just stunk. Maurice was planning something else for Rodriguez and it was something bad. He just knew it. He also knew he had to do something about it. And with that decision, Hector entered the path of no return. He didn't expect to cross Maurice and get away with it. He didn't know what he was going to do, but he figured a good first step would be to go over to Rodriguez's apartment. The Mexico idea just popped into his head on the way over. He thought it had played pretty well. He knew Rodriguez would be suspicious of him trying to help, especially if it was against Maurice, so he had to come up with something that would protect Rodriguez from Maurice even if it was extreme. Hector felt the threat was that real. If he was wrong, Paul would be fucked with the police over jumping bail but not irretrievably and he would still be able to return the house and car to him. Not a great scenario and not great options, but better than being dead. His conscience was clear. He had done the best he could do. He drove to his favorite Buster Burger and let his mind go blissfully numb as he inhaled the perfect combination of chocolate shake, double-double, and fries.

CHAPTER EIGHTEEN

By six in the evening, Sam was just about done wrapping up his work before heading off to meet Sarah for dinner. Since his nap, he had finished a discovery request and some research on *Blue Grass Pictures*, and even started work on *Rivas,* Maurice's personal injury case. With Simon out, he figured he better allow plenty of time to prepare for the upcoming status conference.

Rivas looked pretty run-of-the-mill. Rainy day, lots of traffic, going north on Sepulveda, truck hits Rivas going only about ten mph. Rivas gets whiplash, back issues—really minor stuff. Damages were only a couple grand on the car, but fifteen thousand for medical. Looked fine except the physical therapy bills seemed high based on the injuries. If he was expected to settle this case, he'd have to do something about these numbers, since no skilled defense lawyer would recommend paying these amounts. He studied the bills carefully, checking for duplicate bills or charges. Finding none, he analyzed the treatments—hot pack, cold pack, ultrasound, massage—nothing out of the ordinary. Great, Sam thought. My first P.I. case, supposedly an easy one at that, and I already have a problem with it. Sam continued to parse through the file, looking for any notes from the investigator that would explain the high physical therapy bills. Nothing. If there was a reason the bills were so high, that would at least give him something to argue at the status conference. As it was right now, he didn't know squat. No notes from the investigator, no Simon to ask for advice. Shit, and it was almost half past six. Sam decided to give Rivas a quick call. If it was a choice between running afoul of some pedantic firm policy and bad lawyering, he was going to pick the former, every time.

He easily found the phone number on the physical therapy bills and dialed.

"Hello? Is this Angel Rivas? This is Sam Morrow calling from Cabot, Strickland & Baines. I'm working on your case with Simon Streit. Do you have a moment to talk?"

Angel paused. He didn't know what to do. He wasn't supposed to get phone calls from anyone, but maybe they'd changed the policy and hadn't told him yet. He was just supposed to fill out the paperwork, being especially careful to connect the right social security number with the right policy. Did he say Simon? Simon was his guy. He always worked with Simon. If he said he was with Simon, he must be OK. He didn't want to get in trouble for not talking to this guy and risk losing the best job he'd ever had. "Yes," he said. "I can talk."

"Great. Sorry to have to bother you, but I just have a few quick questions about your case. I'm wondering if you can tell me more about your physical therapy. I mean, why you had to go so many times. Was it whiplash and back pain or was it something more?"

Angel felt immediately defensive. "What do you mean? I did it exactly by the book. I put down as many sessions as I was supposed to. No more, no less. Ask Simon. My paperwork is always 100 percent." Angel was getting angry now and upset.

"I'm sorry if I upset you. I didn't mean to. I was just trying to find out if you had more severe injuries than my report reflects. If there is a reason your physical therapy bills are so, well, high." Sam was confused by what Angel was saying, but was most concerned that Angel was getting annoyed. If Angel got irritated enough he might call Simon or, god forbid, Maurice, and complain about him. That would put him in deep shit—not only for calling the client, but for pissing off the client as well. With Maurice's temper, an offense like that would definitely put him in the doghouse and could even hurt his partnership chances. "I'm sorry," Sam said again. "I'm just trying to understand your bills."

Angel was livid. "Are you telling me I don't know what I'm doing? I do everything right. Everything. All the time." Angel had raised his voice a few decibels and was now shouting. "Who are you to tell me I don't know what I'm doing? Huh? Who are you? Who told you to call me? Was it Simon? Did Simon tell you to call me?" Angel was flushed with anger and was walking around the room with the phone at arms' length, yelling at it like it was some kind of pariah.

Sam couldn't understand why Angel had become so enraged so fast. All he had done was ask a simple question. None of the phone conversation made any sense at all.

"Was it Simon who told you to call?" Angel was at it again. "Was it? I'm going to call him and give it to him. Who does he think he is, criticizing me? *Me* of all people? And having someone else do it for him."

At that, Sam jumped into action. "I don't think there's any reason to call Simon, Mr. Rivas. I'm sorry I upset you. It won't happen again. I . . . "

"Better not," Angel said gruffly and slammed the phone down so hard the plastic cracked. Sam stood there in shock. He felt like he had been blindsided by a Mack truck. He had absolutely no idea what had just gone on. He had no idea why Angel had become so hostile so fast and no idea what he had done to cause such a response. It just goes to show how a perfectly good day can turn to shit in a heartbeat, he thought. He was worried. It might actually be worse for him now that Simon was out of the office. If Angel tried to call Simon and couldn't reach him, he might ask to speak to Maurice. Not a happy thought, but all he could do was hope that Angel would calm down before making any phone calls and then just let the whole thing go. Sam glumly packed up his briefcase and draped his suit coat over his arm. He definitely didn't feel like a huge slab of beef now, but he still wanted to see Sarah. He knew he'd feel better just being with her.

CHAPTER NINETEEN

"You're much improved now that you've had a little refreshment." Sarah said as she raised her glass in a mock toast. "To martinis, lawyers' BFF!"

Sam raised his glass in salute. "I am a strong believer in the medicinal powers of liquor, especially as a balm to sooth the inevitable wounds of law firm life."

"Here, here," Sarah laughed as she took a sip of her Cosmo. "So tell me, you think Maurice would really get that bent about a phone call to your own client?"

"Yeah, I know it sounds weird, but they have this whole system for doing these cases, as they say, efficiently. Simon was excruciatingly clear about what the system does and does not entail. What it does not entail are calls to clients."

"God, I hope your Simon isn't as beastly as the Simon I just got on that case I was telling you about. My Simon is a real piece of work. He just hit me with a couple pounds of discovery served *with* his answer."

"What an asshole."

"Thank you. He is an asshole."

"Well, my Simon is actually a good friend of mine. We were going to double date sometime this week, but he got in a little fender bender and is out for a few days. Just as well though, so I can have more of you to myself."

She decided to let that comment pass, acknowledged only by a slight blush in her cheeks. She didn't want to admit, at least out loud, that she felt the same way. They had only been dating a few weeks and the feelings she was experiencing were a little scary. She decided to change the subject.

"Let's order," she said. "A good piece of red meat will boot Maurice right out of your mind."

"That and another martini."

◆ ◆ ◆

For Hector, it was back to tequila and beer. He had a little less than an hour to go before his rendezvous at the fountain. He figured he'd use a few of those minutes reviewing the surveillance pictures from Francisco that he hadn't had a chance to look at yet. He wasn't concerned. Francisco had said that everything was pretty basic, just a few days in the ordinary life of Ms. Sarah Brockman. Hector thumbed through a few weighty stacks of photos and was just about to call it a day when he ran across some lunch pictures from the Hong Kong Koi Gardens. On first pass, it just looked like Sarah having a luncheon date with a nice young man. As he looked closer though, that nice young man turned into Sam Morrow. Hector put the pictures down slowly and took a long swallow of beer. Interesting turn of events, he thought, although no more interesting than the rest of this crazy day. The question was, of course, what was the connection between Sarah and Sam. It had to be friends or something more intimate, since Sam had just started working on the P.I. side of CS & B a few days ago; there was absolutely nothing he could know. And any possible connection with Simon was just too remote. The best explanation had to be the simplest: pure coincidence.

He regrouped the photos with different colored rubber bands and decided to call Maurice anyway. He didn't see anything to it, but there might be something he was missing.

"Hi, sir. Hector calling. I just wanted to tell you about some photos Francisco took the other day. It was Sarah Brockman and Sam Morrow at lunch. What? I don't know, it could be just a coincidence. I'll keep you posted."

Hector downed the last of his beer and got ready for his appointment at the fountain. He always wore a bit of a disguise. He thought of it more as a costume though because it didn't really make him unrecognizable; he just felt like a different person wearing it. And he needed to feel like a different person to do what he needed to do. He carefully combed his hair to the side and donned a three-piece business suit. This time he also took his full camera case and a few additional lenses. He was ready. He drove to the gardens, parked, and walked in. Once again he thought what an idiot he had been to choose the fountain as the rendezvous spot for these exchanges. It was such a beautiful fountain, but now it was forever sullied by what he had done in its shadow. Tonight, at least, he could take heart in knowing that this was the last time its beauty would be tarnished. He was just a few minutes early and he passed the time kicking a small pear-shaped rock around the pavilion. Right at quarter to nine, a man and what appeared to be his son came around the far side of the fountain and approached Hector. The man and Hector nodded to each other in greeting.

"Getting pretty warm for beginning of spring, isn't it?"

"Yeah," Hector said. "Pretty warm." Hector reached into his breast pocket and pulled out a rather plump, letter-sized envelope, which he handed to the man.

"I'll be back here at eleven."

"Eleven sharp," Hector said. The drive to the Beverly Hills Panorama Hotel was under five minutes, so Hector didn't have time to revisit the issues that had tormented him all day. He just kept telling himself that it was the last time, as if that somehow absolved him of what he was doing at the moment. He waited in the car until exactly five minutes to nine and then proceeded to Bungalow no. 8. After a curt tap, the door swung open to reveal Maurice in his dressing gown with a wide smile on his face.

"Appreciate your promptness as usual," Maurice said. "A midnight curfew makes every minute special."

"Yeah," Hector said. He turned to go. He couldn't stand another word from Maurice or another moment in his presence. He walked down the path as quickly as he could without running, but for the first time, the bungalow pulled him back. Maybe it was because it was his last time or maybe it was something deep and guilty within him, but he turned and looked back. He caught the last glimpse of light from the bungalow before the door closed. He could see the two of them starkly in the light, one, a hulking brute of a man and one, barely a shadow. And in that instant, he saw a kind of fear in the eyes of that young boy that would haunt him forever.

He hurried through the grounds and lobby, and finally made it back to his car where he retrieved his camera bag and lenses and put on his fake press tags. Hollywood press people were a common occurrence at the Beverly Hills Panorama Hotel, so carrying camera equipment with the tags wouldn't raise any security flags. This time he walked through the far right door in the lobby and continued to the surveillance spot he had reconnoitered weeks before. It was in a secluded area of the gardens and had a little grassy rise in the landscaping that allowed him to shoot down into the entire bungalow with little difficulty. Thankfully, he had remembered his bottle. He took a couple of Tequila shots for strength and settled in. He didn't have to wait long. Within thirty minutes he had enough shots to sicken even the most jaded street cop. Hector had to look away on a few occasions even with his alcohol booster. And then it was over. He packed up his gear, stowed it in the car, and headed to the lobby to have a quick drink while he waited for the appointed time. At exactly quarter to eleven, he walked back to the bungalow, picked up his charge, and deposited him with the man at the fountain. He had managed to say not one word or even look directly at the boy the whole time. That somehow made the whole event less real. When coupled with the alcohol, Hector could almost believe it hadn't happened at all.

He finished the last of his ritual at home, taking off his costume deliberately, one piece at a time, methodically laying each piece on the bed. When he was finished, he neatly folded the clothes, placed the sunglasses on top of the stack and took the stack down into the basement where he put it in a giant steel drum and burned it. He waited until there was nothing left, and then slowly mounted the stairs, abundantly grateful for the illusion of peace that washed over him.

He had one last matter to attend to before he could call this long day over. He dressed in his usual attire of jeans, boots and casual button-down, made a sandwich to go and drove to the bus station. Paul and Marion were already there waiting for him.

"I'm glad to see you made it," Hector called out as he approached.

"We don't want any trouble," Paul said as Marion nodded. "We just want to live our lives and not worry all the time. If that means Mexico, Mexico it is. We come from there. We have family there. We can go back."

"I'm glad to hear it," Hector said with a touch of a smile, but inside, he was genuinely happy that Paul was being reasonable. He was tired and spent. It had been a long day. He was pleased that he was, at least, able to save someone from Maurice tonight. "OK, good. I'm going to get your tickets to Tijuana. When I come back, have your passports and keys to your house and car ready."

Paul winced at that and pursed his lips into a tight line. What an arrogant fucker, Paul thought. He'll get his. As soon as we get back and get situated, I'll come looking for him and I'll show him the real Paul Rodriguez, the one he should have thought twice about fucking with. Marion, by contrast, was surprisingly calm. Although she was upset at the prospect of losing her house and car, they meant nothing to her when stacked up against losing America. No, she would make the best of it. If she got a house and car once, she could do it again. If she needed to get pregnant to make it all work out, that would be fine too.

The exchange went without a hitch and Hector watched as the bus pulled out of the station. He resisted the urge to wave, knowing that that would be wildly inappropriate, but the relief he was feeling needed some kind of expression. He turned his attention to the other three people watching the bus pull out. Two people were waiving and smiling and the third was running at a dead heat back to his car. Strange, Hector thought. Must have dumped someone he was very happy to get rid of. Just like him, Hector thought, although he knew Maurice would feel otherwise. He considered what he was going to tell Maurice regarding the disappearance of the Rodriguezes. He realized that he had the perfect excuse. The Rodriguezes necessarily flew the coop when he was performing his service for Maurice. Since Maurice had identified Sarah as the more important surveillance subject, Francisco had been tailing her, so he wouldn't get in any trouble either. Perfect. Absolutely perfect. He smiled a big happy smile. He loved it when a plan came together.

CHAPTER TWENTY

Meanwhile, Sarah and Sam had enjoyed a perfectly fabulous dinner of filet mignon and sea bass followed by warm chocolate bread pudding and coffee. By eleven, they were at Sarah's apartment nursing nightcaps.

"You think I'm this super do-gooder who just wants to help people," Sarah said taking a sip of Grand Marnier. "I wish I was that person, but I'm not. I want to make some money too. I want to be able to stop worrying about bills all the time. And," she said with a mischievous smile. "I want a pair of bright red, four-inch-heeled Manolo Blahniks."

"Well, that I can accommodate," Sam said laughing. "And no, I don't think you're a saint or anything, but I do think that you care about people and help a lot of people who would otherwise be on their own. Just look at that new car accident case, the one with the Cook Islands connection. Prime example. Those people would be bereft without you."

"Bereft? I don't think so. If I hadn't taken the case, I'm sure they would have found representation somewhere."

"Maybe, maybe not. In any event, they wouldn't have received as good representation as they're getting with you."

"Oh, Sam, you do flatter me so," Sarah said affectionately. "You're so sweet. You make me feel so much better about my little firm. Like maybe I didn't make a mistake after all."

"Do you really think that?" Sam said incredulously. "I mean, do you ever think you should have stayed at Tate?"

"Only when money is really scarce. Then I think I should have been a plumber."

"Well, that goes without saying for every lawyer," Sam laughed.

"What about you, Sam? Ever think about doing anything different, or are you focused on your big firm partnership?"

"Up until recently, it was all about C S & B. Working the long hours, living the big firm life. But in the last few months, I've been feeling kinda burned out. I mean, I can still get to the office and still put in the hours, but I feel like I'm losing my 'will to bill.' It's scary really. I'm wondering if one day I'm just going to walk away from it all and end up in Cabo, in a shack, living on beer and fish tacos." Sam manufactured a small, weak smile that made Sarah's heart ache. She moved closer to him on the couch and took his hand.

"I know that feeling. It happened to me too. That's why I left Tate. But I do know that my answer isn't the right answer for everybody. And I think that if I had done nothing and just toughed it out, that feeling would have eventually dissipated on its own. The truth is I just wanted to have my own firm. I like to think I was more running *to* than running *from*."

"You're so cool." Sam said.

Sarah looked up in surprise at such a spontaneously nice comment. It was if the words had just popped out of his mouth. He was smiling comfortably now, looking at her with a mixture of admiration and appreciation. She liked how his look made her feel.

She stood up to refresh his glass and he caught her hand and held it. His eyes paused briefly on their entwined hands and then slowly traveled up her body resting at last in her eyes.

And then his lips were on hers. Hot, hungry lips. Greedy lips. Pressing hard onto hers, taking her breath away. They had kissed before but it wasn't anything like this. The glass she was holding slipped through her fingers and fell noiselessly to the carpet where they soon joined it.

And after the tidal wave had passed, Sam held her close and stroked her hair, wishing they could stay that way, holding each other forever.

Eventually, Sarah whispered, "I wonder what our law school classmates would say if they saw this?"

"I think they would say, 'Took you two long enough,'" Sam laughed. "We were probably the only ones who didn't know we liked each other."

"Really? You think it was that obvious back then?"

"Based on what just happened, I expect our pheromones were giving us away to anyone within a ten block radius."

"Interesting use of the facts, Mr. Morrow. You win. Whatever prize you want, you got it."

"Better watch it, you'll spoil me."

"No more than you've been spoiling me."

"I would give you the world if I could," Sam said so tenderly that a tear welled up in her eye and slid down her face where it was gently caught with a kiss. Suddenly, Sarah's body stiffened and she pulled back in alarm.

"What was that?" she asked. "Did you hear anything?"

"What do you mean?" Sam asked standing up and putting on his pants. "Did you hear something outside?"

"I'm not sure, but I think it sounded like footsteps coming up the stairs."

Just then, the doorbell rang and someone started knocking furiously. Sarah jumped to her feet and Sam started looking around for any kind of makeshift weapon.

"Sarah, it's Duane. Are you there? Hello?"

"Oh my God," Sarah said exhaling in relief. "What in the world are you doing here so late?" she exclaimed as she unhooked the safety chain.

"Well, I tried to call, but your cell phone must be either broken or turned off, if you know what I mean."

"Oh, speaking of which, I'm Sam Morrow," Sam said as he put out his hand.

"I'm so sorry," Sarah said as she made the introductions. "I'm a little scattered."

"Understandably so," Duane said with a nod to Sam.

"So what's going on? What is it that can't wait until morning?"

"It's Paul Rodriguez. He's gone. I was keeping a stiff tail on him today after we found out he was out of jail, and he and Marion hopped a bus going to Tijuana at midnight."

"Oh shit, you've got to be kidding. This is bad."

"I know. I alerted the police and they said they'll try to get someone on it, but made no promises. Thank the governor for the cutbacks. But in any event, I called a bail bonds service in San Diego and they'll pull 'em off the bus there before they cross over into Mexico. We should be fine."

"Can they do that? I mean, has Rodriguez violated anything before he leaves the country?"

"Yeah, he isn't allowed to leave Los Angeles County. So, technically, we could get him as soon as he gets into Orange County."

"Why don't we do that?"

"Well, if we grab him in San Diego, right before the border, it will be clear to the judge that he was trying to flee the country. That will make it worse for him at the hearing. He'll definitely get his bail revoked and who knows what else."

"I agree," Sarah nodded. "What an idiot. What was he thinking?"

"Probably just got scared and let his fear do the talking."

"Right. Well, he's going to wish he'd been a little less spontaneous. Please let me know the minute your guy picks them up, no matter how late it is. And yes," Sarah said with a smile, "I'll make sure my phone is on."

"Appreciate it. Sorry to intrude. Good night."

"Good night," Sarah and Sam said in unison as the door closed behind Duane.

"Wow, what a weird turn of events. I guess you know which case that is."

"Sounds a bit familiar," Sam said. "But I'll promise to forget everything I just heard if you come over here and give me one of your extra special sugar kisses."

"Ooh, you're a ruthless negotiator. But if I must, I must." And she gave him a thoroughly luscious kiss, plus a few more.

◆ ◆ ◆

Sarah woke with a start about three in the morning. She had reluctantly said good night to Sam at around one and poured herself into bed within a few minutes after that. She lay in bed willing herself to go back to sleep until she remembered Paul Rodriguez's wild ride. She must have set her internal clock for Duane's call. The bus should be arriving in San Diego any time now. She lay in bed a few minutes, calming herself down. No use being sleepless the rest of the night for just a phone call. Eventually, she got up and made herself some Ovaltine. Not the trendiest drink around, but it really did a good job on frayed nerves. Finally, her cell phone rang.

"Thanks for calling, Duane. I don't think anyone's getting much sleep tonight."

"The Rodriguezes weren't on the bus," Duane said flatly.

"What do you mean they weren't on the bus?" Sarah said nervously. "How could they not be on the bus?"

"I don't know. All I know is that they weren't on the bus when it pulled into San Diego."

Sarah was being very careful choosing her words. She was sure Duane felt terrible even though she would have agreed to the course of conduct as well. He was the type that took his work very personally and she didn't want to risk offending him. "Any chance the bail bondsman made a mistake?" She knew that was a borderline question, but she had to ask.

"No," Duane said curtly. "They're professionals. They knew

who they were looking for. The Rodriguezes must have gotten off at another stop."

"I guess so, but that doesn't make any sense at all."

Silence.

"Sarah?" Duane's voice was so quiet Sarah had to strain to hear it.

"Yes?"

"I'm really sorry this happened. It's my fault. I just want you to know that I'm very sorry. I also want you to know that I'll find them." Duane's voice started getting stronger and more sure. "I don't know how long it will take, but I'll find them. I promise." He finished on a flourish sounding like the usual, self-confident P.I. Sarah knew so well.

"I know you will, Duane, but don't think anything about what happened. This was the right thing to do. Plus, if you hadn't been tailing Rodriguez like you were, we never would have known he ran anyway."

"Thank you for saying that. Now I got to get to work. I'll call you when I know anything."

Sarah flipped the phone closed. "Shit," she said to her half empty cup of Ovaltine. There was nothing she could do; whatever was going to happen was going to happen without the involvement of Miss Sarah Brockman. She crawled back in bed and fell into the deepest sleep she'd had for many months. Ovaltine and exhaustion, a perfect combination.

CHAPTER TWENTY-ONE

Sam wasn't as lucky and had been plagued by vague, flitting worries for the few fitful hours that he slept. When he awoke, he realized that he was concerned about the Simon situation, but also worried about Sarah. There was something about that car case she was working on that was starting to bother him. Maybe it was just the fact that her private investigator had showed up unannounced in the middle of the night and left them both feeling a bit unsettled. In any event, there was nothing he could do about any of it now. He decided to get himself into the office as quickly as he could so he could get out of work earlier and see Sarah. He called her even before returning Alexander's call and confirming their lunch.

"Guess who?"

"Guess who?" Sarah asked with mock incredulity. "You've been wanting to call me since you woke up this morning and all you can come up with is 'guess who?' Pretty pathetic, Sam. Pretty pathetic."

"You're being a little harsh, don't you think? I mean, after all, I'm triangulating on just a few hours sleep."

"OK, you whiner. I'll take pity on you just this once and throw you a bone. Just make sure it doesn't happen again."

"Yes, your Royal Lusciousness. Anything you say. Anyway, the reason I was calling, before I was so roundly excoriated, was to see how your day was going and to make sure you missed me. Do you miss me?" He said playfully. "Do you?"

"I do, I do, Sam. I miss everything about you. I miss those things about you that nobody else even likes. I miss . . ." she caught herself and felt her face grow warm under an involuntary blush. "What I meant was, I miss the cheese and veggie omelet you should have made for me this morning."

"Hey, wait a minute. You're the one who kicked me out last night and now you're sorry. If you're lucky, maybe I'll make it for you another time. My culinary skills will shock and amaze you."

"OK, if you say so. I'll definitely keep that in mind," Sarah said laughingly as she started flipping through the faxes that had arrived overnight and this morning. "Oh great," she said sarcastically as she came across a one-page letter. "I just got a humiliating offer in that case we were talking about last night."

"Really? How much are they offering?"

"Two grand. Can you believe it?" Sarah said indignantly. "Two grand for almost killing a poor sweet guy walking across the street. Can you even believe it?" Sarah was getting more and more enraged as she thought about Murray, Alice, and Andy and what they had been through and what they were still going through. She dreaded even having to tell them about this offensive offer. "Who does Streit think he is?"

"Who? What did you just say?"

"I said a two grand offer from that asshole Streit."

"*Simon Streit*?"

"Yeah, Simon Streit from the Bicknel Law Firm. Do you know him?"

Sam was hyperventilating. He eeked out an "I'll call you back" and hung up the phone. His head was reeling. He felt like someone had slipped him a mickey or ecstasy or worse. Luckily he had closed his door before calling Sarah. He slumped in his chair and tried to still his lolling head. He felt like his understandable, predictable world was collapsing around him and he didn't know how to make it stop.

After what seemed like a long while, his head started to clear and he was able to sit up in his chair. He had so many questions, he didn't know where to start. And underlying it all was a vague sense of disappointment and sadness that one of his very best friends had somehow let him down. The fact that Simon had kept whatever he was doing a secret from Sam made Sam realize that he couldn't go to Simon to find out what was going on. And whatever was going on probably wasn't good. It just didn't make sense. The most likely explanation was that Simon was moonlighting for Bicknel to make some extra money. But why would he need extra money? He was paid handsomely at C S & B and he was on partnership track. He was taking a huge risk for not much upside as far as Sam could figure. Plus, he hadn't changed. He was the same old Simon. If he was under some kind of extreme financial pressure or was doing drugs or something, Sam thought he would have noticed it. No, nothing made any kind of sense. He resolved to find out what was going on. After all, Simon was one of his very best friends. They had started at the firm together, been in the same summer class.

There was a lot of history between them and all of it was good. He needed to put aside any ego-driven feelings and try and help Simon. That's what a good friend would do. He looked at his calendar—nothing on for tonight. Lorraine had told him that Simon was doing much better and hoped to return tomorrow. Sam decided he would stay very late, after everyone had gone home, and poke around in Simon's office. If he got caught, he could just say he was looking for something on one of the personal injury cases. Not James Bond, but it should be sufficient.

Sam was feeling better now that he had a plan. He made a conscious effort to put all of it out of his mind and get himself ready for his lunch with Alexander. He was delighted Alexander had called. He really loved the relationship he had with Alexander and he missed seeing him every day around the firm. He returned some phone calls, finished drafting the points and authorities for a brief due later in the week, and was just putting on his suit coat when Alexander poked his head around the door.

"Hi, Sam. I thought I'd pick you up here and we could walk over together."

"Great, Alexander. So nice of you to think of me for lunch. I've missed seeing you."

"Me too," Alexander said with his trademark smile. "I hope dim sum is OK with you. I hope it's OK that I unilaterally picked a spot, but I just really have a hankering for dim sum today."

Sam smiled at that. Alexander was the only person he knew who could carry off "hankering" with a straight face. He was lucky to even know what the word meant. They walked the few blocks to Shun Lee's, engaged in pleasantries and small talk, and it wasn't until they were seated that they moved to anything more stimulating.

"So," Alexander turned his chair so he could face Sam. "Tell me about your new girlfriend. She seemed very nice the other day, and smart too, I might add."

Sam felt an embarrassing blush start traveling up his neck. "Oh . . . well, we just started dating. And . . ." Oh, to hell with it, he thought. He didn't want to be cautious when it came to Sarah. "Well, I really like her. I feel like we've known each other forever. I mean we actually have known each other for a long time. We were in the same study group in law school, but we didn't know each other very well then. We just met again in Judge Schneider's courtroom of all places. Kismet, or at least a happy coincidence.

"That's wonderful, Sam. I'm thrilled for you, and Millie will be too. We were wondering when you might carve out a little free time for yourself and have some fun."

Sam could feel the telltale redness creeping even further up his neck. He felt a little awkward to have been the topic of discussion in the Cabot household. He decided to get over it. "Well, we're having a lot of fun," Sam said with a wide grin. "Maybe you better start worrying about my firm productivity instead."

"Now that would be something. With your work product and billables, you'd have to screw up pretty big for me to worry about you professionally."

Sam's blush continued to creep. "Thank you, Alexander. What a generous thing to say."

"And how are things at the firm? I mean, how are things going over there? I feel like I don't have my finger as closely on the pulse as I used to."

"Well, I can only speak from my experience, of course, and my experience is a bit of a mixed bag right now." Sam watched for a reaction from Alexander. He didn't really know how honest he could be considering their history and the obviously lopsided balance of power. Alexander seemed encouraging, though, and nodded for Sam to continue.

"If the truth be told, I was getting a little bored with some of the work I'd been doing and decided I was ready for a change. And just about when I'd decided that, Maurice called me in and told me I'd be working personal injury on some of his car cases. Frankly, I don't know how I feel about it yet. So far, I only have one 'easy' case that I don't think is too easy anyway."

"Oh, that's interesting."

"Well, it wasn't so much the case as the process. I'm sure you know how Maurice runs his P.I. cases, so I don't need to bore you with those details, but not being able to contact the client just made it difficult."

"Yes, that's very strange, isn't it?" Alexander said carefully. "It almost seems like Maurice is hiding something, doesn't it?"

"Well, that's what I thought originally, when Simon told me how things worked. I've never heard of such a system. And it wasn't that I was discouraged from talking to our own clients; I was *prohibited* from doing so. How can that be good for a case?"

"My thoughts exactly. It almost seems like there's something more to it all, otherwise it just doesn't make sense," Alexander said pointedly, looking directly at Sam. "And I know Maurice enjoys being the major domo of the kingdom. He's the only partner in that department and I know he likes it that way."

"Yes, I know what you mean," Sam said slowly. "He does like it that way, even when he's so busy he can't even see straight. He doesn't want any other partner to step in and help."

"You did call the client though, didn't you?" Alexander asked.

"What?" Sam asked startled at the turn in the conversation.

"I said, you called the client, didn't you?"

Sam didn't know if he was going to get reprimanded by Alexander or if Alexander was going to pass on the news to Maurice. In any event, he wasn't going to lie.

"Yes, I did. I needed some information that wasn't in the file. I didn't think I could run the case well without it, and Simon was unavailable, so I called the client." Sam sat back in his chair waiting to see Alexander's reaction.

"I would have put money on it," Alexander said with a smile. "You just couldn't do a mediocre lawyering job, could you?" He asked paternally.

"I'm glad you understand, although I'm not sure Maurice would. Plus, the whole conversation with this guy was weird. He got all upset when I asked him about his physical therapy bills. All I wanted was an explanation why they were so high, in case opposing counsel asked, but he got crazy and started spouting all kinds of stuff about how his paperwork was always 100 percent and that he did everything right. If it was someone else's case, I would be looking at it hard for insurance fraud, but I checked the intake form and Maurice brought it in himself. I would be hard pressed to tell Maurice that he didn't spot a fraud job."

"You're in a delicate position, Sam. I wish I could tell you what to do or step in and take care of it for you, but that's out of my sphere now. All I can say, Sam, is go with your gut. Sometimes a cigar is just a cigar. But most of the time, it's not."

And with that, Alexander and Sam helped themselves to the rolling dim sum cart and enjoyed a wonderful lunch. Sam had made the conscious choice not to discuss Simon with Alexander. He just didn't know enough to bring Alexander in and couldn't be 100 percent sure he wouldn't be inadvertently ratting out his friend. Besides, Alexander had wanted to know how things were going at the firm; he didn't need to know about some personal moonlighting by one of his associates. Anyway, Sam was almost completely convinced that Simon was just showing very bad judgment. It must be that Simon needed some extra money, Sam thought. God knows for what, but that was the only explanation Sam could come up with. Simon needed extra money and he thought he could make some and not get caught. And, in truth, he was right. He was the only one who had caught Simon and his only concern was that Simon was being foolhardy and ruining his future. Of course, the other looming issue was that Sarah was on the other side of moonlighting Simon. Something would have to be resolved on that front as well. He'd have to tell Sarah sooner rather than later, so everything stayed aboveboard. The last thing he wanted were secrets between them. He decided to tell her what he knew after his little reconnaissance later.

CHAPTER TWENTY-TWO

By seven that evening, Marion and Paul were relaxing by the pool in a mid-sized, mid-priced, mind-numbingly common apartment complex right in the heart of Burbank. Their plan had gone like clockwork. Off at San Clemente, a quick walk across the street, and they were on the Amtrak San Diegan on their way back to LA within fifteen minutes. They had located a cheap, but clean hotel room for the remainder of the night and started their apartment search right after breakfast the next morning. They had found this place by four and even managed to get a month-to-month lease, due to a planned renovation in six months. Perfect, Marion thought contentedly. Absolutely perfect. A glance at Paul told her that he was doing equally well. He was so happy—and proud, she should add—about the baby. It was that male validation thing, she thought. Fathering a child had made him a real man. The endearing male ego made her smile yet another big smile.

"I think we should lay low for a few months or so until this whole thing blows over," Paul said after a sip of his beer. "No reason to attract any attention or take any unnecessary risks."

"I agree. We should just go out and pick up some basic necessities. We'll be fine for quite a while."

"True, but we'll have additional expenses now with the baby." Paul could hardly say the word 'baby' without tearing up. Seeing that, and having listened to him for the past twenty-four hours, Marion decided to get pregnant right away and not claim a miscarriage as she had originally thought. Besides, she wanted children too. It had always been just a question of when. She felt another smile sweep across her face as she thought about how nice it would be to have a family. Everything was going to work out just fine, she thought. Much better than fine, it was going to be great.

◆ ◆ ◆

By this time, Sam had called Sarah back and told her he was unavailable for the evening. He ordered dinner and started working on various matters that needed his attention. Good opportunity to get some billables in while he waited, he thought. By eleven, only a few junior attorneys remained and by quarter to midnight, everyone was gone. The cleaning crew had been through at ten, so no one else was expected. He made one last pass of the floor to double-check all the offices and secretarial bays. He picked up a fresh pad of paper and walked briskly to Simon's office. He thought he looked like the consummate senior attorney stepping in to help Simon out while he was recovering.

Everything was in its usual state of disarray. Simon liked to call it 'organized chaos,' but Sam wasn't sure it was anything but a mess. Piles of papers occupied every available surface and part of the floor, and boxes brimming with documents lined the perimeter walls. He was always surprised not to find half-eaten sandwiches or maybe even some laundry, but he guessed Simon drew the line at things made out of paper. Sam felt a bit of a twinge as he sat down at Simon's computer. He felt like he was hurting his friend and helping him at the same time. Although he mostly convinced himself that what he was doing was right, at least a part of him knew that was bullshit. The truth was he was curious and wanted to know what was going on. He thought this was his best chance to do so.

He turned on the monitor and started typing the various passwords to get first into the firm and then into Simon's personal files. They had first swapped passwords a year or so ago when Sam had been flat on his back with the flu and needed some documents printed and delivered to a client. Sharing passwords had come in handy a few times over the year for each of them and they continued to keep each other abreast of any password updates. Not that Simon's was so tough anyway. Any hacker who knew even a little bit about Simon could probably figure it out within a few minutes. Sam typed in "cozumel" and started scanning Simon's files. Everything seemed to be in its place and was, surprisingly, quite neatly organized. The sheer volume of files and cases was stultifying, but as Sam methodically went through the database, he realized that he was familiar with a high percentage of these cases. Either he had heard about them in the weekly meetings, or Simon had mentioned them himself. In any event, Sam was pleased to find that everything seemed to be in order. Sam then started searching for certain cases by name. Again, he was relieved to find that everything looked perfectly ordinary. Maybe Simon's involvement wasn't as deep as he had feared. By this time, it was almost two in the morning and Sam was starting to lose his enthusiasm. He decided that one cup of coffee would get him through the rest of what he wanted to do without ruining his chances for a few hours of sleep later. He did a few brisk jumping jacks to wake himself up and jogged quickly to the pantry. But in his haste and preoccupation, he didn't take that quick moment to re-check the offices and bays on his way. If he had, he would have seen a man's shadow pass quickly behind one of the bays and duck down out of sight.

Sam made some hazelnut coffee and took the remnants of a few leftover veggie wraps back to Simon's office. He was surprised he hadn't run across *Matthews v. Rodriguez* yet and decided to do a concentrated search. He searched by plaintiff, defendant, and even by date, and couldn't find anything. Odd, he thought. The settlement letter had been generated by a computer. There had to be a file for it. He checked recent deletions, draft documents, and scanned the trash bin. Nothing. He had already found Simon's personal files and there was no settlement letter in there. The only explanation had to be some kind of hidden files somewhere. Sam closed down all the applications until he was back to Simon's password. Maybe Simon had another secret password. That would explain why this file didn't come up on his searches. A bit of a stretch, but it was all he had. He started plugging in passwords he thought would appeal to Simon. Simon had always liked travel passwords, especially adventure destinations, probably because he seemed to live such a non-adventurous life at the office, Sam thought. "Cozumel" was a case in point. Sam started with recent trips Simon had taken. "Telluride,""ElCapitan,""Bermuda." No luck. He started logging in any words he could think of that fit that profile. He had known Simon for a long time, and Simon had taken a lot of trips during that time, many of which they had taken together. Word after word he tried and suddenly, he knew what it was. He logged in "CaneelBay," a place Simon had mentioned on and off for years as *the* place he wanted to go for his honeymoon. Unfortunately, Simon hadn't yet met the girl of his dreams, so Caneel remained a hopeful entry on his wishlist. Suddenly, the screen unfolded to reveal a desktop full of files. There were probably a few hundred in all. They appeared to be litigation matters, except for the last two, labeled "financials" and "other." Sam pushed his chair back and allowed himself a brief moment of self-satisfaction before he scanned the screen for *Matthews.* His eyes jumped right to it. He took a deep breath and opened the file. Everything was there— answer, discovery, correspondence, attorney notes. It was an up-to-date and well-organized file. He just hoped it wasn't all well-organized under the Bicknel Law Firm. He opened the correspondence folder. There was the settlement letter he had seen on Simon's desk that had apparently been sent to Sarah. He opened the answer and discovery folders. The answer had already been filed and served, and Simon had propounded every kind of discovery imaginable. Every pleading read: "Simon Streit for the Bicknel Law Firm." He felt deflated, like a beach ball left behind after summer vacation.

He scanned the rest of the discovery file and then opened the attorney notes. There was only one entry dated just a few weeks ago. It read: "M called. Is really pissed. Wants me to get rid of this as quickly as possible." That was it. Maybe there were handwritten notes in the hard copy file, but that was all there was on the computer. And who was "M?" Sam looked at the clock. It was already four in the morning. He didn't have much time left. Some of the word processing crew came in at five, and even some of the juniors came in by six. Plus, he was starting to get a bit paranoid. He kept thinking he was hearing little scuffling sounds, but when he stopped and listened, there was nothing. He decided he would quickly open up some of the other files and see what they contained. Maybe they could shed some light on *Matthews.* There it was again, rustling, scuffling sounds. This time it was undeniable, Sam thought. There was someone out there. He pulled his hands back from the computer very slowly and focused his attention on the sounds. While the earlier sounds seemed to be coming from the outside bays, these sounds were coming from farther away, but seemed to be approaching. Then he heard it. Footsteps. On the wood floor, the sound was unmistakable. His eyes raced around the room, looking for any possible hiding place. The only option was the couch, but it had been pushed against the wall to accommodate Simon's stacks of document boxes, so there was no space behind it. The footsteps were getting louder and more distinct. He couldn't tell if they had turned the corner and started down this hall yet. If they had, there was no escape. He couldn't know, but he had no choice. He closed the computer, grabbed his pad of paper, and bolted for the door, turning the light off on his way. At the doorway, he glanced to the left. Nobody, yet. He cleared the first secretarial bay and ducked down behind it. Luckily, IT was doing a build-out to accommodate the latest network changes and there was a crack between the partitions just large enough for Sam to see through. As he crouched in the dark, looking through the crack, it occurred to him that his behavior was completely inexplicable. If whoever was out there discovered him, he was toast. Beads of sweat formed on his forehead and upper lip, and his breathing almost sounded like panting. Get a grip, he told himself. Whoever it is will find you because you're an idiot and can't control yourself. Sam used every mental power at his disposal and, finally, calmed himself down. By this time though, whoever it was should have passed down this hall. There was no other way. Sam strained to listen. Nothing. No footsteps, no sounds of any kind. He willed himself to listen as hard as he could. Still nothing. He remained crouched under the secretarial bay, listening and looking through the crack for a long time. Finally, he emerged and walked as rapidly as he prudently could back to his office, where he grabbed his coat and walked right out the door.

He didn't know what to think. Maybe he was so tired and discombobulated by what he had seen that he had imagined the whole thing. But even as he thought that, he knew it wasn't true. He knew the sound of footsteps and he had heard footsteps. He figured that whoever was coming had turned around and gone back more quietly than they had approached, since he hadn't heard any receding footsteps. Even thinking it, it sounded ridiculous. Ridiculous, that is, unless that person didn't want to get caught either. Sam mulled that around in his brain a bit as he drove home. He would catch a few hours sleep and return by ten. Maybe his subconscious would figure out who "M" was while he slept. But at least one thing was certain; he would be visiting Simon's computer later.

◆ ◆ ◆

Simon could hardly believe what had just happened. At least he had been able to get Sam out of his office before he got into the other files, but what he did get into was probably enough to point him in the right direction. His best option now was probably to flee. He could liquidate everything he could and take with him the barest essentials. Once safely in Argentina, he would contact the U.S. authorities, seek witness protection and immunity, and begin the grievous job of turning himself and everyone else in. With Maurice behind bars, Simon thought he at least had a fighting chance of staying alive. He had come to the firm to initiate the first part of his plan—namely, gathering evidence from his computer. He had moved carefully through the halls of the firm, alert for any late night workers. Seeing none, he had cautiously turned down the hall to his own office and was shocked to see a light on in there. He had ducked behind the secretarial bays and scooted—as best he could, in light of the pain he still was in—down to the end of the row, where he could see clearly into his office. He didn't know who he expected to see in there, but he definitely didn't expect to see Sam. There was no good reason for Sam to be in his office, on his computer. If Simon twisted his neck far to the right, he could just make out the computer screen. Sam was in his general password protected firm files. Nothing to be concerned about there. Sam had access to that information any time just as Simon had access to Sam's. Suddenly, Sam jumped up and started doing jumping jacks. Simon dived for better cover just as Sam jogged past him down the hall. The abrupt move had caused Simon a lot of pain, but he forced himself to focus on the situation at hand. Sam was probably just going to get some coffee, Simon thought, since he left the light and computer on. Simon had to figure out what to do. Whatever Sam was looking for, he wasn't going to find it in Simon's general firm files. But Sam probably knew that by now. When he returned, he would probably start looking for Simon's shadow files. Simon couldn't let him find them, but he also couldn't let Sam find him. He was still debating his options when Sam came jogging back, some kind of wrap and coffee in hand. Simon moved himself back into screen viewing range and saw that Sam was searching for *Matthews v. Rodriguez.* Well that explained what he was looking for. But he was never going to find it in those files, Simon thought. The realization made Simon feel a bit more relaxed and he allowed himself the luxury of stretching out his cramping legs. He instantly regretted the slight sounds he had made as Sam lifted his head as if he was listening. After a moment, Sam thankfully focused his attention back on the screen. Simon continued to watch. Soon it was clear to Simon that Sam was hunting for Simon's shadow password. Although Simon watched with interest, he was confident that Sam wouldn't be able to find it. He had probably only mentioned it in passing on one or two occasions since he and Sam had known each other. And even then, not as a password, just as a place he wanted to go. No one had that kind of memory. But he had underestimated his friend. Simon saw the look of apprehension come over Sam's face even before he had typed in the word "caneelbay." Simon saw the word go in and the screen come up. Sam was in. He had to do something now, Simon thought desperately. If Sam got into those files, he would know everything. And Simon couldn't predict what Sam would do with that knowledge. As strong as their friendship was, Sam's moral compass might prove stronger.

In any event, Simon couldn't take that chance. He moved quickly and quietly behind the secretarial bays and back down the hall. He made little rustling sounds with his jacket and then started walking heavily toward his office. He could imagine Sam in there, head up, listening. He moved slowly, giving Sam the chance to get out, praying that Sam would seize the opportunity to escape. As soon as Simon reached the hall corner, he stopped, ripped off his shoes, and began retracing his steps, this time as quietly as he could. He thought he heard Sam spring into action, but the movement was so quiet, he couldn't be sure. He crept back to the hall corner and peered around it. The light was off in his office, but there was no sign of Sam. He was probably hiding in the secretarial bays, just where Simon had hid earlier. Classic, Simon thought wryly. Cat and mouse with his own best friend. He assumed Sam would wait a bit before coming out and it was already so late that Simon decided to abandon his plans to gather evidence and head home.

Simon drove with a heavy heart. He couldn't figure out how Sam had found out anything that would have inspired him to sleuth about on his computer, let alone specifically target the *Matthews* case. But clearly he had. Simon should have known this would happen. The minute he heard that Maurice had brought Sam into the group, he should have stepped up and put an end to it, providing he could have. This glum state of affairs was merely the inevitable consequence of Sam being involved.

Simon thought back to when they had first met. He thought it was strange that he remembered it all so vividly, and he was at a loss to say why. In any event, it was their first day of the CS & B summer program. They were seated across from each other at the conference room table and they took an immediate dislike to each other, seemingly on looks alone. After the introductory remarks, they had discovered a firmer basis founded on law school animus. Simon went to USC. For Sam, it wasn't just the cross-town rivalry between UCLA and USC. He disapproved of USC's privileged, elitist values and what he viewed as an emphasis on law as a tool for making money. Law wasn't a money tool for Sam. It was a sacred calling, a hallowed trust, and it contained within it the duty to make the world a better place. He found USC's values loathsome. But Simon didn't give a shit what Sam thought about USC and its values. Simon was in law school to make money, lots of it. And he had determined that USC was his best chance at getting it.

How their enmity turned into respect and eventually into friendship could soften even the most hardened cynics. Suffice it to say that while they remained true to who they were, a part of each one of them spoke to the other at a deeper level. Out of that spark, a friendship flourished. So it came as no surprise that once Sam found out about something that seemed a bit amiss, he had no choice but to pursue it. And, unfortunately, Simon had no choice but to stop him.

By the time he pulled into his driveway, he knew what he had to do. Sam already knew too much. He had seen the complete file on *Matthews*. He knew about Bicknel and that Simon was working for Bicknel. Even if he told Sam he was just helping out a friend at Bicknel, Sam wouldn't believe it; he had seen the other two hundred plus files. Sam wouldn't let it go. He couldn't. So Sam would keep digging, and eventually he would find out everything there was to know about him, Maurice, and the whole operation. Sam would go to the police, in spite of their friendship, and he, the great Simon Streit, would be stewing in jail for the next twenty years. But as dire as that sounded, the more likely scenario was that Maurice would find out about Sam before the police found out about Maurice. Sam's life was at risk even now. Of course, Simon could turn himself into the authorities here and seek immunity and witness protection like he planned to do from Argentina. This would protect him, but Sam would still be exposed. In all likelihood, the cops would interview Sam and find out that he was only tangentially responsible for Simon coming forward, but Maurice wouldn't see it that way. Maurice would understand that Sam was the primary catalyst for Simon's betrayal and his long arm of vengeance would reach out from jail and crush Sam like a bug. No, there was only one option. Simon needed to stay on with Maurice and Sam needed to join them. And since Sam wouldn't join voluntarily, he would have to be persuaded by the charming wiles of Maurice Strickland.

Simon thought back to how it had happened with him. He had been tapped by Maurice to run some of the car cases. He enjoyed the work and was naturally quite good at it. But he especially loved the contingency structure. There was huge money to be made and he wanted to make it. Doing hourly work, all you could hope for was that you had enough work to bill a lot of hours and that you got your bills paid. From the moment Simon spent twenty hours on a case and earned $370,000 for the firm, he was hooked. Of course, there was the dark side to contingency work that balanced the up side; sometimes you got nothing. Fortunately, Maurice was exceptionally talented at only bringing in the winners. He seemed to have an uncanny ability to sniff out and exclude the dog cases. It was heady work, winning big money all the time, and he kept getting busier and busier. Simon's other hourly assignments began to pale in comparison.

Within a few months, Simon was working almost exclusively on Maurice's car cases and barely had time to brush his teeth. He saw that Maurice was very busy as well and wondered why Maurice wouldn't bring in another associate to help carry the workload. A couple days later, Maurice sent Simon an email requesting his presence for lunch at some place Simon had never heard of called The Lucky Seven. Simon had never been invited to lunch before by Maurice and he was thrilled. It could only be good news. No one took you out to lunch for bad news, especially one of the named partners of the firm. Maybe he was getting a raise or another bonus, although the last one had been substantial, as it was based on the increased revenue he had been bringing in for the firm. But who knew? Maybe it was time for another payday. He was virtually exploding with anticipation.

Finally, the day arrived. He dressed carefully, wanting to appear competent and serious without coming off as too full of himself. In essence, he wanted to convey partnership material. He was in his car and on his way by eleven thirty. Simon wasn't exactly sure where it was and there was no way he was going to be late. He plugged the address into his navigation system and headed out. The further away from downtown he drove, the more concerned he got. He was moving into an area of town that he'd only heard about and certainly never experienced. He locked the doors self-consciously, feeling embarrassed by his stereotypical response. Finally, he was there. It looked like some kind of billiard hall or even an old strip club, he thought anxiously. And it didn't look like it was open or had been open for quite some time. There were no other cars and no lights on. Pyramids of trash dotted the parking lot where the wind had piled the errant litter. The only evidence that this was, in fact, The Lucky Seven was an outline of the name over the door where a sign had once been. Simon was just about to get back in his car and return to the office when Maurice drove up in his silver Aston Martin convertible.

"Well hello, Simon," he called out from the car as he parked. "I'm so glad you found the place. Thanks for coming."

"My pleasure, Mr. Strickland," Simon responded.

"I know you're surprised to be invited to a place like this, but I wanted to show it to you, so I took the opportunity today," Maurice said as he bounded toward the building's entrance. Maurice was buoyant, almost ebullient. Simon didn't know what to make of it. He had heard that Maurice had another side to him that came out either when he was trying to charm some new business or, like a cobra, right before a kill. Simon was definitely unnerved to see it now.

"I'm delighted you asked me to lunch, sir. It's an honor." By this time, they were standing at the door and Maurice was navigating the locks.

"The fact is, Simon, I own this place. I just bought it. But I didn't buy it to open a restaurant if that's what you're thinking. I bought it strictly for its privacy." Maurice looked at Simon intently. "Its privacy."

Simon winced involuntarily at Maurice's scrutiny. Maurice either didn't notice or pretended not to notice and continued.

"As you can see, this building sits on three acres of land. It's on a dead end street and the police precinct is the weakest in the county. It's really a great property," Maurice said as he swung open the door and motioned for Simon to come inside.

It was just like Simon was visualizing; nothing really disgusting, just a number of reminders from its better days. Maurice pulled up a chair to the least offensive table and sat down. Simon did the same.

"You know, I'm very pleased with the work you've been doing on my cases," Maurice began, favoring Simon with a generous smile. "So I've decided that it's now time to advance your position in my little fiefdom at the firm."

At that, all of the questions Simon had about The Lucky Seven went right out of his head. "I'm, of course, delighted. I'm glad I've been helpful to you." He fawned.

"You have been extremely helpful and now it's my opportunity to return the favor. I am prepared to offer you a portion of the profits from all the cases you work on for me. Understand that this is not a partnership with the firm, but rather, a private arrangement I am making with you. Since I control this department, I am able to exercise, shall I say, discretion with regard to how I do business in my department. I have decided that the best way to continue growing my department the way I want to grow it is to share the bounty." Maurice paused for a moment to let that sink in. Seeing that Simon was transfixed by his every word, he continued. "Of course, there will be additional duties and even more work, but coupled with that is the opportunity to make a lot more money. If I'm not mistaken, I think that opportunity holds a special attraction for you, as it does for me, am I right?"

Simon was nonresponsive. He had slipped into a trancelike state, thinking about all the money he could make and what he could buy with all that money. Seeing that Maurice was waiting for an answer, he roused himself. "Yes, sir. I would be thrilled to take on more work and increase my contribution to the firm. I would be very glad to be of service."

"Good. Your share of the profits will be 20 percent, after expenses of course."

It was a great deal more than Simon could have hoped for. He was ecstatic. He couldn't wait to get back to the firm and get cranking.

"I consider 20 percent to be fair in light of the fact that the additional duties you will be assuming are illegal."

"Whaaat?" Simon made a bleating lamb kind of sound.

At that, Maurice became even more animated and appeared to be getting physically excited by what was coming next. "Actually, my dear Simon, you've already been engaged in felonious conduct. You just didn't know it. The only difference going forward is that now you'll know it." Maurice again smiled that broad smile Simon had received earlier, only this time Simon saw it for what it was: a barracuda grin.

Maurice went on to tell him how he had added Simon's name, and even his signature, to all kinds of murky documents that Simon had never seen and, of course, would never have signed. He told how he had even made a few phone calls posing as Simon to further thicken the tar. Finally, and just this morning, he had salted the personal injury portfolio of Simon's files with highly incriminating evidence of further fraud, larceny, and other felonious acts.

"So you see, Simon, you really don't have a choice. No one would ever believe that you weren't involved in all the things the evidence points to. You wouldn't have a chance. And just as your name has magically appeared, mine has magically disappeared. I've done nothing wrong and you've done everything. Rather tidy, I think. But before you think about punching me or anything worse, consider the fact that I couldn't have done it without you. I mean, really. The signs were all there. But you, in your greed, chose to ignore them. That's why I gave you such a big bonus early on. It was a greed test and you passed with flying colors. I wouldn't be too upset about it all, though, if I were you. Twenty percent will prove to be quite a significant sum. It will keep you in your $1,000 suits for quite a while."

So that's how it had gone for Simon. After he went back to the office and opened his files, he saw that Maurice had done exactly what he said and he was locked out from changing them back. He had taken the rest of the day, gone home, and sat morosely in the back yard, thinking about the bizarre turn his life had taken. Eventually, he had come to realize that maybe it wasn't such a bad thing. The situation did put him on the fast track to wealth and prosperity where he had been grunting along at a snail's pace before. Also, Maurice was one of the smartest people he'd ever met. If anyone could keep them from getting caught, he could. Finally, it was just money. They were just stealing some money from insurance companies; it wasn't like they were killing anyone. By about four, Simon had decided to make it work. He had opened a bottle of Stella Artois and started to acclimate himself to his new persona. Simon hoped that Sam would be able to do the same.

CHAPTER TWENTY-THREE

It was one of those perfect LA days. Generally, they occurred in the fall, October mostly, when the marine layer cleared up and the days were still warm and sunny. But today, God had smiled on the City of Angels and blessed it with warmth, a crystal clear lapis sky and bounteous sun. Ariel walked to the garden patio and took a long moment to enjoy the fresh feel of morning. The fact that Maurice had already left for the day was the icing on an absolutely perfect cake. She heard her private line ringing as she made her way back into the house.

"Good morning," she said cheerfully.

"Well, good morning to you too. You sound chipper."

"I am, and happy too. I can see the light at the end of the tunnel. I think we're almost through."

"Closer than you know. The cameras picked up some interesting tidbits last night concerning Mr. Sam Morrow."

"Really," she said quizzically. "Was he caught working too hard again?"

"Well, yes and no. He was caught working hard, but on someone else's matters. Simon Streit's that is."

"Interesting. So that little bee in the bonnet worked. He's always been a smart one."

"He is and so is that Sarah Brockman. He got into the *Matthews* file and opened the attorney notes before something distracted him. I don't know what or who it was, since it was too dark for the hall cameras to pick up, but at least I could see that he got out of Simon's office without getting caught. It makes me uneasy, though. I don't like even the slightest possibility that Sam could get into any kind of trouble or, god forbid, in danger with this whole thing. So, unless you object, I think we need to pick up the pace.

"Oh yes, absolutely. This thing isn't worth anyone getting hurt over. But we better keep an eye on Sam and make sure he doesn't get into any trouble on his own."

"Agreed. So he found the 'M' reference in the attorney notes. I'm sure he's wondering who 'M' is. Maybe you can help him out with that, and also with a particular highly confidential password you and I know so well."

"Great. Will do."

"Call me later. Good luck."

◆ ◆ ◆

Sam noticed the gorgeous LA day too, but for another reason. The sun had crept through his bedroom drapes, pierced his eyelids, and roused him from his troubled, but desperately needed sleep. And there was no going back. His mind was instantly awake, like a brain on speed, running all over the place and trying frantically to put pieces of the puzzle together. He showered quickly, grabbed his last two power bars, and headed into the office. He left a message for Sarah, who was in court until later in the day, and considered how he might be able to take another shot at Simon's computer.

CS & B was unique in that certain passwords were computer specific. This provided an additional layer of protection against hacking, computer fraud, and viruses. All partners and associates passwords were just that kind. Sam called Simon, but learned that he wouldn't be in until the afternoon. After staring at the wall for ten minutes and coming up with nothing, he decided he had to let it go for now and do something about the points and authorities that were due tomorrow. He turned to the credenza and noticed that his message light was flashing. Someone must have called when he was getting coffee, he thought. Maybe it was Sarah. He loved the feeling he got when he thought of her. He hoped it would last forever. He hit the play button only to hear another familiar woman's voice. It was Ariel Strickland. She was going to be in the neighborhood later and wanted to invite him to lunch. The world was always so delightfully surprising, he thought. He hadn't seen Alexander or Ariel for weeks, then they appeared at the Hong Kong Koi Gardens, and now both wanted to have lunch. He looked at the mound of work that still had to be completed for the P's and A's and knew he probably shouldn't take time for lunch with Ariel, but decided to anyway. One thing he had thankfully learned early on in his career was that there was never enough time for all the work that had to be done; you simply had to steal moments for yourself as best you could. He left another message for Sarah, this one specifically inquiring about dinner, finished up some smaller matters, and walked around the corner to meet Ariel.

She had picked one of the firm's most popular restaurants, probably so that if anyone saw them there, they would know there was nothing inappropriate going on. Sam arrived a few minutes early, but knew Ariel would be right on time. She always was. There were so many things he admired about Ariel, big things like intelligence, strength, and graciousness, but also little things like this one. She never kept anyone waiting even though, God knows, just about anyone would wait for her. Sam took up a position at the bar and ordered a beer. Since moving to LA, he had pretty well given up beers for lunch. But today, he decided, was an exception.

He was about halfway through his beer when she arrived. He sensed her even before he saw her and turned to see her enter the room. She moved with a sublime, captivating grace that reminded him of the classic movie stars of the 1940s and 50s. He could see that her entrance wasn't lost on the other men in the restaurant either.

"Hi, Sam," she said as she approached the bar. "I hope I haven't kept you waiting."

"You've never kept me waiting in all the years we've known each other. I wish you would, just once, Ariel, to make up for all the times I've been late."

"Dream on, Sam. You know I never will. I love being perfect." She was clearly enjoying herself and Sam could feel himself getting swept up in her buoyant mood. He smiled and started to relax for the first time in many hours.

"It's so great to see you happy," he said. "There was a period there when I didn't think I'd see you smile again. I guess you and Maurice are doing better?"

Shit. He did it again. That mouth of his just blurting stuff out without thinking. He quickly looked for a reaction, but if anything, Ariel seemed even lighter than before.

"Well, I don't know about *us,* but I'm definitely doing better." She ordered a glass of wine and they moved to their table right by the window where they had a breathtaking view of the courtyard garden.

"Isn't it gorgeous?" Ariel said, turning to him with a look of unfeigned delight. "How did they get all those flowers to bloom so early? And all the colors! I just love it here." She spontaneously touched his hand in an unconscious attempt to more deeply share the beauty she was experiencing. But for the very first time, it didn't happen. Sam didn't feel the intense feelings of want and desire that had defined his relationship with Ariel. He almost pulled his hand back in surprise, but instead, let it lie there, unresponsive on the table, feeling a faint sense of melancholy that his one-sided love affair with Ariel Strickland had finally come to an end.

He had met Ariel about ten years ago in Philly. He had just moved there to start his freshman year at Penn. He was so arrogant and full of himself, it made him wince even thinking about it now. He had been on campus for about two days when he decided to go to Saks to pick up a few things. As he walked by the cosmetics counter, he saw her. Standing behind one of the counters was the most beautiful girl he had ever seen. She looked his age, maybe a little older, and everything about her was perfect—except, of course, for the fact that she couldn't be too smart. After all, rocket scientists didn't work as salesclerks. He'd swaggered over to the counter and proceeded to awe her, he was sure, with his boyish good looks if not his mental acumen and considerable accomplishments. He thought he was really quite impressive. Luckily, Ariel had a sense of humor and a kind heart, so after being introduced to his Economics class the next day as its teacher's assistant, she pretended to be meeting him for the first time when he approached after class.

He loved her from the moment he saw her and, later, as they became friends, he loved her even more. They had lots of fun together and shared many wonderful moments, but nothing came of their relationship. After her graduation, Ariel went on to business school while Sam finished his B.A. They stayed loosely in touch for about a year afterwards, but that too faded, and by his graduation, they had lost track of each other completely. That was until he saw her again at his first CS & B dinner. It was a month after he had joined the firm and it was a lovely formal affair for partners, associates, and their dates. His jaw dropped when he saw her on Maurice's arm. It was sublime providence that their paths had crossed again after so many years and so many miles. She was equally delighted and they had continued a dear friendship. But what he thought Ariel never knew and what Sam knew every time he saw her, was that he was in love with her. Not a friendship kind of love, but a real, man-woman love, the kind of love that doesn't work when the woman is married to another man. Of course, he had never done anything about his feelings for Ariel. He would never create a problem like that for her. But he had nursed his smoldering love and drawn comfort from its well-worn familiarity. To have it suddenly and unexpectedly evaporate was a shock indeed. And then he realized why. His love for Ariel had been supplanted by his love for Sarah. The realization stunned him. And then a tender smile began to fill his face. Ariel stopped talking as she watched it unfold. She saw it, she knew what it was, and she knew what it meant. She knew someone else had spirited away that piece of his heart that had belonged to her. She felt a tug at her own heart, but let that feeling dissipate in her happiness for him. She decided to move on and do what she had come to do. "So, Sam. I'm really not sure where it stands with Maurice. I was looking through one of my memories boxes yesterday and I felt so sad and teary. I even took out the bracelet with our initials on it and started wearing it again. See?" she asked showing him the bracelet. It was a beautiful gold bracelet with the initial charms 'A' and 'M' dangling from it in diamonds. "It's just one of those things about Maurice. He loves initials. I think he has always loved initials. I don't know what it is about initials that he fancies, but he certainly does. In fact," and she lowered her voice, "I'm probably talking out of school, but it's just so funny. When we got married, he already had a full line of his own monogrammed towels, sheets, and even dish towels. Little 'M's all over the place. A little eccentric, for sure, but I always thought it was kind of charming."

There, she saw it. He heard the 'M' reference. Whether he would put it together later on remained to be seen, but she figured he would. She could see him mull it over and file it away for future consideration. Now he just needed a password. She continued.

"I also found so many pictures of us in happier times. I had forgotten that we used to have such fun together. I had reams of pictures of us at our favorite places, even places I had forgotten about. The best one was a picture of us at Yellowstone, camping. It was a crazy spontaneous trip right after we were married and it rained and then snowed and blew sleet all over us, but we thought of it as a great adventure and loved every minute of it. On the last day, we reached the peak of the toughest climb either of us had ever made. The views absolutely took my breath away and were worth every blister and sore muscle we got. I remember Maurice crawling up to the top of this really primordial looking rock and gazing out over the spectacular vast expanse and saying how Yellowstone was engraved in his heart forever. I took a picture of him at that moment that is still my favorite picture of him. I even had a smaller one made that I used to carry around in my wallet. But I guess that was another time," she paused a long moment and then continued much more softly, "and another Maurice."

Sam could hear the pain in her voice and see it clouding her face. It must be hard to lose someone you loved so much, he thought.

"But the saddest thing is not that he's lost to me," Ariel said contemplatively. "It's that he's lost who he used to be. Before I put all the pictures back in the boxes, I showed him that Yellowstone picture. Just to see how he would react. And he was like a kid in a candy store. He got a huge grin on his face and took the picture and started studying it intently. I could see him being drawn back into good memories. He looked at it awhile and then he said: 'Damn, that was a great trip. I think about it often. Yellowstone is special to me because of that hike. I remember the tough climb and standing on that rock. I was king of the world, surveying my kingdom—the center of the universe with the world mine for the taking.' He looked so greedy and voracious as he said it. It was obscene," Ariel said. "He couldn't even remember being moved by the beauty of Yellowstone. His ego has become so overpowering that he created a memory based on his own magnificence. I had to excuse myself after that one and take a long walk around the block."

Sam felt surprisingly uncomfortable hearing those kinds of intimate details about Ariel and Maurice's life together. It's not that he and Ariel weren't close friends; they were. It was just that Ariel had never before talked about private matters concerning Maurice, probably either out of respect for Maurice or out of her desire to avoid an awkward situation for him at the firm. But all that had apparently changed. He decided to step up and be a good friend to Ariel.

"Whatever you decide to do, Ariel, you know I'm here for you," he said.

"Thank you, Sam," she said as she looked him in the eyes and gently touched his hand. "That means so much to me. I really appreciate it." And she let her hand linger on his just another moment to confirm what she already knew. Nothing. No response. She slowly pulled her hand back and put it in her lap. Most of her was delighted that Sam had found someone he loved so much, but if she was honest, she would have to admit that there was a tiny little piece of herself buried deep down that was sad to lose the attention.

◆ ◆ ◆

Sam decided to take a roundabout way back to the office to give himself a little more time to think about everything that had happened at lunch. The main thing, of course, being that he had found out he was in love with Sarah. Funny how those things happened. You're usually the last to know. He let the warm, happy feelings saturate his body. He allowed himself to forget about Simon and the firm, and just enjoy this delicious moment in time. If he kept a journal, which of course he didn't, since he considered it gay, he would write down, "Just discovered am in love with Sarah today." He had no clue as to when he actually fell in love with her, but at least he knew when he discovered it. Sam and Sarah. Sarah and Sam. It sounded good. Hell, it sounded great! Lots of S's and A's. Their names fit well together, just like they did. If he was a chick, he would try out "Sarah Morrow," but he wasn't a chick. It did sound pretty good though. But what if she didn't feel the same way? A sickening feeling suddenly hit him hard, right in the middle of his stomach. He knew she liked him, but love was another thing altogether. He needed to know. He wanted to call her right now and ask her, but restrained himself from such undeniable idiocy. He would ask her tonight at dinner. Now that he had decided on a plan of action, he felt the warm feelings returning until he thought about Ariel and Maurice. It was so unlike Ariel to speak frankly about Maurice the way she had. He didn't know how to account for it. She wasn't tipsy. Maybe she just needed someone to talk to and he happened to be there. In any event, he hoped the whole mess resolved itself soon, one way or the other. He continued walking and thinking and before he knew it, he found himself right in the middle of the jewelry district. He hadn't been in the area for years, but it looked just the same. He wandered down the main drag and stopped for a cup of espresso and a mini

Danish. He knew he had to head back, but he wanted to savor these last few minutes of freedom from the office. As he surveyed the window of the store next door, his gaze fell on a beautiful floating heart necklace. It was mid-sized and platinum, with a few choice diamonds that were suspended in the interior of the heart so they looked like they were floating too. He looked at it a long while in the window before going in. When he went in, he was ready to buy. After a moderately successful negotiation, he was on his way, necklace in hand, to surprise someone very special to him at dinner.

By this time, it was almost three and he wanted to get some work done and see if Simon was in yet. There was still an outside chance that Simon wouldn't come in and he could somehow access Simon's computer and do some more investigation. But no luck. As he approached Simon's office, Lorraine called out.

"Sam, he's in, but don't go in there or even knock. He's got his DND on and he gave me very explicit instructions not to let anyone disturb him for any reason. Except a partner, of course."

"Gotcha. How's he feeling? Did he look OK?"

"Not too bad. Nasty bruises, but nothing that won't heal. Oh, and lots of aches and pains."

"Well, that won't hurt his ability to churn and burn on his computer."

"Funny you should say that. That's all he's been doing since he got in. You can hear the keys click-clacking away."

Sam listened for a few seconds, thanked Lorraine, and walked back to his office. Little chance of accessing Simon's computer today. Maybe he and Sarah would drop by after dinner. He was very interested in getting her take on all of this anyway. He might just be overreacting and acting crazy. Plus, he had to tell her that Simon was on the other side of her case. His phone was ringing when he walked in.

"Hi, Sam. Miss me?"

Sam suddenly broke out in a thin layer of sweat. He was nervous for the first time since they had started dating and he didn't know why.

"You know I always miss you, Sarah," he said a little too seriously.

"OK, OK, I was just kidding. I *know* you think about me every minute of every day. That's why you don't get your work done. Are we still on for dinner or do you need more slave time to finish your P's and A's?"

By this time Sam had shaken off his nerves and was back to his comfortable Sam self. "Of course we're still on. I can't let a little thing like work keep me from seeing you, can I?"

"Definitely not. Let's go to this Mexican trasher I know. Best authentic Mexican food in town, and you know that says a lot."

"Great. Is seven thirty okay? I'll pick you up."

"Perfect. And bring your pj's."

CHAPTER TWENTY-FOUR

And just as a big smile was crossing Sam's face, an even bigger one was crossing Maurice's. God, he felt good. It had been months since he'd felt this happy. Actually, he felt happy and centered and back in fighting form again. He would never allow himself to suffer such an unnecessarily long dry spell again. He had treated himself to a lovely lunch at Cicero's with an old friend from his football days and was now back at the office churning through his calendar and to-do lists like a man on fire. He was relishing his renewed ability to make the strong, definitive decisions he would have wavered over a few days ago.

"Marjorie, will you bring me the *Peterson* and *Moldonado* files, set up lunches with Judge Schneider and Roy Eberton, and the CFO of Midland Industries—I forget his name—and bring my group's pre-bills?"

"Absolutely. Consider it done." Marjorie was delighted to see her favorite Maurice back at the helm again. As busy as he kept her when he was like this, she much preferred it to the Maurice that was a bit sluggish and scattered like he had been for the past few weeks. She took care of his latest requests and then ran over to the deli to get a quick sandwich to go.

Meanwhile, Maurice was studying the pre-bills in front of him and making the same adjustments to Simon's pre-bills that he had been making for the past eighteen months, but this time, all the changes were going to final. Maurice had decided that Simon had to go. The fact that he had considered just keeping an eye on Simon earlier was, to his mind, yet another example of the poor judgment that had plagued him. When he saw the deep, limbic fear in Simon's eyes during the incident at The Lucky Seven, a normal, balanced Maurice would have proceeded immediately with the steps he was taking right now. The fact that he had waited until now disgusted him. He created a duplicate set of bills except that he increased the hours and amounts recorded by Simon by ten percent on average, depending on the wealth of the client. He totaled up the difference between the dollar amount recorded by Simon and the new dollar amount like he had done for the last eighteen months, but this time he totaled all eighteen months and actually shifted the funds in preparation for the wire transfers he would make into Simon's account tonight. He would access Simon's computer later and make the critical changes on Simon's hard drive. And tomorrow, Maurice would "discover" the embezzlement and have his favorite police detectives make the ignominious arrest here at the firm. He considered how absolutely delicious it was going to be and almost giggled out loud. He could hardly wait. He would arrange it so he and the detectives were waiting in the lobby when Simon arrived. Simon would be hysterical and would start hurtling shocking accusations about him and his business, but no one would believe the rantings of an embezzler. Later they would add "and drug addict," to embezzler. Hector was taking care of that right now. It was good to have a felon in your employ, Maurice thought smugly.

Maurice knew Simon had returned to the firm after his "unfortunate accident," but he hadn't seen him all day. He had to acknowledge the possibility, however remote for someone so lily-livered, that Simon was in his office right now emailing files and trying to collect as much evidence as he could to use against him. If he *was* doing that, at least he would have risen in esteem, Maurice thought beneficently, but what a shame to have wasted so many hours on files that were going to disintegrate and take their mother hard drive with them. He could never thank his computer savant enough for this one. When the firm made the switch to computer specific applications, Maurice had used Vincent to infect Simon's computer with the most amazing virus he had ever seen. If anyone tried to send any protected material from the computer to any place else, the virus would activate. The files sent would disintegrate and the recipient computer's hard drive would be completely erased. All in all it was a pretty bad bug. Maurice had been careful to tell everyone in his group that they could not send files to non-designated computers. He never told them why, he just told them no. And no one ever did. Except that Simon might be doing it right now.

He made a last check of his phone messages before Marjorie came back and noticed a reminder from Ariel about the AIDS charity dinner. He had completely forgotten about it and it had been inexplicably omitted from his calendar. He had to go. Everyone would be there. It was AIDS and it was LA. He had no idea why it hadn't made it to his calendar, but chalked it up to the deranged Maurice he had been living with. He would just have to stop by the firm and Simon's computer afterwards. He called Ariel for the particulars.

"Hi, Ariel. Thanks for the AIDS reminder. I had forgotten all about it."

"You're welcome. Is your emergency tuxedo still in your office? If so, should I pick you up at the firm?"

"Yes, I have it," Maurice said double-checking his office closet. Seven is fine." Maurice hung up abruptly, but for once, didn't feel the hostility towards Ariel that had characterized most of their recent interactions. She even seemed nice, Maurice thought. But even bitches can have good days.

He worked hard through the rest of the afternoon, making significant headway on numerous fronts. By eight, he was seated with Ariel, the President of Santa Monica Trust, and two state senators, bored to tears, enjoying neither the delicious butternut squash soup nor the conversation.

Sam, in contrast, was sitting thigh to thigh with Sarah, inhaling two burrito extremes, and enjoying everything.

"It's been a weird couple of days," Sam said, finishing off his first burrito. "I know I shouldn't have told you as much as I have, but I really don't care. I needed to talk to you about it all and tell you what I found out about Simon."

"I have to admit to being in a bit of shock. I don't know what to think about Simon and Bicknel and all of it. But he's one of your best friends. Can you really believe he's doing such under the radar kinds of things and you wouldn't know anything about it?"

"That's what's got me," Sam said earnestly. "I thought I knew him. I mean really knew him, like a brother. That's why I have got to find out what's going on. Maybe I can help. Maybe he's in some trouble that's so bad or so embarrassing that he couldn't even tell me about it. I've got to be there for him as a friend—even if he doesn't want my help."

Sarah put her fork down and turned to Sam. "You know, there could be more to this than either of us is thinking. There could be something really big or really bad. It could be dangerous. I mean whatever Simon is into, he's taking a huge risk, so there has to be an equally big reason for why he's doing what he's doing. I think we should be careful."

It was the use of 'we' that got him. All of a sudden, Sarah had made them together in this. He wasn't alone any more. He didn't feel quite as scared. But, even so, he couldn't risk Sarah.

"I don't think you should get involved in any of this, Sarah," he said emphatically. "Like you said, this could be dangerous. Who knows what's going to crawl out from under the rocks I'm going to dislodge."

"I know," Sarah said, giving him a spontaneous hug. "That's why I like it all so much. Cloak and Dagger. I can finally release my inner Nancy Drew. This law thing is just a cover for my real aspirations." She smiled and hugged him again. "Besides, what else would I do while you're off playing Sherlock Holmes?"

Sam wanted her with him. He always wanted her with him, but he had real concerns about her safety. "I tell you what. We'll evaluate as we go. If anything seems too scary to me, you have to pack it in. Promise?"

"I promise. But you have to remember that Simon is the

schmuck who made me that $2,000 offer. I have my own axe to grind with him."

"OK, OK. So what do you think about this whole 'M' thing? I mean, according to the file note I found, it seems like Simon is working for someone. That he's not the only guy involved in whatever this is."

"Right. Don't you think it's someone in the firm?"

"Yeah. It just makes sense, since all Simon's files are on the firm computer. If 'M' was on the outside, wouldn't he use his computer at home?"

"Yes, I think he would. So is 'M' the first or last initial? I think we could just go through the attorneys at the firm and see who fits."

But the second Sarah said 'initial,' Sam knew. "It's Maurice Strickland," he blurted out.

"You've got to be kidding," Sarah said in disbelief. "*The* Maurice Strickland? You've got to be kidding," she said again subconsciously lowering her voice. "Why do you think so?"

"Well, I had lunch with Ariel Strickland today and she mentioned that Maurice has a thing for his initials. That he monograms everything with M's and that it was a bit over the top. Seems he had a full set of monogrammed linens even before they were married."

"That does sound strange, especially for a guy. But why would Maurice want to get involved in anything even the slightest bit shady? I mean, he's a named partner at the firm for God's sake. He makes millions of dollars a year. Why would he risk any of that?"

"Good question. But if you know Maurice even a little, it

makes perfect sense. See, Maurice's whole life has been about competition and winning—his football career, his law practice, hell, even his wives. He sees the world as a zero sum game and he will do whatever it takes to get his share."

"That's pretty harsh. Is he really that bad?"

"Probably worse. Like I said, I don't know him that well." Sam shifted in his seat and continued. "I think he fancies himself to be Alexander the Great or some kind of master of the universe. He even talks in military jargon. You don't notice it until you start working for him and then you notice it all the time. He says things like 'this will take out their artillery' or 'we need to firebomb the other side.' Not bad in and of themselves, but it shows you how he thinks. Anyway, my point is that he's never satisfied, he always wants more. And there's a certain limit to how much 'more' you can get when you work in the typical partnership law firm. If you have partners, you share. Maurice probably doesn't want to share."

"Maybe. I mean, I can see it, but it's a lot of risk."

"Yeah, but it could be a lot of reward."

"OK, well, he's our prime suspect."

"Plus," Sam added. "He works with Simon all the time, so there's already an established connection."

"Well, what do you want to do?" Sarah asked expectantly. She actually was feeling rather Nancy Drew-ish and wanted to get out there and start nosing around.

"I was thinking I wanted to go back to the firm and see if I could get on Simon's computer, but I'm concerned about him showing up. Actually, he might still be there now since he was in there all day working."

"What about Maurice's computer?"

Sam let the question lie there between them, growing more portentous by the second. Finally he said, "If we get caught, it'll be my job and possibly my career."

"I know. I shouldn't even have said it. I was just thinking out loud. It's too much risk, even for your best friend."

Sam looked deeply at her for a long time. "You'd do it. You'd do it for your friend and not think twice about it."

"No . . . I . . . I mean . . ." Sarah tried to deny it, but they both knew it was true. "What I mean to say is that it's different for me. I love the law, but I love lots of other things as well. I *would* be happy being Nancy Drew," she said with an impish smile.

"You're so sweet to me, and kind," he said, taking her hand. "I know you wouldn't think any less of me if I decided to do nothing. But I would think less of me and that's really all that matters. I need to find out what's going on and try and help Simon, because that's the right thing to do."

He gently placed her hand in her lap and put his napkin on the table. Now that the decision was made, Sarah watched transfixed as everything about Sam started to change. He squared his jaw and stiffened his body. His eyes became piercingly focused. He looked like a man ready to do battle. And, of course, he was.

"Now you see why you need me," Sarah said pithily. "I can be the lookout. But if it happens that Maurice is coming and we can't get out in time, we can always jump on Maurice's couch and pretend we came into his office for some fooling around. From what you've told me about Maurice, he might even give you a raise for that."

"Very funny. And probably not far from the truth. In any

event, it would give us a bit of a chance. Plus, it'd be a hell of a lot of fun."

Sarah wacked him with the stack of extra napkins on the table and then proceeded to give him a big, juicy kiss. "Oh, it's going to be fine, you'll see. Remember, there's still a chance we can get onto Simon's computer."

"Yeah, but we'd never even find the couch with all that mess in there. We'd have to roll around on the floor."

They both started laughing, grateful to break the tension with the image of them rolling around, over, and through Simon's clutter.

"Shit," Sam said as Sarah looked up startled. "What about the password? We need Maurice's password."

"I forgot all about that. I don't suppose you can divine Maurice's the way you did Simon's?"

"Highly unlikely, since I don't know squat about Maurice other than he's frequently an asshole and likes to travel."

"Isn't that enough? I mean, we can at least try."

"Definitely. Although we should consider the fact that he might have a shut-off trigger in place that activates when anyone makes more than a certain number of unsuccessful attempts at logging in a password. Sometimes these triggers shut down the computer and call security at the same time. Not a happy scenario for us. Frankly, I was surprised that Simon didn't have one."

"Well, that gives us two chances. Better odds than Vegas. Do you think anyone could help us? I mean, do you think Ariel Strickland would help?"

"Knowing Maurice and his marital history, I doubt Ariel even knows what the password is. Besides, it wouldn't be right to get her involved. She's got her own Maurice troubles to deal with."

"Alright. So we're back to us. Where does he like to travel? Any special places you know of? People usually use passwords that retrieve warm memories for them because they get a feel good injection every time they log on. Who doesn't want that? So Simon's password was rather predictable. Although it was still amazing that you found it," Sarah added quickly.

"Well, he likes adventure travel. We always have to hear about his exploits when he gets back. But that really is consistent with his personality and his master of the universe psychology. He likes trips where he's challenged and triumphs. Like this Yellowstone trip Ariel was telling me about. He and Ariel did a really challenging hike and, at the end, Maurice stood at the top and declared himself 'king of the world.' That's pretty much in line with who Maurice is and what he values."

"Well, maybe the password *is* 'Yellowstone.' It fits all the requirements."

"It could be, but it could also be hundreds of other places he's visited. Plus, Ariel was with him on that trip and she's someone who doesn't arouse the warmest thoughts right now."

"True. And why did she bring that trip up anyway? Were you comparing notes on great vacation getaways?"

"No. It was kinda' weird, actually," Sam said reflectively. "Ariel was talking to me about her relationship with Maurice, something she never does. And she was saying how sad it was and how she had started to wear the bracelet with their initials on it again, and how pictures of good times they had spent together made her sad. And she talked about this picture of Maurice in

Yellowstone. She said it was a very special place for him."

"It sure has all the earmarks," Sarah said. "I say we go over to Maurice's office and try it. First, we can look around the office for any clues as to anything else it might be, but it'll be quick. We can be in and out of there in a few minutes if it doesn't work."

"OK, let's go for it. It feels right to me. Let's stop by O'Riley's for a while though, so we'll get to the firm after all the drones have left."

"Deal. But you better produce the $1.00 you owe me for the last game or I'll tell everyone you're a darts welcher."

"'Welcher' isn't a word."

"Sometimes I really hate lawyers," Sarah said in her most exasperated voice as she threw a withering look Sam's way and marched out the door.

◆ ◆ ◆

Maurice had just about finished his desert and was plotting his escape before all the awards and speeches began.

He turned to Ariel and spoke loudly enough that everyone at the table could hear. "What a fabulous event this has been," he said, looking around the table and appearing to beam with delight. What a huge success for AIDS LA. But I have a mountain of work at the office that I need to get through tonight. Ariel, do you think you can catch a ride home with the Reynolds?"

Ariel knew the scenario well. Maurice made his excuses and orchestrated a graceful exit only to leave her holding the Strickland bag, so to speak. But this time, Maurice's early departure wasn't an option. "Actually, dear, we've been invited to another event afterwards that I've already accepted. I really can't disappoint the governor."

Ariel saw his eyes light up as his whole body became instantly energized. "Oh, I'm sorry, I didn't know," he spoke ingratiatingly. "Well, I certainly can't disappoint the governor, can I? So I guess I'll just have to stay up a bit later."

He sat back in his chair, quite satisfied with his performance, and looked approvingly at Ariel. Good job, my dear, he thought. He had been trying to wrangle an invitation from the governor since the election three years ago, with no success. How Ariel managed to pull it off, he'd be most interested to hear. He felt a momentary pang of remorse as he considered his imminent divorce. Not a pang of conscience over his well-hidden assets, of course, but a sense of loss at having to lose such a valuable business partner. Oh well, he thought. Couldn't be helped. Besides, maybe his next wife would be an even better social gymnast.

Ariel watched derisively as Maurice immediately re-engaged himself in the table conversation with a new zest and commitment. His motives were so transparent, it was surprising to her that everyone didn't see right through his feigned interest and synthetic sparkle. But she, of course, knew him much better than they ever would. He was behaving exactly as she had anticipated. She hated having to give up her contact with the governor for Maurice, but it was absolutely critical that he be contained for the evening. And so here they were. A few more hours of dinner and speeches, a few hours at the governor's, and he should be hammered enough to forget about the office, go home, and just pass out on the couch. That was the only weakness in an otherwise perfect plan, but she would do her best to keep his drinks freely flowing and generously fortified. It would be fine, she told herself.

◆ ◆ ◆

Meanwhile, Sarah had decimated Sam at another dozen or so dart games and Sam put down his darts in a sign of surrender.

"I give up. You're merciless. You've taken my little darts-playing heart and stomped on it, so I have no other alternative but to give you this." Sam took the floating heart necklace from his pocket, dangled it on the end of a dart point, and gave it to her.

Sarah squealed in delight. "Oh, it's so beautiful. It's so delicate and perfect. I absolutely love it!" she exclaimed as she watched it turning on its chain. "It looks like a heart floating within a heart. And the crystals are gorgeous. Here, help me put it on."

"Diamonds," Sam said.

"What?"

"Those are diamonds, not crystals."

Sarah's face blanched as she took the heart in her hand. "Oh no, Sam. I can't accept anything like this. It's too much. I mean it's absolutely extraordinary, but it's just too much. Thank you, Sam. Thank you so much," Sarah said as she placed the heart in Sam's hand. "But I just can't accept it."

"How could anything possibly be too much for you, Sarah?" Sam said gently as he turned Sarah around and fixed the clasp around her neck.

Sarah touched the heart lying perfectly in the hollow of

her neck and allowed it to linger there for a moment before renewing her protestations. But it was too late. Sam wrapped his arms around her and pressed his body against hers in a full body hug as he nestled his head next to her ear and said. "Sarah, I love you."

He didn't know he was going to say it and Sarah couldn't believe she heard it. They both pulled away and turned to look at each other.

"I . . . ah . . . Sarah . . ." Sam tried to speak first, but before he could give it another go, Sarah said. "I love you too."

Sam couldn't believe it—any of it. He grabbed Sarah, spun her around and kissed her euphorically on the lips. They started giggling and everyone in the bar thought they were completely smashed. Eventually, they collapsed in a heaping pile in their booth and tried to catch their breath.

"You know, Mr. Morrow. If that was a ploy to get me to accept that necklace, it worked! Don't ask me why. It probably goes back to things my mom told me about loose women. In any event, I would be honored to wear it and I will love thinking about you every time I do." Sarah fingered the heart again as if trying to memorize every feature. "But you really did out do yourself, crystals would have been just fine."

"Oh, *now* you tell me." Sam laughed as he wrapped Sarah up in another deep hug.

"Well, I don't know about you, but I would sure like to blow off our 'mission' tonight and have a little celebration," Sam said with a wink and a smile.

"Me too, but honestly, what do you think? Is time of the essence or are we just being drama queens?"

"A sobering question, my sweet dear. I know we have to stick with our plan. I feel like things are escalating. I don't know what Simon was doing in his office all day, but I'll bet it has something to do with this."

"I agree. If it seemed unusual to you, then it's suspicious. Let's go. It's late enough even for the drones at CS & B. We'll just have to make some time for ourselves later."

It took less than fifteen minutes to get to the firm with no traffic and, as they approached, Sarah started trying to force herself to concentrate on the job at hand. But she was so happy and so in love. She kept sneaking peeks at Sam and touching her necklace to convince herself that it wasn't all just a wonderful dream. It was clear to her now that she had loved him for a very long time—all the way back to law school. She even remembered the first time she met him. Everything about him had seemed familiar to her. His prepossessing smile, the way his hand rushed through his hair when he was thinking, even the smell of his cologne. She felt that they had met before. And now this. She'd have to find that Louis Armstrong "Wonderful World" song and play it over and over.

"OK, let's park in the building like usual. First, we'll go to my office like I forgot something that I need to pick up. We can do a little recon from there and then hit either Simon's or M's office when we think it's clear. Are you sure you want to do this? There's a gigantic part of me that doesn't want you involved."

"I know, but I have to be. It's my case. He's your friend and you're my, oh God, do I call you my boyfriend?"

"Yup."

"OK, boyfriend, so I need to be in this with you. Besides, we get to be super sleuths. How often does that opportunity come along? Right?"

"OK."

◆ ◆ ◆

"OK, Ariel. You said the governor was going to be here. I don't see him. I haven't seen him and we've already been here for two hours. I'm not even sure this is his party. If he doesn't come real soon, I'm leaving."

Maurice was getting testy and quite unpleasant, Ariel thought. Not uncommon for him. But it was still far too early to release him and all attempts at getting him incapacitated with booze had failed miserably. If anything, he was getting more sober as the night wore on. She needed to come up with something quick. She saw her contact at the bar across the room and went over for an update.

"Hi, Stan. Thanks again so much for having us. The party is a fantastic success. I hate to inquire, but do you know when the governor might be arriving?"

"No problem, Ariel. Actually the governor just called and said that he will be here, but not for another hour and a half. He got held up at a fundraiser for Tom Moray. You know Tom, don't you? In any event, he promised that he'll make our little shindig."

Ariel thanked Stan and wound her way back across the room to where Maurice was standing, tonic water in hand, looking more surly by the moment. She realized as she approached, that Maurice didn't have an hour and a half in him and she diverted herself to the powder room where she could have a quiet moment to come up with a new plan. Whatever it took, she thought. She had to buy a little time. She sat down at the vanity next to a gorgeous, willowy redhead, late twenties, who was freshening her lipstick.

"Hi," Ariel said genially. "Wonderful party, isn't it?"

"Very wonderful," the woman said in a thick Russian accent. "I love parties."

Ariel considered the woman in the mirror and decided that she was her best option.

"You are very pretty. Are you from Russia?"

The girl smiled warmly. "Yes, I am. Moscow. Here I have been six months."

"Your English is quite excellent for being here such a short time."

"Thank you. That is very nice of you to say it. I learn English and then I become movie star."

"Well, you are certainly in the right town for it. Do you have a boyfriend?"

"Yes, I have many. I like them all." By this time, she was smiling broadly and had clearly warmed to Ariel.

"My name is Ariel," she said as she put out her hand.

"And mine is Natalya," she said, taking Ariel's hand in her own. "Happy to see you."

"Likewise," Ariel said smiling. "Say, I was wondering if you would like to make a little extra money and help me out at the same time?"

"What you mean?" Natalya asked looking concerned. "I have green card. I do legal things only."

"Oh, no it's nothing like that," Ariel rushed to assure her. "No. It's just that I am here with my husband, Maurice, who is a really nice and wonderful man. But he is crazy about the Russian people, and Russian women in particular. He loves Russians. I was just wondering if you might meet him and just talk to him for a while. It would make him so happy. Nothing like you do with your boyfriends. Just talk."

Natalya studied Ariel's reflection in the mirror for a long time. "It is strange. It is not right. Just talk to a man? For money? Nyet. I don't think so."

Ariel could feel her opportunity slipping away. The fact was Maurice liked Russians just about as much as he liked everybody else. If there was something they could do for him, he liked them. If not? He didn't give a damn. What he did like, however, was variety in life and savoring as much of it as he could particularly in the form of pretty young women. And Natalya offered just about as much variety as anyone could desire, especially in comparison with Ariel. She was everything Ariel was not. Tall and thin where Ariel was more voluptuous and womanly, redheaded where Ariel was blonde, and exotic where Ariel veritably defined an American Barbie doll. Yes, Maurice would definitely be interested in her. Now, if she could just get Natalya interested in him.

"I will pay you $500 for two hours of your time. Just talking. Stay here at the party and enjoy each other's company. I've got to dash away for a few hours and I just want to make sure my husband has a nice time. Otherwise, he won't want to go to another one of these parties with me and I love to go to them."

Natalya didn't flinch at the $500. Apparently, she was used to making a lot more for her time. "Just talking," Natalya repeated musing about it out loud. "Strange. You're sure nothing more?" She asked still looking perplexed.

Ariel immediately understood. Her request was so alien to Natalya that it was making her uncomfortable. Ariel needed to reformulate it in a way that Natalya could understand. "Oh, sure something more. If you two hit it off in the conversation area, there might an opportunity to get to know each other better in a more private way later on."

Natalya's face instantly brightened. "Yes, I see. OK, I get it. What about you too? I like to party."

Ariel managed to stifle a giggle and turned it into a generous smile. "What a sweet offer, Natalya. Not tonight, but maybe another time. Thank you, though. Oh, one more thing. Don't tell Maurice anything about our little arrangement. Let him think he still has his chops." Seeing a blank look from Natalya, Ariel clarified. "Let him think that he's still an attractive man that you find sexy. It does a world of good in bed," Ariel said conspiratorially.

It was Natalya's turn to giggle. "Oh, you're so funny. You're a good wife. He's very lucky."

He doesn't even know how lucky he is, Ariel thought slyly. Just a few more days and it will all be over. Ariel paid Natalya as agreed, plus a few more hundreds in case things progressed as anticipated, and identified Maurice for her as they left the powder room. Natalya started to walk toward Maurice as Ariel started to walk to the lobby, cell phone in hand. She could see Maurice notice Natalya with marked interest so she speed-dialed his cell and watched as he answered.

"Hi honey," she said not being able to resist a little comedy. "Michael called from maternity and said it could be any time now and to hurry. He said Liz is pretty nervous, so I'm already on my way. Oh, and the aide said that the governor will absolutely positively be there in about an hour or so."

"Of course I want you to be there with your sister," Maurice said, "but I thought she wasn't due for two weeks?"

"That's the concern, she's having contractions. Anyway, got to run. Don't wait up for me. Have fun." Ariel watched as Maurice closed his phone and greeted this night's enchantress with a mega watt smile. Where does he get the energy? Ariel thought as she slid out the door. Too bad she was going to have to miss the governor.

◆ ◆ ◆

Meanwhile, Sarah and Sam were progressing quite nicely. They had decamped in Sam's office and Sam had made a little sortie out to check on Simon. He returned with the news that Simon's door was shut, the light was on and, although hard to tell, there seemed to be some sounds coming from the room. They decided to go to Plan B. Sam picked up some documents and a legal pad, grabbed a prop cup of coffee from the pantry, and made a pass by Maurice's office. Everything looked quiet. The door was open, the light was out, and the trash can had been emptied. By all appearance, it looked like Maurice was gone for the night and the cleaning crew had come and gone. Sam rapidly checked the rest of the floor. Empty. Quiet. Time to make their move. Sam returned to his office and together they went to Maurice's.

"I'll stand right inside the door where I can see anyone who comes down the hall," Sarah whispered.

"OK. See the couch? If anyone comes, dive-bomb the couch. I'll join you and we'll play some hanky-panky. We can't hide, because if we got caught, there's no explanation for that. I learned that last night with Simon. I think the couch is our best option."

"Not to mention the most fun," Sarah said lightly. "OK, let's get started."

Sam moved around the heavy mahogany desk to the computer on the return. What a gorgeous work space, Sam couldn't help but think. He hoped this little exploit wasn't his ticket out of the big leagues forever. He sat down and began going through the log-on sequence. When it came time to type in the password, he looked up at Sarah standing by the door. They locked eyes in silent prayer as he typed in "Yellowstone."

"Oh my God, it worked!" he almost shouted, but caught himself in time. "I can't believe it!"

Sarah was silently cheering, jumping up and down, and waving a big thumbs up sign. They could hardly believe it. Sam watched the opening sequence with fascination. The screen became completely black and then a small gold 'M' appeared in the top left corner and started moving to the center, growing larger and larger until it eventually took up the whole screen. It vanished and was instantly replaced with a combination of speeding images culminating in a picture of Maurice standing on top of a giant rock in a beautiful setting with the words "King of the Universe" scrolled at the bottom. Sam felt momentarily embarrassed, as if he had just seen Maurice naked—although it struck him as even more intimate than that. After a second or two, the image dissolved into the directories. Sam scrolled through, finding most of them either familiar or self-explanatory, with the exception of a folder named "Obelisk Holdings" and one named "Personal Injury." That had to be the folder he was looking for. Opening it only led to more folders, which eventually led to countless files. There had to be thousands of files, each appearing to be a different personal injury case. Sam had no idea Maurice had been generating this kind of volume for the firm. Granted, some of the files stretched back a few years, but it was still an impressive amount of cases. He checked his watch. It was already one thirty. Time was passing much faster than it felt. He had to get his arms around this as quickly as he could. He decided to search for Sarah's case. Since he was already somewhat familiar with it, it might help him understand what was going on.

It came up in a folder named "Real Cases." It was odd that he hadn't noticed that folder before and odd that a folder would be named "Real Cases." *Matthews* was in there and so was the case he had been assigned. He opened *Matthews* and saw the same documents and entries that he had seen in Simon's office. There was nothing new and nothing different. But his case was another story. Under the "Notes" section, Maurice had typed: "Blended case. First matter for Sam Morrow. Simon supervising. Evaluate in one month and consider bringing him in." What the hell did that mean? Sam thought. "Bringing him in." To what? Sam motioned for Sarah to come take a look. She made one last scan of the hall and walked over to the computer.

"That is strange," Sarah said after studying the screen. "What does he mean by 'real cases?'"

"I don't know. And what about 'bringing him in'? It sounds like some kind of a spy movie."

Sarah went back to her post as Sam continued opening files. They were all car accident cases. Lots and lots of them. Some were soft tissue injuries and some were life changing catastrophic injuries. Some involved many victims, some just one. Just about every kind of make and model of car was involved at just about every time of day, in every kind of weather, in just about every place in the city. The only commonality was that it was always CS & B representing the plaintiffs and Bicknel representing the defendants. Always. Sam walked to the door to tell Sarah what he had learned.

"Well, that's impossible," Sarah said. "There is absolutely no way that Bicknel could be on the other side of each one of these cases. Bicknel is just not that big a firm, much less the only firm in town. I don't know exactly how many lawyers they have, and they aren't listed in Martindale Hubbell, but I went by there the other day on my way home to serve my own set of discovery and the office left me underwhelmed. There was just a small reception area with crummy everything and a receptionist looking bored. I didn't even see anyone else. It reminded me of one of those old Western buildings with false fronts—even less there than met the eye."

"Interesting. Yeah, I had never even heard of Bicknel before your case. I will definitely do some major research on Bicknel and try and find out who and what the hell they are."

"I'll help," Sarah said and gave him a kiss on the cheek. "Better get back at it. The morning crew will be coming sooner than we want."

Sam spent the next hour or so opening files and comparing cases, but didn't learn anything more than he already knew. He was exhausted and he could see that Sarah was drooping as well. He was ready to call it a night when he scrolled by a folder called "Templates" that he had passed by earlier. For some reason, it looked much more interesting now than it had looked a few hours ago. He opened the folder and the files stood in neat, recognizable rows. There were templates for letterhead and various form letters, pleadings, discovery forms, corporate minutes and bylaws—just about everything any lawyer could possibly desire. Sam was intimately familiar with just about all of them. As he scrolled down further, he noticed that the templates started repeating. Sam hunched over the computer screen and studied the rows of files carefully. Except for some corporate and tax forms, Maurice had a complete set of duplicate templates. Sam anxiously opened the duplicate letterhead template. Instead of the elegantly scripted Cabot, Strickland & Baines letterhead he was expecting, "Bicknel Law Firm" screamed at him from the screen.

All of a sudden, he pushed back hard from the computer as if he'd been slapped, jumped up and ran for the door.

"Oh my God, Sarah. We were right. It's him!" Sam exclaimed as he grabbed Sarah by the shoulders and fixed his eyes intensely on hers. "Maurice is the 'M.' He's the one. Whatever it is, whatever they're doing, he's the guy Simon is reporting to." Sam was breathless with excitement and barely managed to squeeze the last sentence out before leaning hard against the doorjamb.

"What? Are you kidding? How?"

"Here. Come look at this." Sam led Sarah to the computer screen. "Bicknel Law Firm" stood out just as menacingly, splattered across the top of the letterhead in its bold, chunky type like it had when Sam first saw it in Simon's office.

Sarah gasped. "Bicknel. Bicknel Law Firm. He's part of Bicknel, too."

"Has to be," Sam agreed. "Otherwise, why would he have the letterhead on his computer?"

Together they opened a few more of the duplicate files. Everything was Bicknel. Bicknel pleading templates, discovery forms, even insurance company form letters. Sarah made a quick dash to the door to listen, but everything was quiet.

"What's this one?" Sarah asked when she returned. "It says, 'police reports.'"

"Well, let's open it and see."

"It's just like it says, a template for police accident reports," Sarah noted. "LA County. Looks official. Looks like any police report I've ever seen."

"Yeah, even down to the seal."

"What could Maurice possibly be doing with this?"

"No clue. Maybe . . ."

"Oh shit!" Sarah yelped as she sprang for the door. "There's someone coming!"

"Hit the lights! Run!"

Sarah raced for the lights as Sam logged off the computer, pushed the chair in, and dived for the closet with Sarah right behind. They closed the door and stood, panting, in the dark, trying desperately to tame their rapid breathing. Within a few seconds, they heard someone enter the office. They could hear one pair of heavy footsteps circling about the room. They would both agree later that it sounded like a man—a big man. It sounded like Maurice. Rustling papers. The sound of a file drawer being opened. Telephone messages being torn out of the spiral binder. It had to be Maurice. Sarah and Sam looked at each other in the light coming from underneath the door. They wore identical expressions of alarm and disbelief. Sam squeezed Sarah's hand in comfort and reassurance and she smiled as best she could in return. More file cabinets, more rustling, and then suddenly the sounds stopped. They waited expectantly for the light to go off. Sam checked his watch—3:30, then 3:35, 3:42, then 3:50 a.m., and still the light didn't go off. Sam was getting fidgety. He didn't know how much more of this he could take. Maurice had almost certainly just left the light on. That would be something Maurice would do. He would view energy conservation as beneath him, something that little people did. Definitely not something a 'king of the universe" would trouble himself with. Plus, it was getting late—far too late to be hiding in Maurice Strickland's closet. Sam silently asked Sarah if she wanted to risk it and go. She nodded yes. They opened the door ever so slowly and Sam peered out. No one. He listened. Nothing. He took Sarah's hand and together they walked out of the closet, down the hall, and back to Sam's office, where they collected their things as rapidly as they could and almost ran for the car.

As soon as they were in the car, all the tension erupted and they started talking a mile a minute.

"I can't believe what just happened. Oh my God," Sarah exclaimed. "It was right out of the movies!"

"I know. I know. What was the chance Maurice would actually come back to the office at three in the morning? I almost died."

"Me too. That just tells us more of what we already know: he's a wacko. Hey, what the hell happened with our little couch hanky-panky scenario? We both ended up in the closet."

"It's called panic. Anyway, it worked out OK. If he would have suspected anything, he would have checked the office. Probably the first place he would have looked would have been the closet, so I think we can feel pretty good about being undiscovered."

"I agree. I don't know what happened with the closet. All I know is that it worked out. If we got caught though, I was prepared to say we were just having a little fun on the couch and ran into the closet not to get caught playing hanky-panky. I think it was at least arguable."

"God, what a night. It's Maurice. 'M' is Maurice. We have to let that sink in. What does it mean? But more importantly, what the fuck is going on here? What's the deal with Bicknel and police accident reports? Does any of it make any sense?" Sam asked, looking thoroughly frustrated.

"No sense at all," Sarah said. "Right now the only thing I know for sure is that I love you." She turned to give Sam a kiss and her hand reached up subconsciously to touch her beautiful floating heart.

"Oh my God, it's gone!" Sarah cried out as her hand scoured frantically over her neck, chest, and the folds of her blouse. "It's not here! It's gone! It must have come off in Maurice's office when we ran to the closet. Or maybe it's in the closet. Oh God. It's gone!"

"Don't worry, honey," Sam said soothingly. "I'll get you another."

"Oh, Sam, it's not that. That heart was the first thing you ever gave me and you gave it to me on the night you said you loved me. It can never be replaced," Sarah said sadly as a tear started to cascade down her face.

"Yes, it can," Sam said emphatically. "It goes to the law of floating heart necklaces. If a lost floating heart is replaced within twenty-four hours of said loss with an identical heart, given in the same location with the same words spoken, then it actually becomes the original floating heart. The metamorphosis is so complete that if the original heart is subsequently found, it is determined to be dispossessed of any force and effect and is regarded merely as a pretty bauble that is required to be thrown off the bow of the most proximate large ship at midnight."

Sam stole a sideways glance at Sarah to see if his nonsense was having any impact and was rewarded with the beginnings of a reluctant little smile gently gracing the corners of her mouth.

"Do I really have to throw the original one off a ship if I find it?" Sarah asked wiping her cheek.

"Yes."

"At midnight?"

"Yes. It's the most important part of the law of floating heart necklaces," Sam said with mock sternness. "No exceptions."

"OK. I will agree to comply if the activating facts occur. But let the record show that my compliance will be given under duress."

"So noted."

They both laughed and Sarah reached over and kissed Sam lovingly on the cheek and reached for his hand as he drove. They sat quietly for a few minutes until Sarah suddenly dropped Sam's hand.

"But if I lost it in Maurice's office, he's probably going to be the one to find it," Sarah said anxiously. "He's going to know someone was in there. And he'll be able to find out who. All he has to do is check who was there after he left using the sign in/out sheet and check with security to see who used a keycard on his floor. There can't be that many names and one of them is going to be yours."

Sam felt a little sick. Sarah was right. His trail was easy to find and Maurice would find it. The only redeeming fact was that he was a guy and it was a necklace. Unless he checked the security cameras in the garage, he wouldn't know Sam had come in with a woman. He had been smart enough not to sign Sarah in at the front desk and the unfailingly incompetent building guards hadn't caught it. There was still a little hope.

"It's going to be fine. I didn't sign you in. Maurice won't know I was here with a woman. He'll be looking for someone who would wear a heart necklace and, last time I checked, that wouldn't be me."

"Good, good. We have a chance. Thank God there aren't cameras in the firm, just the garage."

"They're talking about putting them in the firm, but haven't done anything yet. I feel a thousand times better. Now if we can just figure out what in the hell is going on."

"We will. We just need to think outside the box. But more importantly, we need to decide on some serious breakfast right now."

"I hear you. IHOP on the right. Pancakes here we come."

If they knew that Maurice had just been at that same IHOP less than ten minutes ago, they would no doubt have lost their appetites. But by this time, Maurice was wending his way home, thinking of the delicious night he had enjoyed and the many more to come. He put Natalya's number in the stack of phone messages he had retrieved from the office and concentrated on his driving. He had done what he needed to do on Simon's computer and would call his friends over at the precinct as soon as it was a more reasonable hour. He wasn't sure who would love the arrest more. He would love it because it was Simon and Simon had caused him just a little too much angst lately. The cops would love it because it was some fancy pants lawyer going down in flames. In any event, it was definitely going to be one of his most excellent days. And he was going to enjoy every minute of it.

◆ ◆ ◆

Meanwhile, Simon had left the office at two thirty in the morning and made trips to various ATMs to get as much cash as he could from all his accounts in case everything went down the shitter. As much as he wanted to believe it all was going to be OK, there was a huge part of him that didn't believe Sam would go along with any of it, even when faced with the virtually insurmountable frame job Maurice was sure to do on him. No, he had no choice. He had to be ready to escape to Argentina in a heartbeat. He had gathered as much evidence as he could and emailed it all to his home computer. When he got home, he would transfer everything onto two disks. One he would put in his safe deposit box at the bank, with instructions to send it to the police if anything happened to him. The other disk he would send to his contact in Argentina in case he ended up having to make a break for it. He couldn't believe he hadn't thought of collecting evidence earlier. What a fucking idiot he was. He knew Maurice's true colors right from the start. His method of recruitment told Simon everything he needed to know about who Maurice was and he had done absolutely nothing to protect himself. Well, at least he was doing something about it now. He pulled into his driveway at about half past three, still buzzing with adrenaline. Within five minutes, he was in front of his computer ready to copy. He turned on the monitor and logged onto his computer. There they were in his inbox, a veritable swarm of emails with files attached. He felt limp with anticipation. Just a few more minutes and he would be safer than he had been in a long time. But as soon as he opened the first email, he knew something was terribly wrong. The screen went instantly blank and then the computer itself went silent. There was no hum, no buzzing, no sound or activity of any kind. He felt a lump of hysteria beginning to rise in his throat as he stared at the screen. And then he was on automatic, springing into frantic action, rebooting, turning the computer on and off, unplugging it, doing anything he could think of to bring the computer back to life. But it remained dark and dead. And he was starting to feel the same way.

He stopped his frenzied machinations and sat quietly in front of the screen. And in the quietness, he remembered Maurice admonishing him not to send those files out of the office to any other source for any reason. Now he knew why. Of course, he would get his computer guy to come out and try to resuscitate the computer, but he was 99 percent certain what the outcome would be. He suddenly felt very old and very tired. As the exhaustion from the last forty-eight hours finally overwhelmed him, he fell asleep where he sat, the screen blankly staring back.

CHAPTER TWENTY-FIVE

Just as Simon was going to sleep, Marion was waking up. She had slept fitfully, dreaming uncomfortable dreams. When she awoke, she woke with a start, her last dream still available to recall. She was alone in a very narrow, shoebox kind of room that had only one tiny slat of a window at the very top of one of the walls. She could hardly breathe. Her head was spinning. She was beyond claustrophobia and was reaching a state of panic. She rushed to the walls, pouring over them with her hands, desperately looking for an exit. Suddenly, a small wooden door appeared. But the minute she turned the knob, it vanished into the wall and she was left alone, trapped and terrified.

She lay on her sweat-soaked pillow, trying to figure out what any of it meant and finally just attributed it to new surroundings and the scare of the last few days. She got up to splash some cool water on her face and realized, in the gray morning light, that the apartment had a distinct shoebox kind of shape to it. As if on cue, she started to perspire.

"Don't be so dramatic," she told herself. "This is an apartment, not some bad dream. Get over it." She scanned the apartment with a dispassionate eye and willed herself to relax. But even so, she still felt a tug of claustrophobia and wondered if there was more to it. She thought about all the changes that had happened so abruptly and how her life had changed irretrievably, forever. She let herself feel bad.

She loved Paul. She would always love him. She watched him with a smile as he lay sleeping, her heart full of tenderness and prayers for him. She hoped he would heal soon. She wondered if she would ever again live the kind of life she had been living. She thought about her beautiful house and all the exquisite things she had found to put in it. She wondered if she would ever see any of it again. And then she thought maybe there was a way that she could. If she could have just a few of her most precious pieces, she knew she would feel better, she would feel more at home. With just a few things, she might be able to chase away the shoebox. She decided to make one last trip to her house.

CHAPTER TWENTY-SIX

Simon woke with a jolt as his arm dropped down and nicked the chair leg. Nothing had changed. The computer was still dead. He got up and walked outside in the hope that the pre-dawn coolness would clear his head and shake the demons from his heart. But the air seemed cold and inhospitable, and it did nothing to dispel his darkness. He waited for the sun. No matter what horror mankind was wreaking on the earth, it never disappointed. It always appeared, where and when it was supposed to. Predictable. Certain. Secure. Comforts he needed desperately right now. He hoped the sun would bestow even the most meager portion on him. But the sun was mute with her gifts and, for the first time in his life, Simon felt completely and infinitely alone.

He was terrified of his future. He had to assume that Maurice knew what he had tried to do. Maurice wouldn't go through all the trouble of setting up a major bomb like that on the computers and then fail to install an automatic alert. No way. Maurice probably knew what he was doing the second he e-mailed his first file. And if Maurice knew that, he was most likely planning some kind of unpleasant outcome for Simon right now. The truth smacked Sam right between the eyes and sucked the air out of him. He knew that he had no choice. He was out of time. He had to save himself.

"Maurice? Simon. Sorry to call you so early, but it's important. It's about Sam Morrow."

Maurice had been expecting the call. The moment his iPhone confirmed that Simon was attempting to e-mail files, he knew a call would necessarily be forthcoming. Maurice moved out of the hallway and into his most comfortable chair in the study. It would be interesting to hear how Simon was going to make the worm turn.

"Don't worry about it. Any time is the right time when it's important." Nice touch, he thought. What a fabulous team player he was.

"Thank you. Anyway, I didn't think this could wait. I caught Sam Morrow poking around on my computer in our special files."

It was Maurice's turn to be startled. "Sam Morrow? When? How did he get in?"

"I have no idea. All I know is that I came to the office late two nights ago to pick up some documents and I found Sam on my computer searching through our files. I don't know how long he had been there or what he had discovered. I got him out as quickly as I could by making some noises down the hall and giving him the opportunity to escape, which he took, but not before closing down the computer. So I really don't know which specific files he was looking at. All I know is that he was in our private files."

"Fuck. Why are you just telling me about this now? And

how did he get your password? Did you leave it out? Did you fucking tell him what it was?" Maurice almost screamed the last sentence he was so pissed. It had to be Simon's fault. There was no way Sam could have figured out Simon's password on his own. Simon must have told him, either intentionally or inadvertently. Fucking idiot. Maurice couldn't wait for him to be gone.

Simon was flabbergasted. This was not how this call was supposed to be going at all. He was expecting congratulations for first, discovering Sam and then getting him out quickly before doing any more damage. He couldn't believe Maurice was blaming him for any of it. "I . . . uh . . . no, I didn't leave my password out. It's not written down anywhere. Absolutely no one knows it but me. He just figured it out on his own."

"I find that very hard to believe. Either you gave it to him, were so sloppy that you left it out, or are so stupid that you picked a password that anyone could figure out. In any event, you're in very deep fucking trouble." Maurice spat the words out, intending them to do as much damage as possible.

By this time, Simon was visibly shaken. Everything had gone to shit. He felt like a snake on the highway, each passing truck running over a piece of him until there was nothing left except his small, sad little head. A part of him could hear Maurice still carrying on, but a larger part was detached, recalibrating the changed circumstances in his mind. The more he thought, the stronger he got. He was down, but he wasn't dead. Not yet. He still had one hope left. Argentina. He tuned back into Maurice's tirade just as Maurice was winding down.

"So that's what we're going to do. Hector will be there in five minutes to pick you up and take you to the office where you'll wait for Sam and take him over to The Lucky Seven. I'll bring him in just like I brought you in. It'll be one happy little family. You will tell Sam nothing other than you two have a meeting that just came up. I will take care of the rest when we're all together."

"OK, Maurice. Whatever you say."

When Maurice spoke again, his voice was much softer and sounded almost normal. "Maybe it's not such a bad thing after all, Simon." He paused while he appeared to ruminate. "My profit was starting to get limited by lack of attorney help. I was going to bring him in eventually, just not quite this fast. Maybe it's not bad that it happened now."

Simon's ears perked up. Maybe there was hope for him still. Argentina was, after all, not his first choice. Maybe it could work out and they could all just keep working together and make lots of money. The wrench in the plan was, of course, Sam. Simon issued a silent prayer that Sam would just accept his fate, take it in stride, and become one of them. But deep in his heart, he knew that was extraordinarily unlikely.

He closed his phone and went inside to change his clothes and brew a quick cup of coffee. Hector was at the curb before he was done.

◆ ◆ ◆

Now refueled with pancakes and coffee, Sarah and Sam were even more riled up by what they had seen. Too agitated to sleep, they had decided to go home and change clothes, get the work done that needed to be done at their respective offices, and reconvene later to plan their next move.

Sarah practically glided into her apartment. She knew she must be exhausted, but she was still so high on adrenaline that she felt she could go another week without sleep. She had never felt the way she did in her whole life and she prayed that it would never end. She quickly showered, changed, and made her way into the office. If she focused on what she absolutely had to get done, with Christine's help, she could be done by three. With a few hours sleep, she could be with Sam again by seven or eight. Just thinking of Sam brought a luminous smile to her face. Maybe she could get done even earlier. She dictated a few letters, finished drafting a small breach of contract complaint, and had just enough time to make it to court for the *Matthews* eight thirty status conference without a mad dash. But it wasn't until she got to the courtroom that she realized she had drawn Judge Schneider. She had been so busy and involved with Sam that she hadn't checked the assignment when it came in. No matter. There was nothing she could have done about it anyway. At least this way she saved a few moments of premature worry and teeth gnashing. She checked the calendar and saw that hers was the last case of the morning. Great, she thought sarcastically. Since Schneider didn't let lawyers come and go from his courtroom, she could plan on at least an hour of wait time before her matter came up. She started working on some papers she had brought, but her attention, which was usually so reliable, kept wafting up to the bench. Finally, after a few frustrating minutes, Sarah put down her papers and watched the proceedings to try and find out what was diverting her attention.

From her perch at the back of the courtroom she couldn't hear everything that was being said, but she could clearly hear the court orders. Curiously, every order was the same. Discovery cut-off dates, trial dates, settlement conference dates were all the same. It was if Schneider was using a pro forma template to move identical cases through the pipeline. Then she noticed that the same two lawyers kept appearing for the plaintiff and the defendant. Nine cases had been heard and in each case, it was the same two lawyers. She strained to hear the names of the firms and, only hearing pieces, moved up a few rows to hear more clearly.

"Thomas Cook appearing on behalf of Cabot Strickland & Baines for the plaintiff."

"Jerrod Moore appearing on behalf of the Bicknel Law Firm for the defendant."

Sarah was stunned. She sat motionless, frozen by what was playing out right in front of her. Eventually, she was able to reach her legal pad and a pen and wrote down the names of the cases and lawyers she was hearing. There were only two more cases before her case. She started to notice something else strange—Judge Schneider. He wasn't his usual churlish self. He was almost jovial, joking with the two lawyers and acting collegial instead of like an impartial judge. Quite unusual and, Sarah thought, inappropriate. She began collecting her things to walk to the lectern and make her appearance, but as soon as the case right before hers concluded, Judge Schneider immediately stood up and walked out of the courtroom, as did the two lawyers at the counsel tables. Sarah gathered her things and walked briskly to the clerk.

"Excuse me. I'm Sarah Brockman and I'm here for case no. 10 on the eight thirty calendar. I'm wondering how long it's going to be before the judge returns."

The clerk looked surprised and started nervously flipping through some kind of court-generated schedule. "Oh, I'm sorry, but there must be some kind of mistake," she said sheepishly. "What case did you say you were here on?"

"*Matthews v. Rodriguez.*

"Oh. Well, you're not supposed to be here. That case is scheduled for next Tuesday, April 5th at 8:30 a.m."

"I don't mind coming back, but you can see my court notice," Sarah said as she thrust the paper into the clerk's hand. "It says today."

The clerk appeared even more nervous and the paper began to quiver ever so slightly in her hand. "Like I said, there's a mistake. Next Tuesday at eight thirty." She handed the paper back to Sarah as if it was a hot potato and walked as quickly as she could out of the courtroom and into the private judicial chambers in back.

Sarah stood there. Something weird was going on. She didn't know what it was, but felt certain it wasn't just her imagination. She wasn't supposed to have been here today and she wasn't supposed to have witnessed what she did. That seemed clear from the clerk's reaction. But what did she witness? She really didn't know. She saw Schneider being uncharacteristically nice to two lawyers who were representing lots of clients. What did it mean? Why was the clerk so queer? She had no answers to any of these questions, but knew she wanted to tell Sam as soon as possible. She walked purposively out of the courtroom and onto the street, where she placed a call to Sam on his cell phone. No answer. She called his office. No answer, but it rang through to his secretary.

"Good morning, Joanne. This is Sarah. I'm looking for Sam. Has he made it in yet?"

"Oh, hi Sarah. Yes, he's already been in and gone. He went to a meeting with Simon out of the office. I don't know how long he'll be. Do you want to leave a message?"

"Yes, thank you, Joanne. Just tell him I called and to call me as soon as he can." Sarah closed her phone and stood motionless as a feeling of dread washed over her body. She called Joanne back.

"Joanne? Hi, Sarah again. Sorry to bother you, but do you happen to know where the meeting is?"

"No bother at all, but I don't know. Just some place out of the office."

"I understand. Thanks again." She placed a call to Simon's secretary, but she wasn't coming in until noon and by then the meeting would probably be over. She felt impotent and at a loss about what to do. She left another message on Sam's phone and drove back to her office, willing her phone to ring.

◆ ◆ ◆

Finally, Maurice had convinced himself that the whole situation was not only manageable, but preferred. Why wait to bring Sam in anyway? He had picked him because he was almost perfect for the job in skill set and situation. The only characteristic Sam lacked was an apparent lack of greed. Greed was what got Simon over the hump and greed was what made this whole business flourish. Maurice wasn't sure Sam had the deep pool of greed required to thrive in Maurice's world, but he would certainly find out.

He got to the office in plenty of time to do what he needed to do on Sam's computer. Hector had already taken Simon and Sam over to The Lucky Seven with a stop for breakfast on the way. That would give him enough time to work his sleight of hand on the computer. It was amazing how far a little computer expertise could carry you, Maurice thought cheerfully. With Sam on board, he would make even more money. He really could be king of the world. Maurice stopped by his office to drop off his emergency tuxedo and fresh shirt. Just part of good planning, he thought, as he fingered the condoms in his pocket. There was a chance he would see Natalya later and even a chance would motivate him to be prepared. He slipped the tuxedo into the closet and turned on the light to make sure it hung straight and wouldn't wrinkle later. As he adjusted the sleeves, he saw something sparkling on the floor and bent down to find a heart necklace. He placed it flat in his hand and noted the beautiful curves and design. He also noted the diamonds. His jaw tightened as he stared at the piece in his hand. This was not something a cleaning woman would have lost. It was also something that wasn't here yesterday when he took his tuxedo from the closet or he would have seen it then. No. Whoever lost it, lost it last night. And that meant that someone was in his office, after hours, doing god knows what. The necklace also meant that it was a woman.

He scoured his brain for evidence of the necklace on anyone at the firm. The woman had to work at the firm. Even the mediocre security team that the building provided wouldn't let someone without proper credentials into Cabot Strickland & Baines. He didn't think he had ever seen the necklace before. He liked to think he would have remembered it, since he was a bit of a connoisseur concerning gems and jewelry, and prided himself on noticing details. No, he had never seen it. No matter. All he had to do was check the sign-out sheet. Even if the person had come during business hours and just stayed late, the sign-out sheet would show who was here after hours. He paged the head of security and had the sheets on his desk within five minutes. There were fourteen women who had signed out after hours last night. He made photocopies of the relevant pages and then called Ahmad to see who had used their security card on his floor. Six names. All associates. Not one who was suspicious in any way. In fact, he barely knew four of them and the other two were juniors who seemed to be content to put in their hours, collect their paychecks, and go home. One other name, however, caught his eye. Sam Morrow. He came in at eight and left at 3:50 a.m. Of course he had used his security card on Maurice's floor since it was Sam's floor as well, so that didn't help one way or the other. But 3:50 a.m.? That was an odd time to be leaving the firm, especially since Maurice monitored Sam's workload and knew that he wasn't so busy as to require almost an all-nighter to get his work done. Most telling, of course, was that Sam had been snooping on Simon's computer and had found his way into the secret files. Last time he checked though, Sam hadn't taken to wearing jewelry. Nevertheless, Maurice had to assume it was him. Sam could easily have made it by the downstairs security without signing a woman companion in. God knows, he had done it enough times himself. If Sam had been in his office, he had been in it for one purpose only—to tie him to Simon and whatever scheme Simon was involved in. There simply was no legitimate reason for Sam to be there. The thought gave Maurice pause. He moved deliberately to the computer, where he flipped on the monitor and began running the advanced history search he had installed a few months ago. His computer savant had suggested it and, God knows, Maurice took everything Vincent said to heart. He was, as usual, delighted that he had.

He pulled the computer use history from the time he left the office the night before until this morning and winced as it came up. Three full columns of opened files leered at him from the screen—each one of them part of his private enterprise. Goddammit. That fucking Sam Morrow. Why couldn't he just have left it alone? But as he asked himself the question, he already knew the answer. Because it was Sam Morrow. Had he taken the time to really think it through before he had so impetuously appropriated Sam, he would have known that Sam was not the man for the job. He now remembered how important service and pro bono work was to Sam and how that was why he had selected CS & B in the first place. A person like that simply doesn't do the kind of work he required. He would have recognized that if he hadn't been so unbalanced at the time. He knew he had made a stunning error in judgment. But the difference was that this one could cost him everything. He sat back heavily in his chair and contemplated his options. There always were options. Sometimes you just had to look a little deeper.

◆ ◆ ◆

By this time, Simon and Sam had finished their coffee and Hector was just about done with his steak and eggs. Sam still didn't understand why they had left the office so early and why Hector was with them at all, but he knew and liked Hector. He figured it would all be explained soon enough. He was more concerned about Simon. Simon was acting strangely. He seemed preoccupied and hyper, almost manic. Sam decided it could be a consequence of the pain pills he was on, but resolved to watch Simon carefully. Finally, they were ready to go.

"So, Sam. Do you see the world as black and white or with a bit of grey thrown it?" Simon was resuscitating a conversation he had started at the beginning of coffee. "I mean, do you think that basically good people can sometimes behave a little off the mark and still be good people?" Simon asked earnestly as if he truly cared about Sam's answer.

"I think good people sometimes do bad things and vice versa, I suppose. And I think there's a lot of gray. Sometimes goodness itself is a moving target."

Simon visibly relaxed. It was if he had been holding his breath. "Yeah, that's what I think too. And sometimes things happen that you don't expect, and they snowball and get out of control and you hope everyone remembers that you tried to do the right thing, even though it may not come out exactly as you wanted." Simon spewed out the words with such intensity and frenzy that both Sam and Hector turned to stare at him.

"Calm down, Simon," Sam said. "I think those pain pills are really whacking you out. After the meeting, I think you better go home and chill yourself out a little."

Sam's look, even more than his words, catapulted Simon back into a closer state of normalcy, and he mentally regrouped and took himself firmly in hand. "Boy are you right, Sam," he said as he managed a nervous little laugh. "I guess those little pills have got the best of me. I think I will take a few days after the meeting and get better."

"Well advised," Sam agreed.

Hector studied both of them behind the cover of his sunglasses. Something was definitely up, he thought. He didn't know what it was, but whatever it was, it was making Simon quite nervous. He determined to ramp up his own antennae and defenses. He checked his watch and hurriedly finished his last few bites as they made their way out to the car. His instructions were to drive them to The Lucky Seven, come in, and wait for Maurice to arrive. Simon was to field any questions from Sam.

As they drove into the seedier part of town, Hector checked Sam in the rear view mirror and could see him begin to look puzzled and then concerned.

"Where are we going?" Sam finally asked.

"To a club Maurice owns. It's major league ratty, but he wanted you to see it, since you'll be working on a case involving it," Simon said glibly. By this time, he had regained his composure and re-convinced himself that this was the best choice for Sam. After all, Sam was the one who got himself into this mess in the first place. He should have just left well enough alone.

"Oh. That makes sense. What kind of case is it?"

Simon was now on a roll. "It's a breach of contract involving the seller's failure to perform certain contingencies in the initial deal. I think Maurice is trying to sell it now, so he wants any legal issues resolved immediately."

"Interesting. Sounds like fun, but this neighborhood is a dump."

"Wait till you see the club." And they all laughed.

The club was every bit as bad as Sam imagined it. Not only did it look thoroughly unkempt and dilapidated, but it had a kind of sleazy air about it. Certainly not the kind of place Sam could envision Maurice owning. The inside was even worse. Broken bottles and glass were strewn everywhere and there were only a few chairs he could even imagine sitting in. Hopefully, he'd get one of those, he thought. The more he looked around, the more unsettled he became. What was he doing here? Why was Hector with them? And where was Maurice?

"What's next? Do I need to do a full tour or is a general idea sufficient?"

"No. This will do. We'll just hang and wait for Maurice, who should be joining us directly. He's actually been really good about time lately, so it shouldn't be long."

Just as Simon said that, Maurice walked through the door. Sam felt an involuntary stiffening as he watched Maurice come in. God, he had to get over that, he thought.

"Good morning, everyone," Maurice called out as he approached. "Thank you so much for coming out to see my little Shangri-La."

"My pleasure," Sam and Simon said almost in unison as Hector mumbled something from the back of the room.

"Please take a seat and we'll begin."

Sam quickly appropriated the best seat closest to him and Simon did the same. Maurice continued to stand.

"As Simon no doubt told you, you believe I invited you here to gain important background information for a new case. That's a lie. The truth is I've brought you here to radically alter your career path forever." Maurice paused to give Sam a moment to absorb what he was saying.

"You see, Sam, I require your services in my most profitable litigation group, one that you've never heard of and one that brings in almost 25 percent of the firm's revenue. It's called the Insurance Fraud Group."

Sam was stunned. He couldn't say anything. He felt like he was trapped in some super slow-mo underwater nightmare.

Maurice was just warming up. He took his jacket off and swung his leg up onto a chair, much like a professor informally lecturing to an intimate coterie of students. "It started about seven years ago, as a natural outgrowth of my personal injury practice. I had started to do auto accident cases a few years earlier as a lark, but when I saw how much money could be made, and how easily, I decided to actively get into the business. It was simple and lucrative, but had its share of headaches, like anything else. One day it hit me that the reason there were so many problems was because there were too many variables involved. If I could just reduce some of the variables, it would be perfect. And so I did. I began manufacturing car accidents. We'd send a couple guys out in cars and trucks and they would cause accidents to occur. Your friend Paul Rodriguez was part of that first version of my business model and, now that I think about it, actually one of my first hires." Maurice paused as if reminiscing about some high school glory days.

"Anyway, eventually I determined that the business model was flawed and inefficient in many ways as well, and that I needed to take clients and accidents out of it completely. That's when I hit on the 'accident-free accident.'" Maurice smiled indulgently.

"It was brilliant, if I say so myself. Why actually have accidents if you can manufacture accident paperwork? Of course, I needed to have both sides of the equation within my control. Otherwise defense lawyers would go looking for plaintiffs and smashed cars that literally didn't exist. And, voila, the Bicknel Law Firm was born. All the plaintiff work was done from my personal injury department at CS & B, while all the defense work was done by Bicknel, who were also my lawyers, working out of CS & B with a sham office for deliveries and whatnot. So both the fictitious plaintiffs and defendants were represented by me, just wearing different hats. You might be thinking, how can something like this work logistically? And the answer, like all answers in life and business, is merely a function of a little financial lubrication. It goes like this: I would decide that it was time for another accident. One of my colleagues would create all the paperwork required for a proper accident, namely, an accident report, hospital invoices, doctors' bills, physical therapy bills, towing costs, car storage, and any other charges. The 'victims' were easily created with the help of legal assistants I had financially befriended in the three big insurance companies with whom I have the pleasure of doing business. The legal assistants not only created the files for the fictitious insured victims, but also referred the cases to my Bicknel Law Firm." Maurice paused and smiled, clearly relishing the opportunity to share the story of his brilliance.

"Plus, I found I needed a little assistance on the bench, in the prosecutor's office, and at the police department. But, like I said, all these problems were easily solved with a little cash. Of course, I needed to keep my numbers within each insurance company's requirements and make sure that there was always a tidy balance between the CS & B plaintiffs and Bicknel defendants. A settlement in favor of the plaintiffs normally meant a generous one-third contingency fee for me and the firm and, in the cases where the defense needed to win, I at least made my hourly billables. So you see, I couldn't lose; it was always a win-win for me. It was just a question of how much."

Maurice stood, smugly, in perfect communion with his universe, arms crossed haughtily over his chest. "Oh," he continued. "I also kept my legit plaintiffs practice going for even more extra cash and to test out people like you before bringing them over to work in my little money factory." Maurice chuckled and forced himself to stop enjoying his elocution long enough to gage Sam's response to his new world. But Sam wasn't about to reveal any of the thousand thoughts that were coursing through his brain, and he remained expressionless and unreadable. It all made perfect sense, Sam thought. Of course Maurice was the mastermind. No one else possessed such voracious greed and hubris. He probably could have figured it out with one more shot at Maurice's computer. But now he had bigger problems to deal with. Couldn't he just say "no?" He shot a sideways glance at Simon. Where did Simon figure into all of this? Was Simon one of them or the Simon he knew as his best friend? Who the hell *was* Simon?

Sam refocused his attention back on Maurice as Maurice continued his discourse. "So, you should be pleased to know that of all the associates in the firm, I picked you to be the next to join us," Maurice said smiling expansively. "Oh, and by the way, if you think you have any choice in this, you would be tragically mistaken. I have taken the liberty of adjusting your computer so that it appears as though you have committed innumerable fraudulent and criminal acts already. If you went to the authorities, you would incriminate yourself to a tune of about seventy-five years. And forget about trying to implicate me. All evidence on my computer, Simon's computer, and the computers of all my colleagues can be wiped out by me with the simple touch of a few keystrokes which, I have been informed, I can now do from a remote location. So your evidence against me would be reduced to some court filings and testimony from Simon that I assure you, you'll never get."

Well, at least that answers one of his questions, Sam thought dismally: Simon was with Maurice. Simon, who had been his best friend and confidante for more than six years. He felt more crushed by this news than anything he had heard so far. He felt like their entire friendship had been a sham. Sam struggled to keep himself under control and focused. He could mourn later; right now he had to save himself. He ticked through his options. He could refuse to do it and, depending on the quality of Maurice's frame job, face jail time, loss of his license, and an unknown chunk of his life. He could agree to join Maurice and risk getting caught, which would leave him with the very same consequences, or he could pretend to join Maurice and try and build a case against him over time. But did he really have any options at all? Out of the corner of his eye, he could see Hector milling around in the back of the room. Why *was* Hector here, Sam thought uneasily. There was no security explanation he could think of that made any sense. Was there some other innocent explanation, or was Hector here to enforce compliance? For the first time, Sam felt physically afraid. He wondered how far Maurice would go to protect himself and his enterprise. He decided to appear to go along and try and reflect upon his options later. Maurice had effectively eliminated any other choice.

"What do I get out of it?" Sam asked in his strongest voice. "I mean, say I come on board and go along with your program. What's in it for me?"

At that moment, Simon knew Sam wasn't coming in. He knew his friend almost as well as he knew himself and he knew that Sam would never care about the money. But what Maurice didn't know, Simon wouldn't tell. He could see that Maurice was skeptical. He hoped Sam saw it, too. Thankfully, he did.

"I need money now. My mother needs to go into a special nursing home to care for her MS. Insurance will only cover part and we can't cover the rest. I need money," Sam said again for emphasis. "And I need it now."

Simon watched Maurice carefully and could see him accept the explanation. If there was any reservation on his part, it was most likely slight.

"Well, OK," Maurice said as he seemed to warm further to the prospect of Sam joining his little club. "There are impressive monetary benefits to our group. Simon can fill in the details, but suffice it to say, you will make at least $200,000 your first year in addition to your regular salary and bonus at CS & B. Not bad for a little paperwork, right?"

"Not bad at all. But you know, this isn't how I thought my life would go." And the sentence hung suspended in the dark and filthy room for a few seconds too long as Simon and a small, quiet part of Maurice silently conceded the same thing.

"OK then," Maurice said petulantly, breaking the spell. "Let's get on with it. I want Hector to stay here and do some clean up work for me. You two take his car back to the firm. I'll be in touch."

Sam almost squealed for joy the moment he stepped foot outside the club. There was a large portion of his subconscious that wasn't sure he would ever see the outside world again. He would deal with Simon somehow on the ride back, although he wasn't sure exactly where to begin. But for this moment, it was enough just to be alive.

Maurice watched through the window as the car pulled away from the club and then speed-dialed a familiar number.

"Yeah, Sandy? Maurice. We're going to have to go ahead. The newbie didn't bite. He's probably trying to find some way to get to the cops right now, even with Simon in the car. You know where to pick them up. Do your best work."

Maurice pocketed his phone and looked around for Hector.

"Hector, finish cleaning up this mess. Your guy didn't do the kind of job he should have done, so now it's up to you."

"Will do. Sorry about that. I thought Williams was good."

"Guess not. Oh, and thanks for all the background information you pulled up on our friend Sam Morrow. It came in handy right now."

"Yeah, I know. But why'd he pick his mother? They're so easy. I know everything there is to know about her. I got another quarter inch of paper on her that I didn't even show you."

"I guess every boy still thinks of his mommy in times of stress."

"Well, it's definitely one of those times."

Maurice watched for a moment as Hector began working, thinking what a waste it was to spend hours cleaning up a place that would be gone by morning. But he needed him out of the car and this was the best way to do it. No matter what kind of cleaning job Hector did, the fact was there was just too much evidence all over The Lucky Seven. In addition to the blood and tissue DNA, which you could never really scrub away, there were lots and lots of fingerprints from people who would soon be dead. Better to torch the place and collect the insurance. By the time anybody in the police department would even think of making any connection, the evidence would be long gone. Maurice congratulated himself on his composure under pressure and unfailingly nimble mind. He had found the only viable solution to the problem at hand and he had seized it and set it in motion. He stood proudly erect as he thought how strong a man he was. He was a gutsy man with brass balls and a strong stomach, who did what he needed to do to get the job done. He picked up his briefcase, scanned the bar one last time, and headed for the door.

Hector thought nothing of it. Even if he hadn't known Sam's mother was alive and perfectly healthy, he would have known Sam was lying by his body language right away. Sam had done as convincing a job as he could muster and, Hector had to admit, it was pretty good for a novice. But that was the point; he was a beginner, and Hector was a pro. He casually considered what Maurice was going to do about this predicament. No doubt he had something else up his sleeve. Maurice never went into any situation without a plan B. He most likely had even more damaging dirt to throw at Sam that even Hector didn't know about. For as much under-the-radar work as he did for Maurice, Hector knew there was an unknown contractor who did even more. He couldn't wait until this was over, he thought, as he scrubbed even more specks of blood off the floor. He could see the light at the end of the tunnel; he could begin to feel how he was going to feel when it was all over. He just needed to keep himself together for a few more days.

◆ ◆ ◆

Sarah knew something was horribly wrong. She didn't know what it was, but she could feel it deep down in her stomach. The feeling had started with the meeting. Although it normally wouldn't have seemed strange to her that a lawyer would be called to a last minute meeting out of the office, in this case it did. She had tried to convince herself she was just being paranoid, but when no one knew where the meeting was and when she couldn't reach Sam on his cell phone, her concern ramped up to full blown worry. There was absolutely nothing she could do but wait. And waiting was not a skill she had. She paced the floor in her office until Christine came in to find out what was going on and offered to help.

"I can't really go into it right now," Sarah said. "But I'm feeling really stressed and worried and I don't know what to do with all this energy."

"I understand if you don't want to talk about it, but then you should do what you usually do when you're wound up. Do something. I don't know what that is in this situation, but I do know that that's the only thing that helps."

"Of course you're right. I've got to do something or I'll make myself and everyone else around here nuts. Let me think about it. Thanks for your help," Sarah said appreciatively. "You're terrific."

Christine closed the door behind her as Sarah considered what action she could take to move the ball forward in their investigation. If she couldn't use the computers at CS & B, the only connection she had was Paul Rodriguez. He was being defended by the Bicknel Law Firm. There had to be some relationship between her case and Maurice and Simon. Plus, they had to find some evidence apart from the computers at the firm.

Memories could be erased, even hard drives could be taken out. As it stood right now, they had nothing. The problem was, of course, that Paul Rodriguez was missing. She decided to drive by his apartment and see if any neighbors might have an idea where Paul had gone. She felt much better having made a decision to do something, and she grabbed her purse and headed quickly for her car.

Sarah found the apartment with no trouble and resolutely knocked on the surrounding doors. Of six apartments, only two answered her knock and they didn't even know who Paul Rodriguez was. Apparently, he had been a very private resident.

She made her way over to the house held in Marion's name on Timberline Road, checking her messages every few minutes and periodically calling Sam's iPhone. Still no word. She pulled up in front of the house and fully understood what Duane meant when he said it was "spectacular." It was. Even though the stack of newspapers at the door was clear evidence that no one had been home, the grounds were in perfect shape. Obviously the gardeners didn't yet know they weren't getting paid. The house was set back from the street and encircled by a six-foot, pinkish hued masonry wall that was just beginning to play host to a smattering of ivy and other creeping vines. Sarah could barely see the neighbors' houses from where she stood on the sidewalk, and from the inside of the compound, she expected they were completely invisible. Not a bad set up, she thought. Especially for someone who wanted privacy.

She leaned against the wrought iron gate to get a better look at the house and felt it move under her weight. It was open. She took a few furtive glances around her and darted inside. She moved cautiously toward the house. She wondered what Sam would think if he knew what she was doing and decided that he wouldn't be pleased. They were already at the point in their relationship where he watched out for her and was proprietary about her safety. This bit of amateur sleuthing would make him even more nervous than it was making her, and that was saying a lot. Her adrenaline was on overdrive and she could feel her heart beating out of her chest, but she kept going. She easily made her way up the side of the driveway and to the house, where she started peering into windows looking for anything that might help her find the Rodriguezes. The house was just as gorgeous inside as it was out and, thanks to the bright LA day, she could see a number of furnishings surprisingly clearly. She looked as carefully and as quickly as she could through the front windows that were visible from the street and moved to the right side of the house where the low-hanging wisteria gave her even more cover. She could see pictures of what must be Marion and Paul in Mexico with the town of "Escondido" prominent in most. She noted Escondido as a likely target and moved to the next window. As she did, she heard the unmistakable creak of the iron front gate opening. She dived behind the oleander bushes that lined the back side yard and cautiously poked her head around some of the thinner branches for a view. A small grey compact pulled up the driveway and parked immediately in front of the door. After a brief delay, a young, pretty Latin looking woman emerged from the car and walked briskly to the front door, unlocked it easily and, with a quick backward glance, disappeared inside.

Sarah was almost giddy with excitement. What was the chance Marion Rodriguez would show up at her house during the exact few minutes that Sarah was there? So low she wouldn't even have taken odds on it, Sarah thought. And it was Marion Rodriguez; Sarah recognized her from the pictures. If she followed her, chances are Marion would take her to Paul. They had fled together, so they were most likely hiding out together. Sarah stood up to a crouch position behind the oleander and planned her exit. She could remain hidden by foliage almost the entire way and, if she moved quickly, she would have very little exposure. She took a deep breath and headed, as quickly and as quietly as she could, to the gate, which she opened easily and ran through. She was in her car in thirty seconds flat. Sarah slunk down in the driver's seat and waited. She didn't have to wait long. Within ten minutes, the grey compact swung out of the driveway and drove right past her. Sarah waited an appropriate amount of time and took a position about five car lengths behind her. It was easy earlier on, but as Marion drove onto the freeway and then to a busy side street, Sarah almost lost track of her several times. Eventually, Marion drove into a particularly nondescript apartment complex and parked at the door to room number six. Sarah stopped a safe distance away and watched as Marion entered the apartment. A second later, she was at the large bay widow, surveying the pool scene below her. In another second, Paul Rodriguez walked over to Marion and gave her a kiss.

Sarah sat in complete disbelief. She wasn't used to manna falling from heaven. She had never thought of herself as a particularly lucky person, but that had totally changed today. She carefully noted the address and even the specific route Marion had taken to get here. No doubt it was the most direct. She called Sam again, desperate to reach him.

"Sam, Sam, pick up, please!" She screamed in frustration.

◆ ◆ ◆

Sam was fumbling for the phone, trying to catch it as it slid across the seat and down to the floor. Simon had been peppering him with questions on the ride back, in a pitiful attempt to try and persuade himself that Sam was coming in. But after a stream of pat answers from Sam, Simon had finally given up and let it go, knowing at a gut level that Sam was never going to come along and never going to change. They had driven in silence for about ten minutes when Simon started acting strange. He kept looking in his rear view mirror and making unnecessary lane changes. All of a sudden, he punched the gas and shot around a garbage truck barely missing the bumper.

"For Christ's sake, Simon. Slow the fuck down!" Sam yelled as the car took another sharp jag and almost hit the curb. "What the hell is wrong with you?"

Sam glanced at Simon as the car careened again to the left. Simon was pale, his hands locked on the steering wheel, sweat beading on his forehead. He darted a quick look in the rear view mirror and rammed the car across the gravel shoulder and onto Mulholland Highway.

"What the hell are you doing?" Sam shouted above the skittering tires. "Slow down! You're driving insane!"

"Ohhh shit!" Simon shrieked. "They're still behind us!"

"Who? What? What the fuck are you talking about?" Sam yelled as he craned his neck to look behind. The dust was thick, billowing up from the gravel, but he could make out some kind of black sedan with two men in dark glasses sitting in the front.

Simon turned the wheel hard, hurling across the double yellow lines and leapfrogging two cars ahead. He stomped the gas pedal to the floor and shot through the narrow, single lane turns on Mulholland. "Motherfuckers! You'll never get us, you motherfuckers!" Simon screamed as he dove through the last opening in the traffic and took off in front of the pack.

Sam was flat in the seat, pressed down by speed and terror. He took a second to refasten his grip on the door and gulp any air he could into his lungs. "Simon, what? What? Who's after us? Shit, Simon, talk!" But it was too late. Sam was thrown against the windshield as the car was rammed viciously from behind. Simon's forehead hit the steering wheel with a ghastly thud but he somehow kept his hands on the wheel and yanked the car off the shoulder and back into the lane. Blood was streaming down his forehead and into his eyes. He clawed at his right eye, trying to wipe a path to see but there was too much blood and too much sweat and his eyes were burning and starting to close up.

The car was fishtailing and he frantically grabbed the steering wheel just as the car was rammed again.

"Motherfuckers! Motherfuckers!" Simon was screaming, fighting to regain control of the car, keep it off the steep hillsides lining Mulholland. Suddenly, he made a hard turn into one of the driveways lining the road and skidded to a sweeping left around the circular driveway. The force threw Sam against the car door and Simon reached over, opened the door and shoved Sam out. Sam hit the ground hard, his head and shoulders crashing to the pavement. He rolled away from the car and ended up under a bush by the fence. The black sedan was right behind. Sam pulled himself even deeper under the bush and could see the sedan clear the driveway and go after Simon, gaining ground with every second. Simon was on the shoulder, the gravel and dust kicking up so bad it was hard to see.

"Get back on the road, Simon!" Sam screamed. The sedan was right on Simon's tail. The cliff at Topanga Blvd. was coming up fast on the right.

"Simon! Simon . . ."

Sam watched the sedan ram Simon one more time, forcing him off the road and over the cliff. The car plunged down the steep incline and rolled end over end, finally coming to rest bottom up on the canyon floor. Sam waited until the sedan was out of sight and then ran, as best as he could, to the ravine. The car had wrapped around the base of a palm tree and looked half its size, the roof flattened to the floor, the passenger compartments nonexistent. The windshield had popped out with the force and was lying halfway up the ravine among shattered glass and a hubcap.

"Oh my God, Simon. Oh my God." Sam fell to the gravel, sobbing hysterically. "Oh my God."

He laid there for some time until his sobs gave way to excruciating pain and overwhelming fear. He stumbled to his feet and backtracked to the last house on the drive. He prayed that someone was home. He rang the bell and waited.

"Oh, dear Lord," called a voice behind the door. "What's happened?" The door swung open and an elderly couple looked at him in surprise and dismay. "What's happened to you?" the man asked.

"Thank you for opening the door," Sam somehow managed to get out. "I'm sorry to trouble you. Please call 911. I've been in an accident and my friend is dead."

"What accident?" the man said, suddenly suspicious. "I don't see any accident."

"The car is in the ravine. I managed to climb out but my friend is still in there."

"Oh my God," said the wife. "Call 911, Eddie. Go on now." She turned to Sam and said, "It takes about fifteen minutes for the fire department to get here since we're so high up in the canyon, but Eddie will call right away."

Sam started. He hadn't thought it through. He couldn't wait for the fire department. He couldn't go the hospital. He needed Maurice to think he was dead too. He needed to buy any time he could for as long as possible.

"Look at me," Sam said to the wife. "I don't think I can wait that long. Is there any clinic close by? Would you be willing to take me?"

Sam knew it was a stretch. He was a mess—a scary, bloody,

unknown mess. He could be an axe murderer for all they knew. But he could see her consider it. Luckily he still had his wallet and he gingerly reached it to show her his ID.

"OK," she said. "Eddie will take you. I'll wait for the fire department."

By this time, the pain was starting to overwhelm his faculties and his self-control. He barely made it into the car and barely made it out when they got to the clinic. He thanked Eddie profusely and watched him drive away. As soon as he was gone, Sam dragged himself across the street to a dimly lit bar, just open for the day, and asked the owner to use his phone.

"Oh, my God, Sam! I've been trying to get you all day. Where are you? Are you OK?" Sarah was talking in a torrent, words spilling out, tumbling over each other. Finally she took a breath and she could hear that Sam had been talking all along.

" . . . and I rolled and hit my head, but I'm mostly OK. Sarah, listen to me and listen to me like your life depends on it because it does. They tried to kill me, Sarah. They tried to kill me and they might try to kill you too."

Sarah could barely understand him, his voice was so choked with emotion. She almost didn't recognize it.

"What do you mean? What are you saying? What's happened?" She was screaming into the phone as if yelling would get a quicker response. She could hardly hear him and her phone kept cutting out. "Where are you?" she screamed.

"At a bar at the corner of Sepulveda and Mantilla. Come quick."

She jammed on the gas and started driving as fast as she could. She didn't think Sam was seriously hurt, but she couldn't be sure. He was definitely in trouble and she had to get there to help. She blew through the yellow lights and snaked a few red, but knew that getting pulled over would be a disaster, so she kept it as close to the edge as she could without going over. Ten minutes later, she was there. She parked badly and ran to the bar. She saw him right away, sitting in the darkest part of the bar, way in the back. He looked awful. His pants and shirt were ripped and bloody, and as she got closer, she could see a lot of scrapes and cuts—big, oozing patches where skin had once been. In truth, he was a lot worse off than he had said on the phone. She ran to his side and cradled as much of him as she could in her arms. If there was any way to heal him with the sheer force of her love, she was going to do it. He reached for her with every ounce of strength he had and they clung together, oblivious to the world.

Eventually, Sam lifted his head and looked at Sarah with so much love in his eyes that it brought tears to hers. She felt as if he had taken her into his soul. And for the first time in her life, she felt true love. They helped each other up slowly and walked to the car. Sam was the first to speak.

"They tried to kill me, and they killed Simon," he said.

"Oh my God," Sarah exclaimed, grabbing his arm and squeezing it until it hurt. "Are you sure?"

"I'm sure."

Sarah swallowed the hysteria that was brewing inside her and tried to appear calm and under control. "Tell me what happened."

He took a sip of the water she offered and started. "I got in to work about eight and started cranking so I could get out early and meet you. Simon came in and said we had to go to a meeting out of the office. Hector came too. We went to this seedy, boarded up club called The Lucky Seven. It was disgusting. There was garbage all over and broken bottles. I started getting concerned, so I asked Simon what was going on. He said I'd be working on a deal that involved this location and Maurice wanted me to actually see the property so I'd know what I was talking about. I couldn't figure out what Maurice was doing having any part of this. But just as I was thinking I needed to get out of there, Maurice showed up.

Sam paused a moment and drank a little more water as he shifted in his seat. "Maurice told me that I had been recruited to join the insurance fraud ring he was running out of CS & B. He also told me not to worry about saying no, since he had gone into my computer and laced it with so much incriminating evidence that if I didn't go along or went to the police, I would be the one going to jail. We were right, Sarah," Sam said turning toward her. "It was Maurice all along, and Simon too. Simon was in on it, too."

Sarah could see that regardless of what he said, the fact that Simon was part of it bothered him more than he cared to show.

"Here's what they did. At first Maurice started with legit plaintiff car accident cases. But when he saw how much money he could make, he decided to increase his bottom line a bit by causing traffic accidents. You know, like the ones you hear about on the news where they pick a victim, box them in, cause a wreck, and collect. Well, after a bit of that, it occurred to Maurice that he didn't even have to stage real car accidents. He just paid off company insiders to create insurance files, submitted false accident reports on their behalf, got the cases assigned to CS

& B from those same company insiders, created the rest of the paperwork, litigated the cases, and voila, started rolling in the dough. All the templates we found were the templates he and others use to create police reports, doctors' bills, physical therapy bills, you know, the like. His special friends in the courts and police department do their share to move things along. And now here's the really fun part. Of course, none of this would work with proper defense counsel on the other side. They would find out right away that it was all a scam. So Maurice created the Bicknel Law Firm. Bicknel is comprised of his lawyers, Simon predominantly, who 'work' the cases from the defense end. So Maurice has all pieces of the pie. He can never lose. If he decides a plaintiff should win, he gets his third from one of his pocketed insurance companies and laughs all the way to the bank. If he decides the defense should win, mainly to keep the numbers on par with the insurance companies' expectations, he still gets to bill the time of his attorneys on the case, so he wins again. He's made millions of dollars every year for a very long time and turned himself into a crooked, but very rich man."

Sarah nodded silently. It all made perfect sense.

"So I just sat there and took it all in. Maurice was really on a roll. He was clearly enjoying telling me how smart he was and how he'd developed this brilliant scam. All I could think of was that I had to get out of there. If I could get out, I'd have options. In there, I had none. So I said I was in. I said I needed money and backed it up with a story about my mom needing money for her multiple sclerosis. I thought Maurice bought it, but I was wrong. He welcomed me into the fold and then sent Simon and me on our way. Hector stayed to clean that dump—

probably to sanitize it of evidence. I have to tell you, Sarah," he said passionately as he took her hands in his, "when I walked out of that room and into the bright sunshine, I thought my heart would explode with gratitude. I wanted to hit my knees and thank God for my second chance. But that second chance didn't last long."

He took another sip of water and continued. "As soon as we got in the car, Simon hit me with a ton of questions, but I just showed how excited I was about the program and didn't really say much. Then all of a sudden, Simon started looking in his rear view mirror and said we were being followed. It was a black car, like an Oldsmobile, with two men in the front. By this point, we were getting to the turns on Mulholland and Simon sped up, trying to shake the tail. But every time he got a few cars ahead of the Oldsmobile, it managed to move up. Soon it was right behind us and then started ramming us. I was terrified. All of a sudden, Simon made a hard turn into one of the driveways lining the road and opened my door and shoved me out. That's where I got these," Sam said pointing to his cuts and scrapes. Luckily, I somehow rolled away from the car and ended up under a bush. The Oldsmobile cleared the driveway and then it was back on Mulholland right on Simon's tail. Simon was doing everything to get away, but he couldn't and he was approaching the cliff at Topanga Boulevard with them right behind. I could see it all. The Oldsmobile caught up to him and forced him over the edge."

"So he's dead. He's really dead. There's no way he survived the crash?"

"No. As soon as they were gone, I ran over as fast as I could and looked down the ravine. The car was way down in the steepest part. There was no way I could get down to it. It had flipped over a bunch of times on the way down and landed bottom up on the floor of the canyon. The passenger compartments looked like pancakes. I don't think a squirrel could have fit in there. I ran back to the closest house and an older couple let me in. They called 911. I said I couldn't wait for the fire department and the husband took me to the clinic right across the street. He dropped me off in front. As soon as he was out of sight, I came here and called you."

"I can't believe what you've been through," Sarah said, holding his face gently in her hands. We've got to get you fixed up. I know you don't want to go, but we've got to get you a hospital. What if something really is wrong?"

"I know, but right now Maurice thinks I'm dead along with Simon. If I surface now, he's just going to play out his plan of framing me. But when he finds out I'm not dead, which will be pretty soon, he's going to come after me with everything he's got. Our only chance is to get evidence against him before he finds me. We've got to find Rodriguez."

"I know and I have." Sarah said it slowly, still hardly believing it herself.

Sam looked at her as if she had two heads. "What did you say?"

"I said I found Paul Rodriguez."

"Holy shit! You've got to be kidding! How did you do it?"

"Well, when I couldn't get a hold of you today I got really worried. Now I know why, by the way. So Christine suggested that I do something instead of pacing my office floor and this is what I did. I went over to Rodriguez's apartment to see if any of the neighbors knew where he might go, and came up with nothing. So I went over to Marion Rodriguez's house and guess who showed up? I know, I should play the lottery today. In any event, I followed her back to their hideway in Burbank and I saw Paul Rodriguez there. He's at an apartment complex in the heart of Burbank not ten minutes from us right now."

"He's my only hope. We've got to get him to testify against Maurice."

"Correction," Sarah said firmly. "He's *our* only hope and he'll testify. I'll bet on it. Think about it. He went AWOL. He had the courage to go AWOL on Maurice. So he's a tough guy, a proud guy and he's not afraid of Maurice. In fact, he probably would relish the opportunity to testify against Maurice—if he doesn't end up dead on the back side. Yeah, he's going to testify. We just have to go get him and bring him in."

"We've got to hustle. No offense, but if you could find him, Maurice might have been able to as well."

They made it to the Rodriguezes' hideaway in ten minutes flat and pulled up just past the entrance to the complex. The rental car wasn't parked in front of the room like it had been earlier and Sarah looked for it around the rest of the parking lot. No car. By this time, Sam had cleaned himself up a bit with the water and some tissues in the glove compartment and looked better, but still the worse for wear. And, over Sarah's strong objections, he insisted that he be the one to go to the door.

He approached cautiously and knocked. No answer. He knocked again and looked in through the open front window. No one. Just then a neighbor came out thinking it was her door.

"They're gone. They left about fifteen minutes ago."

"Thank you. Do you know when they'll be back?" Sam asked.

"No, but they went to the store. Shouldn't be too long."

Sam thanked her and walked back to the car.

"They went to the store about fifteen minutes ago. Shouldn't be long."

"Great," Sarah said. "But what are we going to do if he does agree to come in? Where do we bring him? You said Maurice has friends in the police department. Which department? Which friends? What if we bring him to the wrong place?" She knew she sounded a little paranoid, but it could happen and then they'd all be dead.

"FBI. I've got a college friend in the FBI. Maurice said police, not feds. I think we're clear as far as the FBI."

"Excellent. I mean really excellent." Sarah reached over and squeezed Sam's hand reassuringly. "It's going to be fine. I know it is."

They waited in the car as the minutes ticked by, fifteen, twenty-five, forty-five. Finally, after almost an hour, Sarah recognized the rental car coming down the street. Both of them watched as it pulled into the complex and parked at number six. But since they were so intently watching the Rodriguezes, they failed to notice a dark green Chevy that had pulled up and parked on the street five cars behind them. Had Sam seen it, he might have seen Hector in the driver's seat. As it was, they had no idea that they were both stalking and being stalked.

Sam gave the Rodriguezes a few minutes to put away their groceries and then advanced to the door. If anything went wrong, at least Sarah would be safe and she could go to the authorities. He knocked and waited.

He could see Marion and Paul peeking around the now drawn curtain and knew that they probably wouldn't even open the door unless he could think up something fast.

"Marion and Paul, my name is Sam Morrow," he spoke quietly at the door. "Maurice just killed Simon and tried to kill me. And I think you're next."

The door swung open noiselessly and Paul grabbed Sam and pulled him in. He had him in a chokehold even before Sam's eyes adjusted to the dim interior light.

"Who are you and what do you want?" he said gruffly.

"I told you, Paul," Sam choked out. "I'm Sam Morrow. I'm a lawyer at Cabot, Strickland & Baines. Maurice was trying to blackmail me into joining your insurance fraud ring. When he figured I wasn't going along, he tried to run me and Simon off the road and he succeeded with Simon. Simon's dead."

Paul released the chokehold and looked Sam full in the face. "How do I know this isn't some kind of set-up by the cops or Maurice? And how did you find us?"

Sam could see Marion move ever so slightly away from them. Sam didn't want to get her in trouble with Paul if Paul didn't know she had gone to the house, but there wasn't much he could do to protect her. He had to prove himself to Paul. Then it hit him. "Paul, I've got Sarah Brockman out in the car. Remember her? Her name was on the complaint you got from the process server you beat up. She represents the guy you accidentally hit in the crosswalk, Murray Matthews. Simon was defending you through Bicknel. Why would she be with me if I was with Maurice or with the cops? It wouldn't make any sense." Sam knew it was a little out there, but it was all he could think of on the spot. He could see Paul thinking it over.

"OK. That makes sense to me. Let me see your driver's license and identification from Cabot, then bring her in. I remember her name. If she is who you say she is, I'll listen to you."

Sam showed Paul his identification and then dashed down the stairs and out to the car, where he explained what he had said to Sarah as they walked back to the apartment. She was eager to see Paul and prove her identity. When they went back inside, it was clear Marion had told him about her visit to the house. He was storming about and throwing things, but he didn't touch her. When he saw them, he cooled down almost as fast as he had revved himself up.

"Sarah Brockman?"

"Yes," she said as she handed him her driver's license. He studied it carefully and matched the picture to Sarah. Satisfied, he gave it back to her and said. "What do you want?"

"We want you to testify against Maurice. We want you to come with us to the FBI, where you can tell them everything you know about Maurice and his insurance fraud business. We know you've been with him a long time."

"Long time?" Paul interjected. "Since the beginning. I know more about him and his scam than anyone except Simon. And I would like nothing more than to bring that son of a bitch down. I hate that fucking Maurice. Treated me like shit. Threw me out and spit on me. Asshole. I was going to get him myself later, after we'd settled in some place safe so I definitely don't mind jumping the gun a bit. But if I testify I could be joining Simon six feet under. I need witness protection. Can you get me that?"

"I can't promise you, but the guy we're going to go see is an assistant director at the FBI and we've been friends since college. I think he can get it done. In any event, you'd only need it until we put Maurice away for fifty years. He'll be hard pressed to come after you when he's ninety."

"Yeah, but he has friends. No, I'm going to want it for as long as we live. But what else do you have? What other evidence? If it's just my testimony, you and I both know that's not going to be enough."

Sam and Sarah knew he was right. They hadn't been willing to admit it to themselves, but they knew that the uncorroborated testimony of a criminal wasn't going to carry the show at the trial. They stood there uncomfortably, each trying to think of something to say.

"Well, we have all the evidence on the firm computers," Sarah said.

"Right," Paul scoffed. "Providing it isn't all erased by the time you get there. No, you guys have nothing. And I'm not setting myself up for nothing. Forget it."

Sarah and Sam could see their only chance slipping away and they scrambled to come up with something—anything—to convince Paul to come in. "I know where Simon lives," Sam said. Maybe he's got some evidence tucked away somewhere for protection. I'll go over and break into his house and see what I can find to corroborate what you'll say."

That was what Paul was waiting for. He wanted to see how far they would go. They had to be willing to do whatever it took. They had to be willing to get dirty because Paul knew that you could only trust people who were willing to get dirty. They were the ones who stuck with you when it got ugly and they were the ones who stuck with you until the end.

"Okay. I believe you," Paul said with finality. "Marion, bring me that book bag from under the dresser."

As Marion went to retrieve the bag, Paul sized up his new partners. Nice couple, he thought. Sure hope they're as tough as they're going to need to be.

Marion was back in a few seconds with the bag. Paul reached in and pulled out a thick sheath of documents.

"Do you know what this is?" he asked Sarah and Sam waiving it at them. "Well, do you?" They both shook their heads no. "Well, this is your case. This stack of papers contains all the evidence you were wishing you had just about now. I've got dates and places, people and numbers. I have everything any prosecutor would drool over and it's all evidence against Maurice." Paul put the papers down on the table and stepped back where he could enjoy watching their reaction even more fully. He wasn't disappointed.

"Oh God, this is fantastic," Sarah exclaimed as she started thumbing through the documents. "How did you get all this? How did you do it?"

"I collected various pieces along the way. I've learned in life that while trust in people is a beautiful thing, don't fucking count on it. Better to have a back-up plan."

"It looks like you have a full list of all the fraud cases," Sam said happily. "Plus, is this a list of the 'friends of Maurice' in the court and police department?"

"Yes, but I don't think it's complete. I'm sure there are others."

Sam directed Sarah's attention to one name on the list that

she wouldn't want to miss—Judge Eric Schneider. Sarah shook her head and smiled ever so slightly. She would so enjoy seeing him go down.

"This is fantastic, Paul," Sam said. "We owe you everything. I'll do my very best for you."

"I'm counting on it."

"We've got to go," Sam said suddenly urgent. "Maurice might be looking for me right now. And he's definitely looking for you, Paul. If we could find you, he'll be able to find you too."

"Yeah," Paul said. Once he finds out you're not dead, you're dead. And us, too. Let's go. Now that we know Maurice killed Simon, none of us is safe."

After a quick scan of the parking lot, Paul, Marion, Sam, and Sarah hurriedly made their way to Sarah's car. Goddamn fuckers, Hector swore under his breath. Just seeing the four of them together made his blood boil. Rodriguez must have been stoned out of his mind to get off the bus before reaching Mexico. Jesus Christ. He'd done everything he could for them. Saved their fucking worthless skins. And they went and did this. Fuckers. But as much as he didn't give a shit about what happened to the Rodriguezes, he did care what happened to Sam and Sarah. Hector shook himself clear of his anger and started focusing on the job at hand. He turned up the volume on the audio so he could easily hear what they were saying and motioned the two cars joining him to follow. Ronaldo and Damon pulled in right behind.

"I'm still on hold. Sarah, make a right here," Sam said.

"Fucking FBI. I can't believe we're on fucking hold when we told them it was an emergency." It was that asshole Rodriguez.

The sound of Rodriguez's voice just pissed Hector off all over again, but he kept himself in check and kept driving. He couldn't regret more having put that bug in Sarah's car. He should have told Maurice it was overkill and unnecessary. But he had no idea it would come to this. That's why he had put Francisco on the monitor. He just didn't think Sarah Brockman was all that important. Was he wrong. Without the bug, Maurice might never have found Rodriguez and he certainly wouldn't yet know Sam was still alive. And how in the hell did Maurice even find out? It couldn't have been Francisco. He didn't even have Maurice's phone numbers and he didn't even really know who he was. No, the only explanation was that Maurice was independently monitoring the audio. But to his knowledge, Maurice had never done that before. He'd always had the technology—he'd insisted on lines to his office. But Maurice had always relied on him for updates. So why now? Had Sarah become important to him because of the Sam connection? Or was there a trust issue with Maurice he didn't know about? Was Maurice looking at him closely, too? Hector took a deep breath and let it wash over him. Of course he would have lied about Sam being alive and about the Rodriguezes. Maurice never would have known. But now, because of that fucking bug, they were in a life and death race for the finish. Their carefully constructed plan was in the shitter. A small sigh escaped him as he knew that none of it mattered anymore. It would all be over in a few hours, one way or another.

Maurice had given Hector very clear instructions. Tail them at a discrete distance and wait until they reached a suitable stretch of roadway. Lag behind Ronaldo and Damon as they boxed them in and did a light swoop and crash. The goal was to damage the car without really hurting the occupants. Once they had been hit by Ronaldo, Ronaldo would pull over with them and start exchanging information. Meanwhile, Hector and Damon would keep driving and Hector would alert the police cruiser trailing not far behind. As soon as Maurice's police friend arrived, Ronaldo would take off with the cop's permission and the cop would claim that Sarah's car was unsafe to drive and require that they come with him to the station. And that was it. That's where Maurice's instructions ended and that's what was making Hector so nervous. He had been Maurice's go-to guy almost since the beginning. He had done things for Maurice that he never thought he'd do, but did to protect his little existence in the world. He had humiliated and shamed himself. But he was always on the inside, always the first one called. So why was Maurice calling in the cop instead of him? It was either that Maurice thought he wasn't capable of handling whatever Maurice had in mind or that Maurice had something in mind that he thought was even outside Hector's comfort zone. The thought kept surfacing in his mind as he drove. Maurice had told Hector that Simon had an accident driving back from The Lucky Seven. But did he? And how did Sam escape unhurt? Shouldn't he be in the morgue too, or at least the hospital? Hector felt a shiver run down his spine. He looked at his cell phone, willing it to ring. Everything was riding on the call. The call had to come.

He faulted himself for the whole situation. He should have seen it coming. Instead, he naively thought he was really going to stay and clean The Lucky Seven even after witnessing Sam's dubious performance. Now the whole plan was in jeopardy. Everything they had worked on for months and months would be ruined if they couldn't get that last piece in place in time. He alternated between staring at his cell phone and looking at the two cars ahead following Sarah. They were all still heading down Sycamore, but at Marabell, Sarah made a left hand turn right onto the freeway. Shit, Hector thought. The freeway is always the preferred roadway for the swoop and crash. He could see his guys starting to inch forward in anticipation. He radioed each one and told them that he didn't have a go ahead from the boss yet so they had to hold back. A credible lie, since only he had received the orders from Maurice. Still no call. He thought about how he had looked forward to this day for months—dreamed about it, envisioned it. Every time he had to do something unsavory, he would think about how this day was going to be and he could force himself through it. Now instead of a glorious victory, there was a very real chance that they were all going to go down in flames. Big flames. Big fucking burn you to a crisp flames.

He scanned the freeway. It was perfect for a swoop and crash. There were a fair number of cars, but very few big trucks and no real pockets of congestion. Ronaldo radioed.

"Hector, have you heard from the boss yet? You can see, everything's perfect. We want to go."

"Sorry, Ronaldo. Nothing yet. And you know I can't call him. I'll tell you the instant I know anything."

He had to keep stalling. It was his only hope. But they were making good time. The FBI exit was only two exits away. Hector could feel sweat starting to trickle down his back and his hands getting clammy. If he did nothing and let them go where they were going, Rodriguez would bust the scam wide open and Maurice would go down, but he would go down with him. Plus, there was the possibility that he wouldn't even make it to jail. Maurice would blame him for fucking everything up and sending him to prison for the rest of his life. And his vengeance would run deep. Maurice could easily call in a favor and take him out in prison. And God knows he had a lot of favors to call in. But if he did the swoop and crash, there was a good chance that four people were going to die. He wouldn't do that even to save his own skin. He wouldn't become like Maurice. All of a sudden, his other radio frequency started coming in.

"Hey, is this Hector?"

"Yeah, who's this?"

"A friend. What's going on? I'm at Crenshaw on the 10 freeway. You were supposed to have called me by now."

It was the cop. Hector clutched the steering wheel hard to try and steady himself. "I . . . ah . . . there's not a good spot yet. We're still looking. Shouldn't be that much longer."

"Better not be," the voice said as it took on a steely edge. "Believe me, you don't want to fuck this up."

The radio was silent. He was gone—for now. Hector began staring at the phone with all his might, willing it to ring. He picked it up and checked the reception. Full reception. He started what he thought was praying and kept driving. They were almost in sight of the Staples Center. Once they hit that, it would be one exit to Figueroa, the one they would most likely take. He checked his rear view mirror to make a lane change and saw a police cruiser immediately switch into his lane. Fuck. It couldn't be Maurice's guy. It just couldn't. If it was, he was fucked. Totally fucked. Just then the radio squawked and a voice started coming over the same frequency the cop had used earlier."

"Hector, you fucking cocksucker. I see you. I'm right behind you. I could shoot you from here. I don't know what kind of little game you're playing, but you better call your guys and tell them to move, *now*! Or this will be the last little joyride you will ever take."

The radio went dead and Hector knew he was out of time. He made his decision.

"Hey, Ronaldo? Yeah, the boss just phoned and called the whole thing off. I repeat, it's a no-go. Got that?"

"Yeah, I got it. How fucked up is that? You still got to pay me, you know."

"Yeah, I know."

Then Hector radioed Damon and told him the same thing. He could see them continue on down the 10 as Sarah was making her exit on Figueroa. A quick look back told him that the cruiser was now directly behind him and riding his tail. There was only one occupant in the car and Hector could see him adjust his sunglasses and then reach for the radio. But at that second, his phone rang.

"Hector? We got it! Call 'em off and come in. We got it!"

Hector almost cried into the phone. "Thank God, I'm coming, but I got an angry cruiser on my back who's not going to be happy to . . . oh shit, he's passing me, I think he's going after them himself."

"Hector, listen to me," the voice said urgently. "You can't let the cruiser get to them. If you do, they're dead."

"I know, I know," Hector said as he hit the gas. "I'm on his tail."

"OK, OK, stay calm. You can do this. What's the car number? If you can just hold him off for a few minutes, I can get this cruiser off both your backs."

Hector sped up until he was right in the cruiser's back pocket. He could just barely make out the numbers. "It's 345. Yeah, it's number 345."

"OK, great. If you can keep 'em off for a few minutes, he'll be gone. I promise."

"All right. I hear you. I'm gone." And Hector flipped the phone closed and focused every cell in his body on out-maneuvering the cruiser. It was one car behind Sarah's on a two-lane street. But then the cruiser hit the lights and siren, the car in front pulled over, and it was directly behind Sarah.

"Jesus Christ," Hector heard Paul yelp over the audio. "We've got the LAPD right behind us."

"Shit," Sam said. "What do we do?"

"How far to the FBI?" Sarah asked.

"About five blocks."

"That far?" Sarah said tensely. "I don't think we have a choice. We have to make a run for it to the FBI. Look, there's no reason for this cop to be pulling us over. My tags are current. My blinkers work. I wasn't driving too fast. No, I think we have to assume it's Maurice. We know he has cops on payroll. If we're wrong, we're screwed with law enforcement, but not dead. If we stop now, we could be dead."

"I agree," Sam and Paul said almost in unison. "Let's go for it."

Hector whispered a silent thank you and hoped that Sarah

could hold her own against one of LA's finest, at least for five blocks.

"OK," Sam said. Make a right here and then it's a straight shot to the FBI.

"Got it."

Sarah made a sharp right onto four lane Grand Avenue and started weaving in and out among the cars, putting a little distance between them and the cruiser.

"Way to go, girl," Hector muttered under his breath. "Go, go, you can make it."

The cruiser still had his lights and siren on and was still behind them, but started gaining and then, in a flash, shot through a hole in the parallel lane until he was right next to Sarah. Hector nailed the same hole and landed directly behind him.

"Fuck," Paul said.

"He's motioning us to pull over," Sam said. "I don't know, maybe he's for real. Maybe he's just a cop."

"I don't think so," Sarah said quickly. "It's too much coincidence. I think he's with Maurice. We gotta stay with it."

"God, I hope you're right," Sam said.

"Me too."

"You, in the red Honda. Pull over. Pull over now," the cop yelled through his PA system. "This is the LAPD, pull over *now!*"

"Shit," Sam said.

"I got a hole right up there," Sarah said. "If I can get through to there, it looks like a clear shot to the FBI."

"You're doing great," Sam said. "Keep it going, we're gonna to make it."

But just as he said it, a delivery truck pulled out right in front of them and forced Sarah to skid almost to a standstill. The cop pulled up short too, so they were eyeball to eyeball directly across from each other. Sarah kept her eyes focused in front, but Paul and Sam looked over.

"Oh God," Sam said. "He looks really pissed." But Paul saw what Sam had missed.

"Oh shit, he's got a gun!" Paul screamed. But there was nothing they could do. They were pinned in by the delivery truck and the cruiser. They were trapped.

But Hector had seen the gun come out even before they had and he punched the gas to the floor and rammed the cruiser from behind as hard as he could. The impact threw the cop hard up against the windshield and the gun jumped free. Hector heard it go off but since he wasn't sure the cruiser was undrivable, he reversed and prepared to ram the cruiser again. As he did, he could see that Sarah was making the most of the opportunity and had squeezed by the trash truck and into the other lane. She was making a run for it and she was almost there. They were going to make it. Thank God, Hector thought as he came in as fast as he could from behind. Thank God, the good guys were going to win. He smiled as he crashed into the cruiser one more time enjoying a brief glimpse of the triumph he knew would be his later. But suddenly everything went completely wrong. He had come in too fast. The airbag opened and hit him hard in the face, leaving him dazed and disoriented. He couldn't find his seat belt buckle, but he knew he had to get out of there fast before the cop got to him. He didn't think even the busy public street would protect him. He kept fumbling for the buckle, but couldn't seem to get it open. He started to panic. Now he couldn't even find the buckle. His fingers were like giant sausages. He couldn't see around the airbag to see if the cop was coming. He smelled something burning.

"Oh God," he yelled. "Help me."

Bright red flames were shooting up from the front of his car.

The bullet must have gone through the cruiser's gas tank, he thought wildly.

He started screaming. He couldn't find the buckle. He could feel heat starting to come through the airbag. He could see a man trying to yank open his car door, but it was wedged inwards with the crash. He could see the man motioning him to climb over the seat and get out the back door. He still couldn't see around the airbag, but his fingers finally traced the seat belt down to what he thought was the base. He felt the hard metal of the clasp. He saw the man being pulled away by another man. He saw them running. He pushed the clasp in hard and the belt released. He threw himself over the backseat and lunged for the door handle. He saw people running away, looking back over their shoulders. He saw the fear in their eyes and he knew.

The cars exploded with a blast that shook a five-block radius of downtown and was the lead story on the nightly news. Apparently, the LAPD officer involved had been illegally transporting a wide assortment of firearms and explosives in his trunk that went off in the fire. The cop and the other driver were burned beyond recognition.

◆ ◆ ◆

Sarah, Sam, Paul, and Marion were just three blocks away, racing down Grand Avenue when the blast hit.

"Holy shit," Paul yelled as they looked backwards.

"It's the cruiser and the car that hit him," Sam said. "Oh God, they blew up. There's just a fireball. There's nothing left."

The car became completely silent.

"Did anybody see who hit the cruiser?" Sarah asked. "I mean, it seems really strange that this cruiser gets taken out just as he was going to take us out."

"I don't know. I didn't get a look at the driver, but I think it was just one person in the car," Sam said.

"I think it was our guardian angel," Marion said as she turned back around.

"Here it is, Sarah. Turn in this parking garage," Sam said. "Let's make what he did mean something."

Sam's friend, Jon Masters, came out to meet them the minute they got to the lobby. Introductions were brief as Jon led the group back to a large, interior conference room and motioned for them to sit down at the table. Three other agents came in and took seats next to them.

"So," Jon began. "Sam has told me basically what's going on and why you're here. I think the most important thing right now is to see if we actually have a case. Otherwise, we're faced with a whole other set of problems. Sam said you had some documents that are evidence against Strickland and other co-conspirators," he said, turning to Paul. "Let's take a look at those first."

As all four agents skimmed through Paul's evidence, they saw that Paul had done a superb job of collecting what they needed. They closed the folders and sat back in their chairs.

"So, Mr. Rodriguez," Jon began. "You've done an excellent job getting this evidence. With your testimony, we should have everything we need to put Maurice Strickland away for a very long time."

"Thank you, Mr. Masters. I appreciate your words, but what about immunity and witness protection? Maurice has a very long arm and a lot of friends. Without protection, me and Marion are dead."

Jon looked over at one of the agents sitting there, who nodded his approval. "You've got it. Immunity and witness protection for you and your wife. You've earned it."

Paul appeared to blush a little at the praise and shifted uncomfortably in his chair.

"Thanks. I appreciate it," he said gruffly. "Maurice is a son of a bitch. I'll be happy to see him go."

"We all will," Sam said.

"Thank you again so much," Sarah said turning to Paul. "You've done a great job." And then she said as gently as she could. "You know though, I still will have to prosecute my case against you for Murray Matthews."

"Yeah, I know. I'm sorry about all of that. I wasn't in my right head. I'm sorry he got hurt and hurt so bad. He should get a lot of money. But I just don't have it."

"Hey, Mr. Masters, isn't there some kind of crime busters award Paul could collect for doing all this?" Marion asked. "Maybe that could go to the Matthews."

"That's a wonderful idea," Jon said thoughtfully. "There is a government crime busters award program. A few of my colleagues have used it for their witnesses and the payouts were big. Much more than the State. I'll look into it and let you know."

"Do that," Marion said looking intently at Jon. "I mean, look at everything Paul has done for you. It's the least the government can do for him."

"I promise I'll do everything I can."

"So, what's the next step?" Sarah asked.

"Arrest warrant. Let's move it. There's a real chance Maurice knows something about all of this already. He's got people all over the city. I'll swear out a warrant, get it signed and be back here in fifteen minutes. I'm sure you two want to stay," Jon said turning to Sarah and Sam, "but if you want to go," he said to the Rodriguezes, I'll have a car and one of my best men take you to a hotel right now."

"Great, let's go," Paul said as they headed for the door. "We're done for now. Good luck."

"Thanks."

Jon rushed out the door immediately after the Rodriguezes and was back in twelve minutes flat, warrant in hand.

"OK, let's go get him."

Sarah, Sam, and Jon rode in one car, and two other cars with two men each made their way to the other side of downtown. Within a few minutes they had descended on the venerable law firm of Cabot, Strickland & Baines. Sarah and Sam were so excited they couldn't stop talking. They couldn't believe what was happening. And they couldn't believe they were largely responsible. They waited until everyone had assembled in the lobby and went up together. Sam had called Maurice's secretary earlier and confirmed that he was in the office. Since there was only one entrance, they decided to call Maurice to the lobby and arrest him there. Sam was delighted they were doing it that way—the more public the better. Maurice had defiled his friend and then killed him. He had tried to kill Sam, too. He had damaged, probably forever, the reputation of the firm that Alexander had built with love and vision, and he had broken Ariel's heart. All in the name of money. A dose of public humiliation didn't even come close to what he deserved.

They stood in the lobby while the receptionist buzzed Maurice's secretary.

"Evelyn? It's Suzie. Sam Morrow and some gentlemen are waiting for Mr. Strickland in the lobby. Do you want to come out and bring them back or is Mr. Strickland going to see them in the conference room?" Suzie listened a few moments and then hung up the phone.

"Mr. Strickland has gone to an appointment out of the office. His secretary thought this afternoon was clear, so there must have been some kind of miscommunication. She's terribly sorry and she's coming out to speak with you and reschedule."

"No problem, Suzie," Sam said quickly. "I'll go back and talk to her." Sam walked as fast as he could to Evelyn's secretarial bay, scanning Maurice's office on his way. Empty.

"Sam? I'm sorry. I must have made a scheduling error. I have nothing on Mr. Strickland's calendar for this afternoon."

"No mistake. This is a last minute meeting," Sam said.

"Do you know what time he left?"

"Oh, just about ten minutes ago."

"Did he leave with his trial case or any documents, if you know?"

"Oh, yes. He had his trial case with him and it looked pretty heavy by the way he was carrying it."

"I'm sorry to be such a bother," Sam said apologetically, "but did you notice if he was on the computer a lot before he left?" Seeing her quizzical look he added, "it's important."

"Why yes. He was busy in there on it for about the last half hour."

"Thanks a lot, Evelyn. Let me know when he comes back, will you?"

"Sure, no problem."

Sam walked hurriedly down the hall to his office where he called the building's lobby security.

"Hi, is this Manny? Hi, Manny, it's Sam, Sam Morrow. I was wondering if you saw Maurice Strickland leave about ten minutes ago?"

"Oh yeah, Sam. He was out the door in a hurry about then. I mean, as fast as he could go with that heavy lug of a suitcase he was carrying."

Sam thanked Manny, hung up the phone, and sprinted for the lobby.

"Maurice is gone. He left the building carrying a heavy trial case about ten minutes ago."

"Shit," Jon said. "Let me call it in. He's still gotta be in his car. Maybe somebody can find him."

"Where else could he go, Sam?" another agent asked briskly. "His home? His mistress's home? Think, Sam, think. If we lose him now, with his resources, we'll probably lose him for good."

Sam went over the options in his mind. "All I know about is his home and a club he owns in East LA called The Lucky Seven."

"Where is it?"

Sam forced himself to quiet down and think. "It's at 1250

Tujunga Drive." The agent quickly called it in, but both knew it was a long shot. Maurice wouldn't hide out at a place Sam knew about, but it was one of the few options they had.

The lobby was instantly turned into a kind of operation headquarters, with agents manning their cell phones and radios, sending alerts to the airports, trains, and bus stations, trying to track down Ariel, doing everything they could think of doing to find Maurice Strickland. Sarah was doing everything she could to stay out of the way. She considered what Maurice was doing right now. Probably driving down some open freeway with the top down, smile on his face, wind in his hair, planning how he was going to spend all his millions. The thought made her perilously close to sick, but that was probably because she was just an inch away from being right. Maurice was, in fact, in his car driving down a freeway, but he didn't have the top down. Instead, he had Aerosmith cranked up until it shook the dashboard. For someone who had so narrowly escaped a catastrophic fall, he was feeling all right. He had designed an exit strategy about three years ago when he had amassed enough of a fortune that he wouldn't care if he needed to leave the United States. Of course, most of his money was in the Cook Islands. He had just swung by and picked up another $800k and was now on his way to the Santa Monica airport, where he had a private plane standing by so he wouldn't have to go through any airport security. It would take him to a tiny airport outside of Half Moon Bay, where another private plane—this one a seaplane—would take him to a yacht waiting for him four hundred miles off the coast. He could imagine their little faces, all screwed up with frustration, all the cops scouring the airports, checking the train stations, alerting the borders. But the coast guard was no match for the breadth of the Pacific, and no one would imagine that he would be four hundred miles out to sea in a few hours.

It was a good plan, a well-conceived plan. He felt quite sure it would work. But there was something he was forgetting. He couldn't put his finger on it, but he felt a nagging sense that there was something. He turned down the music and went through his checklist. No, he had done everything he needed to do. Did he have everything he needed to have? Maurice froze. Shit. He had forgotten $500,000 in the hidden drawer in his office. Shit, shit, shit. How could he be so stupid? He should just leave it, he told himself. He was almost at the airport and on his way to freedom. He had more than enough to last him the rest of his life. But his other voice, his louder, rapacious voice needed more. How could he leave $500,000? *His* $500,000? He had worked hard for that money. It was his money. He had to get it.

He certainly couldn't go in the front way. He had to assume that either the feds or cops or both were looking for him. But they didn't know about the service elevator. Most people didn't. He only did because it was right on the other side of his office. He could easily slip in and out without being seen. Once in the office, all he had to do was open a drawer and get his money. He could do it. He had to do it. He had to have his money.

By this time, all the agents had gone off in different directions, pursuing whatever thin leads they could come up with. Only Jon, Sam, and Sarah were left in the lobby.

"He's too smart and he's got too many resources," Sarah said bleakly. "If we don't find him in the next hour, he'll be gone for good."

"Next half hour," Jon said. "He can cover a lot of ground in a half hour. However," he said trying to sound brighter. "By now we have men at all the airports—LAX, Burbank, even Orange County. We've got the train station covered and alerted the border. We've got an APB out. I think there's a good chance we'll find him." He said it as enthusiastically as he could, but no one believed him. "Sam, is it OK if I stay here and use your conference room as another command post? Would the firm mind?"

"No. I don't even need to ask. I'll just sign it out for the rest of the day and it's yours."

Jon set up shop in the conference room while Sam and Sarah sat glumly in the lobby. Neither could do anything but wait. After twenty minutes, Jon came out and reported that no one had made any kind of contact or found any new leads. Jon joined them on the couch.

"This doesn't mean that your efforts were wasted," Jon said to Sam and Sarah. "We might find him and, if we do, we might be able to extradite him. At the very least, he's not going to cause any more harm in this country."

They knew it was true and they knew it was over. They decided to pack it up and go outside to clear their heads. A little California sun might really help. As Sam picked up his cell phone, he saw that it was vibrating. Apparently, he had accidentally pushed the ring change mode in all the commotion.

"Hello?"

"Sam?"

"Yes. Who's this?" He thought he recognized the voice, but wasn't quite sure.

"Maurice Strickland has just left his office on the service elevator," the voice said urgently. "Listen to me and do this now: take the main elevator down to the lobby. Make an immediate right when you get off and run as fast as you can down the long corridor. Take your first left and follow it around to the back. The service elevator is there. It's far from the lobby, but it's a slow elevator. You can make it. Go! Now!"

Sam dropped the phone and ran for the elevator, yelling at Jon and Sarah to run. They dashed into the open elevator and pushed "lobby," praying that it would go straight down. Sam told Jon what had happened.

"When we get down, Sam, you and Sarah stay in the lobby Here's my phone. Press this button. Tell them to send back-up here immediately."

"I'm coming with you," Sam said emphatically. "I hereby release you and the government from any injury I might suffer. Sarah, will you make the call?" She nodded yes and said. "But I'd rather come with you."

"Okay," Jon said looking Sam in the eye. "But this isn't kid's play. You really could get hurt."

"And I could get run over by a bus. Let's do it."

As the elevator door opened, Sarah stepped aside to make the call and Jon and Sam ran around the corner to the service elevator. They could hear the bell signaling that the door had just closed. As they turned the second corner, they could see Maurice walking away from them down the hall that led out to the garage. Jon drew his gun.

"Maurice Strickland," he barked. "This is the FBI. You are under arrest for the murder of Simon Streit. Drop your envelope.

Lie down spread eagle with your face on the floor. Do it! Now!"

Sam stood transfixed. Every action had turned into super slow-mo. He watched Maurice hear Jon's words, take them in, and digest them. But instead of dropping to the floor, Maurice began to turn ever so slowly to face them.

"Well, well," he said. "If it isn't Sam Morrow. What a pleasant surprise." He was full front now, holding a thick bulky envelope in his right hand and his car keys in his left. "You'll have to introduce me to your friend," he said as he started to move toward them.

"Not one more step, Strickland" Jon growled. "I said: spread eagle on the floor. Now!"

"Testy, isn't he?" Maurice said with a smirk. "I'm sure I would be too in his situation." With each word, Maurice advanced toward them, step by step, closing the gap until he was no more than ten feet away.

"I'm going to shoot you in the leg, Strickland. One more step and I'll pull the trigger."

And as Jon moved the gun down from the kill zone to his leg, Maurice dropped the envelope and revealed the palm sized Beretta he had been hiding. Sam saw the bright red fire from the gun even before he heard the deafening explosion.

"Ugh, aawwh," Jon grunted as the bullet dug deep into his chest. His gun skidded across the floor as Jon clutched his chest and started to pitch forward. A terrifying arc of blood spurted out and covered Sam as he dove for Jon, frantically trying to catch him as he fell. They both landed with a thud on the cold marble floor. Jon was making horrifying sounds, gasping and struggling for his life. Sam could hear people screaming and running toward them from the main lobby. And he could hear Maurice approaching.

"You know the security guards don't carry guns, don't you?" he asked smugly. "There's absolutely nothing they can do and I dare say, with that group of cowards, they wouldn't do anything even if they could." Sam looked up to see Maurice standing directly over him, looking at him intently like he was some kind of a specimen on display.

"It's a shame really. You would have been so good. But I guess it's my fault. I knew who you were. I knew who you were from the moment we hired you. I shouldn't have hoped you would change."

He raised the gun and pointed it at Sam's head. Sam closed his eyes and braced for the explosion. It seemed louder than the first—closer, more vicious. But instead of his life passing before his eyes, his only thought was of Sarah. Sarah. Her sweet face, her beautiful smile, the love he had for her. But where was the pain? Where was the white light? His eyes burst open. There was a pool of blood forming on his left and Maurice was lying in the middle of it.

Sarah rushed over to him, Jon's gun still in her hand. "Thank God you're alright," she cried as she hugged him with every inch of her being. "I love you more than anything in the world. I never want to let you go." She released him gently, stood up, and yelled to the people rushing in: "Don't just stand there. Someone call 911. There are two people who've been shot. Move it! Do it! Now!"

EPILOGUE

The man in row three was breathing so hard, the flight attendant thought he was going to have a heart attack. She approached cautiously being careful not to startle him. "Are you OK, sir? Is there anything I can get you?"

"No, I'm absolutely fine. Thank you." He smiled reassuringly. "I'm just so excited to be going to the Cook Islands."

She looked at him quizzically, so he added, "I'm getting married."

"Oh," she exclaimed. "How exciting for you. Have a beautiful wedding and honeymoon." She smiled broadly and touched him warmly on the shoulder as she made her way to the galley and returned with a bottle of champagne.

"Our compliments," she said, pouring him a glass.

"Thank you," Maurice said. "That's so kind of you. I will remember Cook Air every time I come to the Islands." It *was* nice of them, Maurice thought as he savored his first taste. What a perfect way to start out the rest of his life.

He had spent fifteen long years in Cold Springs Penitentiary. He beat the Simon Streit rap thanks to his top flight defense attorney, but ended up with twenty-five to life for wounding that FBI agent. In retrospect, it was good he hadn't killed him. And, although he never could get the time of day with the outgoing governor, thankfully he knew the newly elected governor quite well. Even so, it had been fifteen long years. Hard to believe. Fifteen years for making a little bit of money off insurance companies that never even missed it. Well, he was done crying over spilt milk. That was all over now and he was poised to begin his new life. He tried to calm his breathing a little so he wouldn't actually have a heart attack, but there was nothing he could do about the huge smile on his face. He was two hours away from collecting fourteen million dollars.

No one had ever found it. Not Ariel, not the police, not the insurance companies. Ariel had probably tried the hardest, but all she got in the divorce was a fraction of the house, since he owned it before marriage, and half of what was sitting around in their joint accounts, for a total of about $600,000. Not much for almost ten years of marriage. And he'd got her on that, too. After his arrest, he had filed for divorce immediately to get in under the ten-year mark. Brilliant. He never lost his edge, he thought. Even under the most stressful situation imaginable. He took a moment to appreciate himself again. In fairness though, he had to admit that parts of the whole deal had been rather unpleasant—the police escorting his ambulance from the building, being handcuffed, the trial itself—not a lot of fun. But the divorce trial was another story. Watching Ariel's face when she got her puny distribution? Priceless. He still chuckled about that. And now he was free. He was free and on his way to collect fourteen million dollars. He figured he could live out the rest of his life in luxury and leisure. Fourteen million could do that. That money was the only thing that had kept him going for those long years in the pen. He had envisioned it sitting in his box at the Bank of the Cook Islands waiting for him. He enjoyed another glass of champagne and watched as the plane made its slow, sweeping descent into Avarua Airport.

As soon as the plane touched down, he was back to crazy again. The luggage took forever and the taxi couldn't drive fast enough. It was a gorgeous, clear day with just a few big puffy cumulus clouds gracing the horizon, but he saw none of that. All he could see was the money, *his* money. Finally, after what seemed like an eternity, the cab pulled up in front of the Cook Islands bank. Maurice lurched out of the taxi and was almost running for the door when he caught himself, and by sheer strength of will, forced himself into a normal pace. The bank looked exactly the same as he remembered it—nothing extraneous, nothing luxurious, just a utilitarian box of a room with a giant vault at the end. He bypassed the teller windows and made his way to the manager's desk, where he took a seat in one of the client chairs and waited. Within a minute, the manager approached and greeted him.

"Good afternoon, sir. I'm Anthony Lavero, the Bank Manager. How can I help you?"

That was another thing Maurice remembered that he liked about this bank; they never wasted his time on chit-chat or needless paperwork. In and out. Business was all that mattered.

"I'm Maurice Strickland and I would like to access my safe deposit box."

Maurice couldn't believe he was actually saying those words

for real. He had dreamed of this scenario for fifteen years. To actually be living the dream was spectacular.

"Of course. Do you have your number and key?"

"Certainly. It's number 54987232 and here's the key." Lavero wasn't even surprised that Maurice had the number memorized. Quite a commentary on banking in the Cooks, Maurice thought.

Lavero took Maurice's key, got his own, and looked up the box location in his folder.

"Fine. Come with me."

Maurice left his luggage at the desk and trailed closely on Lavero's heels as they moved toward the vault. He felt completely conspicuous, as though all eyes were watching his walk to the vault. But as he looked around, he could see that no one was watching him at all. He just felt like they were. They arrived at the vault and Lavero opened it with a series of combinations and keys. The door swung open and the cool damp air that wafted out from the opening was exhilarating, not so much for its coolness, although that was refreshing, as for its uncommon appearance here in this tropical paradise. Maurice drank it in, relishing favored smells of his prior life that he had almost forgotten.

"It's nice isn't it?" Lavero asked, noticing Maurice's response to the air. "It's the coolest non-refrigerated spot on the island." They moved inside the vault and stopped about midway down on the right wall. "Here it is Mr. Strickland, 54987232. It's a big one. I'll roll it out for you and then you can use this private room in the back."

Maurice was exploding with anticipation. He could hardly breathe. Even his palms were sweating. Thankfully, Lavero seemed unaware of Maurice's condition as he continued to release the box from its brethren. He rolled it into the back room for Maurice, turned on the light, motioned for Maurice to come in, and closed the door behind him. Maurice was alone with his box, his fourteen million dollar box. It was a big box, but even in large denominations, fourteen million dollars took up a lot of room. He wished he had one of those fabulous Cohibas he used to smoke during his law firm days to celebrate. No matter, maybe he could find one later. He unrolled the large canvass duffel bag he had brought to carry out his cash and propped it open against the legs of the chair. He was ready. He slowly lifted the lid a little, wanting the moment to last forever. He leaned forward in his chair to catch the first glimpse of green, but he couldn't see any. He leaned farther; still no green. He stood up, ripped the lid completely off and stared in. Nothing! No money! No nothing!

"Awgh . . . Ah . . . Ugh . . . " Maurice was screeching at the top of his voice, horrific, awful screams that flew from the vault and ricocheted all over the bank. Lavero came running in as fast as he could, followed by other bank employees who gathered at the mouth of the vault, waiting to see what had caused such a derangement.

"Mr. Strickland, Mr. Strickland, what's going on? What's wrong?" Lavero was yelling too, trying to get Maurice's attention without getting too close and getting in the path of a crazy person. Maurice looked possessed. His hair was sticking out in every possible direction, like a mad Albert Einstein. His face was such a deep red and contorted in such a grotesque way that he was barely recognizable.

"Wha–at?" Maurice stopped screaming long enough to turn his attention to Lavero.

"I said, what's wrong? Why are you so upset?"

"Where's my money? There's no money! Where's my *fourteen million dollars*?"

At that, the crowd gathered at the entrance to the vault expelled a collective gasp and started jabbering away.

"Shut up," Maurice yelled at them. "Get them out of here," he yelled to Lavero. "Out! Now!"

They scampered away to their respective work areas as Maurice turned back to Lavero. He was a little quieter now and contained.

"Mr. Lavero, I left fourteen million dollars in this box fifteen years ago. I have paid all the safe deposit fees as they came due, as I have any other taxes and fees that accrued. As you can see, there's nothing in this box. There's supposed to be fourteen million dollars in this box. I would like to know where my fourteen million dollars is." Maurice was acting perfectly calm now and was sitting, hands clasped in front of him, like a model schoolboy.

Lavero went to the box and looked deep inside. Seeing something, he reached all the way in and came up with a sealed legal-size envelope, which he handed to Maurice.

"I guess I missed that," Maurice said churlishly. "I'll take a look."

Lavero excused himself and backed out of the room, closing the door behind him. The envelope looked officious, addressed to Maurice L. Strickland, with some kind of seal on the back. He opened it and found a nicely typed letter on some kind of charity letterhead.

"Dear Maurice:" the letter began. "If you are reading this

letter, let me be the first to extend my congratulations. Obviously you have served your term and are a free man. I am sure you have been looking forward to the drama of this day for a very long time and I'm certain this letter won't disappoint. You see, my dear Maurice, it was us all the time. You thought it was Sam and Sarah, but it was us. And, my dear, there is no money—at least, none for you. It has been spent on all the good causes you so embraced when you first joined Cabot & Baines. Remember all the platitudes, all the promises you made about how 'being good meant doing good'? Well, Alexander always believed you. We wanted to make sure your legacy rang true to the real Maurice Strickland, not the one who stole, cheated, lied, and killed. Take a moment and look at the picture on the second page. See that building? See Alexander and me waving at you from the front of Wonderland Kids Care for Cancer? You built that complex and provided all the facilities and equipment. Many people are very grateful for that building and would thank you from the bottom of their hearts, except that you donated everything anonymously. That's just like you, isn't it? You might be wondering about now how we found out about you and how we retrieved the money. I'll give you a few hints. All the fairy tale and nursery rhyme statues scattered all over the firm were really hidden cameras and microphones. While it's true that Alexander is a gifted sculptor, he had another, less artistic goal in mind when making these. You see, he was suspicious of you for a long time. And remember when Alexander helped all the partners set up these accounts and trusts in the Cook Islands? What he didn't tell you was that he set up a trust within the trust to actually hold all your goodies. So when you signed up 'A.C.' to be your managing agent, you also signed him up to be your managing agent of the Rabbit Hole Trust as well. Unfortunately, you didn't know Alexander had appointed himself to be the beneficiary. Oops. Also, you don't really think Paul Rodriguez was able to find, let alone gather, all those documents himself do you? As things developed, he just ended up being the perfect front man. Which brings us to the third point. There's nothing you can do. If you would be so kind to take a look at the picture on the third page. Do you recognize yourself? Do you recognize yourself doing unspeakable acts with that poor, sweet little boy? I do, and I think everyone else would too, especially the police. Great photographer, too. Those are pictures taken by Hector. That's right dear, Hector. So you see, if you try to do anything from there, either I or my executor, as the case may be, will send those pictures to every newspaper, every television station, every cable station, every person you've ever worked with, been friendly with or met on the street. You would be known forever not just as a liar and a thief, but as a molester of children—whose father and uncles would undoubtedly enjoy making your acquaintance. If you try and come back here, the police have already been alerted and they would arrest you as you stepped off the plane. Pretty tidy package, don't you think? I worked on it a long time. Too bad you didn't marry stupid.

And me, how am I? So kind of you to ask. I am remarried to a most exquisite gentleman who adores me. I think you've heard of him. Alfred Winter? That's right, the Australian billionaire, Alfred Winter. And I'm the CEO of Vonair Inc. I think you've heard of them too. Much more interesting than going to garden parties.

So good-bye, Maurice. I know you have to race out and find a job. You did bring enough money for a few stiff drinks though, didn't you?"

Maurice folded the letter neatly and returned it to the envelope. He studied the picture of Ariel and Alexander deeply, as if trying to capture forever all the creases and shadows in it, the graceful curve of her throat and the angular strength in his face. He stared at the picture a very long time, turning his head this way and that, consuming every detail. Finally, he was finished. He placed it in the envelope along with the third picture, closed the clasp, and walked out of the private room, through the bank, and into the brilliant colors of the Cook Islands sunset. If he had thought about it, he would have been surprised that there weren't police outside waiting for him after his extraordinary display, but he didn't think about it. He wasn't thinking about anything. For the first time in his life, his mind was completely blank.

He kept walking, down paved streets and gravel streets and dirt streets with tufts of protruding grass. There were stores and little shops, restaurants and gas stations. And of course there were banks, lots and lots of banks. Eventually, he found a sandy knoll right by the water with exactly the right elevation, so that when he sat down, he could see the entire coastline stretching from end to end. He let the warm summer air lift his hair and ruffle his collar. He took off his shoes. He made a little boat with the envelope and carefully folded each of the three pages separately into little stick people, which he placed in the boat—a man and a woman in front and another man far in the back. He walked to the shoreline, waded slowly out and placed the boat in the water. He watched in the moonlight as the gentle waves caught it and carried it out into the current. Such a happy little group bobbing along until a wave caught the stern and washed the third little man out to sea.

◆ ◆ ◆

The newspaper write-up was brief. Unidentified man found on Sandy Hook Beach at six o'clock yesterday morning by surfers Mark Agnew and Jeff Reneker. Cause of death not yet confirmed, but appears to be shark attack. Coroner says bite marks are consistent with a great white, but Mike Allister of the Department of Fish and Game has issued no surf or swim warning due to the rarity of great whites in the area and their transitory nature. All records of reported citings and taggings indicate that the few that appear just pass through on their way to the rich feeding grounds off the coastal waters of New Zealand.

Great whites are known not only for their impressive size, but for their intelligence and surprising cleverness when pursuing their prey. According to shark researchers, great whites typically circle their prey deep underwater for a length of time while they determine the prey's maneuverability. As soon as the shark can predict the prey's likely path, it comes up rapidly and attacks the prey from the underside. The rapid underbelly attack generally insures success due to the fact that the prey never sees the shark coming.

ACKNOWLEDGMENTS

My profound appreciation and gratitude to my husband Jerry for his generous spirit, brilliant editing, and boundless love, encouragement, and faith. Thanks for the gift of time and space. Thanks for being amazing.

To my sisters Gwen and Kaarin, awesome women, sisters and friends. Gwen, always uplifting, always encouraging, always keeping me gently accountable. And Kaarin, my steadfast believer, who is kind and inspiring beyond measure. As one of my first readers, she helped me carry on, and put herself on the line with the first public reading of *The TimeKeepers* at her book club. Thanks to them both for their limitless love, faith and courage.

Thanks to my Mom and to my Dad, of blessed memory, for a lifetime of love, joy, guidance, support, and for their abiding belief that their daughters could do anything. There's literally nothing I can say that would be suitable thanks.

To Kathy Walker, my best friend forever and then some, for her unending faith and encouragement. To Jennifer Wolfberg, a dear friend, who gave me a laser beam boost when I needed it most.

Thanks to the Highlands Ranch Book Club Girls, the first book club to read the book, for their comments, terrific questions, and for embracing the book.

Thanks to my fabulous book team! To Jeniffer Thompson, Julio Pompa, and the rest of the gang at Monkey C Media, for guiding the process, producing a book cover, logo design and interior design that are perfect, and for other adds too numerous to mention. Thanks to Helen Chang and Laurie Aranda, my editors at Author Bridge Media. Thanks also to Corinne Moulder and Sarah Miniaci at Smith Publicity. Corinne, for her enthusiasm and focus on this project and Sarah, for knocking it out of the park as my publicist. She committed all her skills and talents to getting the word out about *The TimeKeepers*, and she did. For that, I am forever grateful. Special thanks to Blendi Reynolds, a gifted photographer, for her amazing photos and artistry and to Nina McNamara, and Maureen and Arthur Yannoukos at Anvil Nation, for a truly spectacular website. Thanks to Alexia Chalita, for her skill and creative energies on the social media aspect of the team, and to Jen Sincero, a special Badass high five.

Finally, to those who love thrillers, thank you!

CPSIA information can be obtained
at www.ICGtesting.com
Printed in the USA
LVOW12s1704080817
544250LV00001B/59/P